ONE
INNOCENT
COMMENT

ONE INNOCENT COMMENT

A Novel

BY K. RAY CARTER

PALMETTO

P U B L I S H I N G

Charleston, SC

www.PalmettoPublishing.com

Paperback ISBN: 979-8-8229-5751-0
eBook ISBN: 979-8-8229-5752-7

To my parents, who always believed in me, encouraged me to believe in myself, and taught me to be brave-especially during the tough times. Until we meet again, hugs.

And to my brother. You always wanted the best for me, even when we didn't always agree on what that meant. I miss you dearly.

CAST OF CHARACTERS:

Utopia Energy Team:

Mason Williams	Project Manager
Alex Sheppard	Project Engineer
Paul Carter	Purchasing Manager
David Coleman	Attorney for Utopia Energy
John White	Maintenance Manager
Maggie Carpenter	Special Project Coordinator/ Budget Director
Baron Pruitt	VP at Utopia Energy

Chinese Manufacturing Team/Tiger Eye Members:

Zhang Han	Chinese team leader
Zhang Chen	Zhang Han's son/member of Tiger Eye Enterprises
Fu Ling	Tiger Eye founding member
Lin Hong	Han's choice for plant manager

The North Koreans/CIA Players:

Kim Cheol-su	North Korean Minister of Foreign Affairs;
Sang-hee	Kim Cheol-su's wife
Joo Chan	Assistant to Kim Cheol-su; CIA informant
Tae Wo	Chinese hotel manager in Pyongyang; CIA; handler of Joo Chan
Li Jie	Chinese hotel supplier in Dandong; CIA: handler of Tae Wo

The Muslims:

Cai Yi	Chinese middleman (Muslim)
Mohammed Aghasi	US citizen/Muslim extremist/ Plot ringleader
Tarik Aghasi	Brother of Mohammad
Habib Aghasi	Cousin of Mohammad & Tarik/ Professor & head of Iran's nuclear research

The FBI:

Dan Kardan	FBI Agent; boyfriend of Sara
Jim Keith	Dan Kardan's supervisor at the FBI
Brad Robberson	Interpol's Fusion Task Force Member
Joseph Lee	FBI LEGAT in Beijing

Supporting Cast:

Sara King	Maggie's best friend
Collin Wu	Brother-in-law of Alex; brother of Lilly
Lilly	Chinese translator;
Rachel Montgomery	Mason's mistress

CHAPTER 1

"What you are asking for will not be easy or inexpensive to obtain," Han explained, speaking quietly. It was a sunny afternoon in Beijing and the outdoor café afforded them the best opportunity to blend into the landscape.

"If it were easy, I would not be asking for your services," Cai Yi retorted. "As for the price, I don't recall asking how much it would cost. The briefcase at my feet has one million U.S. dollars in it. That is just to talk to you today, so please be assured, money is not an issue."

Han looked around, still uneasy to be meeting with someone of Yi's reputation. Cai Yi did not travel in the same circles as Han, so it came as a surprise when Han was contacted by the Muslim extremist. Han and Tiger Eye Enterprises had their hands in many different pots, but for the most part, they did not get involved directly with the kind of people that Yi represented. They didn't mind skirting the edges of legitimacy on occasion, but they were intensely particular with whom they did business. However, Han's curiosity had overridden his normal warning system.

"Finding a secure source could take a great deal of time, even if it can be done at all," Han continued. "I cannot guarantee that I can even supply what you want at any price."

"That is understood, but my clients have faith in me and I have faith in you," Yi replied. "All that is asked at this point is whether or not you are interested in finding a supplier. If you are, then the details can be worked out later."

"I will discuss this with my colleagues to see if they are interested in your offer," Han said. "How can I contact you?"

"I will contact you-in one month," Yi answered. "If you decide that we can do business, then I will share my number with you. Until then, you do not need to know how to find me. It is in both of our interests to keep it this way."

With that cryptic response, the Muslim left the table, disappearing into the throng of people on the sidewalk. Han sat there for a while, trying to absorb what had just happened. He was accustomed to large amounts of money, both in his daily career and his interest in Tiger Eye Enterprises, but a million dollars just to talk was impressive, to say the least. He knew that Yi was serious with his proposal and obviously had the money to back the undertaking. The question was just how far he could be pushed financially.

CHAPTER 2

"Is your passport current?" Baron casually asked as he searched through papers on his desk.

For a moment, Maggie wasn't sure she had heard him correctly. "Well, yes, but why would you ask?"

"I'd like for you to join the China Project. The team needs a fresh set of eyes. You already know as much background about the project as anyone in the company, so I'd like you to consider actually getting involved firsthand," he explained as he gave up the search. "I know that this would require your being gone for extended periods, and we would have to work out some kind of adjustment in the workload here, but I would consider it a personal favor if you would consider joining the team."

Baron spent the next twenty minutes going over every argument Maggie could possibly have made-had she had the presence of mind to think of anything. She was stunned. In all the months of planning and preparation, she had never thought once about the possibility of actually having to travel to China. She was a behind-the-scenes kind of person, an organizational and financial wizard. She was an expert at arranging introductions, meetings, logistical matters. She always seemed to put the right group together to get the job done. But she was not a frontline soldier-even if it was a backseat frontline position. China. Why in the world would she go to China? She had no desire to spend extended periods of time in such a crowded place, working with people she barely knew, surrounded by sights, sounds, and smells that she couldn't identify.

China. Maggie could feel the fear rising into her throat and she struggled to hang on to her composure. She hated these panic attacks, never understood where they came from, and certainly didn't seem to be able to control them. They had started after Tom died, and while they occurred less and less often these days, she knew this one was gaining speed fast.

"Baron, I don't know what to say. I am truly flattered that you asked-you are asking aren't you? I mean, this is my choice isn't it?" Maggie's breathing became shallow and rapid. "There won't be any problems if I decide to decline, will there?"

Maggie had the deer-in-the-headlight look that Baron had seen before. She felt trapped and that was the last thing he wanted. He didn't need her to freak out about this. He knew that she didn't handle new situations well-at least not in the beginning. But given enough time, she adapted quite well. Baron needed her to be on this team, needed to have someone he trusted to sort out all of the conflicting information that was crossing his desk.

"Absolutely not. I would never force you to join the team, but I would really like you to give this some serious thought. I need you to keep track of everything. It's getting more and more complicated, and I am having trouble disseminating all of the figures coming to me from different sources. There's a problem somewhere, but I don't know where, nor do I have the time to micromanage this team. There are more projects going on than just China and I have to keep up with them as well. But China could be in trouble, so before I push the panic button, I need to know the cold hard facts. You've been in on this from the first meeting and you know as much or more about the project as anyone else in the company. Maggie, I wouldn't ask if it wasn't important. The company needs someone to sort everything out and it would give you an opportunity to travel again. I know how much you and Tom loved to go places, and I know that you haven't been anywhere except your ranch since he died. It's a win–win for everyone," Baron calmly answered, hoping to stop her fear. "Look, there's a long weekend coming up. Why don't you take a couple of extra days and give this some thought? If you have any questions, all you have to do is call me. But for now, find somewhere quiet and peaceful and think about this whole idea."

Maggie's pulse began to settle as Baron's voice slowed and lowered. Her breathing returned to normal and she went back to her office fully intending to pour herself into her work and think about this mess later. It didn't take but a few minutes for the futility of that notion to take over, so Maggie had Anne call the airline while she cleared her desk and called Sara. She knew her best friend would understand and help her make a decision. She and Sara would have a nice long dinner and then she would pack and go to the ranch in the morning. It had been too long since she had been to Montana, and Maggie knew she would feel better once she got there. The ranch was one of the most peaceful places Maggie had ever been and she knew the panic she was feeling would go away once she was there. She could make a rational, logical decision at the ranch.

CHAPTER 3

It was one of those transitional evenings. Early September. Summer was slowly slipping away, yet it was not quite fall. Wrapped up on her porch swing, she was watching the sun sink into the dip in the mountain pass. Soon she could watch the same spot to see if snow was headed her way. Soon she could be listening to the howling wind instead of the night bugs. But for tonight it was the orange and pink streaks across a turquoise sky that kept her lingering in the night air, reluctant to go indoors. There was a soft breeze stirring the pine trees, just enough to make Maggie pull a light blanket around her shoulders. Coming back to her grandfather's ranch had been exactly what she needed. Grandpa Riley had left the place to Maggie along with enough money to run it for several generations. It was a beautiful spot, high in the Montana Rockies, and Maggie always came here when she needed refreshing. The house sat in the middle of two thousand acres of pristine forests and rolling mountain valleys. This was the place where she had spent some of her happiest days growing up. Her family had always come here for the holidays, snowed-in around a crackling fire, roasting marshmallows and playing board games together. Summers provided cool relief from the hot city streets. Now it was the place she came to escape the noise of life.

Maggie was on the waning side of forty-seven. She had grown up as a positive, self-assured, purposeful person. The glass was mostly half full. But lately something was missing and she felt half empty. She really wasn't one of those melancholy women, wondering where she had taken a wrong turn. She was a realist. There had been lots of choices and she recognized where each of them had been in her life-good and bad. Of course, the gift of hindsight painted very clear pictures. She wished she had that gift right now-the vision to know what she should do about China. Try as she might to focus, it seemed easier tonight not to think about it, not to make any decision. Tonight she was too caught up in being at the ranch. She was happy to be surrounded by the peacefulness of the front porch. She didn't often feel this way, and when these moments came they always surprised her. Sometimes it seemed she had been mourning forever, so to find a night of honest contentment was a pleasant event.

Tom had been gone a long time, but every day Maggie thought of him; missed his laughter; ached for his touch. She had never prepared to be a widow this early in life and frankly didn't care for the title. Maggie and Tom had had a perfect, but short, fairy-tale marriage. Life with Tom was all she had ever wanted. He was unlike anyone she had ever been involved with, not that there had been a long list. He was professionally successful, financially secure, and very comfortable in his own skin. He made everything seem easy. But when Tom was diagnosed with cancer, all of his wealth and brilliance couldn't stop destiny. Maggie had been crushed. It had been a long and torturous death. Unable to stand the familiar sites, she had fled to the ranch in the early days after the funeral, to the place where she had felt protected as a child. Ken and Bonnie Aldridge were the caretakers at the ranch. They had been there when Grandpa Riley was alive, and they loved the place as much as he had. For a long time, they were just about her only contacts. She had isolated herself, dealing only with the lawyers when absolutely necessary. Ken and Bonnie had allowed her to mend at her own pace, encouraging her when she reached out and giving her the privacy to retreat into quiet solitude. And Maggie had healed a lot since those first days, even though she still had her moments. On one hand, she missed the friends and constant activities that had filled her and Tom's life. The friends were still there, but being odd man out was no fun at all and it had become increasingly easier to decline the invitations. On the other hand, she had a lot of time on her hands. While she managed to fill her days working, the evenings echoed with silence.

She had come to the ranch to escape, to have time to think. She loved her job, loved the people she worked with, but still she needed a refuge. She had come back here for a few days to think about Baron's offer. China. She had never been to China, had never even thought about going to China. Third World Communist countries were not on her short list of exciting places to see before you die. Try as she might, she did not have one positive thought about the country. She also knew that her fear was taking over. Maggie was quite happy in her comfort zone and fought like a scared cat when someone tried to push her out of it. Like now.

So... Baron wanted Maggie to pack up her life and trek off to a country she knew nothing about to work for weeks at a time. Was he crazy or what? She was quite happy here. America was a good place. She felt safe here. Besides, all her friends were here-especially Sara, her best friend since first grade. While she knew the other team members, they were not her friends. They were not Sara, whom she had just known would agree with her. Boy, had she been wrong about that! When Maggie told her about Baron's idea, Sara jumped on the bandwagon.

"Oh how wonderful! You are so lucky," Sara had screamed as she headed for Maggie's closet. "When do you leave? Do you have anything to wear? We have to go shopping".

"But Sara, I don't know if I want to do this. I'm scared. I don't like traveling alone, or Chinese food, or places where

I don't understand the language. I don't handle roughing it at all."

"Ok, first of all, you are not alone. There are five other people on the team. Secondly... well, I don't have an argument about the food, but you will have an interpreter and as far as roughing it-you're staying in a suite at the Crowne Plaza. How rough can that be?"

"I thought you would be on my side," Maggie whined as she put back the clothes Sara had thrown on the bed. "I thought you would understand."

"I do understand, Mags. More than you give me credit for. You are scared to leave the safe little world you have let yourself live in since Tom died. You've put up these walls that no one can penetrate, that are too high for you or anyone else to climb over. You hide in there with your memories of Tom, surrounded by his friends. It's where you needed to be at first, but Maggie, it's been seven years. It's time to start living again, taking risks, and finding new adventures. It's what Tom would have wanted."

Sara's words had echoed in Maggie's thoughts over and over since she had escaped Houston for the refuge of the ranch. On some level she knew Sara was right. She knew she needed to do this but was still scared. She knew that in the end she had to go. It was one of those things she would regret years from now if she let herself walk away from it.

Besides, it's what Tom would have wanted.

CHAPTER 4

Maggie extended the holiday weekend into the rest of the week. She had stayed gone on the premise of first making a decision about China, and then making all the arrangements for her personal life to continue uninterrupted while she was half a world away. The truth of the matter was that those arrangements were all handled by phone and fax and had taken less than a day to complete. For hours she roamed around the ranch, questioning her sanity one minute and planning with anticipation the next. Soon her mind was exhausted from the roller coaster and she settled down enough to call Baron and accept the assignment. He sounded pleased with her decision, although he didn't seem surprised. Maggie had to smile to herself at how well Baron knew her. He'd never doubted that she would take the job.

She spent the next couple of days truly enjoying the ranch. She and Bonnie went into town to pick up mums and pansies for the fall flower beds. Maggie had been intrigued with Jasmine, Montana, since she was a child, growing up in a large city. Jasmine was straight out of a Laura Ingalls Wilder book: it was the perfect small town with a feed store, drug store, grocery store and a vet-a self-contained little world, where people swept off their front porches while they waved at everyone who drove by. When Grandpa Riley was a young man, he would come to this area to hunt every fall. It was his "down time" from the stress of running a Fortune 500 company, and eventually he bought two thousand acres and built the ranch house in the dead center of the property. He'd adopted Jasmine as his second home and was extremely involved in the town's affairs, even from thousands of miles away. Everyone in town liked Riley Davis and the feeling was quite mutual. When the family all came to the ranch for the holidays or summer vacations, Maggie and Grandpa Riley were inseparable. Maggie would horseback ride with him, accompany him when he checked on the stock, and always went to town with him for supplies. That was her favorite time. They would shop for everything on their list and then they would go to the diner for lunch. Maggie thought the diner was the neatest place she had ever been. The two of them would sit at the counter on red-seated bar stools that swiveled. Maggie could order anything she wanted and Grandpa Riley would order the same thing.

Maggie stilled loved Jasmine and still sat at the counter when she went to the diner. There were a lot of people who still knew Maggie, and the ones who didn't weren't strangers for long. If some of the old timers didn't introduce her, she would make a point of introducing herself. Just like Grandpa Riley used to do. It was a fun game for her, one that did not fit her everyday character at all. In Houston, she was friendly and outgoing, but she did not put herself out there in front. But Maggie felt safer and more secure in Jasmine, and her personality was more laid-back and open whenever she visited the tiny town.

After Maggie and Bonnie had the ranch house looking festive, she spent the rest of the time horseback riding in the afternoons, and when darkness came she would wind up in the library reading one of the hundreds of volumes from the shelves. Sometime during the early morning hours the grandfather clock would wake her from her dozing, and she would climb the stairs to bed. By the time she had to go back to Houston, she was rested and comfortable with her decision. While she still had some insecure thoughts about traveling to

China, she was focused and determined to be able to bring a realistic report of the project to Baron.

CHAPTER 5

"Gentlemen, I have made a deposit into Tiger Eye's Miscellaneous Funds Account," Han began the meeting. "For one million US Dollars."

"Where did you pick up that kind of 'miscellaneous' money?" one of the men asked lightheartedly.

"It seems that having tea with me is now worth quite a handsome sum. You might want to keep that in mind the next time you call me," Han joked back.

"Perhaps you should share a little information on who would think your time is worth so much money," suggested one of the other men.

"A few days ago, I had tea with Cai Yi," Han explained, and waited for the buzz to settle down. "It seems he is interested in using our services. The million was just to listen to his proposal and to assure me that money was no object to his client."

"With all that money at his disposal, why would he come to us?" asked another attendee. "We are not known for working that deeply in the shadows. Tiger Eye has never dealt with the lower end of the food chain."

"That is precisely the reason he came to us," Han continued. "We are legitimate enough businessmen who have managed to fly below most radar screens. We are discreet; no one thinks of us first when something shady has occurred."

"That is not a bad thing. It keeps us in a positive bargaining position with our own government, and out of sight of most of the countries we do business in," replied the other man.

"I am not saying it is a bad thing. You have not even heard what Yi wants," Han patiently said. "At least listen to the proposal."

The five men agreed that they should at least hear Han out. He had led them through many years of prosperity and had never had a deal go bad yet. They owed him the respect to listen.

"Cai Yi has a client. I don't know who they are or where they are located. It seemed better not to know too much, so I didn't ask too many questions," Han began. "His client wants to acquire weapons-grade plutonium. They are willing to wait however long it takes to get it. They want to know if we are willing to locate a supplier and to arrange for delivery of the material."

"Since when are we in the nuclear weapons business?" asked one of the men, although several chimed in when he asked the question. "Have you gone mad? This is way out of our league."

Han waited for the murmuring to quiet down. These men were the core founders of Tiger Eye Enterprises, and they were reacting from the same viewpoint he had been wrestling with for several days. This was an unknown area to them, but it wouldn't be the first time that they had diversified into the unfamiliar. He had argued all sides with himself since meeting with Yi. In the end, it was strictly a business decision, and that was what he needed the rest of the board of Tiger Eye Enterprises to understand.

"I have not gone mad, but I have allowed myself to consider all aspects of his proposal," Han explained. "If we could pull this off, there would be enough money in this one project for the six of us to walk away very, very rich men."

"Are you forgetting that we have no clue where to get plutonium?" another man asked sarcastically. "And did it occur to you that they might be planning to use it on our own people? It's not that I'm terribly patriotic, but I am concerned about my family's well-being."

"I don't have the answer as to where they are planning to use it," Han admitted. "While that would certainly be one of the conditions nice to know before we move forward, we probably don't want to know too much. He is determined to acquire the product, so it will be used regardless of our participation. As far as a supply, that of course would have to be researched. You never know what is available until you start shopping for it."

"Even if we could acquire the material, how would we deliver it?" one man asked. "We can't just ship radioactive materials through our freight companies. We would be risking everything we have spent years building."

"I can't answer that question until I know where we would be shipping the plutonium," Han confessed. "But I have to know if you want to pursue this matter at all before I can know if the details can be worked out. We need to decide if this should move to the exploratory stage or be vetoed by the board tonight. We have less than a month before we have to let them know if we are willing-and able-to proceed."

Han and the other men discussed the situation for more than an hour. Sometimes the conversation became quite heated but in the end, their greed won out. They knew that at least they had to explore the possibility of being able to manage something of this magnitude. They had to know if they could really become filthy rich.

CHAPTER 6

"Mason, I've been going over and over these numbers and they just don't make sense," Baron began as he paced around the conference room. The other team members had not been asked to join this meeting. Baron didn't care to have an audience when he knew that he was going to have to get ugly. Getting in someone's face was one thing, but he didn't make it a habit to humiliate them in front of others as well.

"If you would forget all the garbage the others have given you and look at my figures, it would be perfectly clear," Mason yelled. If he had clenched his jaw any harder, his teeth would have exploded.

"Well, that's the problem now, isn't it? I'm having trouble believing that their numbers are garbage," Baron snapped.

"Maybe the problem is that you don't understand what it takes to build a plant in China. Maybe you have no idea of how the Chinese operate and have put your faith in people who don't have a clue either," Mason blew up, knowing he was pushing Baron's patience to the edge.

"I put my faith in you when I put you on this committee and look where that's got me. You've been in-country for almost a year, and we are no closer to producing compressors than when we conceived the idea," Baron snapped back.

"Well if I'm doing such a lousy job, what's your brilliant plan to save the day?" Mason asked, his tone dripping with sarcasm.

"What I should have done to begin with. I am adding Maggie Carpenter to the team, and for the moment, leaving you on it. But that could change at any second," Baron firmly announced.

"You're kidding me, right? What business does Maggie have working on this team, other than to be your little spy?"

"Mason, you are teetering on the edge. One more remark like that and you will not only find yourself off the team, but out of a job as well. We all know that Maggie's skills are just what this team needs. You would do well to rein in your attitude and use her expertise to pull your butt out of the huge crack you've got it in," Baron threatened in a tone that told Mason the conversation was over.

Slamming the door as he left the conference room, Mason stormed off the floor and out of the building. He was fuming as he moved through the lunch crowd and headed to Murphy's, one of the local watering holes. There he spent the afternoon drowning out the anger and drinking his way to a powerful hangover. He truly hated Baron. Not just because of today's argument, but because Baron had the position and prestige that Mason believed belonged to him. In Mason's opinion, Baron was Vice President because he brownnosed the President and CEO of Utopia Energy. They had all been friends for years and Mason found them to be elitists. What Mason refused to accept was that Baron had paid his dues and had made millions of dollars for the company. His position with Utopia was well earned. But what really set Mason off was that Baron didn't coddle to him. Mason was used to people accepting his opinions and advice. He had bluffed his way to a high-profile job, using whatever means–and whomever-possible. But Baron didn't buy into the façade. He thought Mason had been promoted beyond his capability and he made no effort to suppress his belief. Baron had not yet convinced his superiors that Mason was a fraud, but he continued to march toward that goal and Mason knew it.

Sometime after the end of the business day, Mason staggered back to his office to sleep for a couple of hours. He knew that when he finally went home-late again-there would be another blowup with Cynthia, but he was just sober enough to know that he had no business behind the wheel of his car. Mason and Cynthia had already had a fight this morning over her plans for the Labor Day holiday. Her family was having a big weekend party at the lake house and "everybody who's anybody" was going to be there. Cynthia demanded that Mason be there for the entire weekend, while he kept insisting that he had to work on the China Project and that he needed the quiet time in town. He promised to come up on Monday for the big barbeque, although that had not appeased Cynthia-not that she could ever be appeased. In all fairness, Mason admitted that most of the time he enjoyed Cynthia's parties and her friends. And he thoroughly appreciated their luxurious lifestyle that was made possible by her allowance from Daddy, not by what Mason brought home. She was Daddy's Spoiled Brat and thought everything should go according to her plans. But not this time, Mason mused. This weekend was his to spend as he saw fit, and that was with Rachel, not Cynthia. He and Rachel had already made plans to be together and he needed to be with her. He needed to be excited by her. He needed to touch her hard, svelte body. Rachel was his fantasy, his escape, and he wanted that escape more than anything right now.

CHAPTER 7

"Alex, have you got a minute?" Baron asked as he stuck his head into Alex's office.

"Sure, come on in, if you can find a chair. I have things a little spread out." Everyone at Utopia Energy knew about Alex's "spread out" work style. His office was always in such disarray, but it worked for him. Somewhere in all those piles, he could locate any piece of paper that was needed.

"I wanted to tell you myself that I have asked Maggie Carpenter to join the team. I think a new perspective could be good for the project. She is a numbers person, so please share with her the notes and figures you have and why you feel that they are closer to reality than some of the others that have been floating around."

"Well, Baron, I think that is a great decision. She will be an asset to the team-or at least to some of us. I'm not sure everyone is going to see her presence as a 'new perspective'. I hope you have warned her that not everyone may be happy with their new teammate."

"We both know you are talking about Mason. Yes, I painted a pretty clear picture for her. And I have told Mason. He didn't seem too pleased-to put it mildly. But he will have to get over it. We have to get a handle on all of the bureaucratic chaos so you can build a plant. Enough is enough. Maggie is quite capable of handling Mason. But just in case I'm wrong, watch her back for me, okay?" Baron asked as he got up to leave.

Alex smiled at his old buddy. Always the knight in shining armor. "Not a problem, Boss. I'll keep an eye on things."

Alex stopped for a moment to study this bit of news. Maggie Carpenter. Well, wasn't that an interesting turn of events? So Baron is sending in his own General! Whatever it took to get Mason off his butt and get the plant construction started, Alex would welcome. It would also give Alex a chance to get to know Maggie better. He and Tom had worked together for years, but Alex had not ever really worked with Maggie or socialized with them as a couple. He had, however, envied them from a distance. Maggie and Tom were the perfect couple, always smiling and laughing, so obviously in love. It had never been like that for Alex and Amanda. It had started out that way for Alex, but when he looked back on it now, Amanda had never been in love with him. He had just been a way for her to hurt Parker. Well, she had accomplished that, Alex sneered to himself. Amanda was not a path he wanted to go down right now, and he shook his head as if to clear his thoughts. Maggie. Yes, Maggie would be good for the team. Her skills were well known throughout the company and the project needed someone who could pull Mason back into the fold. And maybe Alex could form a friendship with her that would make the trip more tolerable than it was with just his male team members. They weren't the most fun guys to travel with, even though he got along with them well enough in a work environment. Alex wondered how Mason would behave with Maggie along. Until now he had been a blowhard with a big ego who played more than he worked. It would be interesting to see if he would toe the line a little better with Maggie in their midst.

CHAPTER 8

Han entered the banquet hall with the rest of the members of his group. They were in North Korea to negotiate with Kim Jong-un to allow international talks to take place concerning his government's forays into the world of nuclear aggression. Han was somewhat amused and often aggravated at the wheels of diplomacy: Here they were, ready to offer shiploads of food in exchange for the North Koreans just agreeing to talk to another group. It was not the way businesses were run, but Han reminded himself that governments were never as efficient as businesses. That is why they needed him on the panel. If a deal could be struck, no one in the Chinese government had the capability to implement delivery of such vast supplies. So they turned to the private enterprise entities that they worked so hard to suppress. The irony was not lost on Han.

Just as his group came into the room, they were greeted by the North Korean delegation and divided up with each Korean man playing host to his Chinese counterpart. Han was led to the head table by Kim Cheol-su, the top government official for the summit.

"Today was a very productive session, don't you think?" the North Korean asked his guest. They were attending one of the many banquets planned during the ten days that the Chinese delegation was in Pyongyang.

"Yes, I do. It would be nice if the rest of the negotiations went as smoothly," Han replied. "Perhaps it would be best if the two of us were drawing the plans up instead of having to try to please such a large group."

"You sound more like an American businessman than a government representative," Kim Cheol-su laughed. "Neither of our regimes would allow such a thing. After all, we might have an original, unsanctioned thought."

"You are so right, my friend. Individual thinking is not truly appreciated in either of our countries, especially yours," Han agreed, unsure where his North Korean comrade was headed with this conversation and whether or not he should follow him.

"There are many things our current governments do not appreciate," Kim continued. "Perhaps in the future it will be different."

"One never knows. After all, my country is much different today than it was several years ago," Han said. "When I was a child, I would never have thought that I would have the opportunities to travel that I have had in my life. I have been very fortunate."

"Indeed you have. I understand that you went to college in the United States," Kim said. "Did you enjoy living there?"

"It was a very enjoyable time in my life. I learned a great deal about the American people," Han replied. "I am surprised, however, that you were aware of my educational pursuits. You have me at a disadvantage, for I regret to say that I do not know the same about your experiences."

"Forgive me, I did not mean to make you uncomfortable," Kim apologized. "I am afraid our intelligence people always brief me on any visitors I will be meeting. It's only a formality. I was just curious as to your travels. I often wonder what it would be like to live in another place. I have, on occasion, been a part of a delegation to the United Nations, but I have not been able to experience much of the surroundings of New York. It is always a very busy trip."

"New York is an exciting place. You should try to make time for sightseeing when you are there," Han suggested.

"Perhaps when you travel again, I could arrange to be on business there, and we could spend a few hours seeing the city."

"We might be able to make that work," Kim lowered his voice. "A close watch is kept on my activities, but since we are working together here, it would not be such a big thing for us to have dinner in New York sometime."

"We will just have to work that out," Han smiled. "Time and patience usually win out if one can keep a goal in mind."

The two men continued their conversation over the course of the banquet, finding out that on a personal level they had many things in common. Han was surprised to find that Kim was quite a forward-thinking man, especially for a citizen of North Korea. Most of the people in this country were so suppressed by the government that even an independent thought was outside the realm of possibility. Here was Kim, the Minister of Foreign Affairs, wondering aloud to a Chinese visitor about how life is different in other places and planning an unsanctioned trip. Han was astute enough to realize that this man was not a robot of the state and that he wanted more freedom. That fact alone could be exploited under the right circumstances.

"Tomorrow we have only a half-day session. Perhaps you would be gracious enough to show me around your city," Han suggested.

"Absolutely. What would you be interested in seeing?" Kim asked, surprised that his Chinese guest wanted to sightsee in Pyongyang.

"Whatever you wish to show me will be fine," Han replied. "However, if possible, I would like to see the Juche Tower and perhaps the Kumsusan Memorial Palace."

"I am sure that can be arranged," Kim answered. "There are also many historical sites around the city that you may find interesting. It will take more than just an afternoon to see them. Perhaps we shall take a day's break from the negotiations. The others can handle the minor details."

"I agree with you. I will look forward to our sightseeing time," Han said. "It would be a shame to visit your city and never actually see it."

The rest of the evening was spent enjoying the entertainment that had been arranged for the Chinese visitors. By the time the group retired for the evening, Han was feeling slightly smug about his budding friendship with Kim. Han perceived that his Korean counterpart was not quite the government puppet that he pretended to be at times. It would be simple enough to find out during their non-working time. If Han was correct, Kim could be easily manipulated with relatively little effort. Han had been on the lookout for an opportunity to find a supply source for Yi, and he had a feeling that Kim might just be the answer.

CHAPTER 9

Ending a particularly tedious session, the Chinese left for their hotel after lunch. Kim had arranged for a government limo to pick Han up after he had had a chance to refresh and rest for a brief time. Han was excited about their outing; he had always been fascinated with historical places as well as non-historic, yet significant sites in foreign countries. Well aware that few outsiders ever even entered North Korea, Han was sufficiently humbled that he was not only being allowed to visit important sites within Pyongyang, but that his host was a top government official who, no doubt, had other responsibilities more important than being a tour guide.

"I trust you had a few minutes to rest before we start our afternoon activities?" Kim asked as they headed toward Kumsusan Palace.

"Yes, thank you. I needed the break," Han replied. "Sometimes the details of these agreements become entirely too wearisome."

"I agree. We all know that the end result will work out, but there are times when I think the entire process will break down over some mundane detail," Kim added. "I am sure that it is an attempt on someone's part to justify their presence at the negotiating table."

Han just laughed. Kim's attitude about the sessions was the polar opposite of that of his fellow countrymen, who seemed so intent on holding some imaginary position of power. The truth was that the North Korean people were starving and their government needed this arrangement with the Chinese to go forward at all costs. The Korean demeanor of truly having something to negotiate with was almost humorous to Han. While Kim Jong-un wanted the world to be afraid of his nuclear capability, China was neither afraid nor impressed. Beijing had the ability to crush the tiny country with little effort, but that would not be in their best interest on the world stage. Appearances were very important to the Chinese authorities, and they wanted the rest of the world to see them as contributing to the collective good. In reality, Han knew that his country feared massive waves of refugees from North Korea if there was not enough food for the people in their own country. It was more practical for China to export food to Pyongyang than to deal with the Koreans fleeing into Manchuria.

"Are you sure you were not born in the West?" Han amusingly asked. "You do not have the attitude that your comrades seem to possess."

"My comrades, as you put it, are still very much under the illusion that the government knows best," Kim replied quietly. "They are mostly military men who are well cared for. They do not have, or choose to ignore, friends and family members who are hungry, who go to bed each night without enough to eat and with no idea where tomorrow's food will come from."

"But you are different. You appear to live in the reality of the situation," Han commented. "What happens if you are suddenly out of the good graces of the government?"

"That thought has occurred to me, I assure you." Kim said as they left the car and walked toward the entrance of the palace. "I have, over the years, tried to arrange for other options, should I find myself in precarious circumstances. I have cultivated many friends on the outside."

"You are either confident or extremely foolish to share such information with me," Han warned. "You might want to be more careful to whom you speak so freely."

"Let's just say that I am well informed of my audience's allegiances," Kim smiled as they entered the palace. "However, while we are inside the building, let us speak only of the memorial itself."

With that admonition, Kim proceeded to explain details of the building they were visiting. Once the reported official residence of Kim ll-sung, the palace was now his final resting place. Viewing the embalmed body lying in a glass sarcophagus was common to Han, who had on many occasions visited Mao Zedong's body in Beijing.

After a couple of hours inside the Palace, the two men made their way back to the waiting car. It had been a pleasant afternoon, but Han had promised to meet his team at the hotel for the evening meal and night was fast approaching.

"Tomorrow we have no meetings. I would like to take you on another tour of my city, and then perhaps you will join my family for dinner," Kim offered. "I would like for you to visit in my home and to get a taste of Korean hospitality."

"I would be honored to join your family and would love another day touring your city," Han sincerely replied. "It has been a very interesting and informative afternoon. I look forward to getting to know you better tomorrow."

After making time arrangements for the next day, Han went to his room to freshen up before dinner. It truly had been an enjoyable day and an interesting one as well. Han had a feeling that this friendship was going to end up being very profitable for both men.

CHAPTER 10

"This is a pleasant surprise. I didn't expect to see you here tonight," the manager commented to the well-dressed gentleman sitting at the restaurant bar. "Are you staying for dinner?"

"Not tonight," the man replied. "I just stopped to inquire as to how your fellow Chinese guests are doing."

"Your boss seems to be keeping them quite busy. They leave early in the morning and return late," Tae Wo replied. "I didn't know that checking on my hotel guests was part of your job at the ministry."

"Let's just say this has been an interesting visit, and I wondered if you might have sensed the same thing," the man said quietly. Joo Chan had worked as the scheduling secretary for the Minister of Foreign Affairs for more than a decade. He had been a CIA informant for much longer.

"It is a nice evening," Tae said as he looked around the somewhat crowded bar. "Why don't we take your drink to the patio?"

The two men meandered onto the patio. It was a beautiful evening and Tae was surprised that there was no one else enjoying the outdoor seating. Just as well, he thought, one can never be too sure who is listening.

"It is much quieter here," Tae commented as they sat down at a table in the corner of the patio. "So tell me, what has happened to make you think that this is anything more than official government meetings?"

"These meetings have been planned for weeks and have been given a level of great importance. Kim Cheol-su has been personally involved, making sure every detail has been addressed. Yet now that the discussions have begun, he seems to have found better pursuits than going to the meetings."

"What kinds of pursuits?" Tae asked, leaning in closer to his companion.

"Playing tour guide for one of the Chinese leaders, Zhang Han" Joo replied. "Do you know him?"

"I know who he is." Tae answered. "Why would either one of them miss the meetings to go sightseeing?"

"Ah, I think that is a very good question," Joo whispered, looking around for any listening ears. "Kim seems very taken with his new friend, whom I understand is not really a government official. He is head of a company that would bring food into the country. They have become quite close in the past few days. I have had to arrange for a limo to drive them around as well as getting them access to some of the more restricted sights. I have never known Kim to take this kind of interest in a foreign dignitary."

Tae did not respond to this news, but rather the two men sat in silence: one pondering what this might mean, if anything; the other wondering if his companion felt any curiosity about the situation.

"Keep your ears open, there is surely more to this than promoting tourism in Pyongyang," Tae finally commented. "We should get together this weekend for a game of tennis here at the hotel. Perhaps you will know more by then."

The Korean man finished his drink and left the patio through the bar. Tae stayed seated for some time, contemplating what this tidbit of news might mean. Joo Chan had been a confidential informant for Tae's predecessor for years and had a reputation of never passing along trivial information. Joo seemed to have some sixth sense about what was relevant and what could be nothing more than office gossip. Tae had enough confidence in his informant to know that there was news to be passed to his fellow CIA operative when he traveled to the border city of Dandong next week. Until then, he would just continue to operate the finest hotel in the capital-which meant that for the moment he would have to give up his comfortable seat and go back inside to see what had fallen apart in the past few minutes.

CHAPTER 11

Maggie was the first person through the doors after security had opened the building. It had always been her habit to come into work insanely early the first day back from vacation. She had always been a morning person, and being alone in the office, with just the hum of the various machines, was her peaceful time. It was her way of refocusing her brain to be back on work time rather than ranch time.

As usual, Anne had all of the pertinent papers in neat and organized stacks. Having worked for Maggie for several years, Anne knew that Maggie would be in at daybreak, so she had made sure everything was in order before she left on Friday. Maggie took her time going through the various piles and making new stacks based on what needed to be done next.

The morning was very productive, but hectic, with Anne and Maggie going over what would need to be done while she was gone, whom to delegate projects to, and trying to gather all of the numbers on the China project that they could find. Finally, Anne decided she was starving and headed for lunch.

"Are you sure you don't want me to bring something back for you?" Anne asked, feeling a little guilty for taking a break when Maggie was still working.

"No, thanks. I will grab a bite later. I really don't want to break my rhythm-slow as it is. I know this is all going to make sense just any minute," Maggie answered, trying to sound more optimistic than she felt. "Go on and take your time. I'll be right here when you get back."

Reluctantly Anne headed out, planning to hurry. She decided she would bring a sandwich back for Maggie, for she knew that Maggie would never stop long enough to go somewhere to eat.

Maggie continued to pore over the vendor contracts that Baron had supplied for her. The more she studied them, the more she understood Baron's frustration. Each contract by itself seemed simple enough, straightforward. But when she tried to put the big picture together, the numbers simply did not add up. Maggie knew that numbers don't lie, but she also knew that people often stretched the truth. Someone on the team, or maybe more than one person, was twisting the numbers to make their part of the project look good and meet budget expectations. The question was who … and why.

Maggie was deep in thought when she heard a knock at her office door. Expecting to see Anne, she was surprised when she saw Mason Williams in the doorway.

"Sit down, please. I thought you were Anne when I heard the knock," Maggie said as she pulled her reading glasses to the top of her head. "How have you been?"

"Well, considering I spend about forty percent of my time in airports and hotels, I suppose I'm as well as can be expected," Mason's tone was uncharacteristically cheerful, as if they were bosom buddies from childhood. "I understand that you will soon be joining the ranks of the walking dead."

"So it seems. I have traveled abroad as a tourist, but this will be my first experience working in another country. I don't really know what to expect," Maggie replied, keeping the tone set by Mason.

"It is much tougher than sightseeing, but I'm sure you will be just fine. If you have any questions while we're in China, just ask. I'll be more than happy to help if I can," Mason offered. Even he knew his attitude had just crossed the believable line, but he was determined to not let her know just how much he resented her addition to the team. Better to let her feel comfortable, to let her guard down. He wasn't about to let a woman have the upper hand, at least not at work, but it was better at the moment to act the part of a team player.

"That's very kind of you. I'll keep that in mind," Maggie said pasting her sweetest smile on her face. "I have just been going over some of the contract proposals, trying to familiarize myself with the vendors and currency exchange. There's a lot of information to digest."

"Well," Mason drawled as he stood to leave, "I wouldn't worry too much about it at the moment. It will make more sense once you are in China. Besides, the rest of the team has a pretty good handle on things, so you can just check with one of us when you don't understand something. I'll go now, just wanted to welcome you aboard." He left so quickly that Maggie didn't have an opportunity to respond to his patronizing attitude.

Maggie despised that "don't worry your pretty little head about it" routine that so many men relied on whenever they encountered a woman that was as smart, or smarter, than they were. Those kinds of men could never deal with a woman with brains. Intellectually, Maggie understood that some men were extremely insecure and therefore acted like jerks. Emotionally, they infuriated her. Determined to erase Mason from her conscious thoughts, Maggie turned back to the reports she had been studying before Mason's interruption. She might be confused over the numbers and specifications, but Hell would freeze over before she would ask Mason for one bit of assistance.

Over the next half hour or so, each one of the team members dropped by to welcome her to the project. Unlike Mason, they all seemed genuinely pleased that she would be joining them, and with each visit Maggie felt increasingly better about the whole assignment. Baron had been correct when he'd said that she was already well educated on the overall scope of the project, and she had tried to keep up with progress, or lack of, as the case seemed to be, but she had not had an opportunity to look over every contract proposal. Not being familiar with the Chinese culture and mindset, she had found that some of the notes from the negotiations seemed totally alien. There were demands–and concessions–that would never be a part of contract talks in the United States. She finally set all the paperwork aside and decided to take a break. Her eyes needed a rest and the band playing in her head really needed to go away. It was still basically lunchtime, and the office was relatively deserted, so she decided to shut her door, close the window blinds, and spend a few well-deserved minutes relaxing on the couch in her office. She knew if she dozed off, Anne would make enough noise when she returned from lunch that Maggie would wake up and rejoin the working world. That was her last conscious thought as she slipped off into dreamland.

CHAPTER 12

Han and Kim spent the next day touring several sites in Pyongyang, including the Juche Tower, completed in 1982 to commemorate Kim ll Sung's seventieth birthday. The men ascended the tower and were rewarded with a spectacular view of the city.

"I can only imagine how beautiful the city is at night from this vantage point," Han reflected, looking out on Kim ll Sung Square. "I'm sure the tower itself is a stunning sight in the evening as well."

"It is, on the rare occasions when it is illuminated," Kim replied, speaking quietly so that the accompanying guard did not overhear. "Despite claims to the contrary, it is seldom lit-power shortages, you know."

Han just nodded with a knowing look, not risking any more conversation on the subject. He had found the North Korean government to be very touchy about the country's image. In some ways they thumbed their noses at what the international community thought, but in the next breath, did everything in their means to promote an illusion of power and stability.

The rest of the afternoon was spent at the Grand People's Palace of Studies in Kim ll-sung Square and at the Rungrado May Day Stadium, the world's largest stadium, capable of seating 150,000 spectators. Han was sufficiently impressed with the facility, careful not to make any mention of the generals who had been burned alive at the stadium as punishment for an alleged attempt on Kim Jong-il's life. Han saw no need to push the bounds of their newfound friendship.

At the end of the day, Han spent a pleasant evening in his host's home, meeting both Kim's wife and young son. The house was somewhat opulent for North Korean standards and Han found the food to be the best he had experienced during his visit. Han had enjoyed the time that Kim took to show him the sights of Pyongyang, and he was acutely aware that this was not the normal routine for visiting dignitaries. He was also quite aware that Kim Cheoul-su was not your ordinary Communist official. Something was different about Kim, and Han knew in his heart that whatever it was would come in handy someday. In appreciation for their hospitality, Han invited the entire family to visit his home in Beijing. He was convinced that under the façade of the current negotiations, Kim would be able to accept an invitation to travel to China for further talks. Because of Kim's status and the friendly relationship between China and North Korea, Beijing would be considered a "safe" place to allow Kim's family to accompany him. Any issues that might arise could be quickly dispelled by Han's status within his own government.

CHAPTER 13

"Have the men made all of their contacts?" Mohammed asked.

"Yes. I have confirmed that each of them has recruited four other soldiers in separate cities. We have twenty men in place," Tarik answered. "Only the five know us directly and they are the most dedicated. They will not fail the mission and will sacrifice themselves for the cause. The others, should they waver, cannot lead anyone to us. We will be safe, alive to plan another operation."

"It would be nice to think that this attack would be the one that would bring the infidel government to its feet," Mohammed sighed. "But we know that they are a stubborn enemy. Unfortunately, they do not realize the depth of patience and resources of Allah's forces. They may win battles, but we will win the war."

"The cities that you picked for destruction will strike the Americans at their very core," Tarik praised. "The only better detail than the cities, is the timing. Striking them at the height of their Christian holiday is brilliant."

"Yes, it is a symbolic statement, but I fear one that will be lost on the Americans," Mohammed clarified. "They are far more interested in their economy than they are in their religion. Perhaps that mindset is what keeps them from understanding our dedication to Allah."

On the wall of the den in the brothers' home was a US map with pushpins marking twenty cities in the middle of the country. Big cities were marked: Dallas, Denver, Kansas City, Nashville, and Birmingham. But there were also smaller towns like Poteau, Oklahoma; Marshall, Missouri; and Cleveland, Mississippi. The biggest marker on the board was the most important site to the entire mission: Bentonville, Arkansas. Mohammed had saved this location for his most committed follower. This was the one place where the plan must succeed.

Bentonville, Arkansas, was truly the heartbeat of America. Many thought that attacking Washington, DC, or New York City would bring down the country, but Mohammed knew differently. To destroy America's economy, to stop the supply of goods across their country, and strike fear in the heart of the people nationwide-that would bring down the country. To target WalMart Stores on the busiest shopping day of the year and to destroy their Corporate Headquarters in Bentonville would devastate the entire country economically, psychologically, and with the use of atomic weapons, environmentally. Their government, still intact, would be rendered useless.

CHAPTER 14

The weekends were fairly quiet for Tae. Hotel business was brisk-if you could call it that-during the week with business-men. By the weekend they were on their way home, and Tae and his staff had plenty of time to get ready for the next week.

Tae spent the morning finishing the monthly reports that he would mail to the hotel owners in Beijing. Being a hotel manager was an interesting cover for a CIA agent, but Tae would have preferred an assignment somewhere other than Pyongyang. North Korea was a very gray country, both in surroundings and in the people's personalities. They were so oppressed it would take generations to bring laughter back into their lives. Tae had replaced the Agency's previous operative almost five years ago. This was not an environment where agents could stay for years at a time. The government was too suspicious and controlling, so the CIA's Langley Headquarters moved people in and out every few years. Fortunately, there were several natives in well-placed positions that could bring each new agent up to date on the workings of the govern-ment: North Koreans whose allegiance was pledged to the United States.

Joo Chan was just such a person. His long-time position within the Foreign Affairs Ministry had been a great asset to the US government. Information about what was going on inside North Korea was so scarce and hard to get, and Joo was one of the few assets the Americans could truly count on for accurate information. That fact made Tae restless as he waited for Joo to join him for their scheduled game of tennis.

Tae was anxious to find out if Joo had any more information about the Minister and the Chinese entrepreneur. Their friendship was an interesting development, considering that the North Korean government kept such a close eye on its people, even one as important as Kim Cheol-su. North Korea's obsessive fear of the outside world prohibited its citizens from developing very many relationships outside of the Hermit Kingdom.

Tae's assistant knocked on the office door to inform his boss that Joo had arrived. Tae locked the reports he should have finished in his desk and headed for the locker area to change clothes. Joo was waiting for him when he came outside.

"It's a beautiful day," Tae commented as they headed for the tennis court. "I'm glad we have a chance to be outside and enjoy the fresh air."

"It would be better if the sun was shining, but yes, it is a good day to be out. Unfortunately I cannot stay too long. The minister has given me extra work to do and I must head back to the office when we are finished," Joo commented.

"The Chinese meetings are over. That should have let things settle down, and yet you have to work this afternoon?"

"Kim has accepted an invitation from Han to come to Beijing next month. I have to clear his calendar and reschedule all of his appointments," Joo replied as he causally bent down to tie his shoe. "There is much to do to before he and his family can leave."

"His family is going with him?"

"Yes, at the request of Han. He wants Kim's wife and his wife to have time to get to know each other and enjoy the city."

"Is it normal for his family to travel with him?" Tae asked, trying not to sound too astonished.

"It is not even normal for Kim to accept such an invitation for himself. To have his wife and son travel with him is extremely odd," Joo explained. "I am telling you that this whole situation is strange. Something is going on, and it is anything but official business."

The two men turned their attention to the court and before long were in a fast and heated match. Neither one spoke again during the game, but the situation with Kim and Han never left either of their minds. When the game was over they headed, hot and sweaty, back to the locker room. After showering they met on the restaurant's patio for lunch.

They carried on an innocuous conversation while their food was being delivered. Joo was hungry for any information that his friend could bring him from the outside world. Tae always came back from his weekly border visits with something for Joo. The last trip he had brought him a portable CD player along with a healthy collection of CDs, ranging from exercise routines to symphonies. Stuck in the middle of the stack, disguised as Alan Jackson's newest release, was a CD that contained the latest issues of _Newsweek_, _U.S. News & World Report_ and the _Washington Post_. Joo was a news junkie, which was a difficult addiction to feed living in this country. Were it not for his CIA connections, he would be as uninformed and brainwashed as the rest of his nation.

"Is there any chance that Kim will take you on his trip to Beijing?" Tae quietly asked between bites.

"Not at all. In fact, he is not even taking a security detail," Joo replied in a hushed tone. "He is a trusted comrade, but this is beyond protocol, even for him."

"How is he getting away with such a plan?"

"He hasn't yet, but I suspect he will. No one except the Chairman himself would question Kim, and their relationship is very solid," Joo continued. "There will be no one watching the visit."

"Oh, that's not true, my friend," Tae corrected. "There will be plenty of eyes and ears recording Kim's trip. He will just think he is on his own."

CHAPTER 15

The trip to Dandong the next week followed the same routine that Tae had established years ago. He spent the day visiting the various vendors that supplied all of the wares needed to run a hotel and restaurant. It was essential for Tae to make his purchases in the border city, since obtaining any of his necessary supplies in North Korea was just not possible. Tae never minded the weekly trips because they afforded him the opportunity to acquire luxury items for himself that were only available on the Chinese side of the border. It also allowed him to catch up on the lives of his friends and, most importantly, to make contact with his fellow CIA operative, Li Jie.

The hotel supply made the perfect meeting place for the two undercover agents; Tae needed supplies weekly and Li had worked as the supply house's manager for years. It was easy for the two men to pass information while they went over the hotel's invoice. When the merchandise was delivered to Pyongyang, anything extra that Tae needed was hidden safely among the hotel's provisions.

Tae passed along the information that Joo had given him and asked for any news from Beijing that might explain the budding friendship between the high-ranking Korean and the successful Chinese businessman. His fellow agent had not heard of anything brewing, but promised to make some calls to his network of informants to see what might be happening. With any luck at all, he might have some news to share with Tae on his visit the following week.

Finishing their business for the hotel, Tae spent the rest of the afternoon visiting his favorite lady in Dandong. They had been meeting every Wednesday for the past five years, and while Tae knew that she was not in love with him, for an afternoon he could fool himself into believing otherwise.

CHAPTER 16

Morning came very early for Maggie. After a thirty-hour flight, they had arrived at the hotel around two o'clock in the morning and had to be in their first meeting at seven. Luckily the meeting was being held at the hotel, so Maggie didn't have to allow for travel time. Good thing, she thought. She would have loved to hit the snooze alarm. She didn't know how they all managed this routine. This was her first trip, but the rest of the group had been to Chengdu on several other occasions. How did they ever get used to this jetlag?

Maggie had known the other team members for several years. Alex Sheppard was the project engineer; Paul Carter, purchasing manager; David Coleman, attorney; John White, maintenance manager, and Mason Williams the project manager. They all worked out of the corporate office, but rarely did they all work together on a daily basis. Baron Pruitt, Vice-President of Global Operations, had handpicked each team member and even though Mason was the project manager, all team members individually reported to Baron from time to time, a practice that irritated the control freak in Mason. Maggie wasn't certain what the problem was, but Mason had an issue with Baron for sure. For Maggie's part, she and Baron had been friends since she and Tom first got together. Baron and Tom had been great friends, fishing partners, respected colleagues. Both couples had spent many happy hours together. Baron had kept a protective eye on Maggie since Tom's death, and it was because of her loyalty to Baron that she found herself walking in a daze this morning.

Today's meeting was supposed to iron out some of the labor issues that were holding up progress. The Chinese were insisting on having labor housing provided by Utopia Energy. The bulk of the workforce would have to be bused in from the rural regions of Sichuan Province. They would spend the week working at the plant and then would have to be bused back to their villages for the weekend. Utopia was expected to build dormitories to house the workers during the week, which would send the project way over budget and delay completion of the plant by at least six months. Six months might as well have been six years. They needed to be online as quickly as possible. There was such a backlog of compressor orders stateside that Utopia Energy had taken a drastic step. Two drastic steps, actually. The first was the decision to manufacture natural gas compressors in-house rather than being dependent on increasingly unreliable third parties. The second was to locate a plant in China. Even with all of the add-ons that the Chinese wanted, it would still be cheaper to produce the compressors in Chengdu than in Houston, or in any other American city. And while the Chinese government openly courted Western businesses with many attractive offers, they were cutthroat negotiators when it came to the details. Maggie continued to be amazed at what the company was expected to do before they ever even paid a single yuan in wages. Besides transportation and housing, they were expected to provide an on-site cafeteria that operated around the clock to provide meals for three shifts, and to have a medical staff on duty during all shifts. The Chinese government was also urging, although not terribly strongly, that Utopia Energy set up scholarships for its worker's children to allow them to leave the villages and attend various universities. These types of issues were slowing down the negotiations for the actual plant-architects, building contractors, electricians, the list was endless. The team had already been working in-country for months and there was yet to be one compressor manufactured.

Maggie was nervous as well as tired. Even though she had worked on mountains of details back in Houston, actually being at the negotiation table was so different. She prayed that she could keep up, would understand what was occurring, and would be able to answer intelligently when questioned. She silently chastised herself for her self-doubt. Logically she knew that she was well informed. Professionally, she was always prepared. Emotionally … well that was another story.

With no more time to worry, she headed out the door. Just as she reached the elevator Alex Sheppard came around the corner. Maggie did not know Alex very well, but knew enough to admire his work ethic, not to mention his contagious smile that was greeting her.

"Good Morning. Did you sleep well?" Alex inquired as he punched the Down button.

"I guess so. My body's not sure if it is morning or night, so I'm having a little trouble focusing."

Alex smiled knowingly, "It will get better, I promise. Unfortunately, it will happen just as we leave for home."

Maggie wasn't sure if she wanted to laugh or cry over Alex's comment. Afraid it might be true, she just sighed as she and Alex entered the elevator and headed for the meeting room.

CHAPTER 17

Zhang Han was an odd sort of man. He kept the other members of the Chinese negotiators at arm's length. Very proper, but never truly personal. At the bargaining table, he was ruthless, unyielding, and stoic; when they visited vendors, he was more outgoing but definitely in charge; when they attended a social event, he was cordial and friendly-the perfect host. As President of Beijing Financial, China's premier banking institution, he wielded an extreme amount of power, which made his presence on this project in Chengdu seem very strange to his fellow team members. It seemed beneath his status to leave Beijing to work directly on the details of such a project, large as it was. But he did bring some valuable tools to the table. His knowledge of American culture was extensive and his English was impeccable, thanks to years of study in the States. He had graduated from Harvard as well as the Wharton School, making lots of contacts in America. After working at several prestigious US banking houses, Han had decided to return to China, where he used his education and greed to become a very wealthy and powerful man. He had learned well from the Americans. Han was as expert at following the Chinese customs and traditions as he was ruthless in his quest for power and money, letting no one stand in his way.

Han also prided himself on his intuitive understanding of the Americans. He could discover their weaknesses after spending just a few hours listening to their constant chatter. Americans were experts at bragging about how wonderful and successful they were back at home. Most of the Chinese believed them; they had no proof otherwise, and were mesmerized by American tales of greatness. Han however knew firsthand what blowhards most of these businessmen were, and Mason Williams was no different. In fact, Mason was almost too easy, Han had decided. He could use that arrogance to accomplish this latest job. He would let the other Chinese team members deal with the actual negotiations and he would work on Mason Williams. When he had Mason where he wanted him, then Han would step in and finalize all of the details. This was going to be even easier than he had hoped.

"Mason, my friend, tonight I would like to take just you out for dinner and a tour of the city. Your fellow team members all seem to have scattered anyway," Han said to Mason as they were leaving the conference room for the day. "I will pick you up in an hour."

"Sounds great to me," Mason replied. He was not looking forward to dinner with his traveling companions, or a boring evening in the hotel either. Han's offer sounded interesting.

Mason went to his room to clean up, thinking about the evening. The Chinese delegation had taken them out to dinner many nights, but it was always such a big group. Mason never felt like he got a real taste of the culture. He had always loved international travel and made it a point to avoid the typical tourist traps. While he usually managed to visit the major points of interest, his real love for traveling abroad was to get off the beaten track and see how the people of a country really lived. He liked to barter in the markets and buy interesting handmade pieces for his home and office. Cynthia never cared for the road less traveled, preferring instead to hit all of the popular hot spots, so traveling for business allowed him the kinds of experiences he preferred. He hoped tonight would be somewhat the kind of evening he would like. He was well aware of the wealth and influence of Han; he was among the country's elite, so it wouldn't be an evening at a sidewalk café watching the locals interact. But China's new privileged class was interesting to study as well. While Han had studied at prestigious institutions in the United States, his level of education and wealth was unique to most Chinese. He was in the ultra-high class of Chinese society. Mason was curious as to how that status compared to his own social group in America.

Han picked Mason up at the hotel and had the driver take them to a very high-end restaurant. Han was the perfect host, helping Mason read the menu and making suggestions he thought his guest would enjoy. Han seamlessly reverted to his American persona and entertained Mason for hours with tales of Chinese history and culture. The conversation flowed very easily, with Han explaining the different courses as the beautiful waitresses served them. They were in a private dining room with their own wait staff, and Mason could only assume that most locals who dined there did not get the same level of service.

After dinner, Han had the driver take them on a short tour of the city, where he pointed out places of local interest and history. The city was stunning at night. There were lights everywhere and the streets were crowded with people out window shopping. Chengdu during the day was the complete opposite of the city Mason was seeing tonight. Centered in the heart of an industrial mecca, Chengdu was dirty and polluted. The river that flowed through town was filthy with debris and the air quality was horrible unless it had rained. There were areas that presented themselves better, areas that catered to Western visitors, but they were small and isolated. What Mason saw tonight was a vibrant and exciting cityscape, and he was amazed at what the darkness had covered up.

"We do not meet tomorrow for any work sessions," Han said. "It would be an honor to take you to visit some of our more important sites in the city. I thought perhaps you would enjoy a visit to Wenshu Monastery. It took three hundred years to build but was finally completed in 907. It is the best preserved Buddhist temple in Chengdu."

"I would very much like such a visit," Mason sincerely replied. "I enjoy any type of sightseeing, but I especially enjoy visiting historical sites. Thank you so much for the offer."

"I will pick you up around eight tomorrow morning," Han continued. "If there is time, we will also visit the giant pandas at the breeding and research center. It is a very popular place and there are many other animals besides the pandas. You will enjoy it."

"I'm sure I will," Mason answered. "But if we are going to get started that early, perhaps we should call it a night. It has been a long day and I am not over the jet lag yet. I would like to get a good night's rest before we set out on these great adventures."

"Of course. I had forgotten that you have just arrived after a long flight," Han apologized. "We shall head back now."

Back at the hotel, Mason thanked Han for a most wonderful evening and headed inside for the evening. As his driver headed for home, Han reflected on the night. Whether Mason realized it or not, tonight was business, but it had nothing to do with the plant. Tonight was the initial investment that promised plentiful future dividends. Han had been correct in his assessment of Mason as the person on the American team who had the biggest ego and would therefore be the easiest person to exploit. What he hadn't counted on was that this plan might even turn out to be enjoyable in the process. All in all, this evening had been a pleasant experience, which was somewhat of a surprise for Han. He had enjoyed using his American language skills again in a social environment, and Mason was a charming and intelligent man who seemed to appreciate learning about Chinese culture.

As the driver returned to the bank's Chengdu penthouse, Han felt pleased over the success of his evening. As the Americans would say, he had set the hook. Now all he had to do was reel Mason in.

CHAPTER 18

Alex always hated the first day back in China. His body was screaming for sleep but his brain had to be alert and focused on the meetings. Why Mason never built in a day of rest before the meetings started was beyond Alex's rational thoughts. It was as if he was on fire to get this over with and get back home. He wasn't sure why Mason had ever accepted this position. At first Alex thought that Mason wanted time away from home, from the wife. But whenever they got here, Mason was rushing to get started and get home. Maybe he had a lover, Alex wondered. He wouldn't put it past him. Not that Alex cared one way or the other. He just wanted a day to acclimate before they started negotiations. Apparently, it didn't matter what Alex wanted.

What he wanted right this moment were his materials estimates from today's meeting on the vendor they were going to visit tomorrow. He searched his computer and even went through all of his paper notes. He really needed those numbers, but they were no where to be found. Tired, jet lag still in firm control of his body, everything was a struggle for him. He couldn't be ready for tomorrow's vendor visit if he didn't have those figures. What he really wanted to do was to close his eyes for just five minutes. But if he did that, it would be all over until daylight.

There was one solution. Alex was sure that Maggie had the figures-Maggie kept up with everything. Alex knew her room was two doors down, but it was getting late and Maggie was probably exhausted also. She might even be asleep.

Still … he needed those numbers before morning. In the end, he found himself heading for Maggie's room.

CHAPTER 19

Maggie didn't think she had ever been so tired. This morning she had had that same thought, but now she was sure it was true. The day had been excruciating. All the others at least had met together before, had been in these kinds of meetings, and they all seemed to know the ropes. She struggled to keep up, to act as if she understood why they were jumping from one detail to another. She had never seen such strange negotiations. One minute everyone was civilized and going over the numbers and specs. The next minute, hands were being slammed down on the table accompanied by angry outbursts that seemed to embarrass their translator. She didn't need a translator to understand her team members' responses. And then, as if nothing was wrong, they would all go to lunch together, laughing and carrying on as if they were old friends. It was all bizarre. Maggie felt so out of place. First she was new to the group, to the country and its customs. Secondly, other than the translator, Lilly, she was the only woman. In Houston that never really felt strange to her. Maggie worked in a male-dominated industry and she was quite comfortable being the only female in the room. But in Chengdu, it was not the same situation at all. Even in the "good old boy oilfield" women were respected and treated as ladies. Here she seemed to be an inconvenience to the Chinese hosts. It was a very lonely feeling.

She was so tired of feeling lonely. When would it end? She had convinced herself that this assignment was the right thing for her. She had thought she would be so engrossed in the work that even her nights would be too busy to think about Tom. She would be too overwhelmed to be able to socialize, so turning down invitations would feel justified. Well, she was overwhelmed, that was for sure, but it wasn't helping. At least not tonight. Logically she knew that the exhaustion was responsible for most of this pity party, but the truth of the matter was she wanted Tom. She could be anywhere in the world, dealing with anything, if he had just been there. Everyone thought she was so strong, but they were wrong. She was an emotional disaster. The only person who really understood that fact was Sara. If only Sara were here to talk to her, she pouted.

Sara had always been able to read Maggie. Sometimes it was infuriating, but most of the time it was a comfort to know there was one person in the world who would love you, defend you, make excuses for you, even when they thought you had gone over the deep end. Sara and Maggie had been friends since they were six years old. They liked the same clothes, cried at the same movies, and occasionally had the same taste in men. They had gone to the same schools together until college and even with thousands of miles between them, they remained close. After graduating, they had both come to Houston. Maggie had gone to work for Utopia Energy in their financial center and Sara had taken a job teaching. Through the years, Maggie had worked in various capacities within the administration and now was the Special Projects Coordinator and Budget Director in the Worldwide Operations Center. Sara had spent the past twenty years as a history professor at Rice University. After a long and messy divorce in her early thirties, Sara had dated a variety of men before she met Dan Kardan, an FBI agent. The two of them seemed to be a perfect fit. Neither one was interested in trying the marriage thing again, yet they enjoyed being together.

Maggie was trying to calculate the time difference to decide if this would be a good time to call Sara, when she heard a knock on her door.

"Sorry to bother you. I know it's late-but" Alex stopped midstream when he saw Maggie wiping tears from her face. He didn't know what to do. "What's wrong? Are you okay?"

"Of course. I'm fine. It's just my allergies," even though her sniffle and stutter said differently. "What do you need?"

"I can't find my notes on the materials estimates from today's meeting. I was hoping I could get you to send me your files. But if this is a bad time … "

"Don't be silly. Come on in and I'll do it right now." Maggie said as she turned back into the room, wiping tears from her face.

Alex tried to make small talk as Maggie got her computer out and made a copy of the notes. Maggie struggled to converse with Alex, but it was obvious that her mind was elsewhere.

"Maggie, I really don't mean to interfere, but clearly something's wrong. Please let me help. I know we're not close, but we're a long way from home and a person can always use a friend."

Maggie tried desperately to hang on to control, but in the end she just couldn't hold back any longer. Her back to him, Maggie started shaking as the tears flowed. Unable to even get a word out, she cried so hard she was gasping for breath. Without thinking, Alex crossed the room and took her into his arms. He stroked her hair, not speaking, just letting her sob uncontrollably. Several minutes passed before Maggie was able to breathe normally enough to be able to talk.

"I thought this trip would be good for me; I thought I was ready to do this, but now I know I'm not. I should have stayed in Houston. This is just so hard because I am so lonely. I miss Tom even more here than I do at home. But now I'm stuck halfway around the world, with no one to talk with, afraid to venture out of this hotel room, not even knowing what I'm eating."

"I know how it feels to lose someone you love-maybe not to the same extent that you do, but still I understand the emptiness. You and Tom were the perfect couple that all of us hope to be a part of someday. I can't make your pain go away, but I can listen."

As Maggie reached for another Kleenex, she let Alex's words sink in. She truly needed someone to listen, to be near, to ease her loneliness. Alex was not the person she would have liked to turn to at a meltdown moment, but Sara was a world away. Alex was here. For the next hour Maggie emptied her aching heart, talking about Tom, crying over the loneliness. Through it all, Alex listened, asking questions at appropriate times. Soon they were sharing stories of their individual times with Tom, and before long Maggie felt better, even managing an occasional laugh. Alex had been good medicine.

"It's late and morning is almost here" Maggie said. "Thank you for listening and sharing. I really do feel better-even though I still don't know what food I'm eating."

"That I can help you with-if you will trust me enough to leave the hotel," Alex assured her. "I know where we can get a close resemblance to American food. Tomorrow night we'll go to dinner."

"I hate being trouble to you, but honestly, I would love to have dinner with you. Thank you for taking pity on a whiney woman," Maggie replied, sincerely appreciating Alex's offer.

"Trust me. I am the one who should thank you. Having dinner with a beautiful and intelligent woman is not something I usually get to do on these trips, so please understand that the pleasure is mine," Alex smiled as he opened the door to leave.

As exhausted as Maggie was physically and emotionally, she had a difficult time going to sleep that night. Down the hall, Alex too found sleep hard to achieve.

CHAPTER 20

The vendor visit ended earlier than expected, so Maggie took advantage of the extra time to take a long bath before dressing to go out with Alex. Her body clock seemed a little more in control today and she was excited about going to dinner. She hoped that the food was really the semblance of American food that Alex said it was, as she slipped into the warm bath water. Maggie had to admit that it wasn't just the food that was causing her to look forward to the evening out. While she didn't know Alex very well, she knew of him and was anxious to talk to someone without a translator. Alex had a reputation at Utopia of being a stand-up guy, one you could count on to follow through. He was also a favorite subject of the females throughout the company. Alex was handsome, to be sure, but he was also known as a really great date, a gentleman with lots of fun in his system. In other words, a good catch. There were many rumors about his past, why he wasn't married. It was known that he was divorced, but no one could come up with any of the details. It had been an early marriage for him and no one at Utopia, or Houston for that matter, had dug up any dirt on the subject. They weren't going to get any from Alex. His past love life was not a subject he ever discussed.

None of that mattered to Maggie. She was not interested in dating Alex. She was just interested in a nice dinner with a familiar face. Of course, she wasn't immune to his handsome features. Alex wore a short salt and pepper beard, had gorgeous black eyes and a smile that could out-shine Vegas. And wasn't every girl attracted to a little mystery in her dinner companion? Maggie giggled at her thoughts. She must truly be running on sheer adrenaline to be having such silly thoughts. Sara would try to read more into the situation, Maggie knew, but logical Mags would not be taken away with such nonsense. She did know she could be taken away with the warmth and relaxation of the water. She could feel her body relaxing and her mind was struggling to keep from slipping into sleep. Knowing she could not dare take a nap, Maggie left the bath and continued to dress for the evening. She decided to wear her shoulder-length hair down, since she usually pulled it up during working hours. Down was more casual she thought and they had already agreed not to get dressed up. Jeans and a nice shirt would do just fine. Maggie had no idea how good a "nice shirt" could look on her. Her chestnut hair and green eyes both sparkled and her smile was contagious. The fact that she was oblivious to her beauty added even more charm to the whole package.

She was just putting on a bracelet when Alex knocked on her door. When she opened it, Alex was taken back for a moment. He had never seen Maggie in anything but her work outfits, and this laid-back version caught him off guard. She was beautiful.

"Wow, you look great," Alex sputtered. Realizing the tone he used, he quickly tried to fix his faux pas. "I mean, you always look wonderful, it's just that I've never seen you with your hair down. It looks….great." He knew he sounded stupid, but he didn't know what else to do without sticking his foot deeper in his mouth.

Maggie laughed at his apparent embarrassment and charmingly relieved the situation. "I guess I should give more thought to Casual Fridays around the office. Obviously I have not grasped the concept. Let's go to dinner, I'm starved."

Recovering from his outburst, Alex led them out of the hotel and through several winding streets. Chengdu had a very active night life and there were lots of people out window shopping and enjoying a large selection of restaurants, none of which looked appealing to Maggie. Finally after what felt like miles, Alex ducked down a tiny alley that opened into a courtyard. The entire courtyard was an outdoor restaurant called Pete's. It was packed. As Alex looked for a table, Maggie realized that all of the patrons were Western. A young Chinese man came running to the front, calling Alex by name.

"Alex, you come again. How wonderful to see you," he said as he extended his hand in a very American shake.

"Ah, Pete. It's good to see you again also. We were hoping you would have room for us tonight," Alex replied. Then turning to Maggie, Alex introduced their host. "Maggie, this is Pete Chan, the owner of this wonderful little secret."

Maggie and Pete exchanged greetings as Pete led them to a small table in the back of the courtyard. It was a beautiful evening with a perfect temperature for sitting outside. Maggie was amazed as she studied the menu. Not only written entirely in English, the entrees were all very familiar. Her biggest problem was making a choice. Alex laughed at her comments as she continued to change her mind. Alex explained how Pete had gone to school in America and then came back to China to open a restaurant that catered to Western visitors to the city.

"How do you know about all of this stuff? I mean, I can't even say 'Good Morning' and you know all about the owners of these restaurants half way around the world....I'm just amazed."

"Well, don't be too impressed. After all, these folks speak English," Alex mused.

"Yes, but you open yourself up to strangers, engage them. I just try to roll myself into the smallest possible ball and hope that no one notices," Maggie confesses.

"Well, you're wasting your time, sweet lady, because no one could miss you. You're beautiful and intelligent and have a smile that lights up a room. There's no way that you can hide."

Blushing, Maggie quickly changed the subject. "So tell me about your family," Maggie said as she took a bite of the wonderful bread that had been brought to their table.

"Do you want the G-rated version or do you want all the dirt?" Alex teased.

"Oh the dirt of course, every filthy little detail"

"Well, I have three sisters, all married, five nieces and three nephews. They all live in Houston, so I spend a lot of time at little league games for a guy who doesn't have any kids. And we don't even want to talk about dance recitals. My parents have been married for sixty years, they've lived in the same house for the past thirty years and they go to church every Sunday. That's pretty much all of the dirt."

"You never married?" Maggie asked without thinking.

"Once in another lifetime," Alex replied quietly, but with a tone that told Maggie that the subject was off limits. "What about your family?"

"Much smaller than yours. My brother lives in Florida and my folks live in Nashville. We don't see each other very often. Major holiday kind of stuff."

"Sounds sad. I never liked living away from all of my family. Although, sometimes they can be a bit overwhelming."

"Well from what I've seen, you handle overwhelming quite well. This whole project for instance. You seem to have a pretty good grasp on everything, and I seemed to be bogged down in the details."

"Oh, don't be too sure about my grasp. I do know what I need in place to build compressors, but that doesn't mean that I understand all of the procedures to get there. There are a lot of games that have to be played with the Chinese to make this all happen, and frankly I just don't play games. Never have. It's just not my style."

About that time their waiter brought their food and Maggie let the subject of the project drop. Tonight she just wanted to enjoy the wonderful food, perfect weather and very interesting dinner companion.

They spent the rest of the meal discussing a variety of subjects from the mouth-watering food to favorite vacation spots. Maggie found herself enjoying the evening far more than she had expected to, far more than any evening she could remember in the past few years. Alex was a charismatic man who had a way at keeping the conversation flowing and comfortable. For his part, Alex was caught up in Maggie's charm. Her laughter was genuine and warming and he found himself trying to find ways to keep the evening from ending.

But eventually, Pete made enough noise with his cleaning ritual that Maggie and Alex realized they were the only patrons left in the restaurant. Reluctantly they walked slowing back to the hotel, taking in the sights of the city and enjoying each other's company. Maggie was sure she could never find her way back to Pete's, so she made Alex promise to take her back before they left for home. It was a promise he was more than happy to make.

Back inside Alex walked Maggie to her room and saying goodnight, he gently kissed her. Maggie's heart momentarily skipped a beat. It was one of those kisses that could be taken more than one way. On one hand, it was very innocent, very proper and meaningless. On the other hand, it was very sweet and somewhat lingering. It was a kiss that could promise more. As Maggie closed the door and leaned against it, she found herself smiling and hoping that it was the latter of the two options.

CHAPTER 21

"Are you sure you weren't followed?"

"I was very careful, but we don't have much time. Do you have something for me?"

"Yes." he said as he handed her the envelope. In return, he pocketed a small package into his jacket pocket. "Are you okay?"

"I'm fine, but this makes me very nervous. We can't be seen together."

With that short exchange, she was gone. Alex was always surprised by how quickly she disappeared into the crowd. He tried each time to pick her out of the hundreds of bodies around him, but he was never able to locate her. It never ceased to leave him with an uneasy feeling that he was being watched while at the same time he was unable to see his contact.

* * *

After hours of tedious negotiations and a splitting headache, Maggie thought the lunch break would never arrive. It had been a very discouraging morning; the Chinese were being difficult to say the least. The whole team was frustrated, on edge. Everyone except Mason. He seemed to be disconnected from the process. When asked a question he seemed lost for an answer, as if he had not been listening. Maggie didn't know what his problem was but she felt too overwhelmed to deal with his issues. She had her own work to try to wade through to be able to try to make sense of the numbers that the Chinese were trying to write into the contracts. Drafts submitted from different vendors were so contradictory that it was like comparing apples to oranges. The proposals might have all been for the same job, but the details were so varied that it was difficult to tell what the true costs were for each segment. Maggie knew it was going to be a long process and not one she could do alone. She would need to ask for Alex's help to be able to decipher what they were really being asked to purchase. She would talk to him this afternoon about getting together to go over the paperwork.

She decided that some fresh air was what she needed. Maggie picked up a sandwich from the dining service and went to the park across the street from the hotel. It was a beautiful, well cared for area that was popular with the lunch crowd. Everywhere there were people on benches or blankets, some reading, some talking intimately between stolen kisses. There were children playing on the swings and teenagers skateboarding. Except for the sea of Asian faces, Maggie could have been in any park in America, she thought as she unwound listening to the sounds of the city. There were the usual urban noises of cars and horns mixed in with the birds chirping and children laughing. The whole atmosphere was refreshing to her troubled mind and soon she found herself totally immersed in the pace of the park. She realized that the pounding in her head had eased and for the first time since being in China, she was enjoying her surroundings. It felt good to be still. Maggie watched the people around her with great curiosity. Unable to understand what they were saying, she made up scenarios in her mind for different people. The older gentleman sitting on the next bench was all alone in the city. He and his wife had often come to this park, and since she had died, he came alone to feed the birds and remember his beloved mate. The young mother reading to her toddler was the wife of a banker. Her life was one of relative ease and comfort, so she had time to take the baby to the park and spend hours laughing at all of his discoveries. The couple in the flower garden, walking closely and deep in discussion were planning…..Maggie suddenly stopped her day-dreaming when she realized that this couple was different from the others. This man was clearly not Asian and from this distance looked remarkably like Alex. As they came closer, she saw that it was indeed Alex and the woman he was with was Lilly, their translator. They did not see Maggie as she watched them continue their conversation. It seemed like such a private moment that Maggie felt she was intruding by even being in the park. Alex and Lilly spoke briefly and Lilly turned and quickly walked away. Alex lingered in the garden for a few moments, checking is jacket pocket and turned to walk back towards the hotel. As he came out of the garden area, he saw Maggie sitting on the bench. Unaware that she had seen him with Lilly, he walked over to her and casually sat down.

"Come here often?" he joked.

"Actually this is my first visit, but perhaps I'll do this again," Maggie answered, unsure how to react to what she had just seen. "How about you-is this one of your frequent haunts?"

"I walk in the park as often as I get a chance. It gets me away from the others and lets me relax a bit. I don't care for the usual evening entertainment provided by our Chinese friends, so I come here instead and run. Running clears my head."

"I understand about needing your head cleared. That's why I'm here. But what do you mean about the usual evening entertainment?" Maggie questioned.

"Let's just say it's not something they would include you in, and trust me, you're glad they don't. It's about time to get back to work. Can I walk you back to the hotel?"

Maggie knew Alex had politely side-stepped a subject that he did not want to discuss. From his tone she was sure she could fill in the blanks with any number of activities, and Alex was correct: she didn't want to know the details.

As they headed back, Alex made small talk about nothing in particular. Maggie wanted to ask about his encounter with Lilly, but wasn't sure how to bring up the subject. It was a most unusual circumstance as the Chinese translator never interacted with the team except in her official capacity. She was always with them during the meetings and when they visited a vendor. When the entire team joined their Chinese counterparts for dinner, Lilly came along to interpret. But in all of these times, she never relaxed with them, never just visited, never divulged one item about her personal life. She seemed very tense, like she was afraid. All of that made her appearance with Alex very odd.

CHAPTER 22

"Shall I pick you up in about an hour?" Han asked Mason, slapping him on the back as they gathered their briefcases. It had been a particularly fruitful afternoon session and members on both sides of the table were feeling pleased with the progress.

"Sounds great. I'll look forward to it," Mason answered as he walked toward the door.

Neither man realized that Maggie was still in the room and had observed this comfortable exchange between them. How strange, she thought. She had not been aware that the two men were socializing in the evening hours. But for that matter, she hadn't paid attention to what any of the others did at night. She had been too wrapped up in enjoying Alex's company each night for dinner. They had a wonderful time together—at least she thought so—even on the nights when they actually worked on the project. Tonight would be one of those evenings. Maggie was concerned about one of the bids from the electrical vendors and Alex had offered to go over the figures with her.

Mason and Han went to a new restaurant almost every night. Han was the perfect host, and Mason looked forward to the evenings with him. They had been to several places of historical significance--Han seemed able to arranged after-hours tours—and on Saturday they had traveled to the Great Wall. Mason was in awe over the trip. It had been a place that he had always wanted to visit and it made the weekend stay-over worth it. It was this part of the project that was worthwhile and made the rest of it palatable. As far as the details of building the plant went, he wasn't really that interested. It was a job. It did get him away from Cynthia and it did allow him to visit wonderful places, but that was about all he got out of the experience. He had long ago quit worrying about the corporate ladder. As much as it irritated him that Baron had the position Mason wanted, he had to admit that he had a pretty cushy job and he intended to exploit it for all he could. If Utopia wanted Baron at the helm, then fine. Mason would take all the advantages he rightly deserved and would contribute only enough to stay under the radar. It was a shame, he thought occasionally, that he had lost his fire for the work. He was once a shining star for the Company, but now he only cared about himself.

"Tonight I have a special activity planned for us," Han explained as they were leaving the conference room. "I do hope you like to take some risks, have a little excitement in your life."

"As long as I come home with all of my body parts intact, then I am up for anything," Mason's ego boasted. "What did you have in mind?"

"A friend of mine has opened a new casino. He caters to our Western tourists, so I thought you would feel comfortable there," Han explained. "It is a short ride away, but well worth the trip."

"Your friend sounds like an astute businessman. I enjoy a night of gambling from time to time, as do a lot of Americans. I'll meet you downstairs in about an hour," Mason said as they shook hands and each headed his separate way.

CHAPTER 23

When they got to the casino, Mason was speechless. His first thought was that they could have been in Vegas. Chengdu was not shy about lighting up the city, but this was way over the top. There were so many flashing lights that Mason wondered if it was visible from outer space. Inside the casino, the activity was buzzing. There were people everywhere and for the first time since he arrived in China, Mason was sure there were more westerners than Chinese. English seemed to be the language of choice. The girls were beautiful and the drinks were free and plentiful. Mason thought he had died and gone to Heaven.

"This is unbelievable," Mason remarked with a tone of awe. "We could be in the best casino in Vegas—you would never know we're in the middle of China. Your friend is a genius."

"Don't tell him that; he's already hard to live with," Han laughed. "He is quite proud of his little place here and loves all of the tourists who have made him very rich. All he needs now is Wayne Newton."

Mason had to laugh. His host was correct though: it felt just like home. American influences were everywhere in Chengdu. The depth of U.S. investments in the city would have stunned most Americans. There were many Western industries and financials institutions that had come here to do business, but they were definitely upstaged by this Chinese businessman. This was over the top. He had every nuance nailed to perfection.

Mason and Han worked their way through the casino, but ultimately spent the better part of the evening at the blackjack table. Han made sure Mason's drink was always fresh and that he had the attention of more than one beautiful woman. Mason loved to gamble, loved the excitement of the game, and in the end he had walked away with a few more dollars than when he arrived, not that it was his money that he was using to gamble.

The evening was certainly more interesting than dinner at the hotel with his co-workers would have been. The adrenaline alone kept Mason going for hours, but eventually even he had to give in to his fatigue.

"Han, this has been a fantastic evening, but I have got to call it quits," Mason conceded. "I am at the end of the road."

"Ah, my friend. You Americans really need to learn how to pace yourselves," Han laughed as they headed for the limousine. "I may have to introduce you to some Chinese herbs. They will give you more endurance."

By the time they got back, Mason was on the edge of total exhaustion. He never even changed out of his clothes, just crashed across the bed. He missed the morning team meeting and didn't join the negotiations until close to noon. Interestingly, Han had arrived early, looking very alert.

"So glad you could join us," Alex snidely remarked as Mason interrupted the meeting with his entrance. "I trust everything is well."

Mason just glared, knowing that he had no defense that even sounded reasonable. "Sorry, I am late. Please carry on."

The other team members glanced at each other with looks of disgust. It wasn't as if Mason was essential to the proceedings, despite his lofty title, but it would have been better had he tried harder to participate. The Chinese also seemed aggravated. They were very much into appearances, and would have never showed up late for the meetings. The only person who did not seem bothered was Han. In fact, he seemed quite undisturbed about the whole matter.

It turned out to be a terribly long day for all involved. After extensive and sometimes tense discussions, they had finally come to terms on several of the more arduous aspects of the project and, by the end of the day, a great deal of progress had been made. By late afternoon, everyone's mood seemed lighter and more relaxed. Even Lilly seemed more relaxed. Maggie had talked to her a little during the visit, but had never brought up the meeting between Lilly and Alex in the park. They both still acted a little awkward around each other, although they did pass glances and smiles fairly frequently. Maggie was curious, but did not feel like it would be appropriate to ask questions of either one of them.

"Alex, do you have a moment?" Maggie asked as Alex returned to the conference table to gather his paperwork. He had been speaking quietly to Lilly just before he came back to the table.

"Sure, what's up?"

"I have a couple of reports that I need help deciphering. I was hoping that you would have a few minutes to go over them with me—if you don't have other plans," Maggie answered, nodding her head and looking in the direction of the doorway.

Alex followed her movement and saw that Lilly was the object of Maggie's gaze. "No, not really. I was just asking her for directions to a particular restaurant. If you'll go with me, we can go over the reports you have questions about when we get back."

"I don't want to interrupt your evening plans. We can talk about them before the meeting tomorrow."

"You would not be interrupting. As a matter of fact, I was just getting ready to ask you to join me for dinner. I'm famished and I know you would like this restaurant. Please, say you will go with me," Alex added.

"All right. Will you starve to death if I take a few minutes to freshen up?" Maggie teasingly asked.

"I can probably survive for another half hour or so. I'll pick you up at your door."

Maggie hurried up to her room, really wishing she had time for a shower and a nap, but knowing there wasn't time for either one. She quickly changed clothes and was freshening her make-up when she heard Alex's knock.

"Ready?" he asked when she answered the door.

"Of course. Did you think I was going to let you die of malnutrition?" she joked.

They left the hotel and wound their way through the city's streets. Maggie never ceased to be impressed at how comfortable Alex felt with his surroundings. He always gave off an air of confidence that she wished she had. When they arrived at their destination, Maggie couldn't help but laugh. They were standing outside of a T.G.I. Friday's.

"How in the world did you know this place was here?" Maggie laughed.

"The Internet, how else?" Alex answered. "I was hungry for one of their steaks, and thought maybe, just maybe, there was a Friday's here in Chengdu. So, I Googled and here we are."

"Remind me to always take you with me on my international trips."

"I'm sure we could work out some arrangement," he said smilingly as they were shown to their table.

The aroma was magnificent. Suddenly Maggie realized that she too was hungry. It dawned on her that her lack of appetite on the trip was probably due to the smells assaulting her nose. She didn't want much to eat in a place where the smell drown out any thought of pleasing tastes. But this evening was wonderful and the food was superb. Maggie and Alex settled into comfortable conversation. The evenings they had spent together in China had given them a relaxed relationship. There was no agenda on either side except to enjoy the evening. They had learned a lot about each other and were amazed to learn how much they had in common. There was a level of trust building with each other and they each had a growing respect about the other's work ethics and abilities.

As the evening progress, the restaurant grew more crowded and the noise level increased accordingly. By the time they were ready to leave, they could hardly hear each other across the table. As soon as they walked out the door, they were struck by the difference in the noise around them. Although the streets were always full of people, they were not all trying to talk to each other at once.

"That was a wonderful meal, but honestly, I could have done with a little quieter atmosphere," Maggie commented as they walked back to their hotel. It was an early fall evening, and the weather was pleasant.

"I agree. I'm ready for a more sedate setting myself. Let's head back and go to work on those reports," Alex replied as he put his arm around her to steer them around an approaching group of people.

Alex's act of protection was not lost on Maggie. When he had touched her, she felt a chill up her spine. It was a response that both pleased and puzzled her, for she had not been expecting such a sensual reaction. She pushed the thought to the back of her brain as they entered the hotel and headed toward her room to retrieve the paperwork that she wanted to discuss.

"Do you want to go back to the conference room, or will it be okay to work here?" Maggie asked.

"If you are comfortable working in your room, I'd rather do that. I have had enough of that meeting room for one trip."

They spent the next two hours going over some of the electrical contracts for the plant. The construction could begin without these contracts being complete, but sooner, rather than later, they needed to be awarded. Maggie was familiar with the language used by electrical contractors, but when the Chinese translated their proposals into English, they sometimes were quite confusing. Maggie and Alex worked until they were both too tired to care anymore. Alex stood and stretched his back as he prepared to call it a night.

"You have brought up some interesting points with all this, but honestly, I am too exhausted tonight to be able to sort it all out. I'll send some emails tomorrow to get more information, and then we can make an educated decision on the electrical contractors for the plant. But it's just not going to happen tonight. We both need to get some rest."

"Oh, you're right. I never planned to get this involved in this mess tonight. I thought it would only take a few minutes to work out, but was I ever wrong about that," Maggie agreed as she walked Alex to the door. She had not realized just how tired she had become.

"I will see you bright and early in the morning, pretty lady. We have several details to iron out before we can move on to the next group of contracts," Alex said. He turned in the doorway and bent down and kissed her on the cheek.

Maggie didn't know what to think of his kiss, but decided she had too much to do before morning to spend much time day-dreaming about it. After all, she reasoned, it was probably nothing at all. Just a sweet gesture by a gentlemen. She turned her attention to a hot bath and a well-deserved night's sleep.

CHAPTER 24

"David, John and I are going to dinner in the hotel dining room in a couple of hours. Do you two want to join us?" Paul asked Maggie and Alex as they were all leaving the meeting.

"I'm good with that plan. It will let me get to bed earlier. I'm beat," Maggie answered.

"Me too. Sounds good. See you there," Alex joined as they entered the elevator.

Maggie used the time before dinner to take a quick shower and nap. By the time she went downstairs, she was feeling more rested. The men were already seated when she entered the dining room and were quick to motion her to the table. Maggie knew all of them from the office, but had never socialized with any of them, except for her dinners with Alex since they had been in China. She wasn't sure how she would fit in, but soon found her worry to be unnecessary. They were a comfortable group of men who were courteous to include Maggie in their conversation, asking her opinions and attempting to get to know her as well.

"Where's Mason? Did he not want to join us?" Maggie asked.

"In previous trips, he would occasionally go to dinner with us, but most often ate in the hotel here alone. Even if we were at a different table in the same room," David explained. "I guess we're not his preference in dining companions."

"I haven't seen him in the evenings at all on this trip. I thought the three of you had been going out," Paul smiled. "We haven't seen much of you either.

"I have been dragging Maggie out of the hotel to show her around at night, but we haven't seen Mason either," Alex clarified without acknowledging Paul's insinuation. "Of course, we haven't seen any of you out and about. Have you eaten in this restaurant every night?"

Having changed the focus away from Maggie and himself, Alex chided the trio as they listed all of their excuses for not leaving the hotel. Alex gave them a hard time over their lack of adventure and then told them about several places near the hotel that they should try. Maggie noticed that he did not tell them about Pete's cafe. Lingering a while after dinner, Maggie excused herself for the evening. Alex offered to walk her to her room, leaving the others to themselves.

"That was a very clever diversion with Paul tonight, after his comment about not seeing us," Maggie teased as they left the restaurant. "Are you always so chivalrous?"

"Paul was trying to go down a road he had no business traveling. I just took him on a detour," Alex replied.

"So, where do you think Mason is at night?" Maggie asked.

"Honestly, I hadn't given it much thought. As you can probably tell, I don't care much for Mason. He has no business being on this team; he doesn't pull his share of the load, but he wants to act like the big shot who's making it all happen. So as long as I don't have to deal with him, I don't care how he spends his free time," Alex replied tersely.

"It was just a casual question, Alex. Sorry I pushed your button."

"No, don't be. I'm the one who should be sorry. I have just been so aggravated at Mason. He comes dragging in every morning, looking like he hasn't slept at all; he adds nothing to the discussions; never says a word to anyone on the team, just glares at us when we ask him a question, and then visits during breaks with Han, as if they were old friends. I just don't understand why he's even here."

"I know. His behavior is not what I expected at all. And you're right-he and Han do seem rather chummy," Maggie added.

"Well, I still shouldn't have blasted you. Forgive me?" Alex asked with a smile that already knew the answer.

"I guess I have to forgive you. Who else will take me to dinner if I don't? It sure won't be those other guys-they're as cowardly as I am about venturing out," she laughed. "Good night, Alex."

Maggie thought about what the others had said about Mason's lack of camaraderie as well as Alex's opinion as she got ready for bed. She was concerned about Mason's behavior with the Chinese, wondering if his actions were affecting the negotiations. Perhaps that was why the Chinese were being so difficult. She had thought it was a cultural issue, but perhaps not. This was a situation that she would have to pay closer attention to and, if necessary, talk to Baron about when they returned home.

CHAPTER 25

Maggie couldn't believe that they were finally going home. The team had been in China for two weeks, but it felt more like two months to her. They had worked fourteen hours most days, tedious, intense work. Every detail to actually get the plant started had been ironed out, but not without a lot of concessions, in Maggie's opinion. Overall though, they were leaving with a workable plan. Soon the construction phase would begin and with any luck they should be producing compressors in a few months. There were still a lot of details to be worked out. All of the parts vendors were not in place, but at least most of the contracts for the building itself were completed. In the end, the construction bids came in just below budget, but Maggie knew that there would be plenty of unexpected problems that would push the costs over the amount allotted. She had already spoken with Baron about all of this, and even though they were a long way from negotiating prices with the parts suppliers, they at least felt good with Phase 1. They had long ago committed to this project, and even though all of the numbers weren't in yet, they knew they were not turning back. What Maggie knew that the other team members did not was that the budget for the project had plenty of unpublished padding in it for unexpected complications. Maggie knew that this was not the only project in the works, just merely the first, and that Utopia Energy was plotting a course in an entirely new direction from their past. If all went as planned, in fifteen years Utopia Energy would be the premier compressor supplier worldwide, in addition to all of its exploration and production business.

But that was the future. Maggie refocused her attention on the present project: finishing her packing and getting to the airport on time. She was not looking forward to the long flight, but at least when it was over she could sleep in her own bed. The thought of familiar surroundings warmed her heart and speeded up her progress. She needed to meet the team in the lobby in half an hour. She checked her watch and decided that there was time to grab a sweet roll in the hotel restaurant.

Apparently Maggie wasn't the only one with a growling stomach. When she walked into the restaurant, the rest of the team members, except for Mason, were already seated at a table.

"We left a seat for you, but weren't sure how long it would take a woman to pack," Paul Carter, the purchasing manager, ribbed her. "You know, women pack a lot of stuff when they travel."

"I think if you will check, you'll find that I have the same number of suitcases as the rest of you," Maggie chided back jokingly. They had all developed a comfortable relationship during the past two weeks.

"Oh sure, but our bags are much smaller than yours," he replied, feeling quite pleased with his comeback.

"Well then, in that case, you won't mind helping to carry my luggage," Maggie promptly answered.

Laughing at the way Maggie had backed Paul into a corner, they all conversed easily as they finished their breakfast. The car that took them to the airport arrived before Mason had joined them. Alex was about to ask the concierge to telephone Mason's room when the elevator opened and Mason, looking worse for the wear, joined them. His surly mood matched his physical appearance, and the other team members just looked at one another and grinned. Many of the mornings during this trip, Mason had joined the meeting looking a bit hungover, but this morning was the mother of them all. It was not going to be a pleasant flight for Mason.

When they arrived at the airport, they were pleased to find that there were no delays. The flight was long enough without having any extra time added to it. Settling into first class, Maggie found herself next to Alex for the return trip. It was a pleasant surprise and she found herself a little excited at the prospect of getting to visit with Alex for such a long stretch. Alex, too, was happy to see that they were going to be traveling companions. This had been a tough trip for all of them, but Maggie's presence had seemed to make the visit more pleasant. The guys all seemed to be on their best behavior, which had cut the gripe sessions down to a minimum. Alex and Maggie managed to talk their way through several hours without even mentioning business. Conversation was easy for them and before long they were both fighting sleep. Somewhere over the Pacific, they both drifted off into dreamland.

After changing planes in San Francisco, Maggie fell right back to sleep, but Alex knew enough to stay awake and try to get his body clock started back on Texas time. He smiled as he looked at Maggie sound asleep next to him. She would learn how to make the transition, but it would take a couple of trips. Alex couldn't help but think how beautiful she was, even after being on a plane for almost thirty hours. He was going to miss not working closely every day, but they would be headed back to China soon enough.

When they landed in Houston, Maggie was sure there wasn't a bone in her body that didn't ache. Waiting for the luggage to arrive, she truly wanted to just sit on the floor and cry. There wasn't even a drop of adrenaline left.

"Do you need a ride home?" Alex asked. He was tired also, but had done this trip enough to know to keep pushing.

"No thanks. Sara is picking me up. I hope she hasn't been delayed," Maggie answered, too tired to think about what she would do if Sara wasn't at the pickup area.

"I'll go with you to make sure she's there. I don't want you waiting alone for her, and you sure don't need to rent a car and try to drive to Katy," Alex announced as if she were some helpless damsel.

Maggie didn't argue with him, which indicated just how exhausted she really was at this point. Any other time she would have explained quite plainly that she could drive herself home. Luckily, there was no need for any further discussion. When they arrived at the pickup area, Sara was waiting.

"Hey there, world traveler," she said as she greeted Maggie with a big hug. "It feels like you've been gone forever."

"I have been," Maggie weakly replied as she introduced Alex to her best friend.

"We'll all have to get together sometime when you both are not so tired," Sara declared as they loaded Maggie's bags into Sara's car. "Do you need a ride, Alex?"

"Thank you, but no. I have my car here. In fact, here's the shuttle to long-term parking, so I'd better be going," Alex replied. "I'll see you Monday, Maggie."

"Sure. Have a restful weekend," she offered, smiling. She wasn't sure if she should shake his hand, the situation feeling somewhat awkward.

"Nice to meet you Sara. I hope to see you again," Alex said, as he leaned down and gave Maggie a quick kiss on the cheek and he was gone.

As Sara and Maggie made their way out of the airport complex, Sara was full of chatter and questions. Maggie just had to laugh at her energy. Maggie had only been gone two weeks, but Sara had "tons of stuff" to tell her. The trip from the airport seemed to fly, with Sara keeping the conversation going all by herself. When they got Maggie's luggage inside,

Maggie took a deep, soul-filling breath. It felt great to be home.

"I know you're tired. We'll get together on Sunday and you can tell me all about your great adventure-starting with that gorgeous hunk back at the airport." Sara smiled, looking over at Maggie with a knowing look that only best friends have with each other.

"Sunday. No problem. But don't get your hopes up about the gorgeous hunk. There's nothing to tell," Maggie replied as she walked Sara to the door.

"Whatever you say, my friend," Sara winked. "Whatever you say."

Maggie went back in the house and curled up in a blanket on the couch. It felt so good to be inside, still and quiet. No airport speakers, no plane roar, no conversations in foreign languages. Just peace. Yes, it was good to be home. She knew that sleeping in her own bed would feel like heaven, but the couch was as far as she managed go. Tomorrow she would have to pay bills and return calls, but for tonight she was too wiped out to even move. She had thought she would read, but her eyes and her brain would not focus. More and more she found her mind wandering to Alex. Had he made it home safely? Was he as exhausted as she was? Was he thinking about her?

Maggie shook her head to clear it of such foolish thoughts. Going down that fantasy road was a trip she didn't need to take. She was acting like a teenager. She wasn't ready for someone new in her life. She wasn't ready for the headaches that always come with a relationship. Besides, Alex had never given her any indication that he was interested in her romantically. Sure, he flirted. Lots of guys flirted. Most of them, actually. But it was harmless and didn't mean anything. More than likely, Alex didn't mean anything by it either. She knew this whole line of thought was just the result of jet lag.

Monday she would go into the office and everything with Alex would be back to normal, professional. Being in China was not real. Being in Houston was very real, very normal. Monday … it was her last thought as sleep finally claimed her.

CHAPTER 26

"It has been a while since my visit to Pyongyang. It is good to see you. I trust your trip was as pleasant as possible," Han said as they all settled into the limo. "I would have been happy to send a jet for you. It would have been much faster."

"Yes, but my government would never have let my family travel on a plane that someone else was supplying," Kim explained. "The train seems much safer to them-the destination is not likely to change as it could with a plane."

"Well, we wouldn't want to do anything that would upset your leadership," Han said, smiling at Kim's wife and son. "After all, we would love to have you return again soon. My wife has too many activities planned for just one visit."

Han continued to chat with Kim's family on the ride from the train station to the hotel. He had arranged for his North Korean guests to stay in a luxury suite at one of Beijing's finest hotels. It was important to show them the kind of life that was available outside the austere country they called home. If things went as Han had planned, Kim would find it impossible to turn down a chance at a better life.

When they arrived at the hotel, Han accompanied them inside to be sure everything was exactly as he had requested. When he saw that they were settled into their suite, he prepared to leave.

"I will return in about two hours to take you to my home for dinner," Han explained. "That should give you some time to rest from your long train ride. Is there anything you need before I leave?"

"No, my friend. Everything is just wonderful," Kim replied. "We look forward to dinner and the opportunity to meet your wife."

Han left the hotel, feeling optimistic about the evening. He genuinely liked Kim Cheol-su and wanted to return the hospitality shown to him on his visit to North Korea. More important, Han felt that Kim was fertile ground for exploitation. Kim did not seem to buy into the party line of propaganda and, while careful, communicated his discontent with his government's behavior, if only in his tone of voice. It would take time to develop the type of relationship that would be needed to even see if Kim was able to deliver the plutonium that Tiger Eye was looking to obtain. But Han was a patient-and calculating-man, especially when there was so much to be gained.

Han was so busy thinking about the steps of his plan that he had failed to notice the gentlemen who not only followed him out of the hotel's lobby, but was close behind as Han's car wove its way through the afternoon traffic.

CHAPTER 27

"Have you heard anything else from your source?" Li Jie asked quietly as they went over the hotel's invoice.

"No. I was hoping that you would have some information from Beijing," Tae replied. "There has to be something in the works; for Kim to travel unescorted even to Beijing, is unprecedented. Joo never passes along inconsequential information. If he is suspicious, then there must be more to this trip than what the surface shows."

"Beijing agrees with you. Several weeks ago, Han was photographed meeting with a known Muslim extremist, Cai Yi. We were following Yi at the time and have had no idea why the two men were meeting. We kept a tail on Han after that, but there has been nothing unusual in his routine since that first meeting. Now Han is making friends with a high-ranking North Korean."

"So, suddenly a successful, but harmless, Chinese businessman has expanded his circle of friends to include Communist leaders and underground terrorists," Tae reflected. "Why doesn't this all seem like a random coincidence?"

"Who thinks it is?" the undercover agent asked. "No one in Beijing has a clue as to what may be going down, but everyone feels there must be something sinister in the planning. The Muslim movement does not have a footprint within North Korea, much less a radical arm. Even if they did, what would they need from Han?"

"Maybe Han needs something from the Minister," Tae rambled, his mind bouncing from one thought to another.

"But what could he want? Is he acting as a government official or a private businessman?"

"If Kim has something Han wants, why would Kim need to travel to Beijing?" Li Jie asked. "Are you sure his family is traveling with him?"

"That's what my contact told me," Tae answered. "Apparently Han requested that they come along. He wants their wives to get to know each other. There's no way that can be part of the official food-exchange business."

"I'm sure you are right about that. If you hear anything else, you find a way to come back to Dandong. The embassy is anxious to hear anything else that you can find out. I am to contact them with any new information."

"I'll do that. If anything surfaces, I will make an emergency trip for supplies." Tae replied. "If not, we will wait to see what happens on the Chinese side of the border."

Tae stopped to visit to his lady, but instead of staying the entire afternoon with her, he found himself leaving after only an hour. He could not keep his mind from wondering what might be unfolding within the Ministry of Foreign Affairs. The entire situation with Kim and Han was just too suspicious to ignore. Korean officials did not socialize with Chinese businessmen; they did not visit each other as a vacation destination. Even the concept of a vacation was alien to the people of North Korea. There was something brewing and Tae wanted to be the one to find out what; he wanted out of Pyongyang and if he could uncover a major event, it might just be his ticket to a better assignment. He had spent his entire career in both Asia and Southeast Asia, but his stint in North Korea had been the most emotionally difficult. He was ready for more color, more activity. When Tae returned to the city, he would contact Joo. It was time they had lunch together and time for Tae to turn up the pressure on his contact.

CHAPTER 28

"Are you awake yet?" Sara asked. "It took you a long time to answer the phone."

"That's because I kept thinking it was the alarm and I kept trying to hit the snooze button," Maggie admitted. "What time is it anyway?"

"Close to noon, sleepyhead. Dan and I started to bring you breakfast, but we figured you might want to sleep through that meal."

"I'd like to sleep through the next two or three meals, but I guess I should get up and try to move around," Maggie said, yawning as she sat up. "I ache all over."

"Well that's what you get for jet-setting all over the globe," Sara teased.

"Trust me, it is not some glamorous photo op. This is tough."

"I'm really not making fun of you. I can only imagine how awful you feel, but you are right: you need to get up and get moving. Why don't you take a shower and go through your mail and then tonight go to dinner with Dan and me? We're dying to hear all about your trip."

"You may be dying to hear about it, but I'm sure Dan won't be all that interested. It's not very exciting," Maggie answered. "But I will accept your invitation as long as you promise to take me somewhere they serve real steak and potatoes."

"You're on-we'll go to Saltgrass. Pick you up at seven," Sara said as she ended their phone call.

Maggie managed to drag herself into the shower and stand there for at least twenty minutes. She couldn't remember when hot water had ever felt this good. After dressing she opened all the shades in the house to let the sun in. She was amazed at the sky. Even with the pollution from the Houston, compared to Chengdu, this sky was clear and fresh. After a shot of caffeine, Maggie started her laundry and tackled the stack of mail. It was mostly junk, since almost all of her bills were bank drafted. She decided to make a quick trip to the store so that there would be food in the house for the week. By the time she returned, she was ready for a nap. It hadn't taken much effort to wear her out. She wondered how she would ever get through the work day on Monday. After a short nap, she hurriedly got ready for dinner and was just finishing her hair when the doorbell rang.

"Wow, you look much better than you did last night," Sara joked as they headed for the car. "You need to be sharing whatever it is you're taking."

"Don't let looks fool you. I may fall asleep during the middle of dinner, so you two had better keep it lively," Maggie warned.

Dan had made reservations, so they didn't have a long wait when they got to the restaurant. The place was busy and the crowd was noisy, which worked great for Maggie. She felt her adrenaline pick up as she began to eat.

"This is so wonderful. We may have to come back here tomorrow night," Maggie managed to laugh between bites. She had forgotten how completely comforting real live American food could taste.

The three of them had a very relaxing meal, as they always did. Maggie never minded being "single" when she was out with Sara and Dan. It was more like three separate friends than one couple and one single. She was comfortable with them both.

"So tell us what China is like," Dan urged.

"I can't really tell you much. We changed planes in Beijing and when we got to Chengdu we spent most of the time in the hotel. Sometimes we went to a vendor's location and we went out at night some, but I really didn't get to sightsee at all. It's a very crowded place with horrible air quality," Maggie explained. "But there were some interesting moments."

Maggie went on for the next hour or so telling them about going to dinner at Pete's Café and having breakfast at Starbucks. She had been amazed to see lots of familiar American logos whenever she was out with the team or when she and Alex ventured out for something different from the hotel food.

"Sounds like you and this Alex guy spent a lot of time together," Sara commented with a conspiratorial tone. "Maybe this job assignment has some perks you didn't think about."

Maggie tried not to smile, but failed miserably. Just thinking about Alex's kindness to her warmed her heart. "He's a really nice guy, but don't get too wound up in anything. He was just being nice to me since I fell apart that first night. It's just the way he operates."

"Yeah, and giving you a kiss at the airport was just him being a nice guy also?" Sara questioned. "It didn't look like a pity gesture to me."

"You always make more out of things than there really is, so just let this one go. Our relationship is purely professional."

Sara was about to keep digging when the waitress interrupted with their desserts. Maggie was glad for the intrusion. Alex was not a subject she wanted Sara to get hung up on. She loved Sara, but sometimes she went overboard with her need to fill Maggie's life with a man. Maggie knew that Sara's intentions were heartfelt and because of that Maggie overlooked a lot of her matchmaking attempts. Sara just wanted Maggie to have someone special in her life so that she didn't feel so alone. What Sara didn't understand was that Maggie had already had that special person and the chances of another one seemed pretty slim to her. Most of the time she went along with Sara, just to keep the peace. But not with Alex. He was her business colleague and Maggie didn't need that complication in her life right now.

Dan managed to keep the rest of the evening's conversation going with tales of his latest office stories. FBI Special Agent Dan Kardan was always good for some interesting laughs. He never told any of the details of his cases and only talked about investigations that were closed. While he never gave specifics, he could keep the stories coming for hours about the dumb things that criminals did. Tonight he knew that he needed to get the subject off China and Alex before Sara pushed Maggie too far. He loved Sara, but understood that she sometimes crossed the line with Maggie. Maggie, sensing his intervention, mouthed a thank you to him when Sara wasn't looking. It wasn't the first time he had bailed Maggie out and she was grateful every time he did so.

Before long, Maggie was struggling to keep from yawning, so they all decided to call it a night. Maggie barely remembered the drive back to her house and was relieved that Dan was driving. After their goodbyes, Maggie headed for bed, so tired that she never remembered her head hitting the pillow.

She was still in that comatose state when she heard a rude, blaring sound. It took a few minutes for her conscious mind to realize that the alarm clock was going off and to register that this was a work day. Dragging herself into work was harder than she ever remembered. She tried to get there early, and managed to do so, but not by much. She had barely sat down at her desk when Anne arrived. Luckily Anne had learned that the trick to getting the China team moving again that first day was caffeine, and lots of it. She came in with the biggest and strongest Starbucks had to offer, followed by chocolate-filled donuts. Maggie just looked at her like she had lost her mind, and then burst out laughing as she took the coffee from Anne. It was good to be home, even if she was going to have a sugar crash in a couple of hours.

The morning went by like lightning. Maggie had spent two hours in Baron's office going through a debriefing. She really didn't have the answers to all of his concerns, but they both felt she was beginning to get a grasp on the numbers. A lot of the problems stemmed from calculation differences in currency and in the fact that more than one vendor's bids were being turned in by different team members. There definitely was a communication problem within the team and as much as Maggie hated to say it, she felt that Mason promoted the confusion. It was as if he was a one-man show, sitting in at the bargaining table all day and then going out with the Chinese at night and negotiating another deal completely. Sometimes the results were better, sometimes not. She wasn't sure how to handle the issue since the Chinese seemed to really like Mason. There would have to be more thought and study before they knew what course to take.

Maggie worked straight through lunch, trying to get through the backlog on her desk. Even though most of her workload had been delegated to others, there still was an enormous amount of work that needed her attention, not to mention answering questions from those who had taken over her other projects. By the end of the day she was exhausted again. It was all she could do to get into the house, kick off her shoes, and stagger to the couch. Within seconds, she was out like a light.

CHAPTER 29

Alex poured himself a drink and settled into his favorite chair. It was a wretched night with howling winds and rain. While Houston weather never came close to the cold he had experienced during college in Boston, there were still nights like this that were just as miserable. But Alex really didn't care tonight; the bad weather would give him a good excuse to rest up. His body still hadn't recovered from the jet lag and his muscles truly ached. A long, quiet evening sounded wonderful. Of course, it would be even better if he was cuddled up with Maggie. He wondered if she ever had the same thoughts about him and was afraid he already knew the answer. Maggie was still in love with Tom and would always be. Theirs had been a magical marriage and Alex couldn't blame Maggie for never wanting anything else. But still, he wanted her. After spending so much time with her during the past two weeks, he found that she was constantly in his thoughts and filled his nights with warm sensual dreams. He knew inside that she never thought of him in that way, but just the idea that she might was enough to take him into a fantasy world.

Alex hadn't felt this way about anyone in a long time. After Amanda, he hadn't allowed himself to let anyone get too close. There had been other women, companions, but nothing more. Alex always managed to gracefully end each relationship long before it got too serious. He had remained friends with many of the women he had been with and even met them for occasional lunches. His friends were amazed that he managed to sidestep any serious relationship while maintaining a long list of dinner date choices. For Alex it was easy: He never led women on, never promised or insinuated more than was there, and was always a friend first. It kept things simple. But with Maggie … it was different. He wanted to hold her, laugh with her, protect her, grow old with her. He was mesmerized by her hazel eyes and addicted to her deep, soul-filling laugh. She was good and honest and he trusted her. There was no agenda with her. She was just living her life and Alex knew he wanted to be a part of it.

But Maggie was off-limits. Or at least it felt that way. Maybe that was just Alex's perception-or the perception of the office. She and Tom had been a larger-than-life couple and it was hard not to look at her as Tom's wife, even though he had been gone seven years. She had always had her own place at the company, separate and apart from Tom's, and she was liked and respected. But there was an unspoken hands-off rule. It wasn't that she made that rule, but rather it was more out of respect for a friend and colleague who was no longer with them.

The absurdity of that whole concept was very obvious to him, but some part of him bought into it. He dialed Maggie's number before he had time to talk himself out of it. He was about to hang up when she fuzzily answered the phone.

"Did I wake you?"

"Alex? What time is it?"

"It's about 8:30, but you sound like you were asleep"

"I guess I was. I came in from the office and laid down on the couch for a few minutes. I guess I was exhausted." Maggie yawned.

"It's difficult to get back into a routine after traveling halfway around the world. Your body just doesn't adjust very quickly," explained Alex.

"My body doesn't do anything quickly anymore," Maggie reflected as she slowly sat upright, back and neck aching. "What's up?"

"I, uh, well, um, I just wanted to make sure you were home. The rain is really coming down," Alex stammered, suddenly unsure of himself.

"That's so sweet. It was just starting to rain on my way home, but it sounds much worse now. I'm glad I'm in for the night and I don't have to fight this mess again until morning. I heard it was supposed to do this all day tomorrow."

"Yeah, I heard that too. I guess I'll let you get back to sleep. Sorry I woke you but I'm glad that you're in and safe." Alex hesitated, not wanting the conversation to end.

"Thank you so much for calling. It's been a long time since someone checked on my well-being. I really appreciate it," Maggie quietly said. She knew her tone was a little more serious than she intended, but Alex's concern touched her heart in ways she couldn't understand.

At a loss for a proper response, Alex ended the call with a promise to stop by her office in the morning.

Still groggy from sleep, Maggie laid the phone down and immediately fell back into dreamland. Alex, on the other hand, was way past the point of sleep. He was too tired to sleep and too tired to think logically, but the weariness did not stop his mind from wandering back into fantasyland. Somewhere in the quiet of his living room his body finally gave up the fight, and he slipped off into the night.

CHAPTER 30

Early the next morning, Han took Kim to his office at Beijing Financial where they spent the morning going over some of the logistics for the first shipment of food into North Korea. Because of his position on the government panel, Han was able to secure the transportation contract to one of Tiger Eye's companies. It was a very lucrative deal for the business and allowed the government to let someone else deal with the details.

"So, you own part of the company that will be delivering the food to my country?" Kim asked. "How did you manage that deal?"

"My government is very interested in being perceived as an important influence in the world," Han explained. "But they do not really want to manage the specific details of an agreement."

"I did not realize that they allowed such independence among the people," Kim replied. "That would never happen in my country."

"It is not a well-known, or even widespread, practice here," Han continued. "They are only tolerant with those they feel they can trust. As long as everyone plays the game politely, there are no problems."

"It would be nice to be able to just 'play the game', as you put it," Kim reflected. "I think my country would be in better shape to feed its own people if there was more open trade with the rest of the world. But, I am sure they do not care what I think."

"Things are always changing, my friend," Han responded. "One must always be ready to seize what opportunities come their way. You never know what your life may be like tomorrow."

The two men finished their work and decided to spend the afternoon on a tour of the city. Their wives were busy shopping, while Kim's son was taken to the Beijing Zoo by Han's housekeeper. The first stop after lunch was Tiananmen Square, where they were invisibly shadowed by two tourists loaded with guidebooks and the latest in digital camera equipment.

"This is one of the most prominent sites in our city," Han explained. "The Tiananmen was first built in 1417 during the Ming Dynasty and has existed in its present form since around 1901. It is the largest square in the world–440,000 square meters."

"I have seen many pictures of this place," Kim told his host, "but I never realized how massive it is. It is amazing."

"Today we shall visit the Mausoleum of Mao Zedong," Han continued. "I can get us to the head of the line, but I am afraid we will have to pass through quickly. There are so many people who come here each day that they have to keep the line moving at a swift pace."

What Han did not tell his visitor, or perhaps did not know himself, was that the people were pushed through quickly so that they would not get a good look at the corpse, said to either be decaying rapidly, or not to even be real. Mao had wanted to be cremated, but Communist officials had other plans. Unfortunately, their plans for embalming required expertise that they did not have at the time of Mao's death.

Even with the quick viewing, the men's afternoon was coming to an end. Han returned Kim to the hotel and made arrangements for the two families to have dinner later in the evening.

Both Kim and Han felt that their day had been not only enjoyable, but profitable in the sense that a relationship was being formed. Han felt that his plan to use Kim to obtain plutonium was progressing at an acceptable pace. What he did not know was that Kim had ulterior motives of his own. For years, he had been passing out favors whenever possible in exchange for cold, hard cash. He had a healthy balance at a bank in Switzerland, and when the time was right, he would take his family and leave North Korea. He did not plan to stay one day longer than necessary, but at the same time, he knew he had to have enough funds to provide for any situation that might occur with such a drastic move. Kim thought he had perhaps found the final solution for his plan. It would take time, but the rewards were surely worth the wait. Kim had every intention of using Han to finance his defection.

CHAPTER 31

"I'm afraid you've come out on the worse night of the year, although they all seem rough lately. The rain is coming down in sheets," Maggie observed as she looked out the kitchen window. "Good thing tomorrow isn't a work day. It looks like the rain has set in for a while." It had been raining for several days now and didn't look like it was going to let up anytime soon. November in Houston was never what Maggie would call cold, but between the cooler night air and the rain, her fireplace was a welcomed addition to the evening.

"Well, I can think of worse places to be tonight. Thank you for the invitation. Beautiful home, lovely company, great food. That was the best meal I've had in a long time," Alex complimented as he helped clear the table. "Do you cook often?"

"Thank you. And no, I rarely cook. It seems a little foolish to go to much trouble for just one person. It's a lot more fun when you have someone to share a meal with" Maggie replied. "Do you cook?"

"I'm pretty handy with a grill, but that's about it. My side dishes consist of a baked potato and a salad."

"Not a bad combination. I love grilled food, but I'm not an outdoor chef. We'll have to negotiate some sort of joint venture," Maggie suggested. "Make yourself at home while I finish these dishes?"

While Maggie wrapped up in the kitchen, Alex wandered into the living room, admiring the peacefulness of Maggie's home. There was something about a home filled with beautiful wood furniture and with so much attention to detail. There was such craftsmanship everywhere he looked; he wondered if this was Tom's fingerprint on the house.

"What thoughts are you so lost in?"

The sound of Maggie's voice startled Alex. He didn't realize she had been standing there. "I was just thinking about how beautiful your place is, how comfortable it feels."

"What a nice compliment. I'm glad you feel comfy. Here, I brought you some hot chocolate. It seemed like the perfect thing for such a stormy night. Sometime when the weather is better, you must come out and barbeque for me and we'll relax on the patio, maybe enjoy the hot-tub."

"You just name the time; I'll be out in a heartbeat. I could stay here forever. How do you tear yourself away to come into town everyday?" he asked as they sat down in front of the fire.

"Don't get me wrong, I love it here. I love the space and the openness. But unless you have someone to share it with, the silence can be deafening." Maggie's voice dropped, along with her gaze.

Alex didn't know how to respond. Inadvertently he had brought up a sad subject and that had not been his intention. "I'm glad you offered to share it with me tonight. You know, it can get pretty quiet in my condo too," Alex said softly as he reached over and took Maggie's hand.

Maggie's heart was beating so loudly, she was sure Alex could hear it. Maggie was out of practice at having these kinds of butterflies. She hadn't allowed anyone to get close to her in a long time. But Alex was different. She found herself hoping he would kiss her-just like in her dreams. He moved closer to her and put his arm around her, drawing her in close to him. Then he gently kissed her. It was a long, slow kiss. The kind that Maggie could get totally lost in.

"Now, this is a nice way to spend an evening," he whispered in her ear as he continued to hold her.

Their conversation went on for hours, sprinkled through-out with slow, gentle kisses. By the time Alex finally left, Maggie was punch-drunk with emotion. One minute they would be deep in discussion and the next moment they were kissing. It was not urgent, impatient kissing, but instead the kind shared between two people who were very comfortable with each other, who had been together a long time. It was sensual, private. Maggie couldn't explain how it felt even to herself; she just knew it made her feel good.

She had learned a great deal about Alex tonight and his everyday life outside the office. She knew all about his nieces and nephews, his family's traditions, his secret desire to be a Navy Seal. But Alex didn't talk at all about his college years. It was a subject he avoided whenever the conversation headed in that direction. Odd, she thought, but her mind quickly brushed it off. Everyone had painful periods in their lives that they didn't always want to share with others. She knew that feeling as well as anyone, and it wasn't something worth pushing him to talk about.

CHAPTER 32

On his way back from a business luncheon, Han decided to spend a few minutes in the park. He needed a little peace before diving back into the frantic pace of his office. Han's mind had drifted away from even the sounds of the birds and the laughter of the people, when he was startled by the young boy who ran up to him. Looking down into the face of the child, no more than five or six years old, reminded him of his own sons when they were that age. Sweet and innocent and full of questions. This child said nothing, just handed him an envelope and ran back onto the playground.

Looking around, Han saw no one watching him as he slowly opened the envelope. The paper inside was plain, no signature or letterhead, and was hand-printed with tomorrow's date, the time, and the name of the same outdoor restaurant where he and Cai Yi had met a month earlier. He could only assume that the message was from Yi, but the fact that stopping in the park had been an impulse gave Han a alarming feeling. Obviously someone had been following him, someone who used the child as a messenger rather than be seen himself. Which probably meant he would continue to follow Han and did not want to be identified. Han remained on the park bench for several more minutes, casually trying to locate the tail. Unable to decide on anyone, he left the park and headed back to his office, continually aware of the people sharing his surroundings. At one point that thought amused Han: How could you concentrate on any one person in a city of seventeen million people?

Finishing paperwork that needed immediate attention, Han left Beijing Financial and drove to the building that housed the corporate offices of Tiger Eye Enterprises. Although Han did not participate in the daily business of the firm, he did keep an office there and was a frequently seen face in the building.

Han casually walked into one of the offices of his colleagues and closed the door. The office belonged to Fu Ling, one of the six founding members and the one who oversaw most of the operations of the various companies.

"What brings you here this time of day?" Ling asked. "I don't usually see you until closer to quitting time."

"I got a message from Yi today," Han said, handing the note from the park to his companion. "It seems he is having me followed; no one else knew where I was going for lunch, and yet a child delivered a message to me."

"I'm sure that doesn't surprise you, given his reputation as a savvy businessman," Ling replied.

"He suggested we meet tomorrow, and is going to want to know our answer," Han said flatly.

"Just tell him that we are interested in pursuing the opportunity of doing business with him but that we need more details as to how and when and where he wants the product delivered," Ling continued. "If he won't give you enough of the details to help us decide if we can pull this off, then just walk away from the deal."

"He is also going to have to meet our price, which we won't know until we know all of the details," Han added. "You know, this guy is so cryptic and spooky, but for the right price I can get past his personality defects."

The other man laughed and the two of them discussed other business that was going on within their empire. Before too long, they heard the others in the office leaving for the day and decided it was time to head home themselves.

"I will stop by tomorrow after my meeting and let you know what happened," Han offered. "Either way, it will be an interesting conversation."

"No doubt it will be," Ling replied. "With any luck, we will need to call the others together to update them on the project."

"Luck, my friend, will have nothing to do with it," Han commented as they both left the building and headed home.

CHAPTER 33

The waiter had just brought Han's tea to the table when Cai Yi appeared out of the bustling sidewalk crowd. It gave Han a chill, as if the man could just materialize from thin air.

"It is good to see you." Yi greeted Han as if they were old friends. "I like a man who is punctual."

"As do I," Han replied. "We are both busy men with no time to waste."

"Then let me get right to the point. Have you and your associates come to a decision as to my proposal?" Yi asked.

"Perhaps. We have some questions prior to giving you our reply," Han calmly answered. "Our answer is dependent upon your response."

"That is fair enough, as long as you remember to be careful what you ask," Yi warned. "There are many things you do not want to know."

"I'm sure that is true," Han agreed. "However, without some information, we cannot know if our participation is even feasible. We need to know how much of the product you will be needing, how quickly you will want it, and the destination where you will need delivery to be made."

"As I have said before, the time table is very flexible. It could take months or possibly a year. The product needs to be delivered in small quantities to avoid any issues with the authorities," Yi said quietly. "My customer is looking for approximately one quarter of a kilogram."

"An amount that large will take time indeed, but it is not out of the realm of possibility," Han commented.

"The product needs to be shipped to the United States—Houston to be specific," Yi continued. "I understand that you have operations at the port there. All you need to do is get the product to Houston and my client will pick it up at your warehouse."

"You make it all seem so simple," Han snidely remarked. "Are you forgetting that the US Customs stays on high alert for this type of cargo?"

"I am forgetting nothing, my friend," Yi said, leaning in closer to Han. "That is why you were chosen. You and your colleagues are very smart men. You did not get where you are by letting details get in your way. I have faith in your ability to find a way around this little obstacle."

"This obstacle is not so little," Han said under his breath as a couple walked by the table. "How much do you think this project is worth to your client?"

"So, you are interested in participating?" Yi questioned smiling.

"We are always interested in profitable undertakings," Han replied. "The question is whether this one is profitable enough for the risks involved."

Yi slid a piece of paper across the table to Han, who picked it up and looked at the figure, using his best poker face expression. The note had 300 million US dollars written on it. Han was careful to control his breathing. His first thought was that this was going to be well worth the effort, but if they were willing to pay this amount, they would be willing to pay much more.

"I will take this to my associates, along with the details involved," Han very calmly commented. "Meet me here one week from today, same time."

"Very well. I trust we will enjoy working together," Yi said as he stood to leave.

"Enjoyment has nothing to do with this project," Han replied. "This is strictly business."

Once again, the Muslim blended into the crowd immediately. Han sat at the table for several minutes trying to absorb the enormity of the proposal. He resisted the urge to call one of the others at Tiger Eye. He could not be sure that Yi was not watching, and he did not want to appear too eager. What he did not realize was that Yi was not the one watching him. Han was totally unaware of the tourist snapping pictures of the outdoor café.

CHAPTER 34

Han made his way to the Tiger Eye offices, followed by the camera-toting tourist, whose companion had pursued Yi when he left the café. Han, lost in his own thoughts, was not paying attention to anyone in the crowd, but his pace showed a determination to get to a specific place. When he went into the building, the tourist casually stopped on a park bench across the street and took several photos of the building, being sure to get a shot that showed the name of the business.

Inside, Han quickly entered the office of Fu Ling, who did not seem surprised to see his colleague. Ling dismissed the secretary who was in the office and asked her to shut the door as she left.

"I assume that you met with Yi," Ling commented when they were alone.

"Yes, and this is much bigger than we had thought," Han replied. "They want a great deal of plutonium and are willing to pay an enormous amount of American money to make it happen."

"Did he tell you where he wanted it shipped?" Ling asked.

"Houston. He wants us to ship it to our warehouse at the port," Han explained. "His client will arrange for pick up at the warehouse. They need a quarter of a kilogram."

"That's not a small amount. Can you acquire that large a shipment?" Ling asked.

"I'm not certain at this point that I can obtain any plutonium," Han admitted, running his hand through his hair. "I am still working on cultivating a relationship with someone who might be a source. If this falls through, we would have to start all over. I'm not sure where else to even look."

"We must not panic," Ling reassured his friend. "If we cannot rely on the source you are working on, then we will simply pull out of the deal. There is no need to expose ourselves hunting for sources of a product that we know little about."

"You should not be so quick to dismiss this entire project," Han stated. "Yi's initial offer was to pay us 300 million dollars."

Ling sat behind his desk, speechless. That was a massive amount of money, even for these men.

"We need to call the others," Han suggested, finally breaking the silence. "This is not something one or two of us should decide alone."

Ling agreed and telephoned the other four board members. Within the hour, they were seated around the conference table, stunned at the update in the developments that had occurred.

"How confident are you with the source you are cultivating?" one man asked.

"I feel that I am making progress, but at this point I cannot be certain of the outcome," Han answered. "I have yet to even approach the subject."

"When do you have to give Yi an answer?" another member inquired.

"One week from today," Han replied. "Too soon to be able to know if my source will come through or not."

"It is an enormous amount of money to walk away from," Ling commented. "I think we should figure out a way to buy more time before giving a definitive answer."

"I have been thinking about that," Han offered. "I suggest that we tell him that we need two months to see if we can cultivate a source. The million dollars that he has already paid will cover the expenses for that period of research. However, if we see that we can indeed find a supplier, then our price for the project will be 500 million dollars, American."

The men just stared at him in disbelief. The amount offered already exceeded what they had anticipated. To raise the bet that much was an extremely risky move.

"I think it's a reasonable number, considering that we will be taking all the risks and doing all of the work," Han continued. "We could pay my source a few million, which is way beyond his wildest dreams, and still walk away with a great deal of money."

"What makes you think that they would be willing to up their offer that much?" one of the men asked.

"I don't know that they will," Han admitted. "But I do know that you never accept the first offer. Besides, if they could pull this project off themselves, they would not have come to us. We operate on such a different level that no one would ever suspect that we would be involved in anything to do with radioactive material. They need us because they are too close to the fire to be able to do this on their own."

"Assuming Yi goes for your counteroffer," Ling began, "will two months be enough time for you to know whether or not you can bring your source over to our side?"

"I think so," Han answered. "I have already been working on him. Even if we cannot use him for this project, one can never cultivate too many friends in high places. Someday he will come in handy; I just don't know if it will be this soon."

"Let's make an assumption that your source comes on board," Ling continued. "How will we get the product to Houston? I know we have a freight company, but we can't just ship plutonium to a warehouse in the US. There has to be a cover."

"I have been thinking about that as well," Han replied. "My bank is in negotiations to finance an American company to build natural gas compressors in Chengdu and ship them to Houston. I am actively involved in that project and have an idea about how that situation can be compromised to our benefit."

The men were amazed at how circumstances seemed to be falling into their laps. They discussed the subject for another hour or so, before heading for their homes, each of them consumed by a combination of excitement and fear: excitement about the prospect of becoming extremely wealthy; fear of how bad their lives could get if anything went wrong.

They exited the building as a group, totally oblivious to the photographer sitting on the park bench-and equally unaware that things had already gone wrong.

CHAPTER 35

"Good morning, stranger." Anne greeted Maggie with a warm smile and a cup of hot coffee. "Just about the time I get used to you being gone, you pop in again."

"I feel like this is all I do-pop from one continent to another," Maggie replied as she took a deep whiff of the coffee, knowing it was too hot to even attempt to drink. "I get settled back here and then we're off to China again. I'm not sure this is what I bargained for when I signed up for this circus."

"Well, it won't last forever, I hope. I hate it around here when you're gone. No one can figure out anything on their own. All I hear is 'can't you call Maggie' or 'when will Maggie be back?' They don't realize that it's the middle of the night in Chengdu or that work must go on even if you aren't here."

"The problem is that they don't want to make the effort themselves to find what they need. It's much easier to ask me. Unfortunately for them, life is not going to be that way for some time to come," Maggie explained.

"You are so right. This is your first morning back and before you know it, you will be off again. So I guess we'd better start working through this mess," Anne commented as she reached for the pile of papers that Maggie had already gone through, making notes and corrections. "I'll get started on these while you work your way through another stack. Nothing like job security," Anne quipped as she headed back to her office.

Maggie smiled, knowing that Anne liked the challenge of keeping everything going while Maggie was in China.

Anne didn't mind any project you sent her way as long as things didn't get to be routine. She became bored easily and needed new adventures on a regular basis. Maggie also knew that she could depend on Anne to have every detail managed correctly. Anne was focused on the big picture and understood how every detail affected the overall scheme of things. Anne and Maggie made a great team. They approached things the same way and were not satisfied with mediocre performance from themselves or anyone else. Maggie was very lucky to have Anne working for her.

Just about the time that Maggie was deep into the next problem, there was a knock at her door. She looked up to see a familiar face.

"Hey there, pretty lady," Alex smiled as he came around her desk and whispered in her ear. "I missed having breakfast with you."

"I missed having it with you also," Maggie blushed from his closeness. "We had quite a habit going on in China."

"You are a habit I could get used to easily. So much so that I absolutely must have lunch with you today," Alex insisted.

"Alex, I can't get away. There is just too much to do here. I won't get caught up in time to leave again. I would love to have lunch with you, but I really can't. Not today," Maggie explained, hating herself for turning down his invitation.

"Well, kiddo, you really don't have any choice in the matter. Baron wants to have lunch with the two of us to talk about China. I'll be by to get you just before noon," Alex replied, proud of himself for having teased her.

"That's just great," Maggie groaned as she looked at all the work on her desk. Realizing how tacky her comment sounded she tried quickly to make amends. "I'm sorry. I didn't mean that the way it sounded. I always enjoy having lunch with you. I'm just a little overwhelmed here."

Alex smiled, understanding completely how she felt. He usually had that same sense of urgency the first day back, but he wasn't about to let anything come between him and a chance to spend time with Maggie. "No one understands that more than I do, but you have to take a break and eat. Tell yourself it's a working lunch and you won't feel near as guilty for unchaining yourself from this desk."

He kissed her on the back of her neck and was out of the office before she could react. She settled back in her chair and rested her brain for a few minutes. She knew he was right, that she would need the break, and that she didn't have a choice. She also knew that he had broken all chances of concentration with that kiss.

* * *

The morning passed quickly as Maggie and Anne worked their way through tons of paperwork. When Alex showed up for lunch, Maggie had to admit that she truly needed a break. There were too many numbers and details floating around in her head and she need to clear them out before she could face any more. It was much warmer than the weekend had been, and the sun felt good as they walked to a sidewalk café. Baron had already arrived and had secured them a table protected from the wind.

The three of them spent a long lunch catching up on the project as well as enjoying one another's company. Alex and Maggie had both known Baron for a long time, so there was camaraderie among them. Baron felt better about the progress of the plant in China, not so much because Maggie was there now, for he trusted the ability of each of the team members. What made him feel more comfortable now was that he was getting good feedback. The communication process before had been almost nonexistent. Baron felt that Mason was too secretive, maybe hiding something. Mason resented reporting to Baron. It was a never-ending cycle. But Maggie had nothing to hide. She was very secure in her position with the company and had no quarrels with the hierarchy. She was very willing to discuss anything about the project that Baron questioned, and Alex was there to fill in the blanks.

Baron understood that Alex needed the latitude to build the plant to the specifications needed to produce the most efficient manufacturing process. He also knew that Mason didn't always see the big picture and didn't understand Alex's persistence on some of the details. It was obvious that there was a problem between the two men, but he trusted Alex to be demanding enough to get what he needed to do the job correctly.

Each of his team members were exceptionally qualified components of the project, but that didn't mean that their personalities worked well together. Baron had often thought the project would be better if Mason was off the team and Alex was overseeing it. But for the moment, he had not totally convinced the powers that be-although they were coming around to his line of thought with each passing month without production. It would be best for everyone if the group in place could just get the wheels turning and compressors coming back into the US. But Baron was prepared to push the point about Mason if that was what it took to get the job done.

By the time they walked back to the office, Maggie was relaxed and felt much better about her workload. She had planned to work late to try to catch up, but changed her mind after lunch. There was a point when one became unproductive, and she knew she would be there quickly if she tried to work into the evening. Instead, she called Sara and invited her to an early dinner at one of their favorite restaurants. It would be good for just the two of them to get together and catch up on each other's lives.

As Maggie walked out of the office that afternoon, she met Alex leaving as well. They were both accustomed to taking the stairs, mostly because the elevators were slow and crowded. Alex walked Maggie to her car in the parking garage and seemed reluctant to say goodbye.

"Do you have dinner plans for tonight?" Alex asked, hoping she would join him.

"Yes, as a matter of fact I do. I am meeting my best friend for a well deserved girl's night. I would invite you to join us, but you don't fit the criteria of the evening," she joked.

"You are so right. I am definitely not a girl, although it might be interesting hearing what you two talk about."

"You'd probably be bored. You would much more enjoy an evening when Sara's boyfriend is with us. He's an FBI agent. Very fun and very interesting. Maybe we could all get together sometime," Maggie offered.

"Name the place. I've never met an FBI guy. I'll bet he would have good stories," Alex answered. "Just let me know when, and I'll be there."

As Maggie left Houston, and drove toward Katy, she thought about an evening with the four of them. It would be fun and Sara's excitement over Alex would be off the chart. Maggie had to laugh as she thought of Sara's reaction to Maggie's bringing a date. A date? Is that what Alex would be? Maggie's mood sobered as that thought settled into her mind. A date. Hmmm.

CHAPTER 36

"Are you sure it will fit into your truck?" Maggie asked as Alex struggled to get the Christmas tree into the truck bed and secured.

"You need to be more worried about getting it into your house. Trees grow from the farm to the house, didn't you know that?" Alex teased, wishing he had brought along some help.

"It will be perfect, Mr. Crabby, just wait and see," Maggie commented as she tossed her head and got into the truck. She and Alex had spent the morning at the tree farm, looking at every tree over five feet tall. Alex was exhausted by the time Maggie finally found the one she wanted.

In Maggie's heart, she knew this was the perfect tree, albeit very large. This was the first season since Tom had been gone that she found herself looking forward to the holidays. She was so full of Christmas spirit, she was making everyone else nauseous. She didn't care. It felt so good to be alive again, to feel excited over something, anything. She told herself it was because the traveling had made her appreciate home and all of its comforting rituals. Sara argued that it was Alex. Sara could be right, Maggie thought, but she wasn't ready to admit that out loud. Whatever the reason, Maggie was grateful for the peacefulness in her heart.

When they got to Maggie's house, the real struggle started. Just as Alex had predicted, the tree was way too big to go in through the front door. After clearing a pathway through the house, they managed to wrestle the tree in through the French doors off the patio. The tree dwarfed everything else in the living room, but Maggie was delighted. She had always loved blue spruce trees, but this one was Christmas-card perfect. Alex collapsed on the couch while Maggie walked from one side of the tree to the other, lost in her own decorating thoughts.

"We have a problem," Maggie declared as she stared at the huge spruce.

"Besides the fact that there is no room for anything else in here?" Alex sarcastically asked.

"Don't be so negative. With a little rearranging there will be plenty of space. The problem is that I don't think I have enough decorations. We need to go shopping," Maggie explained.

"We have been shopping all day. Can't we take a break first?" Alex complained, knowing full well he would do whatever necessary if it meant spending more time with Maggie.

"Okay. Break first, then we'll head into town for dinner and shopping," Maggie enthusiastically decided. She was having a great time, and she knew that Alex was only halfheartedly griping. He was enjoying himself too much to be very disgruntled.

They both stretched out on the couch and within minutes had fallen asleep. Alex woke first at the chiming of the grandfather clock, but he lay still, holding Maggie in his arms. He loved watching her sleep; she always seemed so peaceful. He knew that he was falling in love with Maggie, something he had never intended to do but was nevertheless helpless to stop. She was the first woman he had let this close to his heart since Amanda. He had always kept his guard up, but with Maggie, it felt different. He knew that Maggie was genuine, that she wasn't out to use him. He also knew that she still had deep, deep feelings for Tom, and he wasn't sure if she was truly ready to move on. He would never push her, but he knew he wanted to grow old with her. Alex was a patient man, and he would give her all the time and space she needed. Besides, he still hadn't told her about Amanda.

Maggie stirred in his arms and sleepily smiled. He wrapped her tighter in his arms and kissed her gently behind her right ear.

"That's a nice way to wake up," Maggie quietly said. "I could stay this way for a long time."

"I have no problem with that plan," Alex replied.

"Aren't you forgetting something very important?" Maggie questioned, grinning widely. "We have shopping to do."

Alex rolled his eyes and laughed. She had so much energy and enthusiasm; he just couldn't disappoint her—even if he would rather stay wrapped up on the couch.

Deciding that Mexican food was on the menu, they headed for La Cocina. By the time they finished their meal, both were feeling more lively and ready to look for Christmas decorations, but their energy ran out fairly quickly. They managed to finish the shopping but agreed to leave the decorating until Sunday.

CHAPTER 37

Alex arrived mid-morning the next day, only to find that Maggie had been up for hours. She had baked Christmas cookies and pumpkin bread and there was fresh coffee brewing. Alex's senses were overwhelmed with warmth and peacefulness.

"This is like walking into a fairy tale. I thought you didn't cook," Alex commented as he tasted some of the bread.

"I said I rarely cook. Besides, this is holiday baking and there is a distinct difference," Maggie smiled. "I love this time of year and all of the smells and sounds. It just felt like we needed treats to get us in the tree-trimming spirit."

"I think you have plenty of spirit, maybe too much for one person. Texas time must agree with you because you're never this cheery in China," he teased, taking a drink of coffee.

"You might be right. I don't like China; it's just a job that has to be done. But this is home and for the first time in several years, this is where I truly want to be. It's hard to explain," she ended quietly.

Before the conversation could get too serious, she grabbed a box of lights and headed for the living room. Following, Alex took Maggie into his arms and just held her. They embraced for what seemed like minutes, then without a word, began stringing the tree with lights. After a couple of hours of hanging every ornament in just the right place, Maggie stepped back to assess their efforts.

"It's absolutely breathtaking, don't you think?" Maggie asked as she cocked her head from one side to the other.

"Breathtaking might be a tad strong, but yes, it's beautiful," Alex answered. "I don't think there's room for another ornament."

Pleased with their accomplishment, Maggie grabbed her jacket and headed for the door. Not sure what he had missed, Alex just stood there with a perplexed look.

"Where are you going?" he questioned.

"I thought we were going Christmas shopping for your nieces and nephews. Don't you remember asking me to help you?" Maggie asked.

"I remember, but are you sure we need to do this today? Aren't you tired?"

"Don't be a Scrooge, Alex. It's Christmas!" Maggie laughed as she headed out of the house.

Laughing at her silly spirit, Alex locked the door behind him, thinking to himself what a wonderful life they were going to have together.

CHAPTER 38

Han arrived at the café a few minutes early. He was determined not to be taken by surprise this time. Yi always seemed to appear out of nowhere and his sudden presence always caught Han off guard.

The waiter came and took Han's order and as he left, Han heard a familiar voice coming from the table behind him.

"I thought you would have seen me when you came in," Yi said, almost lightheartedly.

Angry at being startled despite his efforts, Han slowly turned around to face the voice.

"You are a master at blending, my friend," Han said in the most unconcerned voice he could muster. "Won't you join me at my table?"

Yi very slowly and nonchalantly gathered his jacket and cup of tea and moved to the table that Han was occupying. He seemed almost amused with the whole situation.

"I hope you have good news for me today," Yi said as he sat down.

"I do have news," Han replied. "Whether it is good or not will be for you to decide."

"Well, that comment certainly piques my interest. Please, continue," Yi said in his most polite tone.

"I have spoken with my colleagues, and we are interested in doing business with you," Han began. "There are, however, some obstacles that will need to be overcome before we can be certain that we will be able to deliver your product as ordered."

"Obstacles?" Yi asked.

"Yes. Several, actually," Han quietly continued. "The most important, of course, is finding a dependable supply for the product you need. We have a lead in that area, but as you can imagine, it is not just something one advertises for in the newspaper. We need more time to be assured that the source we are cultivating will be reliable, without whom there will be no point in going forward with the project."

"That sounds reasonable. How much time do you think you will need?" Yi asked.

"We should know within the next two months," Han answered. "It is not something that can be rushed."

"Two months will not be a problem," Yi answered confidently. "What other concerns do you have?"

"One other is how to safely handle the product," Han said. "That, however, is just a technical issue. I have people researching that information already. Another area that I do not have worked out yet is how to get it to your destination. I realize that we can use our freight forwarding business to physically get the product to Houston. The question is having a consistent shipment going to that particular port."

"Obviously you have given this a great deal of thought," Yi commented. "I am confident that you will come up with a solution. But first things first: a supplier. Here is the number to call me when you have secured a source. This is a cell phone so please, be discreet. Just let me know what time and we will meet here at this spot to talk more freely."

As Yi got up to leave he handed Han a piece of paper with the phone number. Han cleared his voice and motioned for the man to sit back down. Once Yi was back in the chair, Han leaned in close so that no one could possibly overhear.

"There is one other obstacle," Han whispered. "Assuming we can get all of the problems that we have discussed worked out to everyone's satisfaction, this will be the price for our services."

Han slipped his own piece of paper to Yi and watched with some amusement the shocked look on Yi's face.

"You have two months to decide whether you wish to continue," Han said as he quietly left the table and quickly disappeared into the crowd.

CHAPTER 39

"My wife is having a wonderful time here," Kim commented as the two men met over breakfast. The restaurant was quite busy, with enough noise that no one could overhear any specific conversation. "She is not accustomed to all of the shopping opportunities that your wife has shown her. I may never get her back on the train to Pyongyang"

"I'm not sure that would be a bad thing," Han said, picking his words carefully. "If she were here, my wife would have a shopping companion, and then perhaps I would not ever have to go with her again."

"I can see your point." Kim laughed. "The problem would be paying for all of their entertainment. I am afraid that I do not make enough money working for the government to support that kind of addiction."

"Well, if that is the only problem, we can make this happen," Han smiled. "I can put you to work today at Beijing Financial making a very handsome salary. Your wife would be delighted."

"Ah, if it were only that simple," Kim replied in a more serious tone of voice. "I am afraid I do not have the skills you would need to make a 'handsome salary' a reality."

"Do not underestimate yourself, my friend," Han said sincerely. "You are an accomplished negotiator with a lifetime of experience. You would be a great asset to our organization-or even at Tiger Eye Enterprises. We are always on the lookout for talented risk-takers."

"For the sake of argument, why would a successful business look for someone who takes risks?" Kim calmly asked. He liked the direction that the conversation was going, but did not want to appear too eager.

"With the right controls in place, a risk-taker can be a company's biggest weapon," Han explained. "It is very easy to become complacent, to do things 'the way we've always done them.' It is good to have someone who is always thinking of new innovative directions that the company might pursue, rather than just being comfortable in the same old rut."

"And you think that I have the tendencies of such a person?" Kim asked.

"Without a doubt," Han answered. "You have had a great deal of practice in having to be both creative and diplomatic as a representative of a regime that holds you to such strict rules. Through it all, you seemed to have developed a healthy level of independent thought. I'm sure that is not very common in your world.

"Perhaps you are correct," Kim replied. "However, one might argue that having an independent attitude is the opposite of healthy in my country. I have to constantly be aware of my surroundings and my conversations. Talking to the wrong person could be highly dangerous for both my family and me. Even talking so freely to you today may get me killed tomorrow."

"You have nothing to worry about from me, my friend," Han tried to assure him. "I am somewhat of a rebel in my own country-I just try to be a subtle rebel. As you say, it makes for a much longer life. Besides, we were only speaking hypothetically. Nothing for anyone to get upset over, right?"

"Perhaps you were speaking in theories, but I am always thinking about my future, about my family's future," Kim said quietly. "The situation in my country is not good and there are no prospects of its improving in my lifetime. My position within the government has allowed my family to live better than most, but it has also allowed me the opportunity to see how people in other countries live. It makes it hard to be happy when I go home."

"It might be better to continue this conversation outside," Han said cautiously, looking around the busy room. "Even here, one can never be too careful. This might be the perfect morning for us to visit the Forbidden City. The Imperial Garden would be a good place for us to stroll through."

The men left the restaurant and Han's driver took them back to Tiananmen Square. Dismissing the driver, the men made their way slowly across the square toward the entrance to the Forbidden City.

"It is much safer to speak outside," Han explained. "I do not fear my government, at the moment, but you are here visiting and we can never be sure who might be interested in the nature of our conversations."

"It is always better to be cautious," Kim replied, casually looking around. There were lots of people in the square, but because of its large size, no one was close enough to listen to the two men. The men made casual conversation until they were in the Imperial Gardens, where there was enough space to not be overheard.

"So, am I to understand that you would consider leaving North Korea?" Han asked as soon as they were alone.

"I would leave tomorrow if the circumstances allowed for such," Kim answered. "It would take a lot of money to be able to live outside of my country. I would have to be somewhere that would not be too close to the regime. I could never escape to China. It would be far too dangerous. At this time, it is just a dream anyway. I do not have enough money saved, and despite what you might think, I do not have any marketable skills that would support my family in the real world."

"What if you had the money-enough to live extremely comfortably for the remainder of your life?" Han questioned. He was trying to control his emotions so that his voice would not give away his excitement. He had never dreamed of having this conversation so soon, but he was not going to turn back from it once the door opened.

"If I truly had the money tucked away in some safe country-such as Switzerland-then my options would be different," Kim said. "I would also have to have a plan to get my family and me out of the country. I have neither of those things."

"Details can be worked out under the right conditions," Han said authoritatively. "Life has a way of dropping opportunities right in your lap."

"Is this what is happening now? Are you my opportunity?" Kim asked, stopping to smell of a blooming tree whose limbs bent deeply under the weight of its white blossoms.

"I try to always be aware of doors being opened in front of me," Han replied. "Perhaps we can work something out, if you are serious. I have no desire to take unnecessary risks, but I am not opposed to them if the return is worth the possible danger."

"I would be quite interested in knowing what you could possibly have in mind," Kim said, trying desperately to control his excitement. He had seen too much and experienced too much on this trip to Beijing. To think that escape might truly be a possibility at this point in his life was almost more than he could stand. He had thought it would take at least twenty more years to even be close to getting out from under his regime-unless of course Kim Jong-un died, and that didn't appear too likely to happen anytime soon.

"What I have in mind is very dangerous; if you were to fail, it would cost you your life, and probably the lives of your family," Han said bluntly, stopping to look Kim in the eye. "Should you succeed, you would never have to worry about money again, and could live anywhere in the world. You have to decide if you are serious. Are you willing to die?"

The Korean man just stood there, not sure of what to say. He had dreamed of leaving his country for years, with his wife and young son in tow. He did not want his son to grow up under the same brutal conditions that most of his countrymen lived with every day. If he got out now, his son would be spared the mandatory service in the world's fourth largest military machine. It was not that he didn't want his son to be brave and patriotic; he didn't want him to die because of the ravings of a madman. Neither did he want him to die because of a mistake made by his father.

"You need to do a great deal of soul searching before you answer that question," Han said, his fatherly instincts coming to the surface. "There is much to think about. I do not participate in whims and I assure you that if we go forward from here, it will not be on some spur-of-the-moment impulse. The rewards are enormous, but the consequences could be deadly.

"We will let this rest for now," Han continued. "Tonight we will dine with the senior members of Tiger Eye and then tomorrow, we will look over the transportation options we have to ship food to your country. Tomorrow night we will all attend your farewell dinner at the embassy. Sometime between now and tomorrow night, we will talk again-when it is safe to speak freely. Until then, measure your courage."

Han called his driver to meet them at the far end of Tiananmen Square. As the two men left the Forbidden City and walked toward the waiting car, Han told Kim about many events that had taken place in the square. He pointed out the different gates and the Monument to the People's Heroes. To anyone watching, Han appeared to be the perfect host, showing his guest the important sites of Beijing. Had they looked a little closer, they would have seen that his guest did not seem to be nearly as interested in being a tourist. In fact, he seemed entirely distracted.

Back at the hotel, Kim remained deep in his thoughts, even when his wife and son returned from their day's activities, full of energy and excitement. Beijing was one big adventure for them and they were soaking in every ounce of its allure. Especially Kim's wife. She was enamored by all of the places to shop, even the ones from America. Whenever she accompanied her husband to the United Nations, she was never allowed to roam freely in New York. In fact, she was rarely able to enjoy any of the magic of that city. But the trip to Beijing had been different. Her country was not as concerned about her husband's trip here to work on the details of the government's agreement with the Chinese. Pyongyang did not consider Beijing to be a place where defection of one of their officials would occur. For that matter, they never considered that Kim would ever betray his country. The North Koreans were mistaken from several view points: Kim was not the faithful servant that he appeared to be and Beijing was very alluring to both Kim and his wife.

Kim chose not to say anything to his wife, even though she was fully aware of his longterm plans. Unlike many couples, Kim and his wife were a team. They had always envisioned escaping the regime and they had worked together for years to make sure the dream came true. But dreaming and reality were not the same thing. Until now, Kim had been able to make a little money here and there, through petty bribery from various foreign officials and businessmen. It was never enough to increase the value of their Swiss bank account significantly at any one time, but over the course of a few years, it was beginning to add up. It had been a game of small risks and small returns. Kim realized that now the game had changed and while he had no specifics, he knew that Han did not dabble in trivial pursuits. Han had not achieved his level of success by being involved in small dealings. When Han warned Kim of the consequences of becoming his partner in whatever plan Han had in mind, Kim knew that the businessman was not exaggerating the level of danger involved. Kim was not ready to share his feelings with his wife; he had to think things through for himself first.

The dinner that evening with the board members of Tiger Eye Enterprises was very pleasant, and under other circumstances, Kim might truly have enjoyed himself. As it was, he could never quite get rid of the nagging feeling in his stomach. Han was the perfect host, introducing him to everyone and making sure he had plenty to eat and drink. The only serious talk throughout the entire evening was the agreement between their two governments and the role that Tiger Eye would play in the implementation of the plan to ship food from China to North Korea. The only time Kim was able to speak to Han alone was as they were waiting for the car to pick them up for the return trip to the hotel.

"Have you given any thought to our conversation from this afternoon?" Han asked casually.

"It is hard to give much thought to anything when you have no details to ponder over," Kim replied. He wasn't about to admit that he had thought of nothing else.

"I suppose you are correct," Han conceded. "One cannot weigh risks against gain when he is unaware of the extent of either one. Tomorrow, when we tour the shipping facility, we will have plenty of time to enjoy the fresh air. It will be a good time to talk."

CHAPTER 40

The morning came very early for Kim. It had been late when he arrived back at the hotel from dinner the night before, and he had been unable to sleep once he got there. The mystery of Han's proposal weighed heavy on his mind. The thought of getting out of North Korea, out from under the thumb of such a mad man, was getting more exciting by the minute. Until now, he had never allowed himself to dwell too long on the possibility of being free. It was always an abstract idea, but never had he been so close to touching, tasting it as he was at this moment.

"I hope you slept well," Han commented as Kim got into the car. "We have a big day ahead of us and you need to be well rested."

"I wish I could tell you that sleep came easily for me, but it did not," Kim replied. "But do not worry, I am quite alert."

The two men spent the morning going over the final details that Kim would take back to his government. After having lunch with some of the officials on the team, Han and Kim drove to the shipping facilities that Tiger Eye owned. It was a very large complex that housed the offices for their land, rail and water transportation methods. Kim was surprised at the number of people employed there and at the size of the operation.

"We need to take a break," Han commented after they had been there for a couple of hours. "It is a beautiful day and we have lovely gardens here on the grounds. Perhaps a walk would be in order."

"I'm sure I would enjoy that," Kim replied and the two men excused themselves from the rest of the group and headed for the gardens.

"How do you like our little operation?" Han asked.

"It is not so little, my friend," Kim answered. "I was completely unaware of the enormous size of your company. Forgive me for not having a better idea of the assets at your disposal."

"This is just one part of Tiger Eye's family," Han explained. "There are several other divisions that are of equal size to this one, although they handle much different operations. That has been the key to our success: We are not afraid to diversify."

"So how do I fit into that diversity?" Kim asked, unable to handle the small talk any longer.

"You have decided that you are interested in doing business with us?" Han asked back, smiling knowingly, yet not sarcastically.

"I have decided to hear what you have to say," Kim explained. "Until I know what you have in mind, I am unable to assess the risks involved. I have to have more information before I can give you a decision."

"That is fair enough. We have a customer who is very interested in obtaining a certain material that is available in your country," Han began as they sat down at a table in the gardens. "They have a great deal of money and patience. They are willing to take whatever time is necessary to assure a safe supply."

"What does my country have that they want?" Kim asked.

"Plutonium," Han bluntly stated. He watched the Korean's face to see what type of reaction that fact would bring. He was not surprised.

"Surely, you are joking," Kim finally replied. It had taken a moment for Han's answer to register with him. He had not been expecting such a bombshell. "Do you have any idea what you are asking?"

"Oh, I am very aware," Han calmly answered. "This is not an impulse on our part. We have done quite a bit of research, and what we are asking for is not impossible for someone of your status to arrange."

"If something went wrong, if I got caught," Kim's voice trailed off as his mind took him down the obvious road of failure.

"Your life would end, no doubt," Han completed his friend's thought. "I made that perfectly clear from the beginning. What I also made clear was the fact that if you succeed, you will be a very wealthy man."

"How wealthy?" Kim asked quietly.

"One million US dollars," Han answered after a moment of quiet. He was willing to offer more, but he wanted to leave room to negotiate. The pause had his intended effect. Han now had Kim's complete attention.

The two men sat quietly for a few minutes, each caught up in his own thoughts, neither aware of the pleasant sounds of chirping birds. To have observed them from a distance, it would have appeared that they were enjoying a quiet moment of peace. In reality, neither one of them was feeling very calm or peaceful. There was a great deal of turmoil going through each man's mind. Han was just as anxious as Kim. Should Kim not take the bait, Han had just exposed himself and the others to great danger. It was a hand he had felt fairly comfortable in playing, but the continued silence from Kim had him second guessing his choice of partner.

"How much plutonium does your customer need," Kim quietly asked, breaking the silence.

"In all, they would need approximately a quarter of a kilogram," Han answered. "They want it delivered in small quantities over an extended period of time."

The Korean just nodded his head, slipping again into deep thought. His mind was reeling over the entire situation. Could he do this? Should he do this? How could he not do this? What if he got caught? What if he didn't?

"You do not have to give me an answer today," Han explained. "There is time for you to think about it. I will be visiting Pyongyang next month. You can have an answer for me at that time. If the answer is yes, then it would be helpful if you also had some plan as to how you would be able to make delivery."

"Next month," Kim repeated. "Yes, that will be better. I need to have time to think about all of this. It is a very serious matter and one that needs a great deal of thought.

"You are correct. You must give this much consideration," Han replied. "While you are thinking, it would do you well to remember one more thing. The choice is yours to make. You can walk away from this deal with no hard feelings on anyone's part. However, if you should do something foolish-like report this conversation to anyone-please be assured that Kim Jong-un will not be your biggest problem. There will be no safe place for you or your family should you acquire a dose of patriotism or conscience."

Kim stared at his Chinese host for a moment, and then nodded his head in understanding. The two men walked back to the complex in silence. Han had the car return Kim to the hotel to get ready for the embassy dinner. He thought it best for the North Korean to have time alone to compose himself before he had to interact with his wife or the embassy personnel. Han needed a quiet ride back as well. It had been an interesting day. He hoped he had made the first step in securing a supplier for Cai Yi's client. More importantly, he hoped that Kim would take his threat seriously.

CHAPTER 41

Kim Cheol-su and his wife, Sang-hee made the rounds of all the people attending the embassy dinner. Sang-hee was quiet and did not engage in any conversation except with Han's wife. The women had spent every day together for the past week while their husbands were conducting business. They had become fast friends. The dinner was very typical of most such events, except that Kim seemed extremely distracted, although no one noticed except Han and Kim's wife.

"I trust you have enjoyed your visit to Beijing," Han commented to Sang-hee as the two couples were waiting for their cars to be brought around to the front of the embassy.

"Very much, thank you," Sang-hee replied. "I enjoyed the shopping especially. We do not have so many stores at home."

"What did I tell you?" Kim joked for the first time all evening. "She will not want to leave tomorrow."

"Well, perhaps another visit in the near future could be possible," Han replied. "I'm sure my wife would be more than happy to have a shopping companion again."

The couples said their goodbyes for the night and Han advised them what time he would pick them up in the morning to take them to the train station. The ride back to the hotel was quiet. Kim mostly stared out the car windows at all the lights of Beijing. When they arrived at the hotel, Kim stopped his wife from entering the building.

"It is a nice evening," Kim explained. "Why don't we go to the park across the street for a little while?"

"That would be nice," Sang-hee replied, thinking her husband's behavior was odd. "We cannot stay long, though. I have to get everything packed for our trip tomorrow."

The two walked silently across the street and found a bench just inside the park. The lights from the hotel lit up the area and even though it was late, the park was fairly populated.

"We need to talk before we get on the train tomorrow," Kim flatly said after several minutes of silence. "Something has happened."

"I know that you have been bothered for a couple of days, especially tonight," Sang-hee commented, her heart beating fast with dread. "What is wrong?"

"An opportunity has presented itself to me-one that could make all our dreams come true," Kim began, as he reached over and held her hand. He knew he had frightened her, but he did not know how else to explain the situation. Besides, he was frightened also.

"If it were as wonderful as that sounds on the surface, you would not be as upset as you are," she replied. "You have been my husband a long time; I know when you are scared. Please tell me what has happened. Tell me everything."

"Han proposed a business deal. It is very dangerous and very profitable," Kim said.

"How dangerous and how profitable?" Sang-hee asked.

"One million US dollars," Kim said quietly. He turned to look at his wife when he heard her gasp. "But if anything goes wrong, we could all die."

Sang-hee just sat there for moments, trying to absorb what Kim had told her. One million dollars was more money than she had ever imagined having in her entire life. They could escape North Korea and live anywhere in the world that they wanted. They were simple people, with few needs. One million dollars was a fortune that they would never spend.

"What do they want you to do?" she finally whispered, almost too afraid to want to know. "What would you be doing that could endanger all of our lives?"

Kim spent the next several minutes explaining everything that had transpired, everything Han had told him. He felt better just talking about it to her. They had always been close and this was not a decision he would make alone.

"When do you have to give him an answer?" Sang-hee asked after listening to her husband's story.

"Next month," Kim answered. "The Chinese delegation will return to Pyongyang to sign the final agreement. I have to give him an answer at that time. If the answer is yes, then he also wants to know how I plan on making delivery."

"Do you have a plan?" she asked.

"No. It has all happened so quickly," Kim answered. "I have not thought that far ahead. I couldn't even decide to do this until I talked it over with you."

"Now that you have told me, what is your decision?" Sang-hee asked, her voice quivering.

"If I were the only one involved, the answer would be easy," Kim replied. "I would find a way to deliver the plutonium, collect the money and leave North Korea as quickly as possible. But my future is not the only one to think about. I do not want any harm coming to you or our son."

"We have known from the beginning of our plan that there was danger involved," his wife reflected. "We have always known that we were taking risks. I realize that this is a more dangerous situation, but in truth, anything that we have already done could have had devastating consequences. They still could if we are discovered. If we are going to die, should it not be for something grand, rather than just the petty?"

Kim just looked at his wife, thinking that she was the braver of the two of them. He knew she would never tell him no, never tell him to walk away from such an opportunity. The fact that she was willing to die with him, for a dream, took his breath away. She was right: They had already put themselves in peril; at least Han's proposal offered great reward.

The two of them talked on for quite a while, going over and over the same conversation they had just had. In the end, they knew they must take this risk. They knew that they would never get such an opportunity and with things getting more and more desperate in their country, they really had little choice. Both of their parents were dead, so it was only the three of them. If they ever hoped to have a better life, it would have to be somewhere other than North Korea. They both felt that conditions in their country were rapidly deteriorating and they might not get a chance to get out if they waited too long. As they headed back to the hotel, the decision had been made. They would commit treason in order to escape the dismal future that awaited them at home.

CHAPTER 42

Han arrived at the hotel the next morning, just as he had promised, to take Kim and his family back to the train station. Han was in a particularly cheery disposition, which seemed to push Kim into an even darker mood. Even though Kim had made the decision to work with Han, he had no intention of letting his Chinese friend know that at the moment. It would be good for Han to wonder, to wait. After all, Kim was the one taking all of the chances. He could at least have some control over when he informed Han that they had a deal. Besides, he still had to figure out a plan.

"It has been good having you visit our city," Han said as they were loading their luggage onto the train. "I will look forward to seeing you next month."

"Thank you for your hospitality," Kim replied. "We will have much to talk about when you visit again."

"I hope you are correct, my friend," Han said, handing the last of the luggage to the porter. "Until then, I hope your plans work out."

Without further comment, Kim and his family boarded the train for the long journey back to their home. It would take them about twenty-five hours to reach Pyongyang. Perhaps in that amount of time, Kim would at least figure out where to start. It wasn't that he couldn't get access to plutonium. The problem was getting it out of the country without getting caught. He had already decided that one million dollars would not be enough to cover the risk he was taking. Han would have to come up with more money.

CHAPTER 43

When the Chinese delegation stepped off the plane at Pyongyang's Sunan International they were greeted with the typical gray sky they had come to expect. It seemed as if the sky had absorbed the color of the country and the people. There was, however, one difference this morning. Instead of just the usual junior government staff sent to collect them, Kim Cheoul-su was there to greet them. The gesture was not lost on Han.

"Welcome back to our country," Kim welcomed the group. "We hope your trip was comfortable, and that your stay will be as well. My staff is here to transport you to the hotel."

As the men headed toward the waiting cars, Kim pulled Han aside and directed him to his own limousine. A shallow conversation continued until the two men were seated and safely behind the glass, out of the driver's hearing.

"It is good to see you again, my friend," Kim genuinely said. "This has been a long month."

"Has it?" Han replied, knowing he had certainly thought so. "Does that mean you have been busy with plans since your time in Beijing?"

"I have had a lot to think about during these days and many risks to consider," Kim replied with a pleasant smile. Even though he knew the driver could not hear their conversation, Kim wanted to project a polite, but superficial setting, should the driver look back in the mirror. He had no intention of getting into a serious conversation at this point.

Taking Kim's cue, Han turned the conversation to other things, pointing to various sites along the road and giving the impression of an interested tourist. Kim responded with explanations about each location. By the time the motorcade had reached the hotel, the discussion had become a history lesson about the northern part of the peninsula. Even when the men exited the car, they were still talking about the ancient times in Kim's homeland.

"There is a welcoming banquet tonight," Kim explained to Han as his staff passed out itineraries to each of the delegates. "My staff will transport the others to the festivities, and I will be escorting you personally."

"I will look forward to this evening then," Han replied as he prepared to enter the hotel. "Perhaps we will have some time to visit this evening."

"Perhaps," Kim smiled, as his driver held the door open for him. "If not, we will make time tomorrow."

With that promise, Han turned to enter the hotel wondering if he felt any less anxious than he had for the past month. He had been very concerned over Kim's answer to their proposition. If Kim did not agree to work with them, then even coming to North Korea could endanger Han's life.

CHAPTER 44

Han greeted each of the delegates, making small talk with them before the session began. He had tried to learn everyone's name from the first visit. He had a theory that everyone who crossed your pathway could someday be important, so networking was something he had learned well during his years in the States. Now he hoped it would benefit his arrangements to get Kim and his family safely out of North Korea. He had been awake most of the night and finally, in the dawning light, a way of escape began to form. He must find a way to talk to Kim alone today and see if he agreed with the plan.

The discussions were livelier than normal, and soon it was time for the lunch break. Kim and Han both joined the rest of the group in a meal prepared by the Chinese Embassy. The luncheon included presentations to the North Koreans of gifts and flowers honoring their talks. By the time the event was over, everyone agreed it was too late to resume talks, especially since there was a similar banquet arranged by the North Koreans scheduled for that evening. Han was anxious to have time alone with Kim, but there was no opportunity to visit with him at the embassy. Han did not even trust walking in the embassy's gardens. His frustration was about to peak when his friend gave them the opening they needed.

"Since we are not going back for discussions, my government has cars ready to take your group back to the hotel," Kim explained. "The same cars will pick them up this evening, but it would be an honor if you would allow me to transport you to the banquet. My wife will be joining us, so we will be bringing our private car."

"That sounds wonderful," Han replied in relief. "I look forward to seeing Sang-hee again. My wife will be disappointed that she is not here also. I think our two wives enjoy each other's company."

"I think they enjoy shopping together," the Korean laughed. "Your wife would be shocked at the lack of opportunity for that activity here. It is probably good that she stayed in Beijing. Until tonight, then."

"Until then, my friend," Han said as he entered the limo with his Chinese team members. He was relieved to know that soon he would be able to talk freely with Kim, and for the first time all day he realized how tired he was from not sleeping the night before. As soon as he returned to the hotel, he headed straight for a nap.

* * *

"I trust you are having an enjoyable evening," Kim casually commented as he and Han mingled through the crowd in the banquet hall. The dinner was over and they were waiting for the entertainment to begin.

"The dinner was wonderful, as usual," Han politely replied as he tried to appear calm and unconcerned about the potential result of this visit. He had tried to read his host's body language since they had arrived, but was unable to come up with any idea of his decision. Han decided that this was probably not someone he should bet against in a game of poker.

"Perhaps you would like a breath of fresh air while we wait for the show," Kim suggested, as he guided his guest toward the door. "If it weren't night we could tour the gardens, but at least we can see the edges from the patio."

The two men took their drinks and casually slipped out the door. If anyone was watching, as they probably were, their activity would seem harmless enough. There was a group of people at the far end of the patio, but not within hearing distance, especially over the music coming from inside. Kim felt relatively comfortable talking here, although he noticed that his friend did not share his confidence.

"It is okay. If we speak quietly, no one will be able to hear us," Kim said, trying to relieve his guest's anxiety. "Besides, what could we possibly be discussing that anyone else would care about?"

"I would like to think that our conversation would be one of great interest to certain parties," Han replied quietly. "Perhaps I am wrong."

"You are not wrong, my friend," Kim said. "We just must be careful as to which 'certain parties' are involved. The ones on your side of the border are more appealing to me, and I'm sure you are waiting for my answer to your proposal."

"Of course I am. I hope you have given this deep thought," Han answered, mustering up as much bravado as he could. He wanted to be the one in control of this situation, but realized that until he knew Kim's answer, he would have to play along at Kim's pace.

"There has been much to consider. What you are asking will require a detailed plan that is extremely dangerous. From my viewpoint, it appears that I will be the one taking all the risks."

"Do not forget that you will be paid handsomely for your effort," Han interjected. "You will be wealthy beyond your imagination."

"Assuming I do not get shot in the process," Kim dryly replied as he guided Han back inside. "It appears that the entertainment is about to start. You wouldn't want to miss it, would you? While you are watching the show this evening, you need to consider one thing: My price is five million American dollars. Are you still interested?"

Before Han could answer, Kim opened the door and they were immediately absorbed into the crowd. What neither one of them noticed was the man who came in the door behind them. From the dark corner of the patio, Joo Chan had heard every word they had spoken.

CHAPTER 45

Han could not have recalled one moment of the evening's entertainment presentation had he been asked to do so. All he could think about was Kim's last statement. The five million was irrelevant; Han was already prepared to pay that amount. The important part was that Kim had named a price. He had made the decision to accept the proposal. Now all they needed was a plan. Han could hardly sit through the show; he wanted to know how Kim intended to transport the plutonium out of the country. The thoughts running through his mind distracted him to the point that he almost didn't move when the lights came back up.

"Well, that was quite a show," Kim remarked. "I hope you enjoyed it."

"Yes, yes, quite a show indeed," Han replied, hoping he would not have to comment further. "I think it relaxed me to the point that I am ready to retire. Perhaps you could take me back to the hotel now."

"I'm afraid I have another stop to make," Kim apologized. "My assistant, Joo Chen, is here to escort you back. I hope you sleep well. I will see you again in the morning."

Han watched Kim exit the banquet hall before he had an opportunity to try to speak privately with him again. Just as quickly, Joo was at Han's side guiding him to the waiting limousine. Joo tried to make pleasant conversation with the businessman, but Han's thoughts were miles away. Somewhere in his subconscious, it registered to him that Kim's assistant spoke perfect English, the one language that Kim and Han had in common. The thought never went any further.

CHAPTER 46

"I need to make arrangements for the Minister and a guest to have lunch in your restaurant today," Joo said, loudly enough that the hotel boss's staff overheard the conversation. "Is this a good time to work on the details?"

"Of course. We would be honored to have the Minister join us," Tae replied, trying not to show his surprise at the Korean's unannounced visit. "I was just heading toward the gardens. Please join me and we will work out your needs on the way."

The two men chatted about the lunch menu as they left the lobby. When they were safely in the gardens, their conversation took a more serious tone.

"What has happened?" Tae asked his visitor. "I was not expecting to see you today."

"At the banquet last night, I overheard Kim and Han discussing a proposal," Joo explained, trying to control his breaths. "I don't know what Kim is planning, but whatever it is, he asked Han for five million American dollars as payment."

Tae stopped walking and just stared at his informant. Five million dollars was a huge sum of money; Tae could only assume that whatever Kim had was of proportionate value. Tae had Joo repeat what he had heard the evening before. Tae was sure that they were onto something of significant importance, but they had no idea what they had uncovered.

"Whatever it is, the risks must be enormous," Joo reflected. "Kim is afraid of getting shot."

"That's why he wants so much money," Tae surmised. "It's his ticket out of Hell."

CHAPTER 47

"We have credible intelligence that security has been compromised at our plutonium storage facility," Kim began the conversation as he closed the door of his office. The major in charge of the site sat in stunned silence. "We will need to make some changes."

"Why is General Sung not here? I have to have instructions from him before I can do anything," the major replied. "I'm sure you understand my orders."

"I understand perfectly, but let me repeat what I first told you: Our security has been compromised," Kim firmly continued. "The fact that the general is not here should tell you something."

Kim sat silently for a few moments, letting the seriousness of his suggestion sink in. He hoped that the major would be a good soldier and carry out his orders without too much questioning. Everything hinged on his believing Kim's story.

"I understand," the major finally replied. "What do you need me to do?"

"First of all, you must swear your allegiance and silence to me. Our country's safety depends on your loyalty. You must not discuss this operation with anyone, including General Sung."

"The general will still be my superior officer?" the now confused major asked. "How am I to do anything without his knowledge?"

"General Sung will be busy with a special assignment and will frequently be away from the base," Kim explained.

"While he is gone, you will execute the plan. It is a long term operation; one that will allow us to secure our materials and gather evidence at the same time. This is a most serious situation and one of grave circumstances should we fail to ferret out all of the traitors. Only you and I, and the Chairman will be aware of what is taking place. Do you understand the confidence that has been placed in your ability to carry out this secret mission?"

The soldier sat staring at Kim for several moments. He had not been aware that the Chairman even knew he existed. To be held in such confidence filled his soul with pride. He was trusted; he was competent. The Chairman knew his name. Kim's well-placed words had the effect that he had hoped they would. He watched in silence as the major's persona changed. Kim's pulse settled just a little.

"Sir, the Chairman has my total devotion and service. Tell me what you need done and it will be handled," the major declared, sitting up straight in the chair. "No one will learn of the mission."

Kim spent the next hour laying out an elaborate plan to convince the major to funnel small amounts of plutonium to Kim under the guise of an order from the Chairman. The reality was that the government had already planned to relocate part of the weapons stock to another location, but the major wasn't aware of those arrangements. The Chairman had appointed Kim to oversee the military's moving of the nuclear material. Kim instructed the soldier to deliver two canisters from each shipment to Kim personally. The reasoning he gave was that the Chairman wanted to have a separate stockpile that was not in the control of the military. The major bristled at this insinuation, but he would never question an order or the logic of the Chairman. At least Kim was counting on that attitude. He had visualized the scenario in his head dozens of times over the past week, trying to locate any point of weakness and eliminate whatever threats of exposure that might arise. Now, he hoped he had thought of everything, knowing in his heart that that was truly impossible.

By the time he had finished the briefing, the major was vowing his unwavering allegiance and secrecy. Kim had made several allusions to General Sung's disloyalty, just enough to deceive the soldier into believing he was privy to catching a traitor. Kim knew that the general had a special assignment in the northeastern part of the country, near the Russian border. He would be gone most of the next year, allowing Kim the time to remove the amount of plutonium that Han's customer was wanting—and the time to have Kim's bank account swell enormously.

CHAPTER 48

Both Kim and Han felt that the negotiations dragged on endlessly. By the time lunch came, they were both ready to escape the meeting hall. Kim had been trying to appear coy since Han's arrival, but now that he had blurted out his asking price, he nervously wanted to know if the Chinese would meet his demand. What if he had asked for too much? After all, five million was far more than he had ever imagined having in the bank. Perhaps he had pushed too far.

For his part, Han was just as restless. He now knew that Kim was willing to be his supplier, for the price Han was willing to pay. He could already count the money being deposited into Tiger Eye's account; he knew exactly how much of it belonged to him. It was time for the action to begin and Han was more than anxious to know what plan Kim had devised.

"I was beginning to think that the morning session was never going to end," Kim commented as the rest of the men were leaving for lunch. "I have arranged to have a wonderful meal prepared at the hotel where you are staying. It is owned by a Chinese company and their chef is from Shanghai. I thought you would enjoy the meal better than what your comrades will be served."

"That sounds delightful," Han replied. "It is not that far away; perhaps we could walk." Han was desperate to have time alone with Kim where they could speak freely. The car was somewhat secure, but not enough for the delicate nature of their conversation. Han wanted to get out of Pyongyang alive and he was very aware of the consequences should anyone find out about what the two men were planning.

As they headed toward the hotel, Han was struck by the despair of the dismal city. There was hardly any color and the monochromatic setting had bled over into the people's demeanor. What few people they passed had such forlorn expressions and never made eye contact. It was not the vibrant city that Han was accustomed to in Beijing, or even the life that the industrial city of Chengdu portrayed, despite its own polluted skies. Pyongyang was cold, even on a summer day.

"Have you considered what I said last night?" Kim quietly asked.

"I'm very certain that your request can be met," Han nonchalantly replied, as he watched his surroundings. His companion walked along as his fellow countrymen, with his head down, but Han wanted to be aware of who was around them. "I assume that you have developed a plan. Perhaps you will share it with me now?"

"I have made arrangements to procure the material you need," Kim began. "I will be receiving small amounts at a time, secured properly from contamination. It would be better for you not to know any more of the details. The less you know, the less likely a path could be followed back to you or to me."

"I agree with you; it is not wise or necessary for me to know how you acquire the product," Han responded. "I would think it prudent, however, for me to know how you plan to get the supplies to me."

"That was the easy part to determine," Kim explained. "Each time your ships return from bringing food to my people, a cylinder of plutonium will make the return trip with them. It will be necessary for someone trustworthy to accompany the shipments each time. I need to know what that person looks like, and I will work only with that person. I will sign for the deliveries with the person you appoint, and I will send a gift from my government back with that courier."

"It is a good plan," Han remarked as thoughts were racing through his brain. "Obviously it would be suspicious if I were to make the trips. That would be totally out of character, even for something as important as this arrangement between our countries. I will send my son, Chen. That would be appropriate and he would be the one I most trusted with this delicate situation."

When they arrived at the hotel, Tae was waiting to greet the two dignitaries and show them to the restaurant's best table. Prior to their arrival, Tae had secured a listening device to the underneath side of the table hoping it would give him some insight to this budding and unusual friendship.

"Do you have a picture of your son with you?" Kim asked.

"Yes, this one was taken about six months ago," Han replied as he slipped the photograph out of his wallet. "You may keep it."

"He is very handsome," Kim remarked as he slid the photo into his suit pocket. "You must be very proud of him. He works with you at Tiger Eye, I presume."

"He does. Someday, perhaps in the near future, he will take over my responsibilities. I'm getting tired, and am ready to relax and travel with my wife," Han remarked as the waiter brought their food. "Perhaps you and your wife would like to travel as well?"

"One never knows what opportunities are going to come his way," Kim cryptically answered. "For example, who would ever think that my new best friend lives in Beijing?"

The two men laughed and continued irrelevant conversation over the rest of their lunch. Tae, listening from his office, was disappointed and aggravated; he had hoped something more tangible would be revealed. Just as the two were being served dessert, Tae's expectation grew a little more optimistic.

"Since you said you were certain that my terms can be met, how will the payment arrangements work?" Kim asked, lowering his voice to a level that Tae had a hard time hearing through the planted bug.

"There is an account set up in Beijing already, awaiting instructions on where to wire funds," Han explained in a whisper to match is companion's. "You give me the information about where you want the money to go, and through a series of complicated nontraceable transfers, you will be a wealthy man. Five hundred thousand dollars will be transferred after each shipment. The contract with your government calls for ten shipments of food. When the last ship returns to Shang-hai, you will have five million dollars stockpiled in a safe place."

Kim just sat there, staring out the restaurant's windows. Five million dollars. He and his family could live comfortably for the rest of their lives–if he could pull this off and get out of the country safely. The seriousness of that thought shook him back into reality. The sick feeling in the pit of his stomach had been a constant reminder for the past month that what he was engaging in could be fatal. Now was not the time to be fantasizing about spending the money.

"I will have a Swiss bank and account number ready for you before you return to Beijing," Kim said. "I have all of this planned out except for how to get my family and me to safety. Once the material is in China, it is imperative that we not be here. The chance that this could be discovered is too great for us to remain in this country. Do you have any ideas?"

"Let me think on this for a while," Han replied. He had assumed that Kim's plan to steal the plutonium would include an escape as well. While he was not prepared to come up with an idea off the top of his head, he did realize the absolute necessity of getting Kim out of North Korea and to a place where his steps could never be traced through Tiger Eye Enterprises.

"We must return to the meetings," Kim instructed as he looked at his watch. "We must follow all of the rules during this visit. We cannot afford for anyone to get suspicious."

With that comment, the two left the restaurant and headed back to the meetings. Sitting back in his office chair, Tae was shocked. Not only was Kim about to become a multimillionaire, but he was going to defect as well. This was big. Tae could feel the sunshine of his new assignment warming him from head to toe. He had to talk to Joo, and he also had to get to Dandong with this information.

Going against his normal behavior and knowing the call would be monitored, he dialed Joo's office. He would have to be careful what he said, but it was too important that he set up a meeting with Joo to wait for their normal meetings to occur. It took a few minutes before Joo came on the line.

"Good afternoon, my friend," Tae greeted him, trying to sound upbeat and casual. "I was calling to see if everything was satisfactory for the Minister's lunch and to thank you for the opportunity to be of service to him."

"I'm afraid that I have not yet spoken to the Minister, but I will check with him at the first possible occasion," Joo answered. He was confused by the phone call, but tried to follow Tae's lead. "Perhaps I could get back with you and let you know if the Minister was pleased. Would that be acceptable?"

"Thank you, that would be just fine," Tae replied. "I will be in my office until late this evening. I look forward to hearing from you."

All Tae could do now was wait. Joo would come to the hotel as soon as it was safe. He tried to busy himself while he waited, but he could not keep his thoughts from returning to the conversation he had overheard. Five million dollars was a fortune to most people, but to a North Korean, it was unattainable, nothing but a fantasy. So what was Kim Cheol-su up to? Where did the Chinese fit in? Was the Beijing government involved or was this strictly a business deal with Tiger Eye? What could Kim have that Tiger Eye could possibly want?

* * *

Several hours later, there was a soft knock on Tae's office door. The office staff had left for the day and no one saw Joo enter Tae's office.

"You are working very late. When do you expect your staff to clean your office if you are here all of the time?" Joo joked as he walked in the door.

"It's clean," Tae replied, understanding the meaning of his companion's remark. "I checked for bugs before you arrived. No one is listening in to this conversation. Did anyone follow you?"

"No. I was very careful. In fact I went straight home after the meetings and as far as anyone can tell, I am still there … sound asleep," Joo explained. "I got here as quick as I could. What did you find out?"

"Whatever is going on, it will become an international incident if they pull this off," Tae started, his mind racing faster than his words. "Not only is Kim asking for five million-for who knows what-but he is planning to defect as well. With his family in tow."

Joo was absolutely speechless. This entire situation was spiraling out of control. What had started as a strange friendliness was now a global issue. Joo's head was spinning. The fallout from such a situation would be far-reaching, and he was way too close not to be contaminated.

"You do realize that whether or not they succeed, my life is now in danger," Joo stated as he started pacing around the room. "Either way, I am a dead man."

"You are not a dead man," Tae replied, trying to calm his informant's nerves. "You know that I will protect you.

What we need to worry about now is finding out exactly what these two nuts are trying to pull off. You have to focus on the immediate problem and not get so upset that you blow your cover. Work with me and we will get you out safely."

"What could Kim have that would be worth that kind of money, especially to the Chinese?" Joo wondered aloud. "We have nothing; we can't even feed our own people. This is incredible."

"I've had all afternoon to think about it and I still don't have an answer," Tae replied. "I was hoping you knew something that could shed some light on this situation."

"Give me a day or so to work on this." Joo sighed, finally calming down just a little. "I am so tired with all the details of the talks that I can't even think straight."

"Don't take too long," Tae warned. "Kim will be passing along bank information before the Chinese leave at the end of the week. We need to figure this one out fast."

The men said goodnight and went to their respective homes. Neither one of them slept well, but they were not alone: Kim and Han each struggled with the passing shades of darkness, both wondering about all that could go wrong and how devastated their lives would be if it did.

CHAPTER 49

Tae decided that the information he had, sketchy as it was, must be passed along to the embassy in Beijing. Something major was about to explode, and he wanted to make sure that it was his hand on the detonator. Making excuses for an unscheduled trip, Tae left early the next morning for Dandong. He had to get word to his fellow agent at the hotel supply warehouse. The trip took no longer than usual, but Tae's anxiousness made it seem endless. When he finally arrived, he had to will himself to act calmly and normally. He could not afford to arouse anyone's curiosity. He did, however, suggest to Li Jie that the two of them go for tea before conducting business.

"You were the last person I was expecting to see," the supplier reacted when they finally sat down at the outdoor restaurant. "What has happened?"

"Nothing-and everything," Tae spoke as he shook his head. "There is something big going down and it has nothing to do with Han and Kim becoming best buds. I don't know any details, but Han is prepared to deposit five million dollars into a Swiss bank account in exchange for material that Kim is planning on smuggling into China. Oh, and Kim wants to defect."

"What could North Korea have that China wants that badly?" Li questioned, stunned at this new information.

"Maybe it's not about North Korea and China. Maybe it's about Kim and Han, a strictly off-the-books deal," Tae suggested. He had had a long time to think about the situation during the night and on the drive to Dandong. He thought he had an idea of what Kim might have-or could get-that Han might possibly want. The problem was that he had no idea how to prove it … yet.

"What are you suggesting? Do you think that this has anything to do with the meeting between Han and Yi?" the agent asked.

"Perhaps. If you have a high-ranking North Korean official who is planning to defect, then what does he have to bargain with? What is the one thing that the rest of the world is concerned about when it comes to North Korea? Nuclear weapons. Maybe that is what Kim has to bargain with for his family's freedom," Tae explained. It was the only thing that seemed plausible to him.

"China has their own nuclear weapons, so they would have no need for any from Kim," the hotel agent surmised. "But Yi is a different story altogether. I can see where he might want to get his hands on something like that. He is quite a reliable source from what I understand. He could very well have a customer that is in need of just such weapons."

"I think you should take a flight to Beijing tonight," Tae instructed. "The embassy needs to know about this arrangement. With any luck, they will have some insight on the situation that will make sense. I will head back to Pyongyang and wait for more news."

"Be careful. If Kim is desperate to defect, he is dangerous and unpredictable," Tae's friend warned. "He will be taking extra precautions and will be more aware of what is taking place around him. Your contact will have to be especially vigilant."

"That thought has already occurred to both of us, especially to Joo," Tae agreed. "These are times that make you afraid to even breathe too loudly. Believe me, we will be alert."

"Very good. We should return to the warehouse. After all, you can't make an emergency supply trip and then return empty-handed."

* * *

"I was glad to get your call," Yi commented as he sat down on the park bench next to Han. "Two months have passed quickly."

The park was busy with activity. It was a beautiful day, and it was as if all of Beijing was outdoors enjoying the sunshine. Han had picked this park because he knew it would be filled with people, and no one would notice two men sharing a park bench. He could have not been more wrong. Sitting across the green was a very curious young couple having a picnic and laughing as they took pictures of each other and of the park's activities.

"It has been a busy time," Han casually replied. "There has been much progress made on your little project. Are you still interested in going forward?"

"If you mean, will my client meet your price, then yes, I am still interested. I presume you have worked out all of the details," Yi answered looking straight ahead as if he were watching some imaginary ballgame.

"The product will begin to arrive in the States within the next few months. It will take ten months to get the amount your client requires," Han explained. "Will that time period be acceptable?"

"Quite," Yi replied. "My clients are very patient and are willing to wait for your plan to work."

"Very well. When each shipment leaves Shanghai, you will wire twenty-five million dollars to this account," Han explained, slipping Yi an envelope with a bank routing and account number. "Another twenty-five will be expected when the shipment arrives in Houston. By then end of ten months, you will have all of your order, and I will have five hundred million dollars."

"It sounds like a workable plan," Yi commented. "You are sure your source is reliable?"

"As you have said before, it is not wise for one to know all of the details," Han replied cynically. "The less you know, the better. However, you can rest easy, knowing that my source is quite reliable and extremely aware of the sensitivity of your project."

"That is all very good," Yi said. "I will advise my client that the plan is in place. They will be ready with the funds at the appropriate times."

Yi stuffed the envelope in his suit pocket as he prepared to leave. He rose and stretched to give the appearance of casualness to the scene.

"There is one more thing," Han interjected before his companion started to walk way. "If the money does not hit this account within forty-eight hours of the shipment arriving in Houston, the product will be returned to Shanghai."

"Understood. Han, my friend, you have nothing to worry about; the money will be gladly paid," Yi replied with a certain amount of amusement in his voice. "You have no idea who you are dealing with."

Across the park, the young couple hurriedly packed their picnic supplies. As the woman gathered everything up, her partner left the park, walking in the same direction as Cai Yi.

CHAPTER 50

"Good evening Mr. Williams. I trust your trip from the hotel was pleasant," a man appearing to be in his fifties said as he sat behind a desk, tapping a pencil on the edge of it.

Mason did not recognize the man who was addressing him, or any of the six others in the room, until one of the men turned around and looked him directly in the eye. Recognition made Mason even more confused. It was Zhang Han. Mason did not know why he was here, but the fear rising in his throat told him this was not a good situation.

"Let's get right to the point of this meeting. It seems, Mr. Williams, that you have a great appetite for gambling," the man behind the desk continued before Mason could say anything. "It's too bad that you are not very good at it. You have run up quite a large bill with us."

Mason looked at the piece of paper that the man slid across the desk. He felt himself gasp as he saw the amount at the bottom of the column. He was puzzled and then angry. First, at Han who had led him to believe that his losses were covered by his Chinese hosts, an entertainment expense from their perspective. Secondly, he was disgusted with himself for being so naïve. He wasn't some wet-behind-the-ears kid. He should have known better. But he had been caught up in the game, in the wining and dining aspect of his job. He realized now that he was in great danger, not only physically but professionally and financially as well. He knew he had to play out whatever cards he had been dealt and bluffing was not an option. Mason kept a close eye on the two men who had picked him up at the hotel, sure that at any moment they would be called upon to use their persuasive talents.

"I had no idea that I owed you so much money. But I'm good for it, don't worry. I'm sure we can work something out," Mason hated himself for the obvious panic in his voice, but the truth was what it was. He looked to Han for some kind of sign of help, but Han turned back to the window, as if he wasn't a part of what was going on in the room. Mason's heart felt like it was going to burst out of his chest at any moment.

"This is a considerable amount of money. You have access to these kinds of funds?" an older man sitting in the shadows asked.

"Well, not all at one time, but surely I could pay you a little at a time," Mason bargained, knowing full well that he was not in a position to do so.

The man behind the desk stood up. "Do we look like a credit card company to you? You are not here to negotiate a payment plan. You are here because you are weak and vulnerable," his voice was getting louder. "You are here because you cannot control your desires. So now, we control you. We will decide how and when you will pay off your debt."

His voice had risen to an angry, but controlled level, which frightened Mason more than if the man had just lost his temper. Mason was quite aware that men in control of their emotions, especially anger, were dangerous, and he had no doubt that this man and his friends were very dangerous indeed.

"What do you want?" Mason asked, deciding to cut to the chase. It was obvious that money was not their focus.

"Oh, we do not want anything from you personally, Mr. Williams. If fact, when you deliver what we truly want, your debt will be erased. We need you to make sure that certain friends of ours get in on the wealth that your new plant will be generating."

"I don't understand. You go to all this trouble and planning so that some of your buddies can get a cut of the plant's profits?" Mason was not following their line of thinking at all. If what they said was true, he owed them several years' worth of salary, and they were willing to wait to have it skimmed off the company's books? That scenario made no sense to him. There was no way he could even make that happen. His job never crossed paths with the accounting side of the business.

"You are right, you do not understand. Perhaps our friend Han can explain it better than I can." The man turned to Han, who had not left his perch by the window during the entire conversation.

"Mason, we do not want your company's money," Han calmly started. "We want a certain company to get your warehousing and shipping contract. You will see that they are awarded the contract without changes." He handed Mason a sheet of paper with the name of the company. "Oh, and one other thing. You will see that Lin Hong is hired to be your plant manager," Han added, pointing to one of the men sitting in the room.

"Han, you know I'm not the sole decision maker. There are a lot of people involved in the process, and I can't guarantee that I can secure a vendor or personnel. You are asking more than I can give you," Mason logically tried to plead his case to the man who had suckered him into this whole mess. He had come to like Han on a personal level, and this betrayal made Mason seethe inside.

"You underestimate your influence, my friend. You have the ability to make this happen, and you will do whatever it takes to see that we get what we want," Han answered somewhat arrogantly. "You have no choice."

"But, why? What could make this so important to you? The profit this vendor would make would take years to add up to the amount you say that I owe. This just doesn't make sense," Mason desperately argued.

Han moved from his window perch, leaned in close and very quietly said, "Mason, this is not a time to try to be logical. While you may find it difficult to trust me at this point, please understand that you do not want to be enlightened as to the true purpose of your assignment. Just do it."

Mason was struck by the determination and the honestly of Han's tone. He realized that this was the end of the discussion and that his future well-being required him to quit trying to make sense of the situation and just comply with their instructions. While they had neither harmed him nor made any specific threats to him or his family, he had no doubt they meant business. The evil spirit in the room was palatable.

The man who had been sitting behind the desk, motioned to the two bodyguard-types who then escorted Mason from the room and took him back to the hotel. After they were gone, the other men in the room began to discuss what had taken place.

"Han, do you think the American will do what we tell him?" one of them asked.

"What choice does he have? Of course he will, but he will have to be watched carefully. We will have to make sure he does not try to play hero and contact any of the authorities. His escort knows to stay at the hotel. If he tries to leave or tries to meet with anyone from the American Embassy, we will know. Mason will do as he has been told, but he may need to be reminded from time to time that this is not a game."

CHAPTER 51

Mason remembered nothing about the ride back to the hotel. His mind couldn't seem to focus on anything except how hard his heart was beating. How had he gotten in this mess? He asked that question over and over again in his head, but in his heart, he knew that it was all on him. He had let his ego control his life. He had loved the attention and prestige that the Chinese team leader had extended to him. He was enjoying all of the perks that Han had put before him. He had been playing the game, and now he realized just how big a loser he had become.

He paced around the hotel room, panic rising with each step. What to do, what to do? He was alternately distraught and then angry. He could not believe he had been so foolish, so stupid. There was no one on the team that he could turn to. Even if he had formed a close relationship with any of the other participants, he would never let them know what trouble he was in. He thought about the American Embassy, but what could he tell them? Han was the only one of the men that he could identify, and it was Han's word against his own. Mason knew he could never come up with a lump sum payment, even if they had been willing to take his money. But they weren't interested in his money, never had been. They had set him up from the beginning and he had played right into their trap.

He needed to think. He needed to sleep, but he knew that wasn't going to happen. The only thing he could figure out to do was to go to the meetings tomorrow and act as normally as he could. He knew Han would be there, and if Mason failed to show up, they would come looking for him. It was best, he decided, to go through the motions and hope that it would buy him some time. The team was leaving in two days. All he had to get through was the meetings tomorrow, and then he would be on an early morning flight the next day back to safety.

But what if they came for him again tomorrow night? What if Han wanted him to go to dinner again? Mason could not risk being kidnapped by those thugs again. Finally in the early hours of the morning, he formed a plan. He would attend the day's meetings to keep Han from suspecting any problems. Meanwhile, he would have the concierge change his flight plans and he would leave as soon as the meetings were over-before anyone could sidetrack him. In his state of panic, it never occurred to Mason that his every movement was being watched.

CHAPTER 52

The man blended into his surroundings well. Sitting in the lobby reading a newspaper, he watched as Mason got off the elevator and walked to the concierge's desk. After a few minutes, Mason headed toward the meeting room.

Putting his paper down, the man strolled over to the concierge, who happened to be a friend, and inquired into Mason's plans. It seemed the American had asked the concierge to change his airline arrangements and have his luggage ready to leave for the airport as soon as he was finished with the day's meeting. After a brief phone call, the man settled back into his lobby chair and waited for the lunch break when he would follow Mason, keeping a close eye on his activities.

When the meeting broke for lunch, Mason went straight to the concierge to make sure everything was in order. Apparently satisfied, he went to the hotel restaurant to have lunch. Preoccupied with his plans, Mason never noticed that he was being watched or followed. He never noticed that his escort had taken his photo with a camera phone. Mason never even noticed that he hadn't touched a bite of food on his plate. He would have missed the beginning of the afternoon session had one of his team members not stopped at his table.

The afternoon seemed to last forever. Each time he looked at his watch it was if the hands were not moving at all. Mason struggled to keep up with the discussions. He would find his mind wandering back to his predicament. He couldn't bring himself to look at Han, who seemed to make a point of trying to pull Mason into the conversation. In Mason's opinion,

Han was overly smug, enjoying Mason's discomfort far more than was necessary. Mason wanted to be angry, wanted to get in Han's face, but fear kept him from doing anything stupid. He knew that he just had to make it through the day, to get to the airport, to get back to America.

Shortly before the end of the meeting, Mason excused himself. When he did not return, the rest of the team thought he had gone back to his room early, and they wrote his absence off as another example of bad etiquette. What his co-workers did not know was that Mason had left for the airport and was on his way back to Houston. And what Mason didn't know was that on the other end of his flight two men were waiting, armed with a photo emailed from China.

CHAPTER 53

Mason called Rachel before he left the airport. He was home a day before he was scheduled to be, so he thought he would spend the night with Rachel. He had missed her. It had been a long two weeks, especially a long two days, and he knew that he would feel better if he could just be with Rachel. He wanted to touch her and excite her. He wanted to know that she had missed him as much as he had missed her. He wanted to know that his touch could bring her to the point of total surrender. He wanted to feel like something-just one thing-in his life was still within his power to control. It wasn't that he wanted to dominate Rachel-he could never do that-but he needed to know that this one part of his life was still intact.

Rachel had sounded excited that Mason was coming over. He could see her smile, and the thought of it warmed his heart. Rachel was definitely the cure for his shaky nerves. He was safe now. Safely back in America. But he was still unnerved by the events of the last forty-eight hours. He knew that his troubles were not over. He was still on the China team and would not be able to stay stateside for very long, but he had bought some time. Time that would clear his mind and let him make a plan. He felt his body relax at the thought of being back in Houston. He was going to enjoy tonight. He would push his problems to the back of his mind and focus only on Rachel's tantalizing body. For the rest of the trip from the airport, Mason thought about how Rachel felt; how soft her skin was to his touch; how sensual she smelled. By the time he reached the condo he was more than ready for a night of ecstasy with his hot, sexy girlfriend. Any remaining thoughts of China vanished the moment Rachel answered the door.

From across the street, a camera whizzed as it captured frame after frame of Mason parking his car, walking to the door, and being intimately welcomed by a gorgeous redhead. The two men turned to look at each other, both wearing a pleased and knowing smile.

CHAPTER 54

Rachel knew that there was something wrong when Mason called from the airport. It wasn't the fact that he had come in early. He did that from time to time so that they could steal a night together before he had to show up at home. There was something else going on; she could hear it in his voice despite his repeated denials. He was different, acting disoriented and unfocused. Whatever it was, Rachel was sure he would tell her eventually; he always did. She would wait until he was ready and try not to worry in the meantime.

Mason had fallen asleep in the chair while Rachel fixed him a bite to eat, and after his short nap seemed to be acting more normal. They spent a while catching up on the past two weeks. Rachel brought him up-to-date on her projects at the museum and he scantily summarized the visit to China, being very careful not to mention anything about his predicament. In time, they had moved to the bedroom, where Mason quickly forgot about everything except Rachel's seductive moaning.

Before long, sleep robbed Rachel of her partner. The stress of the trip finally caught up with Mason and soon he was deep into sleep. It wasn't a restful night though, as he woke Rachel up more than once tossing and turning and having a conversation with someone in his dreams. Rachel couldn't make out many of the words, but from his fitfulness she knew it was not a pleasant dream.

When morning finally came, neither one of them felt rested, but no mention was made of the nightmares. Mason's mood was still dark when he left, but Rachel tried not to dwell on it. She was positive that their relationship was fine. After all, they had spent most of the day together, making love, before Mason gathered his bags and headed home to Cynthia.

The rest of the weekend Mason stayed secluded in his library. Pretending to be working on paperwork and emails, he managed to avoid Cynthia during most of the daytime. He wrestled with plan after plan to eliminate his Chinese problem, but each scenario led to a dead end. He could probably raise the money, at great expense to his ego, if only the Chinese were interested in cash. He could resign from Utopia Energy, but where else could he go within the Houston oilfield and make the salary he was accustomed to, as well as keep the freedom that his current position afforded him? He could ask his father-in-law for a job, but he knew that indebtedness would be far worse than with the Chinese. And then there was Rachel. He had to protect her at all costs, and any change in his lifestyle could potentially threaten their relationship. That was not acceptable to Mason. He knew what a scoundrel he was on many levels, but he would not allow Rachel to be hurt or exposed. Even Mason had a shred of chivalry left in his soul.

Over the next week, Mason managed to get more work done at the office than he had in years. He stayed at his desk most of the day, working on expense reports and answering emails. He sent Jenni for coffee and left for lunch alone, meeting Rachel at the condo everyday. But still his moods worsened. He was constantly after Jenni to provide figures from different reports or sending her on errands that he used as excuses to leave the office. He stayed late every night and looked as if he had slept in his clothes when he came in each morning. By the end of the week, Jenni was ready to scream.

The evenings were just the opposite. Contrary to his normal behavior, he seemed happy, even anxious, to join Cynthia for her social activities. Cynthia could not stand the grey days of winter, even as mild as they are in Houston, so she filled the evenings with dinner parties and charitable events. Truthfully, Mason only used these events to promote his stature in the community. He wasn't all that interested in the details of the evenings, but at the moment they allowed him to escape his reality, just as work and Rachel did during the day. But he hid his indifference well.

To the friends in Mason and Cynthia's circle, Mason was the epitome of their version of the perfect husband, friend, and businessman. He attended all the correct fundraisers, drove the right class of car, vacationed at the hottest ski resorts. Everyone assumed he had "married up" with Cynthia, but they could also see her interest in him: He was charming, good-looking, and smart, and had learned to fit into all the social requirements of Cynthia's family. A self-made man no doubt-but not in the sense normally used. None of them would have ever suspected Mason to have a gambling addiction, much less the extent of trouble he was in. No one had a hint of how scared he was or how much sleep he was losing.

CHAPTER 55

"So, you're off again for China," Baron commented while refilling his coffee cup.

"The team is going, but I won't be this time," Mason casually replied as he picked a donut out of the box. "I will be going to Minneapolis later in the week to meet with Ray Controls about the remote monitoring systems."

"So soon? I thought that meeting wasn't until the end of May," Baron questioned, surprised at Mason's news. "Could it not be rescheduled when it would not conflict with the negotiations in China?"

"It was originally planned for then, but they're moving into new facilities about that time, so their sales department wanted to go ahead and start the preliminary dialogue now. I should be there for three or four days. By the time I get back, the group in China should be finishing up. It really wouldn't be worthwhile to join them at that point," Mason explained.

"Did you tell the others?" Baron asked, still concerned over this sudden change.

"Not yet, but I will later today. I'll get with you when I return and bring you up-to-date," Mason offered, as he left the lunchroom.

Baron returned to his office, concerned about Mason's trip. It didn't bother him that Mason was going to Minnesota, but he would rather he not miss the trip to China. He also wondered if Mason would have even told him about the change of plans if Baron had not run into him. Sometimes Mason acted like a renegade rather than a team leader. Mason's latest behavior did nothing to ease Baron's feelings about him. It was just a matter of time before Baron would have to deal with Mason once and for all. But for now, he would just continue to gather ammunition to use against him.

* * *

Mason had no intention of reporting to any of the team members. He knew they would not buy the story he told to Baron. Technically, he was going to visit Ray Controls, but not on a scheduled trip. He would stop by for a short walk-through while he was visiting Minneapolis. In truth, he and Rachel were escaping for a few days, using Ray Controls as an excuse. Mason did not have the courage to return to China just yet. He had not figured a way out of his dilemma; he wasn't even sure there was a way out. But he did know that he was not ready to face Han or his associates until he had some sense of a plan.

"Don't most people vacation in Florida during the winter?" Rachel questioned as she searched through her closet for something resembling winter clothing. "Why would anyone go to Minnesota in February?"

"I thought you would be happy to run away with me anywhere," Mason whispered as he nibbled on the back of her neck. "Minnesota is where I can make a semi-legitimate trip-and it's definitely not one that Cynthia would insist on joining me for. So, tell me again what the problem is."

"Nothing that a shopping trip won't handle," she murmured as he began to run his hands over her body.

"Well now that we have that problem solved, maybe we should work on our itinerary. Why don't we practice enjoying our luxurious hotel room," Mason teased as he led her toward the bed.

CHAPTER 56

"Thank you for meeting me at the garage," Maggie said as Alex loaded her luggage into his truck. "I had a whole list of things for them to fix while I'm gone. Taking care of a car is not on my list of fun things to do."

"Not a problem. It was on the way to airport," Alex smiled, more than happy to have an excuse to spend time alone with Maggie.

"I can't believe we're on our way back to China so soon. I felt like I was just getting settled back into the office routine."

"That's the way it works. Just about the time you think you can have a life again, something blows up, and you're off again," Alex explained. "I'm betting Baron didn't really point out that part, did he?"

"Now, what do you think?" Maggie laughed. "Baron knows not to tell me everything at one time. He didn't get where he is just because of his good looks, you know."

"You will forgive me if his looks don't do anything for me," Alex joked back. He liked the comfort at which they could talk. It just seemed natural. "At least we were able to be at home for most of the holiday season. I loved going to my nephew and nieces' Christmas activities. And I very much enjoyed spending time with you and being in your home."

Maggie smiled. This had been the best December in several years. For the first time since Tom's death, she was engaged in the traditions and activities instead of retreating into her memories of happier times. She had felt a warmth and excitement in the holidays and she knew it was because of the occasions she spent with Alex. They had enjoyed the season together, which scared her a little when she let herself think about it-which she rarely did.

The trip to the airport continued with an easy, relaxed conversation. Once they were through security, they met up with Paul, David, and John.

"Where's Mason?" Alex asked them.

"He won't be joining us this time," David answered. "Baron told me yesterday as we were leaving the office. He said it was something about meeting with the remote monitoring vendor."

No one said anything, but instead settled in to wait for the flight to be called. Maggie thought it was very unusual that Mason was meeting with Ray Controls at this time. Their initial meeting was not scheduled until later this spring, so there was no need for Mason to be going alone to Minnesota in the dead of winter. Apparently no one else thought anything about it, since no comments were made. Deciding that her curiosity was not going to be satisfied, she focused on reading a magazine she had brought along. She knew she had plenty of reports that she needed to be studying, but she just wasn't in the mood to pull them out of her briefcase.

Try as she might to become interested in the magazine, her mind kept wandering back to Mason's absence. What was he up to? Why was he not joining them? It wasn't like Mason to let others handle things without at least being in the room to take the credit. It was as if he had to justify his existence, so why would he take the chance of letting it look like the team could accomplish something without him? And why in the world would someone go to Minnesota in the winter?

"Are you going to go with us, or just sit in the airport until we get back?" Alex asked.

"Oh, I'm sorry. I didn't hear them make the boarding call," Maggie stammered as she gathered her belongings and got up to join the others.

"I didn't mean to startle you. You looked like you were a million miles away," Alex replied. "Was it anywhere I would have liked to be?"

"Not even close. I was thinking about why Mason isn't going with us. It just doesn't make sense."

"Mason doesn't make sense most of the time," Alex snidely remarked as they found their seats. "It does seem strange, though. I saw him yesterday and he didn't say a word about going to Minneapolis. I'd rather go to Chengdu than be in Minnesota in February."

"My thought exactly. We weren't scheduled to visit Ray Controls until spring. There is no reason to go there now," Maggie continued. "I don't understand what he's thinking, although I really shouldn't care. Our work will go easier without him there."

"Good point. However, I'm sure Han will miss Mason," Alex said sarcastically. "They've become quite the buds."

"You noticed that too?" Maggie asked surprised. She thought she had been the only one who had detected their unusual relationship. It was one thing for your hosts to entertain you, but Han and Mason left the others behind and went out every night. It was beyond the official entertaining limits.

"A little hard to ignore. I wonder what they do. Mason drags in every morning looking like he's been run over by a bus, while Han always looks rested and refreshed. It's strange to say the least." Alex added. "Whatever it is that they do, it keeps us from having to make nice to Mason. I'm good with that."

"So am I." Maggie laughed as the plane prepared to take off. "So am I."

CHAPTER 57

"Where is your friend Mason?" Han questioned the group when they had convened the morning meeting.

"Mason had other duties that prevented him from joining us on this trip," Maggie spoke up for the group. "I'm sure that we will be able to make progress without him. We have a great deal of work on this week's agenda."

"How can we make any progress without Mason's approval?" Han asked haughtily, his tone dripping with contempt toward the American woman. The other members of his team sat speechless, looking down at the table.

"Han, please understand that we are a team, and as such we all have the capability to make decisions for the project," Alex firmly interjected, matching tone for tone. "Mason's lack of attendance will have no effect on our negotiations."

"This is unacceptable," the Chinese leader erupted as he slammed his fist on the table, got up, and stormed out of the conference room. The other members of both teams sat quietly for a few seconds, stunned at Han's outburst.

"It seems that both of our leaders have chosen not to attend today's session," Alex commented in a controlled voice. "However, as far as I can tell, we still have work to do and decisions to make. Is everyone ready to begin?"

At loose ends about what other options were available, both teams agreed to continue with the work. As Maggie had pointed out, there was a lot of work on the schedule for the week and they did not have the luxury to take off or to come home without any progress accomplished. The talks were lively and often heated as they discussed what was needed versus what was feasible. By the end of the day, however, both sides could see that great strides had been made despite the fact that their respective leaders had not participated. Maggie couldn't be sure of the Chinese team's feelings, but as far as she was concerned, the whole project would go smoother if Han and Mason never returned.

Realizing the jet lag was really beginning to take its toll, everyone agreed to adjourn early and start again in the morning. The American team all decided to stay in the hotel and meet later in the dining room for dinner.

"I don't know about the rest of you, but I thought today's session went very well," Paul commented as they finished ordering their meals.

"I agree. It was the best one-day meeting we've had during this whole process," Attorney David Coleman added. "Maybe we should send Baron an e-mail suggesting that Mason just stay Stateside from here on out."

"Ah, but then he would be stuck with Mason, rather than us," Alex laughed. He knew that Baron had little use for Mason.

The group laughed over a few more anti-Mason comments and then the conversation settled into a quiet rhythm of stories about home, families, and how much they hated the food in China. After a couple of hours, they all decided they had better turn in for the evening or risk going to sleep at the table. Alex walked Maggie to her room, as his habit had become whenever they were in Chengdu.

"Now that it's just the two of us," Maggie whispered as they walked down the hallway. "What do you make of all the drama today?"

"That's not where I hoped this was going when you first started that sentence," Alex flirted. "But to answer your question, I'm not really sure. The whole Mason story about visiting

Ray Controls sounds bogus to me, but I'm more than happy not to have to look at him this week. However, I would never have predicted that temper tantrum that Han threw. That was amazing."

"It was so sudden, like something just snapped," Maggie added. "He just exploded. Did you watch his team members? They were caught totally off guard, just flabbergasted."

"It was bizarre to say the least," Alex continued. "I wonder why he flew into such a rage."

"Well, the two of them had become quite chummy during the past few months, but still, the whole thing was just a little weird," Maggie said.

"It doesn't make sense. I know that they go out every night we are here, but I wouldn't think missing his dinner partner justified that kind of outburst," Alex remarked. "Maybe their relationship has gone to another level."

"Now I know the jetlag has kicked in. That is one road we don't need to go down." Maggie laughed as they reached her room. "Say goodnight Alex."

With that small note of levity, Alex gave Maggie a kiss on the forehead and headed toward his room. Neither one of them remembered their head hitting the pillow.

CHAPTER 58

Han was furious. He had known that he might have to remind Mason from time to time of their little deal, but he had not planned on such cowardly behavior from the American. Did Mason not have any pride? Did he think he could just run away? Mason Williams had no idea whom he was dealing with and how far the arms of Tiger Eye Enterprises actually reached. He was such an amateur.

Using the ride from the hotel to calm down, Han was in much greater control when he arrived at his office. He could see no need to alert the others yet. He had options he could exercise with Mason before having to inform the others of the situation. Picking up the phone, he dialed the international number from memory.

"It is good to hear from you, my friend," the voice answered. "I trust you are well?"

"Very well, thank you, but I am in need of a favor," Han replied. "I have a little job for you."

"Always happy to help in any way possible," the voice replied. "Just tell me what you need."

Han spent the next few minutes explaining what he wanted done. When he ended the phone call, he felt much better. Still aggravated, but better. The American would learn that there was no escape from his predicament; there was no place he could hide.

CHAPTER 59

"The other man in the picture is Zhang Chen, the son of Han," Li Jie told him. Tae was on his weekly visit to Dandong. While he could risk an occasional email out of North Korea, receiving one from outside the country was too dangerous. He had had to wait until this trip to get a reply.

"Well that answers one question," Tae commented. "Han had given Kim Cheoul-su a photograph of his son when Han was in Pyongyang with the delegation. It seemed very strange at the time, but now makes perfectly good sense. Han was giving him a visual of his contact person."

"Has your informant found out anything else about the Army Major?" the other man asked.

"Only that he visits Kim a few days before every food shipment arrives. He arrives with a box and leaves without it," Tae answered. "My bet is that he is delivering Kim's part of the arrangement and I would bet my next assignment that it involves nuclear material."

"Too bad that no one will take the opposite bet," the man joked. "You are never going to get reassigned to your dream island."

CHAPTER 60

Maggie decided to head back to her room for the lunch break. Her massive migraine suppressed any desire for food, and all she could think about was lying down in a cool, dark room. She wasn't sure what had brought on the headache, but she knew if the pain didn't subside soon she would be vomiting up her guts. Not a pleasant thought, she mused as she made her way to the lobby.

Just as the elevator arrived, out of the corner of her eye, a movement caught her attention. Next to a bank of phones, a couple stood, huddled close, whispering, and looking at something the man was holding. Vision blurred by the headache, it took her mind a few moments to process the scene. The couple, so obviously hiding from public view, was Alex and Lilly. They seemed to be happy, sharing some sacred secret as they continued to look at whatever Alex had in his hand. Maggie was too sick to be able to determine what they were looking at, and even if she could have seen things better, the elevator doors closed, drawing a curtain over the scene. As she held onto the rail inside the elevator, her mind was reeling. In between the constant pounding in her head and the nausea in her throat, there was the bewildering thought of Alex with Lilly. Close. Whispering. A new feeling, a sickness, hit the pit of her stomach, one she knew had nothing to do with her migraine.

Crawling into bed, cold rag over her eyes, Maggie could not get her brain to stop. How could he do this to her? How could he flirt and kiss and caress with her? How could he have coaxed her into letting her heart open up again? How could she have been so stupid? All this time, all these trips, she had basked in the warmth and excitement that comes when a relationship is new. She had clung to every word, every touch. Yet all the while, Alex had a thing going on with Lilly. Maybe he had been seeing her even before Maggie joined the team. They had seemed so comfortable together. At least today they appeared that way. Other times, Lilly had seemed uneasy around Alex, determined not to be seen alone with him.

Somewhere in the dark of the room, alone in the quiet, Maggie's headache broke. It still hurt if she moved, but as long as she remained still, the pain stayed at bay. What didn't leave her was the pain in her heart. More rational than she had been at the height of the migraine, she realized that it wasn't just the thought of Alex with Lilly that filled her with fear. It was the realization that she had let herself fall in love with Alex.

* * *

"Has anyone seen Maggie?" Alex asked as the afternoon session was about to begin.

"Didn't you have lunch with her?" Paul asked. "I thought you two had a standing date."

"Very funny. No, I did not have lunch with her, and it's not like her to be late," Alex retorted.

One of the Chinese members, overhearing the conversation, told Alex that he had seen Maggie heading toward the elevators just after the morning meeting had ended. Assuming she had gone to her room, Alex went to the lobby to call her. After several rings, a quiet voice answered.

"Maggie, are you all right?" Alex asked, concerned over the tone of her voice.

"No, not really. I have a terrible headache," she answered. "I think it will be best if I skip the rest of the afternoon. I really don't think I'm up to being there."

"Is there anything I can do for you?" Alex inquired. "Do you need any medicine?"

"I have taken all I can for a while. I will be fine, but I need to sleep it off," she said. "I really don't feel like talking right now."

"I understand. I'll check on you later," Alex replied as he heard the phone click in his ear.

Worried, he returned to the meeting room. He knew Maggie had been somewhat removed from the morning discussions, but she hadn't mentioned anything about not feeling well. He chastised himself for not paying better attention. He should have known that something was wrong when she didn't take part in the deliberations. He decided to try to wrap the afternoon up as early as possible and then he would check on Maggie. He didn't like the thought of her being alone when she was ill.

CHAPTER 61

Maggie stirred. She had heard a sound that caught her attention, but she quickly slipped back into the darkness of sleep. There it was again. She heard something but was so groggy she couldn't process any logical thought. The noise became louder, more insistent. Slowly her mind rose to a level of awareness that let her process what she was hearing. The door, she thought. Someone was pounding on the door.

Weak from the headache and the medicine, she finally got the door open, relieved to have the noise stop. Standing on the other side of the door was Alex. He wasn't alone. Next to him stood Lilly and some man she had never seen before. Her mind instantly reeled. How could he dare bring his lover with him? What kind of jerk would do such a thing?

"Maggie, are you okay? I tried calling the room, but your phone was always busy," Alex said as he looked across to the nightstand and saw that the phone was off the hook.

"What is she doing here?" Maggie asked, her voice dripping with unspoken accusation.

"Lilly came with me to see if you were all right. She brought her uncle-he is a doctor," Alex explained, taken back by Maggie's attitude. He had never seen her act rudely toward anyone, and this obvious disdain toward Lilly surprised him.

"Doc-" Maggie tried to say as her body swayed in the doorway.

Grabbing her by the waist, Alex was able to keep her from falling to the floor. She collapsed in his arms as he picked her up and carried her to the bed. Lilly was quickly at her side, feeling her forehead.

"She is burning up," Lilly informed her uncle, as he was opening his bag to retrieve his stethoscope.

Quickly the doctor came to the bedside, felt her skin and listened to her heart. After taking her temperature, he asked Lilly to bring a cool damp cloth for her forehead. He reached into his bag and pulled out a syringe.

"Wait just a minute, doc," Alex said protectively as he stepped between Maggie's bed and the doctor. "Exactly what kind of shot are you planning on giving her?"

"Your friend has an extremely high fever and this shot will help bring her temperature down," he patiently explained. "I believe that she has the flu. She is dehydrated as well. I would prefer to take her to the hospital, but usually Americans are not very open to that suggestion."

"You're right-she's not going to the hospital. I will take care of her right here, or will get her on a plane to the States," Alex said, worriedly looking at Maggie as she moaned.

"She cannot travel. She is too sick and you cannot expose other people in the airport and on the plane," the doctor firmly replied. "If it is the flu, as I am confident it is, she will be okay in a few days. But we must get the fever down and you have got to get her to drink a lot of fluids."

Looking at Lilly for her reaction, Alex stepped aside when Lilly smiled and nodded to him. After giving Maggie the shot, the doctor left instructions with Lilly to call him should Maggie get worse during the night.

As Lilly walked the doctor to the door, Alex turned to Maggie and washed her face and arms with a cool rag. The gesture seemed to calm her down and her moaning stopped. Alex looked up as Lilly walked back to the bedside.

"Alex, I know you are worried about her, but you have to trust Woo Su," Lilly said, trying to comfort him. "He is a very good doctor, who was educated in America. He did his residency at Johns Hopkins. He is far more Western than most of our doctors here in China. In fact, it is our people who are often distrustful of him because he does not follow traditional Chinese medicine."

"I'm sorry, Lilly. It's just that she seems so sick, and I would feel better if we were in Houston," Alex replied, running his fingers thru his salt-and-pepper hair. "I don't know your uncle, but I do trust you. Forgive me for being rude."

"It is okay. You are a good man who is concerned for his friend," Lilly gently responded. "I will go now before the hotel fills up with the evening crowd. I should have left with Woo. Try to get her to drink plenty of warm tea. You know how to contact me should you need me during the night?"

"Yes, I have your number in my room. But you are right, you need to go before anyone sees you on this floor," Alex answered. "Thank you for your help and for your understanding. I will see you in the morning."

"Alex, tomorrow is the weekend: we will not be meeting, remember?" Lilly reminded him.

"Of course. I am just tired … and worried," Alex said. "I will see you on Monday."

Lilly opened the door and slipped a look down the hallway before leaving. It was important that no one see her near any of the American's rooms. She had taken a big risk even coming here with Woo. But what else could she have done? Alex asked for her help, and she would do anything possible for him. Woo would only assume that she was helping because of her translator job with the negotiation team. He was her father's brother, but that did not mean she would trust him with her personal secrets.

Back in Maggie's room, Alex refreshed the cool cloth for Maggie's head. He was terribly worried about her and didn't feel at all comforted by the doctor's visit. He did agree that

Maggie was entirely too sick to travel, but at that moment he would have given anything to have had her safely back in the US. He didn't even know who she would want notified in her family if he did have to take her to the hospital. Her friend Sara would know, but he wasn't entirely sure he knew how to contact her.

Realizing that he was letting fatigue give in to panic, he got up and walked around the room, stretching his muscles and formulating a plan for the evening. He always felt better when he had a plan. That thought brought a smile to his face. What a joke, he thought. He had never "planned" on falling in love with Maggie, yet here he was-totally and completely in love with her. As he looked at her feverish face, he knew he had to make sure she got well enough to travel on Wednesday. He had no intentions of depending on the Chinese medical community to care for his Maggie.

Alex slipped out of the room quietly and went to his own room to change clothes. He gathered up his computer and enough work to keep him busy while he sat with Maggie. He would not leave her alone tonight. When he got back to Maggie's room she was still sleeping. As he spread his work out on the desk, he called room service. It was going to be a long night and he was already hungry. Just in case she woke up, Alex ordered some gelatin and a pot of hot tea. It was all he knew to do … besides wait.

A few hours later, Maggie stirred. It took a few seconds for her to comprehend her surroundings. She finally remembered that she was in China, but what in the world was she doing in Alex's room? She watched him while he worked on his computer, totally unaware that she was awake. Something was wrong, she thought. She felt terrible. And she had no idea how she gotten into Alex's bed.

"Hey there," she said weakly. "What are you doing?"

"Well, you decided to wake up finally. I was beginning to think you were going to sleep until morning," Alex said as he crossed the room and sat down on the bed beside her. "Are you feeling any better?"

"I feel awful. What's wrong with me?" Maggie asked, too tired to even try to sit up. "How did I wind up in your room?"

"You're not in my room-I'm in yours. You have the flu and have had a very high fever. The doctor gave you a shot to help bring your temperature down, but you've been asleep for a long time," Alex explained.

"Doctor? What doctor?" Maggie asked trying to search her mind for any memory of going to a doctor's office.

"Lilly's uncle is a doctor and he came here to see about you. He says you are dehydrated and need to drink as much as you can. I had some tea brought up but it's cold now. I'll call room service for another pot," Alex said.

"I had a dream about Lilly. About you and Lilly. I saw you in the lobby and it looked liked the two of you had some secret you were talking about," Maggie said as she snuggled to find a comfortable position. "I don't remember much more about it."

Alarmed, Alex hesitated, not knowing quite what to say. He didn't know that anyone had seen him and Lilly together, especially not Maggie.

"Dreams are funny sometimes. I'm sure it was because of the fever," Alex tentatively answered, wondering if it would still feel like a dream when she was well.

Maggie slipped back off to sleep as Alex called room service for another pot of tea. He would probably have to wake her up when it came, but she had to start getting some fluids in her. After at least twenty minutes, the tea arrived and sure enough, he had to wake Maggie up to get her to drink. When she awoke this time, she seemed to have forgotten all about their earlier conversation, which made Alex feel a little better.

"I need to lie back down. I'm really not feeling well," Maggie said as she sat the tea cup on the nightstand. She had managed to drink one cup of the tea but had not touched the Jell-O that Alex had ordered for her. "I hurt all over; my skin even hurts where the sheets touch it."

"That's the way the flu works. If we can get your fever down, the rest of the symptoms will ease also," Alex tried to comfort her as he pulled the covers up around her shoulders. "Is there anything else I can do for you?"

Maggie had already fallen asleep before she ever heard his question. Realizing that he too was exhausted, Alex shut down his computer and settled into the overstuffed chair next to Maggie's bed. He might not get the most refreshing night's sleep, but he would be here if she needed him. He had no intention of leaving her alone.

CHAPTER 62

Three hours had passed when Maggie's moaning woke Alex. She was in that stirring phase, not quite awake, but no longer sleeping. When Alex touched her forehead to check her temperature, she opened her eyes. A weak smile came over her face.

"Good morning sleepyhead," Alex teased as he pushed the hair from in front of her eyes. "How are you feeling?"

"Like I've been hit by a train." Maggie answered, closing her eyes again.

"I know, babe. You've had a rough time. Do you think you could sit up in the bed long enough for some breakfast?" Alex asked.

"Don't even mention food. I can't eat anything," she groaned.

"I know, but you need to get some liquids in you. Otherwise you'll stay dehydrated and the fever will go back up," Alex gently explained. "I need you to try to a least drink some tea. I'll have them bring a fresh pot."

When the breakfast tray arrived, Maggie not only drank the tea, but managed to eat a bite or two of toast that Alex had ordered for her. She continued to sit up and talk with Alex as he finished his food. It wasn't long, though, before she was exhausted and slid back down in the bed. In just a minute she was asleep again.

Alex quietly left and went to his own room for a quick shower and change of clothes. Just stirring around made him feel better, and by the time he returned to Maggie's room, he felt refreshed. She was still sleeping so he settled down at the desk and resumed the work he had abandoned last night. Several hours had passed when Maggie woke again, this time remarkably alert.

"You look like you're feeling better," Alex commented as he crossed the room to her bed. "I think the sleep was exactly what you needed."

"It was the only thing I was capable of doing," Maggie laughed. "It's a good thing it was what my body required."

"How about something to eat? Maybe some chicken broth?" Alex asked.

"That sounds good to me, but first I need a shower-badly."

Alex helped her out of the bed and held on to her as she steadied herself. Once she seemed to have her legs back, she headed for the shower while Alex ordered a light lunch. He hadn't realized how long he had been working and was surprised that he hadn't been hungry earlier.

Room service arrived just about the time Maggie emerged from the shower. She looked exhausted. Alex helped her to a chair at the desk and cleaned off his work material to make room for their food.

"I had no idea how weak I was," Maggie commented as she took a sip of tea. "That shower just about did me in, although I at least feel clean again."

"Worrying about whether you feel clean or not is a good sign," Alex mused. "When a person is as sick as you have been, clean is the last thing they care about. After you finish eating, you'll be ready for a nap."

"It seems like all I've done is sleep. What day is it, anyway?"

"It's late Saturday night. You've missed the better part of two days," Alex explained. "But you're doing much better. If you take it easy, you'll be up and around in no time."

"Well I can rest one more day, but then I have to go back to work on Monday. I already missed the last half of the Friday session," Maggie commented. "In fact, I really wasn't there mentally during the morning meeting."

"I knew you were quiet, but I had no idea you were so sick. You should have said something to me," Alex said. "We will talk about whether you join us on Monday when it gets a little closer. The last thing you need is a relapse. We're going home on Wednesday, and you are going to be well enough to travel."

"Surely I will be fine by then. I just need to rest tomorrow and I'll be ready," she determinedly said.

Alex smiled at her declaration, made with a weak voice and a body that could barely stand on its own. She was one tough lady, he thought. He realized that the past seven years had made her that way. With no one to take care of her, she had had to learn to push on, to take care of herself. The realization saddened him. He wanted nothing more than to change that life for her.

CHAPTER 63

"You need to come with us," the bigger of the two men explained.

Before Mason could think to protest, a limo pulled up beside them and the armed men quickly loaded Mason into the back seat and then took their appropriate spots as the car left the parking garage. Mason found himself sitting between the two guards, facing an Asian man whom he did not recognize.

"Mr. Williams, how are you this fine morning?" his host casually asked, as if they were meeting for an early breakfast.

"I would be better if I knew what this was all about," Mason feigned ignorance, though in his mind he felt sure he knew why these men had changed his morning routine.

"Well, perhaps I can help you with that problem," the Asian man continued in his most polite tone of voice. "But first, let me introduce myself. My name is Mr. Wang. I am a business associate of Zhang Han. I am sure you remember Han."

Mason was silent. He figured it was better to say nothing.

"Han was concerned when your team returned to China last month and you were not with them. He was worried that perhaps you had taken ill. So, he asked me to check on your well-being," Wang continued as he handed Mason a thick manila envelope. "As you can see, I found you in excellent health."

Mason opened the envelope and pulled out what appeared to be fifty or more photographs of Mason taken during the last month all over Houston. They had been taken as he entered his office building, as he lunched with business associates, as he pulled into his driveway. Just as he was about to cop an attitude, he saw the pictures that made his heart stop. Rachel. Mason with Rachel. At the condo. In very compromising positions. He knew his life was over. There was no running away from these people. He had thought he could come back to Houston and be safe. But now he knew that would never be true. They knew about Rachel. One wrong move and his life would be completely destroyed. He knew he would do whatever they wanted.

"You seem at a loss for words," Wang chided. "Mr. Williams, just in case the photographs have not made your situation perfectly clear, let me explain. You cannot run away from your obligations. It is a small world and Han has friends in every corner of it. It is not his desire to further complicate your life, however he is concerned that you are not planning on holding up your end of the arrangement that the two of you negotiated. But, as you can see, Han is a very resourceful man, and he is not without the power to make your life-business and personal-shall we say, miserable. You will honor your commitment with Han, or your life as you know it will cease to exist."

"What do you want from me? I am only one person on the team and I can't control all the contracts," Mason shouted, fear filling every word. He hated himself for sounding so weak and pitiful, but he had no control over his demeanor.

"Mr. Williams, there is no need to shout. We are all gentlemen here. I merely need to be able to assure Han that you are very much aware of what is expected of you and that you have every intention of fulfilling your end of the bargain," Wang calmly replied.

Mason slumped in the seat, defeated and frightened. Somehow deep inside him he found enough ego left to control his response. "Please tell Han that he has nothing to worry about. I will honor our agreement."

About that time the driver stopped the limo and Mason was let out of the car precisely at the point where he had been abducted. Before pulling away, Wang tossed the envelope at Mason. "You may keep these. I have many more," Wang said with a smile on his face as the driver pulled away.

CHAPTER 64

By Monday morning, Maggie was ready to do anything other than rest. She had certainly enjoyed Alex's undivided attention for the weekend, but by late Sunday afternoon, she had to get out. After much pleading, she persuaded Alex to go on a short walk in the park. She needed the fresh air, although it was a bit colder than she had expected. They did not stay out long, but it was enough to lift her spirits.

However a short walk in the park was not the same as spending several hours at a conference table, trying to concentrate on the details of the negotiations. By the lunch break, Maggie was worn out. Making Alex promise to give her a wake-up call, she decided to go to her room and rest for a few minutes. She was certain that a short nap would get her through the rest of the day.

Alex decided to join the other team members in the hotel restaurant for lunch. While going through the buffet line, he heard a familiar voice.

"I was surprised to see Maggie this morning. She must be doing much better," Lilly commented nonchalantly as she filled her plate with fruit. "She will be ready to travel, no doubt."

"Yes, she is better-thanks to your uncle. Please forgive me for acting rudely toward him. I really do appreciate what he did to help Maggie," Alex replied. "There is something you should know about, though. Maggie saw us on Friday, in the corner of the lobby. She thinks it was a dream, or at least that's what she thought Friday night. I'm not sure what she thinks, now that the fever is gone."

"This is not good news. We must be more careful. We must not let her-or anyone-see us again again. I will tell you goodbye now, Alex. Travel safely and come back as soon as you can. I will miss you."

With that comment, she was gone. Alex finished filling his plate and joined his co-workers. He casually looked around the dinning room, but did not see Lilly at any of the tables. He had no idea where she had disappeared to. She was right, however. There could be no more meetings on this trip. They could not take the chance of Maggie seeing them together again. They would have to more careful in the future.

CHAPTER 65

"Are you okay?" Alex asked as they stood just inside the airport doors. Their flight from Chengdu had been very turbulent, and Maggie was pale and shaky by the time they got off the plane. They had a three-hour layover in Beijing before leaving for San Francisco; he hoped it would be enough time for Maggie's system to recover.

"I've been better, but I will make it," Maggie smiled weakly. Paul had gone to find Maggie a wheelchair; she was far too weak to walk through this terminal, although she had stubbornly insisted on getting through the smaller Chendgu Airport on her own power. She hated being a burden to anyone, but especially when all of them were tired and in a hurry to get home.

About that time, Paul arrived back with a wheelchair in hand. The thought of needing to use it irritated Maggie, but at the same time, she was grateful to be able to sit down. The airport was crowded, as usual, and Maggie was thankful that she could just sit and be wheeled through the hallways. In contrast, the airline's lounge was quiet and while the guys sat around talking sports, Maggie quickly dozed off. Alex kept a close eye on her, watching for the fever to return. He would be relieved to get her back to Houston, where he could get her to a doctor that he trusted.

Alex had planned on driving Maggie to Katy when they returned, since her car was still in the shop, but he decided this was not the best solution given the circumstances. Maggie was in no shape to argue when he told her that they were going to his condo instead of taking her home. His next door neighbor, Brad, was a doctor, and he really wanted to have her checked out as soon as possible. On the way Alex called Brad, and he was waiting for them when they arrived. Alex got Maggie settled into bed as he explained all of the details of her illness to the doctor. After listening to what happened and taking her vital signs, Brad confirmed what the doctor in China had diagnosed.

"She has a severe case of the flu. It will take some time before she recovers. Her fever is not too high at the moment, but if it goes up any more, call me," Brad instructed. "Keep the liquids in her as much as you can. If she's not better by the weekend, you will have to take her to the hospital."

Promising to check in on her in the morning before work, Brad left as Alex was getting a glass of orange juice for Maggie. She drank most of the glass before falling asleep. Alex tucked her in before crashing across the bed in the guest room. Neither one of them stirred for hours.

* * *

Over the next couple of days, Maggie slowly improved. Most of the time she slept, but the periods that she stayed awake begin to increase and she even managed to sit in a chair for a few minutes at a time. Alex refused to go to work, leaving her only long enough to go the grocery store. He had called Baron and advised him of the situation and that he was going to do his post-travel reports from home. Brad stopped by each evening to judge Maggie's improvement, and by Saturday night he agreed that she would be able to go into work on Monday for a few hours.

Maggie insisted that Alex take her home on Sunday afternoon. She had mail to catch up on and laundry to do before she could start a new work week. Sara had retrieved Maggie's car from the shop and had filled the house with groceries.

"I don't know how to thank you for everything you've done for me," Maggie said as Alex was preparing to head back into Houston. "Especially in China."

"You would have done the same thing for me," Alex replied as he pulled her into his arms. "The only request I have for my services is that you take it easy for the next few days. No superhuman efforts, okay?"

She was about to agree to his request when he bent down and kissed her. Maggie thought she would truly melt on the spot. It felt like he went on kissing her for several minutes. Eventually Alex slowly let go of her waist.

"Here I have been lecturing you about taking it easy and if I don't leave now, you're not going to be able to keep that agreement," Alex confessed with a regretful smile.

"I know," Maggie whispered. "But just for the record, I plan on being completely healed by next weekend."

"Is that a promise or a threat?" Alex asked teasingly.

"It's a warning. You need to be completely rested," she laughed as she watched him walk toward his car.

CHAPTER 66

"I was getting ready to send the National Guard to look for you," Jenni joked as Mason brushed past her desk, slamming the door to his office. Well, I guess he isn't in any mood to discuss his morning, she thought. It must be nice coming in three hours late with no explanation and feeling free to be totally rude to the one person who covers your tail.

Jenni took a deep breath, knowing it was going to be a long day, and she was determined that her boss was not going to ruin it for her. Whatever his problem was, she wasn't going to get wrapped up in it. She had learned a long time ago not to get caught up in Mason's drama. Mason could be kind and generous, if somewhat distant. She knew plenty about Mason's activities, but figured there was still way more that she didn't want to know. She could live with their unspoken "don't ask, don't tell" rule. Besides, when she covered for him-more and more lately-he usually responded with some gift of generosity. Sometimes it was a day at the spa, sometimes a long lunch for her friends at a fancy restaurant, sometimes a bonus. She long ago had decided that she could deal with his absences and absent-mindedness. If his guilty conscience made him generous with her, then so be it. She could live with a few perks. And today seemed like a perfect opportunity for one of those perks-an early and long lunch was exactly what Jenni decided would be the best antidote for Mason's pouting. She sent the phones to voice mail, called Anne, and headed out to lunch.

Mason stood staring out his office window at the traffic below him, watching another world carry on, a world that seemed so distant from the one he was drowning in. He vaguely heard noises outside his door and decided that Jenni was leaving for lunch. He had been rude to her and she didn't deserve it. He often behaved terribly toward her for no reason. He really didn't mean to take things out on her, but nevertheless, sometimes he did. He knew that he needed to try harder to be more civil and professional with Jenni. After all, his mess wasn't her fault. Mason knew he needed Jenni, although his ego would not let him say that out loud. He also knew that she would not approve of most of his personal activities: out-of-town business trips that were really gambling junkets; long lunches with clients by the name of Barbie or Bambie. And if she knew about Rachel or the condo … well, that would be way more than she would tolerate. Not that he would really blame her. He had not been raised this way. His life had become such a mess. But it was a mess of his own doing and while he knew all the wrongs and rights, he wasn't ready to give it all up. He wasn't ready to give any of it up.

Especially Rachel. Mason had used a lot of women over the years for fun and games, but Rachel was different. She was his soul mate. She was the woman he wanted to sail to Fiji with and never come back. He knew that would never happen, but still, he let himself fantasize about it. He could never be with Rachel. Not really with her. He had long ago set his course with Cynthia and he could not financially or socially end a 30-year marriage to the daughter of the senior partner of the most prestigious law firm in the state. That was not going to happen-no matter how much he truly loved Rachel.

Yes, he had been out of line with Jenni again. He couldn't afford to keep treating her badly-he truly needed her. He would find a way to make it up to her and promised himself, once again, that he would do better by Jenni. He just couldn't focus on work anymore. The details that he used to be able to recite on command were no longer there, no matter how hard he concentrated on remembering them. He knew it was stress-he even knew what the source of the stress was. What he didn't know was how to stop the madness.

He couldn't help himself, he loved to gamble. Not just a little. Not just the recreational gambling that the vacationing tourist indulged in, writing it off as a once-a-year entertainment spree. No, this was the big league. Mason would gamble on anything and everything. It had started with the office football pot, and then it was the Thursday night poker game. He would wager on the local high school games, the Super Bowl, tomorrow's weather. It didn't matter; he just got a thrill from trying to outguess the next guy.

Then Mason started traveling to China, and as Project Manager, the Chinese made sure that his evenings were entertaining. It was harmless at first, a little blackjack, the roulette table, his choice of any number of beautiful women. Every night he and his harem would spend hours gambling. He won some big bucks too. It was such a high. The casino management knew him by name and courted his business with all kinds of free perks. His Chinese hosts would cover the losing streaks he would encounter, and continued to encourage him to play just one more game. For a long time he made more than he lost, or at the least would break even. But then it all started changing.

Casino managers would invite him into private games. Mason's ego grew with every invitation. These games were considered Big Time, and to be asked to join them was a trip Mason couldn't turn down. He did well at the games, winning enough to be taken seriously, but not enough to make enemies. But over time, he had run up a huge debt. He owed more money than he made in a year-and that was not an inconsiderable amount.

Now they wanted the debt paid. If it had only been about the money, somehow Mason could have managed to pay them off. But what they wanted was more than Mason was sure he could deliver. The more he wrestled with the situation, the more he realized that he was in no position to bargain with them. They had him where they wanted him and, even worse, he could see no end to their blackmail. In the end, to save his life or at least his lifestyle, Mason knew he was going to have to make a deal with the Devil.

CHAPTER 67

Rachel took a deep breath, absorbing the aroma of the sauce she had simmering on the stove. It smelled wonderful and she knew it would taste just as good. She loved cooking for Mason. He was always so appreciative and ate with an appetite that defied his toned body. Luckily for him he had inherited slim genes instead of fat genes, Rachel thought. It wasn't that way for her. She could have never eaten half the amount of food that Mason put away and hoped to fit into any of her clothes. She knew she had a great body, but it was from hard work at the gym every day, not from her DNA. She also knew how much her tight body turned Mason on. He loved her, she never doubted that fact. But she was keenly aware that he lusted after her, crazy with desire, never getting enough. That was just fine with her. Rachel loved Mason also, and she lived for the sex. Her appetite in that department was just as insatiable as Mason's. Tonight would be good for them. Usually their rendezvous were hurried, no time to savor the glow. No time to pretend to be a normal couple. But tonight would be different. Cynthia had gone to Dallas for a shopping spree and appointment with her hairdresser-like she couldn't do both of those things in Houston. But Rachel was thrilled at Cynthia's snobbishness because it gave her the entire night with Mason. They would have a wonderful meal, visit and relax like real people, and then end the evening ripping each other's clothes off and making love in every room in the condo. Yes, Rachel reflected as she put the lid back on the sauce pan, tonight was going to be a great night.

Rachel had no illusions about her relationship with Mason. They would never be together, not in the couple sense of the word, she understood that fact. Mason was never going to leave Cynthia. She was his status symbol and he was not going to give up his lifestyle or be alienated from his children, even though they had long since removed Mason from their worlds. It was irrelevant that Mason and Rachel loved each other, that they filled each other's needs. They would grow old together in secret. This was not what Rachel had planned for her life, but plans don't always work out. Rachel never let the bumps sidetrack her. She had learned to roll with the punches. The plan was to find a man to love her and with enough money to keep her happy. The fact that her path to the goal hadn't followed the course that her mother would have wanted did not change the result.

Turning the stove down to simmer, Rachel headed to her bedroom to get ready for Mason's arrival. She had decided on jeans and a white silk halter, simple but elegant, much like the atmosphere she was trying to create. While Rachel wanted the evening to be laid-back and homey, she never forgot that Mason lived on a different plateau. He was used to casual on a much higher level. It was a level that Rachel maneuvered around in very well, even though her childhood had been spent far from the elegance of high fashion. She had grown up in Arizona on a horse ranch. If there was a job to be done, Rachel could do it as well as anyone else there. But she spent her nights looking through art books, sketching her own landscapes and dreaming of working in an art museum. She got her degree in art history and set out on her own. Her first job was at a small art gallery in Santa Fe. From there she went to Dallas and worked at various art galleries and small museums. Then she came to Houston and landed a job at the Chaffee Museum of Art. After five years, she was now the Curator and a well-recognized face in the artistic community in Houston. She worked on several charitable boards and was a formidable fundraiser.

It was at one of these fundraisers that she had met Mason. She had taken a break from the very crowded ballroom and was enjoying the peacefulness of the courtyard. Lost in thought, she had not heard Mason approach and was startled when he spoke to her. He was a charming man and their conversation was easy, not the least bit strained, as it often is when strangers meet. They had discovered that they knew many of the same people and traveled in many of the same circles. Rachel was surprised that they had not previously met, for she was sure she would have remembered such a handsome man.

The following week, Mason showed up at the museum and took Rachel to lunch. They talked about everything: local artists, horses, Houston society news. Rachel was always amused at how much men gossiped. Men usually blamed that character weakness on women, but Rachel's experience was that the men were every bit as guilty as any of the women. The afternoon had flown by and before they knew it, the day was rapidly coming to an end. It had been the beginning of a regular routine for them, meeting once a week at first and then more often. Soon they were unable to ignore the chemistry between them and within a few short weeks the lunches turned physical. Very physical. Before long Mason had moved Rachel into a condo not far from Utopia's building. There were shops and restaurants on the street level, so should he be seen going into the building, he had a ready excuse. It was an arrangement that had worked well for both of them and since the condo was also fairly close to the museum, it was not unusual for Rachel to go home for lunch.

Mason shared his world with Rachel. No subject was off limits. Rachel knew all about his marriage to Cynthia, and was very aware from the beginning that he would always be married to Cynthia, unless of course Cynthia found someone else. Maybe she already had and, like Mason, chose to have her fun without having to deal with the hassle of an expensive divorce. It wouldn't have been the money that stopped her-she had an airtight prenup-but even in this day and age it was tough to be a divorcee in Houston, America. There were still certain stigmas that were alive and well in her social circle. Most of the time Rachel didn't care that Mason had a wife. It was as if Cynthia was just someone that they talked about from time to time. She wasn't real. Sometimes Rachel had to remind herself that Mason was a married man.

Rachel also knew all about Mason's two grown children. His daughter was a lawyer working in the family firm, single and seemed happy to stay that way. Her life was very busy with her clients and friends. She and Cynthia would shop occasionally, but for the most part, Mason only saw her on holidays. His son was a trauma center doctor in Dallas, married to a cardiologist. Their schedules were unreal and when they did take a few days off, they went anywhere except Houston. It took a rare and special event to get them to come home. Rachel was appalled at their lack of caring for their father, but in truth Mason didn't seem too concerned with them, either. It was as if the children had just been another collection in their picture-perfect world. Rachel felt sorry for Mason because there was no bond between him and his children, but Mason never acted as if he cared.

As she clipped her long red hair onto her head, she heard the door open. Mason had arrived. With a quick wisp of fragrance, she left the bedroom to greet him.

"Hey there. How was your day?" she asked as she took his briefcase and jacket.

"Long and very boring," Mason answered. He wasn't ready to tell Rachel about the mess he was in, or about the thugs. He would try to figure this out himself. Otherwise she would just worry, and a nervous mistress was not what he needed. "How was yours?"

"Not too bad. I met with the Neisler Foundation this morning about setting up a grant for a summer program next year. Then I took off early to come home and fix a nice meal."

"It does smell good," Mason commented as he wrapped is arms around her waist and pulled her close. After a long, very seductive kiss Mason managed to break away. "As much as I could go on with this for hours, I really could use a shower. Can dinner wait long enough for that?"

"Dinner can wait until tomorrow if it needs to. Need any help with that shower?" Rachel asked as she unbuttoned his shirt.

"Have you ever known me to turn down your offers of help?" Mason teased as he led her into the bathroom and began to undress her. He would deal with his problems tomorrow, he thought as he felt the warm water hit the back of his neck. Before the shower was over Mason was so wrapped up in Rachel that a couple of two-bit hoods were as far away from his mind as the ladies in China.

CHAPTER 68

"It has been a while since you have been here for dinner," Tae politely commented as he sat down. "You must have been very busy."

"Actually, things have been fairly quiet and routine since the Chinese delegation left," Joo replied. "Which is why today was interesting, out of the ordinary."

"Please, tell me," Tae smiled. Anyone watching would have thought the hotel manager was engaged in his usual habit of mingling with the restaurant's guests. "It must be important to bring you out on such a rainy night."

"An Army Major came to the office today. It is very unusual for a Major to meet with the Minister," Joo whispered. "He has come one time before, several months ago. Kim Cheoul-su met with him privately that time, and again today. No assistants, no secretary. It is very odd."

"How long did he stay?" Tae asked.

"Not long," Joo answered. "He came with a box, but left without it. Afterward, when I went into the Minister's office, the box was nowhere in sight."

"How big was the box?" Tae questioned.

"Not large, about thirty centimeters," Joo replied. "He held it with both hands, as if it were either heavy or valuable."

"What is on Kim's schedule this week? Who is he meeting with?" Tae asked, still smiling, seeming engaged in a relaxed conversation.

"No one this week, but next week the first shipment of food from Beijing arrives," Joo responded. "The Minister plans on meeting the ship in person. That too is very strange. Usually when we receive foreign aid, someone lower in the diplomatic chain oversees the arrival. These things are usually kept quiet. The government does not want the people to know where the food is coming from. They are told that the government is providing such needs from farms in the North."

"What day next week?" Tae asked.

"Thursday night. They plan to dock around 9 o'clock, after dark." Joo informed his CIA handler. "The military will have trucks at the dock to offload the food and take it to government warehouses."

"Do you know where the ship is docking?" Tae questioned.

"Pier 43, on the north end of the harbor, away from the regular shipping lanes," Joo answered.

"Let me know if anything else comes up," Tae instructed. "I have a ship to meet."

CHAPTER 69

Kim pulled the collar of his jacket up as he waited. It was a chilly night, a little too chilly for this time of year. Perhaps it was his nerves, he thought. He was more edgy than he could ever remember. He had taken chances before, but never of this magnitude. This was the real deal. No more small-time bribes with small-time pay. This was the biggest risk he had ever taken. If it worked, he and his family could live a very comfortable life anywhere in the world; if it failed, they would lose their lives. Kim didn't fear for his own life; he had long ago resigned himself to that possibility. But his wife and son did not deserve to die. They had done nothing wrong, and yet, they would be deemed just as guilty should the plan fail. That scenario kept Kim awake many nights. He could not fail, could not let his family down.

He was jarred from his thoughts by the sound of the ship's horn, sounding a safe arrival into port. The government wanted to keep word of the food shipment as quiet as possible and so a night arrival was scheduled. The Chairman did not want the people to realize that they were being fed by the other countries of the world, so the ship had docked at Namp'o, the port city for Pyongyang. It was important to the cause that the people believed that the country was self-sustaining. It was also the fantasy of the Chairman that the common man did not understand. The North Korean people understood extremely well how hungry they were when they went to bed at night and no amount of government propaganda would ease their pain.

Inside the jacket pockets, he curled his fingers around his tickets to freedom. He tried not to think about where they would go, into whose hands they would land. He did not think beyond their current purpose. Watching the deck of the ship, Kim finally found the face he was hunting. Amid all the activity stood one man, quietly observing the pier as if he too were searching for a familiar face. Once the gangplank was lowered, Kim made his way toward the ship. As he was about to board, the man he had been searching for suddenly saw Kim and met him half way down the passageway.

"It is an honor to meet you," the younger man said as he politely bowed before Kim. "My father speaks highly of you and sends his greetings."

"Your father is a good friend, a kind man," Kim responded. "He speaks well of you also. Welcome to my country."

"Would you join me in my quarters while the crew readies for the unloading of the supplies?" Chen asked. "It is much more comfortable there."

The two men boarded the ship and headed to Chen's stateroom. Kim was very surprised at the luxury of the accommodations. He had not expected to see such comfort on a freighter. His surprise registered immediately on his face.

"My father believes that every ship should have a place reserved for greeting honored guests, even on a freighter," the younger man explained. "He considers such comforts to be a necessity."

"Your father has very good taste," Kim replied. "I was not expecting such beautiful surroundings. But then, your father never ceases to impress me."

"My father's good taste extends to his choice of friends," Chen commented. "He considers you to be one. In fact, I have a gift for you from him."

The young man opened a drawer in the cabin's desk and handed Kim a piece of paper with a set of seemingly random numbers. Kim instantly recognized the numbers as belonging to the bank account for Kim's promised payments.

"He said to assure you that this was just the first gift," Chen cryptically said, and smiled. "There would be more gifts with each shipment."

"Please convey my appreciation to your father," Kim nodded. "I have a gift for him as well. I trust you will keep a careful watch on it until you can deliver it to Han." Reaching into each jacket pocket, Kim pulled out two lead cylinders about six inches long. He gingerly handed them to Chen.

"You can trust me, just as my father does," Chen assured him as he deposited the cylinders into a wall safe. "You have no need to worry."

"Ah, but worrying is an art I have perfected," Kim smiled. "My wife considers me to be a master at agonizing."

CHAPTER 70

Parked in the shadows between two warehouse buildings, the camera with night vision capabilities recorded the Minister of Foreign Affairs meeting the shipment of food from China. It was dark, there was no official welcoming. Just a solitary man greeting the relief that would keep a population fed for a few more months. Tae knew that the Chairman did not want a big fanfare announcing the arrival of foreign aid, but to send such a high ranking member of his Cabinet to meet the shipment alone was suspiciously odd, even for this secretive country.

Tae had hoped to catch a glimpse of what the Major had brought to Kim's office earlier in the week, but the man was not carrying any box. He kept his hands in his pockets, but not in a relaxed position; it was more as if he was holding something inside each pocket. When Kim reached for the railing as he walked up the gangplank, the pocket on the overcoat noticeably sagged. There was definitely something heavy in his pocket.

Tae did not recognize the man who greeted the Minister, but he kept snapping pictures of the two men walking along the deck of the ship. Suddenly several large military vehicles pulled up to the dock. Soldiers poured out of the back of one of the trucks and started loading the ship's supplies into the other trucks. There was a lot of commotion and Tae decided it was time to leave. He had wanted to wait for Kim Cheol-su to reappear, but he didn't dare risk exposure. With his headlights off, Tae backed the car between the buildings and left the dock area without being noticed. He went straight to the hotel and emailed the pictures to his contact. He was sure someone there could identify the mystery man.

CHAPTER 71

"I am probably not the best company to be around tonight," Maggie confessed as she kicked off her shoes and crashed on Sara's couch. "It's been another adventurous day at the zoo."

"Maybe you'll feel better after dinner. Dan's out on the patio now cooking the best steaks you've ever tasted," Sara replied. "Sometimes I think his talents are wasted at the FBI. He would be much better at owning a restaurant, and would definitely make more money."

"He would probably not work as many hours either," Maggie added. "How did he manage to get the weekend off?"

"He didn't-he's on call, so just hope he gets the food cooked before his phone rings," Sara answered. "Tell me what's going on at the office that made your day so rotten."

Just as Maggie was about to pour out a whole list of woes, Dan called them to the table for dinner. The three friends had a great rapport and soon settled into a comfortable conversation. As they were finishing their meal, Sara commented on Maggie's relaxed disposition.

"You seem to feel a lot better. What did I tell you about Dan's cooking?" Sara remarked. "I told you it was good medicine."

"What did you need a cure from?" Dan laughingly asked.

"Oh, it's just been one thing after another ever since I took on this China project," Maggie answered. "I am so tired of feeling like I'm the Gestapo."

"Mason again?" Dan asked.

"Who else? It seems that Mason made an after-hours agreement with the head of the Chinese team to give the shipping contract to a particular company," Maggie explained. "It's not a good deal for us, but Mason was obstinate about the deal, totally unyielding."

"I take it that the contractor wasn't the low bid?" Dan inquired.

"Not even close–not by a long shot," Maggie continued. "We finally get the plant to actually produce compressors and I'm afraid the second-class freight forwarder won't get the shipments to the US in a timely manner. It's so frustrating."

"So what does the Great Mason have to say about all of this?" Sara sarcastically asked.

"He just keeps insisting that Tiger Eye is the best company for us to use," Maggie said.

"Tiger Eye is the name of the company that Mason insisted you use?" Dan asked quietly, leaning in toward Maggie.

"Yes. I sure wish I understood what was going on that made Mason so adamant about using them," Maggie said. "It's got to have something to do with his blooming friendship with Han. Those two are practically inseparable whenever we are in China."

"Maybe the two of them are sweet on each other," Sara said mockingly as she cleared the table and the others headed toward the living room.

"I really don't think Han is Mason's type. At least that's not the drift I get from others," Maggie commented. "Mason has a rep of being quite the ladies man."

"Isn't he married?" Dan asked.

Both Sara and Maggie stared at him with a look of unbelief. "Like that matters, mister head-in-the-sand," Sara laughed.

Giving Dan a long dissertation about the abundant occurrences of married men with wandering eyes, the conversation branched off down roads leading away from Mason and Tiger

Eye. But while Sara and Maggie went on to different conversations, Dan was thinking about what he had heard tonight. He needed to do some checking, but he was sure that he already knew what he would find. Tiger Eye Enterprises was on the newly released Homeland Security Watch List.

CHAPTER 72

Dan Kardan had been recruited by the FBI while he was still in law school. It had not been a difficult decision for him: He loved the law and felt he would be more fulfilled upholding it through working at the Bureau than by prosecuting petty criminals in Hometown, America. He had never regretted his choice. His job had taken him many places, but for the past few years, he had worked out of the Houston office. Since 2002, he had been assigned to one of Houston's Joint Terrorists Task Force teams, working closely with other government agencies to counteract threats to US security. Intelligence flowed in from all sorts of sources, and agents were always alert for any unexpected tip from regular citizens-many of whom never realized that they had set off a warning bell.

Such was the case with Maggie. She had not realized that their dinner conversation the evening before had piqued Dan's interest. It didn't take long the next morning for him to confirm his suspicions: Maggie's employer was now on the radar screen of a very sophisticated organization. Utopia Energy had become a pawn for a group whose profile posed a threat to the security of the United States. Normally, this bit of information would be considered a great help to the Bureau in their investigation and surveillance of the group's activities. But Dan did not feel as if he had been handed a gift. Instead, he had a sick feeling in the pit of his stomach. Even though Tiger Eye had been added to the watch list, the Bureau had had no information that they posed a specific threat to America. The fact that they might have compromised an American company certainly raised that possibility. More important, Maggie was too close to the players. Maggie was in danger. Dan had put in a call to Beijing, but Joseph Lee, the legal attaché assigned to the embassy, had not been in his office. Until Dan had an opportunity to talk to Joseph, all he could do was wait.

* * *

Dan had been watching the late news when the phone rang. It was the night desk in the Task Force's office; Joseph Lee had called from Beijing and wanted Dan to return his call. Dan would have loved to call him from the comfort of his recliner, but he knew he needed to call on a secure line, so he'd made the trip into the office.

"I hate the time difference between here and Beijing," Dan chided when Joseph answered his phone. The two had worked together twenty years earlier and were always able to fall into a comfortable conversation.

"I hate it between Beijing and anywhere," Joseph added. "But I can't seem to make the Chinese work on an American time schedule. What's up, buddy?"

"What can you tell me about Tiger Eye Enterprises-besides what's in the official record?" Dan asked.

"For years they have been a somewhat legitimate group of businessmen. The older members were all educated in the West, mostly the US but some in England and France," Joseph said. "Their sons and nephews have been brought into the group now, but the old guys seem to still be calling the shots. Why are you interested in Tiger Eye?"

"Their name has surfaced here through one of my sources. It's probably just a coincidence. What did you mean by 'somewhat legitimate'?" Dan asked.

"They have been businessmen, operating much like they would in a free enterprise country. That's not been a typical way to do business in this country, although there have been giant steps made in that direction in the recent past," he explained. "But Tiger Eye has been known to transport people and supplies, on behalf of the government, to countries that are known bullies in the international playground. Because of their willingness to be smugglers for the Chinese government, they are allowed a great deal of liberty, both as a company and as individuals. It's really an unprecedented amount of freedom in a Communist country."

"'But that background, while not great, does not make them a direct threat to the United States," Dan stated. "What has happened to get them Homeland Security's Watch List?"

"Greed, rather than ideology, would be my guess. They do not appear to champion causes, unless there is monetary gain in it for them. These men have been very successful in Southeast Asia, but by our standards, they are not major players and they know it," Joseph ventured. "Apparently, they are diversifying and stretching beyond the limits of their own government's dark ops."

"Check your computer; I am sending over pictures of one of their generals, Zhang Han. He seems to be the one leading them in new directions," Joseph continued. "The second picture is Han and Cai Yi. Yi is an active political Muslim with ties to radical Islamic groups. Han and Yi have met on several occasions over the past few months, and as best as we can ascertain, for no legitimate reason. At the same time, Han is on a government diplomatic mission to North Korea that is negotiating with the Chinese for shipments of food. It seems that Han and the Minister of Foreign Affairs have become quite chummy. The last picture is of the two of them in Beijing. As you said, it could all be a coincidence; but you know as well as I do that there are few coincidences in the world of terrorism."

"You think Han is working a deal between the Muslim and the North Korean?" Dan asked.

"We haven't been able to ascertain exactly what they are doing, but there's no way that this can be an innocent development. Check out the file I'm sending on Yi. He is a busy man with very bad friends," Joseph explained. "It's a little more difficult to get information on Han. He is a fairly well-placed Party member, so my government sources here pretty much have a 'hands-off' attitude. We have a little intelligence on Kim Cheol-su, the North Korean, but nothing that sheds light on any deal that might be going down. Our source in Pyongyang is just as mystified as we are. He has no insight to the budding friendship between Kim and Han, but is shocked by the development. Read the files I'm sending and get back to me. I would like to hear your take on what our intelligence has gathered. The fact that you are asking questions on your end, adds credence to our suspicions."

"I'm just fishing at the moment. I may or may not have anything viable to add. Give me a day or so to get back with you," Dan replied. "I want to go over all this and also share it with my colleagues here."

"Just call me when you're ready-but don't get me out of bed," Joseph said laughing. "It's okay for you to traipse out late at night, but I need my beauty sleep."

"You couldn't get enough sleep to help that ugly mug of yours," Dan joked back. "Thanks for the help, bud. I'll get back with you soon."

Dan printed out the file that Joseph had sent and settled into reading. By the size of the stack of paper on the printer, he knew it was going to be a late night. There was quite a bit of information on Cai Yi. He seemed to live a fairly fluid life, traveling throughout Southeast Asia on a frequent basis. It appeared that he made a living as a black market entrepreneur, buying and selling whatever was in demand: electronics, blue jeans, drugs, weapons. But he never seemed to actually make any deliveries. He was the middle man. From the records and photos in the file, it was clear he regularly met with representatives of extremist groups-mostly Muslim, but sometimes more ethnic than religious. Homeland Security suspected that he was supplying these groups with weapons and traveling papers. However, suspicion was all they had, for Yi was an experienced chameleon; he faded into the background long before any event occurred that could be attributed to the group he had recently met with. One thing was fairly certain: No one just socialized with Yi; every meeting was about business.

So, Dan thought in the wee hours of the morning, why was Zhang Han meeting with Yi? Until now, Han and his group had operated valid businesses, other than their government work. Their portfolio included construction companies, supply houses, electronic manufacturers. Even the freight forwarding company was a lawful, viable entity, although it was often used by the Communist government for smuggling purposes. Tiger Eye as an entity had never done business directly with Muslim extremists. Something had obviously changed to make Han become bed partners with someone on the level of Yi. Han was up to something, and his choice of new friends had landed him and the group in the cross-hatches of the US Government. The only problem was that, at the moment, Homeland Security had no idea what they were really seeing.

Neither did Dan. He felt in his gut that something evil was in the making and that Utopia Energy was caught right in the middle of it. He had to find the link between Cai Yi, Tiger Eye, and Utopia. There was one there; he just didn't have any idea what it might look like. As he stood up to get another cup of coffee, he realized how exhausted he was. He looked at the clock: It was almost six and soon the office would be filling up with the early birds. Deciding to skip the caffeine, he locked the file in his desk and headed for the house. A quick shower would refresh him for the day ahead. He had to find out a way to determine what Han and Yi and Kim were planning before he could find any link with Utopia. As soon as he returned to the office, he would meet with Jim Keith. It was going to require some upper-end authorization to begin the type of investigation that Dan had in mind.

CHAPTER 73

Armed with the information he had gathered, Dan went to his boss's office shortly before noon. Jim Keith looked up from a desk piled with folders, smiling as Dan came through the door. He and Dan had been friends for years and had worked together in the field many times, before Jim had been promoted to head of the task force. Now, most of his days were spent digging through paperwork and politicking for more money. Seeing a friendly face was a welcomed break.

"Boy, you are just the distraction I needed," Jim said as he pushed his glasses on top of his head. "I think I will see budget figures in my sleep tonight."

"That's why you make the big bucks," Dan tried to joke, but his voice betrayed the lightheartedness of the comment.

"I will choose to ignore that remark, only because you said it way too seriously. What's up?" Jim asked as he sat up straight at his desk.

"I've learned something that I'm sure is important, but I have no specifics as to what is actually being planned," Dan began. "And to complicate the issue, the people involved don't have a clue about what they have become caught up in."

Dan spent the next half hour laying out everything he had learned about Tiger Eye Enterprises' players worldwide. There was some intelligence about the organization, but until now there had been no knowledge of any involvement with terrorist activities. The fact that they were even having tea with Yi changed the entire situation. Because of Tiger Eye's contracts with Utopia Energy, Dan could only suspect that Yi and his associates were planning some sort of presence along the Gulf Coast. Whatever their plan was, it could not be good for the homeland.

"So you think this Mason guy is their contact?" Jim asked after listening to what information Dan had brought him.

"I feel like he is the one they are working through, but he may not be the only one. Maggie seems to think that this was some sort of under-the-table deal that he made, but it could be more complicated than that," Dan replied.

"What makes you think that Tiger Eye's dealings with Utopia is anything more that what it appears?" Jim asked. "After all, until now they seem to have been on the up and up. Perhaps this is just what it appears to be-a business arrangement."

"You may be right, except that now, Tiger Eye seems to be courting a friendship with a known radical. My gut tells me that Utopia Energy is not involved in any terrorist activity-at least not as a company. However, that does not mean that one or more of their employees is not striking out on their own to either help some fanatical group or at least benefit from their activities. Homeland Security did not bring up Tiger Eye's name just to add another group to the ever-growing list of bad guys."

"That could be true, but you know that we have to go on more than your gut feelings. Bring this subject to the task force meeting this afternoon and let's get a team working on it-starting with someone in Beijing. You will need to bring Joseph Lee into the loop on what you are working on here. We need him to be our eyes and ears in China."

"I'll have to find out the names of the people on Utopia's team and get their pictures and bios to Joseph," Dan commented. "He will need to know who all the players are that he needs to be watching."

"Remember," Jim warned as Dan was leaving his office. "Not a word to Maggie. Not even a hint. If she knows you suspect anything, she could inadvertently jeopardize the investigation. There will be time to fill her in later if we find out anything."

"I know, Jim, but at some point we are going to have to bring her on board," Dan argued. "She is our insider, and there are things she could know that would help us."

"Well, for now I'm afraid you'll have to find a way to get her to tell you things without her realizing what she's doing," Jim replied. "Otherwise you could put her in more danger than she is already in."

As Dan returned to his own office, he thought about Jim's warning. He knew Jim was right about how to handle Maggie at this point. It was standard operating procedure, except for one detail: Maggie was not just an impersonal source. She was his friend. Dan knew he would have to be extra careful not to let any of his suspicions show to either Maggie or Sara. Well, he thought as he dialed the phone, now was as good a time as any to get started.

"I was just thinking about you," the cheery voice answered. "What's going on in your world of crime?"

"Slow day on the home front," Dan lied. "I was just thinking about going to Saltgrass for dinner on Saturday."

"It must be slow there if you're thinking about Saturday dinner plans on Wednesday," Sara laughed.

"Why don't you call Maggie and see if she and Alex want to go with us?" Dan suggested. "I think it's time we get to know this guy."

"That's a great idea-as long as you don't grill him too much," Sara warned. "Sometimes you forget that you aren't Maggie's big brother."

"Looks who's talking, Miss Nosey Butt," Dan laughed. "Just call her, okay?"

"Okay, okay. I'll let you know later if it's a date," Sara agreed before they said their goodbyes.

Dan hung up already feeling deceitful. He was going to have to do better than this or he would blow the whole operation before it ever got started. A quick glance at the clock reminded him of how little time he had before the task force meeting. He settled in to making his round of calls-starting with Beijing.

CHAPTER 74

"Do you understand what you are to do? Do you have any questions?" Han quizzed his son.

"Yes. Everything is going as planned. We leave with another food shipment tomorrow morning," Chen answered.

"How much plutonium will you bring back?" another man asked.

"Same as before, enough for one. We will be able to retrofit two compressors out of every shipment," the younger man again answered.

"Do you understand what to do when the compressors arrive?" Han asked his son.

"Yes, Father. Do not worry; we have gone over these plans many times," Chen answered.

All they needed now were the compressors. After eighteen months of negotiations and construction, Utopia Energy had finally shipped their first load of compressors to the United States. Soon they would be running up to capacity of twelve units per month. At a rate of two shipments of plutonium per month, Han would fulfill his customer's order in ten months. It had been a long and often difficult road for Han, but in the end, the Americans had played right into his hands. Mason had been an easy target, and even though he had had to be reined in occasionally, it had all worked out very well. Mason had managed to get the shipping arrangements secured for the company belonging to Tiger Eye Enterprises, despite the interference from the woman on the American team. She had almost ruined everything, but in the end, Mason did whatever it took to save his own skin. Han had to smile. Yes, he was very good at exploiting the weaknesses of the Americans.

CHAPTER 75

The two men took a table in the corner of the cafeteria. Several thousand people worked in the complex, many of them with varying ethnic backgrounds, so to see two Middle Eastern-looking men having lunch together did not seem unusual. In fact, no one was paying any attention to them at all. After several minutes of catching up on their morning's activities, the younger man brought the conversation around to the real purpose of their meeting.

"I have made the arrangements to get to Pickle Lake," Tarik informed Mohammed. "We will fly to Minneapolis, then to Thunder Bay. From there we will take a charter to Pickle Lake, arriving the evening before Habib gets there."

"We are to meet him at the fishing charter's office at the airport?" Mohammed asked.

"Yes, we will be there in time to meet him, and we will all fly out to the cabin together. We will spend a quiet week fishing. On the remote chance that anyone is watching, we will appear to be typical Americans showing our cousin a good time."

"You have the passports ready to exchange?"

"All is ready. Habib and I could pass for twins. He will fly back with you to Houston, and I will leave for Tehran. From there, I will fly to Caracas and wait. When Habib finishes with the bombs, he will fly to Venezuela, where we will switch passports again, and then I will return to Houston to help you finalize our plans," Tarik explained. "It will all work out just fine, my brother."

"I trust it will," Mohammed agreed. "It should not take long for Habib to do his part of the job. We have waited a long time to get some of the materials, but now we have them, so he should be able to work without interruption. When you return from Venezuela, we will begin to distribute the devices. Soon, soon all of our waiting will come to an end."

"In the meantime, we need to visit the tackle shop. We need to have the right equipment to appear to be serious fishermen," Tarik added. "It would look suspicious to take a fishing trip to Canada without the necessary accessories."

"Tomorrow, after work, we will visit the fishing supply store and then have dinner," Mohammed decided. "We will appear to be two guys anxiously anticipating our vacation."

The two of them continued in ordinary lunchtime conversation, being careful to appear casual rather than calculating, should anyone be watching. They were both sure that no one suspected anything unusual, but they were too careful to become complacent. Their mission had been in the making for many years. They were too patient and too smart to allow their behavior to change this close to the completion of their assignment. Their parents had stayed in America after meeting in college, and while they had assimilated into the American culture, they had not lost their passion for their Muslim heritage. Both Mohammed and Tarik had been indoctrinated into a quiet, but passionate radical belief. Tarik and Mohammed were Americans, but they were first and foremost Muslim. With their parents safely relocated in Venezuela, the two men were now left to complete the job they had been groomed for since early childhood. They had no feelings of guilt for what they were about to do. For them, it was a holy calling.

CHAPTER 76

"I can't believe we are actually having lunch in the middle of the week. Do you realize how long it's been since we did this?" Sara asked as the waiter led them to their table.

"Yes, forever. I never realized when I took this China assignment that my life would change so much," Maggie answered. "It feels like I've lost my direction."

"You're not lost, but you are definitely traveling a different road-that's not all bad, is it?" Sara questioned as she looked over the menu. She really didn't need to even open it; for years she and Maggie had been meeting here for lunch-she knew the selections by heart.

"Not really; it's not been as horrible as I had expected it to be. I have learned a lot about the business and even more about international travel. My confidence level has risen, for sure, but I would never let Baron know that this has been good for me," Maggie laughed. "If I do, the next thing I'll know, he will be sending me to Venezuela."

"At least you would be on the same side of the globe," Sara remarked. "I would certainly feel closer to you. I felt so helpless when you got sick and were a world away."

"I was too sick to even know I should have been worried," Maggie replied. "I don't know what would have happened if Alex hadn't been there. He took such good care of me-even after we got home."

"It's obvious that the two of you have reached a higher level than just co-workers," Sara said. "So when do I get to meet this great guy-more than just at the airport?"

"He's coming out to the house this weekend, so why don't you and Dan come over also?" Maggie asked, not realizing how her face lit up at the thought of seeing Alex. The expression was not lost on Sara.

"That sounds great to me. Why don't we go to Saltgrass for dinner? You know how much Dan loves his beef," Sara suggested, thinking how much better it would be if Maggie thought this whole get-together was her idea. "Then we can all go back to your place."

The two friends ordered their meals and spent the rest of the time catching up on each other's lives. Sara was a never-ending source of funny stories from her students. There was nothing like college coeds to put the world in perspective. Maggie thought the exposure to people in their twenties kept Sara young, and perhaps a little isolated from the rest of the world. Fortunately, or not, depending on the viewpoint, Dan's FBI world kept Sara somewhat balanced. They seemed like the perfect couple to Maggie, always laughing and enjoying whatever came their way. Maggie envied the life they had made together.

On the way back to the office, Maggie thought about what she had said about the China project being a growing experience for her. It had been a positive move for her, not only professionally but it had also done a great deal to improve her self-esteem. Instead of hiding within the safe walls of her former life, she had been forced to travel into strange territory and learn to be comfortable with herself in settings that were far from the secure world she had sequestered herself in after Tom's death.

Most important, she was learning to open up her heart again, which had been a mixture of difficultly and easiness rolled into one effort. Only a few people knew that Tom had talked to her at length about what he hoped for her life after he was gone. It had been a very painful conversation for Maggie at the time and for many years afterwards. Tom had wanted her to move on, to live again, and to love someone else. It was a request she found hard to honor. She did not want to love anyone else; she did not want to take the risk of being hurt again. It had been much safer to just live in his afterglow.

Until now. Somewhere in the past several months, she had come to realize that Tom was right. She needed to laugh, to have someone special in her life to share the events of the day. Alex had become that person to her. It had happened so slowly that she had not had time to be afraid of getting hurt. She knew that Alex was as safe a place as Tom had been, even though they were very different men. Contrary to what she had thought she would feel, Maggie had no sense of guilt in loving Alex. Doing so did not diminish the love that she and Tom had shared. In her heart, she knew that Tom was pleased. She wished she could tell him about Alex, but somehow she knew he already was aware, and she could feel his blessing.

Deep in her private thoughts, Maggie had almost walked past her own office when she heard Anne call her name.

"Just going to walk on by when there are beautiful flowers waiting for you in your office?" Anne asked suspiciously sweetly. "If it were me, I would be dying to know who sent them to me."

"Knowing you, the card has already been read, and you know more than I do," Maggie said, laughing as she headed for her office. She had a good idea who had sent them and it made her heart beat a little faster.

"The card was no help at all, and yes, I did look," Anne said disappointingly. "You would think a guy would have the common decency to sign the card in such a way that the rest of us can know the scoop."

Maggie caught her breath as she walked into her office. Sitting on the corner of her desk were a dozen perfect long-stemmed red roses in a crystal vase. They were exquisite.

Maggie hadn't had flowers-much less roses-sent to her in years. She had forgotten how special they can make a woman feel. She reached for the card and reading it, smiled softly. It simply said, "Hi Pretty Lady".

"Well, aren't you going to tell me who they're from?" Anne asked. "And don't pull that 'need to know' line on me."

"They are from a friend," Maggie said without elaborating as she put her purse away. She and Alex had tried to be very cautious at the office to not advertise any type of relationship that might be happening. The other team members, while having their own opinions based on their knowledge of the China trips, were equally discreet.

"That's just great. Here I am, your assistant who is supposed to know everything, and you're keeping secrets from me," Anne dramatically whined as she went back to her desk in the outer office.

Maggie just laughed. She knew Anne well enough to know that she wasn't really upset for not having all the latest news, and she also knew that in time Anne would have to be told. However, Maggie knew that when that time came, Anne would be the consummate professional in regard to her boss's personal life.

Maggie picked up the phone and called Alex's office. When there was no answer, she dialed his cell phone.

"Thank you for the roses. They are beautiful beyond words," Maggie said when he answered. "I'm not used to such romantic gestures."

"I'm glad you like them-and the gesture," Alex replied, beaming at her reaction. "Maybe you will just have to get used to a little romance in your life."

"Maybe. It's been so long, I'm not sure I'll know how to behave," Maggie said, quietly.

"Don't worry. It's like riding a bike, so I'm told," Alex reassured her as well as himself. "Just enjoy the ride. I promise not to drive too fast"

Maggie laughed. Alex always had a way of taking her unexpected shyness and making her feel comfortable with the situation. It was one the qualities she liked best about him. He didn't let her feel foolish.

"Are you still coming out this weekend?" Maggie asked.

"Am I still invited?" He joked back, knowing full well that she was looking forward to the time as much as he was.

"Of course you are. I was just making sure, because I made plans for us with Sara and Dan," Maggie explained. "They want us to go to dinner. I hope you don't mind."

"I think that sounds great. I've heard so much about them, I feel like we are all old friends," Alex replied. "So is this the 'meet the boyfriend' dinner?"

"Is that what you are-my boyfriend?" Maggie laughed, but only half jokingly. She had wondered how Alex viewed their friendship.

"Well, I hope so. I'm not in the habit of sending roses to just anyone," Alex answered. "I was aiming for more than just a business colleague."

"You know you are," Maggie said softly. "Besides, you're too cute to just be a coworker."

"I'm not even going to respond to that comment," Alex sarcastically replied. "You never did answer my question: Is this dinner going to be an inquisition?"

"No. Well, maybe. It could be," Maggie hesitated. "You can never tell with Sara. Sometimes she can be annoying, but she always means well. I just love her anyway-and kick her later."

"I'm sure I can handle Sara. I just don't want to tick off the FBI agent." Alex laughed. "You know, that could be a bad day."

"Well, then, you had better be on your best behavior Mr. Sheppard," Maggie replied. "I have to go now and try to get some of this work finished. Call me tonight?"

"Sure. Isn't that what a boyfriend's supposed to do?" Alex asked with a fake innocence.

"I'm saying goodbye now before this gets totally out of hand!" Maggie laughed and hung up. She took a long look at the roses and decided that she truly did like having a boyfriend.

CHAPTER 77

Habib Aghasi left the stage to the respected applause of his fellow scientists. His key presentation had been the highlight of the symposium, where for four days he had joined his fellow professors and professionals at the World Conference on Nuclear Energy in Ottawa. He had agreed to make an appearance at a reception following the conference, but insisted on an early evening as he was scheduled to fly out early the next morning. His colleagues assumed he was returning to Iran, when in fact he was chartering a flight to the tiny town of Pickle Lake, Ontario. How in the world his cousins had picked a place named Pickle Lake was beyond Habib's comprehension. But he trusted Tarik and Mohammed and felt confident that their plans were well thought out. He had done his research in case the charter personnel were the chatty type: He would be joining friends who were the fishermen in the group, and while he would also be fishing for walleye and northern pike, he was mostly there for the photography. He hoped that this would keep anyone from asking him too many questions about his fishing experience. Should they want to talk about photography, he had considerable experience with a camera and could easily discuss any techniques or subject material.

Photography was truly what he loved to do, but somewhere in his college days he had become quite fascinated with nuclear science. After earning his Ph.D, he had worked for several years in the private sector before returning to Tehran to head the government's nuclear research department. Being highly esteemed in his professional community, he was quick to be used by his superiors as the innocent public face for nuclear responsibility. Privately, he was a senior member of one of the Muslim world's most zealous radical groups. It was Habib who was the contact point between the group and his American cousins. It was Habib who had told Mohammed what materials were needed to produce the desired result, and it was Habib who would build the bombs that would bring the Americans to their knees.

CHAPTER 78

"I'm so hungry, I don't know what to order," Sara sighed as she studied the menu. "Maybe I'll have one of everything."

"You're always saying that, and then you order salad," Maggie laughed at her friend's dramatic attitude. "Someday we're going to make you eat the biggest steak they have on the menu."

"Well, tonight's the night," Sara decided. "Not the biggest of course, but I am having a steak. It's a special night and salads are just not appropriate for special occasions."

"What exactly is the celebration?" Dan asked.

"Getting to meet Alex, silly," Sara explained, astonished that he was not following her train of thought. Sometimes men were exasperating. Then again, sometimes they were gorgeous. Alex certainly fit that description. Sara decided her friend had very good taste in men.

"I can't say that I have ever been the subject of a celebration before," Alex said blushing. "Except with my sisters. They make up opportunities just to embarrass me, and here you've joined right in with them."

The four of them laughed at his comment. They were off to a comfortable start, Dan thought. Alex seemed to fit right in with the tight little group that the three of them had become. He was happy for Maggie, but was having a difficult time just relaxing and enjoying the company. This might be a relaxing evening for the rest of them, but he was working.

"So Alex, tell us about your take on traveling to China so much," Dan said. "Maggie whines a lot about it, but I just mostly check that off to being a diva."

"Oh, you are so in trouble with that comment," Maggie responded. She had no problem with Dan's snide remarks because she knew that he respected and loved her. He just liked to kid around, which was okay with her.

"I'm afraid I am not brave enough to jump into that fire," Alex replied. "In her defense, she does an excellent job at holding up her end of things in China."

"Spoken like someone totally blinded by infatuation," Sara said sweetly. "You can't fool us-we know exactly how thrilled Maggie is with international travel."

"Okay, okay. Seriously now, how do you like traveling so much?" Dan asked, trying to get the conversation going back in the direction he needed it to go. "I would think it would be difficult, considering the huge changes in time zones."

"You're right. The traveling part is tough," Alex agreed. "It takes several days after you're there to know whether it's morning or night, and by that time you are so tired that you don't care. Just about the time your body gets on a Chinese schedule, you leave and head back to Houston. Your clock has a hard time adjusting to it all."

"How do you like the country itself?" Dan continued questioning. "Do you get to sightsee any at all?"

"Sometimes you do. It just depends on the work schedule," Alex explained. "It's a very diverse country and I would like to be able to visit more of it, but so far it's been mostly work. The few people that I've met seem nice enough, with a couple of exceptions."

"One in particular, no doubt," Maggie said under her breath. "Don't let Alex kid you. He's very comfortable there-in Chengdu anyway. That's where we spend most of our time, and he knows his way around the city very well. He interacts great with the locals. I would never leave the hotel if it were up to me, but Alex goes anywhere he wants and seems to know everyone when he gets there."

"She exaggerates. But it's true that I try to move around the city," Alex continued. "I just can't stay secluded inside one building. The other guys on the team rarely venture past the lobby, but I can't do that. I've got to be exploring, checking everything out."

"So how many others are on the team?" Dan asked, glad for the easy segue he needed for the direction of the conversation. "Mason Williams is the only other one I've heard Maggie mention, other than you, of course."

"There are three others," Alex answered. "Paul Carter is the purchasing manager, David Coleman is our attorney, and John White is the maintenance manager. They're a great bunch of guys, just not very adventurous."

At that point in the conversation, the waiter brought their food, and the conversation moved on to other subjects. Dan was satisfied with what he had been able to find out tonight. Years of training allowed him to memorize the names Alex had mentioned. Tomorrow he would start working on their backgrounds. He figured it was a waste of time, since Maggie never mentioned anyone being chummy with Mason except the Chinese team leader. But it was still something he had to pursue. He also had to check Alex's background. It seemed that Alex had found his way around Chengdu. That could be just because of his nature, as Alex had pointed out, or it could be something more cynical. Either way, Dan had to check. Assumptions were not acceptable in his line of business.

The remainder of the dinner conversation flowed effortlessly and freely. Maggie seemed to bask in the easiness of the evening. She was thrilled that Alex and her friends got along so well. She and Sara were able to visit between themselves, since it seemed that Alex and Dan were completely oblivious to their presence. The guys had trailed off into the world of hunting and found out that they had a great deal in common. Before dessert was finished, they were planning a trip to Montana to elk hunt in the fall. The group returned to Maggie's house and continued their visit late into the evening. Finally, Dan ended the night with the excuse of an early morning run into the office.

"So, I guess I don't need to ask how you liked Alex," Sara commented as they pulled out of Maggie's driveway. "You two hit it off like two old buddies."

"He seems like a great guy," Dan honestly answered. "He and Maggie appear to work well together. Maybe she has finally found the person who can make her happy again."

"I sure hope so," Sara replied. "I guess this job in China was a great decision after all."

Dan didn't reply to her comment. He wasn't sure it was a good decision for Maggie at all. Perhaps, though, it was a good thing for the country. Without Maggie being on Utopia's China team, they would not know that Houston was possibly the destination for something sinister between Tiger Eye and Cai Yi. Dan tried to find comfort somewhere in that thought.

CHAPTER 79

The lone boat anchored in the middle of the lake resembled a speck of dirt floating in a bowl of water. The men knew they must be the only people on the entire lake, but just in case they were wrong, they played the role of three guys enjoying a great fishing adventure. They were very careful with the subjects of their conversations, unless they were in their cabin or in the middle of the lake. With no other boat in sight, they felt relatively comfortable discussing their plans.

"We will build the first four units together, for you to learn the process," Habib explained to Mohammed. "It is not difficult, but everything must be done in a specific order."

"Do you really think I will be able to assemble the rest of the devices by myself, once you trade places with Tarik in Venezuela?" Mohammed asked.

"You will have no trouble at all. Once I have taught you the procedures, you will be able to build each unit as your raw materials arrive," Habib answered. "You will then be able to deliver one group at a time to the target destination. When the last ones are complete, you will be ready to execute the plan."

"How long will it take for you to build the first four units?" Tarik questioned.

"Not too long–two, maybe three weeks," Habib responded. "Long enough though for you to get used to island life on Margarita."

"Just don't get too comfortable, my brother. Remember we have a job to do," Mohammed interjected. "There will be plenty of time to enjoy the sun and the water when we have taught the infidels a lesson."

"I have never lost sight of our mission, Mohammed," Tarik retorted. "I was just thinking how much nicer it will be in Venezuela than in this foggy, damp wilderness. You must admit that there are better places to be than on a lake in the middle of the Canadian backwoods."

"True, it does not have the most comfortable weather," Mohammed admitted. "But it is beautiful here, and more important, it's isolated."

"Deserted would have been my take on it," Habib laughed. "Just a bunch of trees and probably a few hundred bears."

"Don't forget the fish," Tarik shouted as he reeled in a huge walleye. "Looks like we have dinner for tonight."

The three men continued their morning fishing trip, enjoying their time together and catching up on family news. The brothers had not seen their cousin in many months, and not since they were children had they spent this much time together. The fact that they were fellow soldiers in the holy war just added to their sense of solidarity.

CHAPTER 80

"I wasn't expecting a call from you, especially at this time of the day-or should I say, middle of the night-for you," Dan joked as he answered the secure line from Beijing.

"Trust me, I'd rather be sleeping, but something's come up that's too big to sleep through," Joseph dryly replied. "I don't know what this has to do with your end of the world, but you can bet it plays in there somewhere."

"I assume you are calling about Tiger Eye?" Dan asked, his interest piqued by his colleague's serious tone.

"Probably, maybe, I'm not sure," Joseph answered. "I realize that's not very definitive, but the pieces of this puzzle are just not fitting together yet. We received intel from an operative inside North Korea that the Minister of Foreign Affairs is planning to defect. Not only is he bailing out of his country, he stands to become a very wealthy man in the process. To the tune of five million dollars."

Dan sat in silence, stunned by this turn of events and unable to comprehend what the connection was between all of the players. His thoughts were spinning around in his head so fast that nothing made sense.

"Let me see if I understand this latest scenario," Dan finally commented. "I have a US company doing business in China that is using Tiger Eye as their freight forwarder. Tiger Eye's leader is not only on the team that negotiated the contract, but he is meeting with both a known terrorist connection and a North Korean official-who now wants to defect with a large amount of money. Do you see this the same way?"

"Except that it seems that he is not just leaving with the money, but rather being paid the money for supplying something to Han," Joseph replied. "The problem is that each one of those connections raises a set of questions. Is there a link between the North Korean, Tiger Eye, and the Muslim extremist or are these separate operations? If there is a connection, what is it? Is Utopia Energy involved or a rogue employee of theirs? Are they just being used in some scheme? Most importantly, will this plan, whatever it is, impact the security of the United States?"

"Is Han the one paying the North Korean, or is it the Chinese government, or even Cai Yi?" Dan asked.

"What we know at this point is that Kim Cheol-su has provided a bank account number for Han to wire funds to, five million dollars total, with installments corresponding with each shipment of food being delivered to the Pyongyang government. We don't know of any connection with the government and of course, the money could be coming from Yi. There must be some connection with Han's son: Han gave Kim a picture of his son to keep—an unusual act for two businessmen."

"You have someone watching the son, I presume?" Dan asked, already knowing the answer.

"Our buddies over at the Agency are doing the leg work on most of this," Joseph replied. "It's easier for them to operate undercover. They are aware that we are working an angle involving your friend's company. We all function very well together here. It's a community effort."

"The obvious thing that Kim would have to bargain with would be nuclear weapons. Does anyone know if he could get his hands on his government's stockpile, and if he could, how he would smuggle something like that out of the country?"

"We have thought of that, of course. Could he acquire such? We don't know," Joseph responded. "There is such little known about the workings within their government. We have a fairly well-placed CI there, but we have not sent instructions back yet as to what information we want him to try to obtain. All of this is raw intel that just came to us this afternoon. We are still trying to work through the thought process."

"Do we have a timetable on any of these plans?" Dan inquired.

"The food shipments will take ten months to complete," Joseph replied. "The first shipment took place six weeks ago. That may give us enough time to find out what is really being planned. Once we have some answers, we can decide what action needs to be taken."

"There are just too many unknowns at this point," Dan commented. "I will take this back to the task force. Maybe among all of us, we can figure something out. I will check back in with you in two days, unless we come up with something sooner."

"That will work. I'll call you if we find out anything before then," Joseph said. "Dan, you know that you are going to have to take a hard look at Utopia. I know this is your friend's company and you want to take the high road with this, but realistically you have to know that they could in some way be involved. You have to make sure you are keeping an open mind."

"You're right, but in my gut I just can't see them being involved in anything covert," Dan argued. "I know this company's history; I know about the management in place today; most important, I know Maggie. She would never tolerate a betrayal to her country. She would have already come to me if she had any suspicions that there was a problem."

"But what if she is being used?" Joseph countered. "For that matter, the entire organization could be being used without their knowledge. They could be being set up by Han or even by one of their employees who is involved with Tiger

Eye, or some terrorist group. These are all things you have to consider."

"We are looking into all of those possibilities, but I am telling you, Maggie doesn't know a thing," Dan replied. "I feel certain that the management is not involved, however, I am not as certain about a single employee or two being in on the plan. We are doing background checks as we speak. They should be ready for us to go over at this afternoon's meeting. Look, Joseph, I understand what you're saying. Trust me, I will not let my personal opinions cloud my judgment, but there are just some things that I am sure about."

"Enough said, my friend. I do trust your judgment, but I want you to realize the ease with which you could be side-tracked," Joseph responded. "Just do what you know best to do. Talk to you in a day or so."

Dan sat quietly in his office for a few minutes after ending the overseas call. He knew that Joseph was right and that others were probably wondering if he could be objective in his assessment of the situation. He understood that it would be easy to have his views marred by his relationship with Maggie, but in his heart he knew this was not the case. He had been an FBI agent for thirty years and was seasoned enough to know that, despite what anyone might think, his job, his country, came first in his life.

CHAPTER 81

"Your shipment has arrived in Houston and is ready to be picked up—the sooner the better," Han spoke quietly across the table.

"I will make the call. It should happen quickly," Yi replied. "Whom should my friend contact?"

"Same as before. He will make all of the arrangements with your friends," Han answered as he slipped a piece of paper to Yi. "Remember, very soon, very quietly."

"When can we expect the next freighter to arrive?" Yi asked.

"In about a month," Han answered. "There should be a delivery twice a month for the next nine months. That should be enough to cover what your client ordered."

"Very good. You are a man of your word, and you can trust that I am a man of mine," Yi responded. "The monies will arrive in your account on schedule."

"I have no doubt. After all, no money, no shipment." Han smiled. "A pleasure seeing you again."

As Han left the restaurant, Yi placed a call to Mohammed, giving him the number that Han had passed to him. Yi was very pleased with the way this whole arrangement was going. His comrades were up to no good for sure, but it was of no consequence to him. He was making an enormous amount of money in this deal, and if his friends in America used the shipments to attack the infidels, then all the better.

CHAPTER 82

The background checks yielded little information that Dan didn't already know, but it did bring the rest of the task force up-to-date on the Utopia players. John White, David Coleman, Paul Carter were all ordinary, tax-paying citizens who served on their local school boards and charitable events. There was nothing more to be gleaned from their personal dossiers. The story was the same with Maggie. Dan had more to offer about her than the official check revealed. That left just two team members: Alex Sheppard and Mason Williams.

Mason Williams was a well-connected Houston socialite whose position with the company seemed somewhat below his community status. That status however was more due to a well-placed marriage than any effort on his part. His photograph was routinely pasted in the social sections of every newspaper in Houston. He and his wife, Cynthia, were seen at all the right parties and often chaired some of the city's more elite functions. He was known to entertain his clients in fine style and to immensely enjoy a night at the blackjack table. In fact, he had the reputation of being quite the gambler and yet, miraculously, did not appear to be in any kind of financial difficulty. That could have been due to his wife's personal fortune as well as that of her family. Regardless, there was no sign of financial vulnerability.

It did seem that Mason enjoyed traveling. According to his passport records, Mason not only traveled to China on a regular basis, but managed to work in several other places as well. The destinations he had traveled to in the past five years were quite a mix. He had hit many of the traditional spots that wealthy Americans like to visit: Rome, Paris, the French Riviera. He had also visited Peru, Russia, Thailand, and several countries in the Middle East-not the usual hot spots for tourism, but that could possibly fall within the realm of his responsibilities at the oil company.

Then there was Alex Sheppard. He seemed to be a man of several secrets. Were they worthy of consideration? Perhaps. Or not. Apparently Alex had been married in another lifetime and had made a concerted effort to conceal that fact. The wife, debutant Amanda Walker, was critically injured in a car wreck that had left her in an almost three-decade coma. She and her lover had failed to negotiate a curve on a dark, icy road, just moments after she had left Alex heartbroken, and stunned to learn Amanda had been unfaithful. The lover had been killed. Her wealthy parents had forced an annulment and had gained legal guardianship over their daughter. Alex left the East Coast and returned to Houston and the security of his family. As far as the Bureau could determine, Alex had left the entire incident in Boston and had never looked back. He was considered one of the city's most eligible bachelors, but one that never flirted with settling down. None of that mattered to the FBI.

What did concern Dan and the other members of the task force was Alex's brother-in-law, Collin Wu. Collin, his Americanized name, had once been a rising star in China's growing space program. He was one of the early pioneers who, unexpectedly, defected to the United States in the late 1980s and promptly found a home at NASA. Ten years later, he had married Alex's sister, Barbara.

Dan was conflicted. He really hadn't expected to find any type of Chinese connection to Alex. He didn't know if what they had uncovered was relevant or not. Was there anything significant about the fact that Alex's brother-in-law defected from China?

The task force decided that several avenues of interest needed to be pursued. They decided to dig deeper into Mason's travel habits. If he was traveling on business then they needed to know what was the nature of the visits and with whom he met in those countries. If the destinations were personal, they still needed to know where he visited. Some of the countries in his records were not places that most Americans would consider a vacation getaway.

One of the task force members was going to do research on the current activities of Collin Wu and also focus on any family dynamics that could connect him and Alex with Han. Meanwhile, Dan would ask Joseph Lee to find out all he could about Wu's history in China and what would have caused him to turn his back on his homeland. Dan also had his homework cut out for him in Houston. He had to try to get more information out of Maggie without her knowledge.

Dan left the office that evening feeling drained. What had started as a curiosity over a chance comment had turned into something that perhaps was vital to national security. When he had heard Maggie mention Tiger Eye Enterprises it had set off a warning bell in his head, but he never would have imagined that one innocent comment would lead him into a world of terrorists and defecting officials from Communist countries. The scariest thought of the entire unfolding drama was the possibility that nuclear weapons might be involved. Dan's mind was trying to sort out all of this, but every time he settled into one focus area, new information popped up that sent his brain into all sorts of scenarios. The only conscious thought that kept coming back was that wherever all of this information led to, it was not going to be good.

CHAPTER 83

The three men stood on the tarmac outside the charter company's building. It had been a productive week for them. They had the appearance of friends who had spent a glorious week fishing and enjoying the great outdoors. After hugging and saying their goodbyes, two of the men boarded a tiny plane headed for Thunder Bay.

The third man gathered his baggage and headed for the waiting area. Two hours later, he also boarded a flight to Thunder Bay where he would make connections that would eventually lead him to Tehran. At that point he would be met by a comrade who would have another ticket ready for Venezuela. Tarik was looking forward to being reunited with his family in Venezuela. His parents had moved there years ago and he was anxious to see them. It would be a short visit, but soon he would be joining them again–this time to stay. He had worried that he would have trouble passing as his famous cousin, but the Canadian officials did not seem to know or care who he was, as long as his papers were in order. He boarded each flight without incident and before the day was over, he was headed to Tehran. He prayed to Allah that Habib's entry into the United States had gone just as smoothly. When he got to Tehran, he would phone Mohammed and find out if all was going as planned. Until he was safe in the air heading toward Venezuela, knowing that Habib had fooled the Americans and was in Houston, he kept his guard on high alert.

CHAPTER 84

Clad in hazmat suits with lead gloves, the two men carefully handled each component as if it were already programmed to explode. They realized that the only item of danger to them at this point was the plutonium, but still, there was a reverence in their activity; it was as if they were touching sacred objects.

"There is no way that any part of the bomb is going to survive to check for even a fingerprint," Habib commented. "I think you are being a bit paranoid."

"It could be that you are naïve," Mohammed responded. "I am more worried about my heath than some fingerprint, but this is not some third-world outpost. American law enforcement is more cunning than they are given credit for on the nightly news. We can take no chances in case something goes wrong."

"Nothing will go wrong. But if you are happier with these silly precautions, then so be it," Habib relented. "After all, I will be living safely in Tehran in a few weeks. You and Tarik are the ones taking all of the chances."

"They are chances we are honored to take if it will shake the arrogance of the infidels," Mohammed replied. "Besides, it will be our comrades who deliver these bombs who are the true servants of Allah, for they will not survive their assignment."

"So tell me how you plan to distribute these after we have them built," Habib requested. "Twenty bombs are a lot to dispense."

"Ahh, it is an ingenious plan," Mohammed began. "We have five men chosen for couriers. Each will deliver bombs to four others whom they have handpicked. Tarik and I have been purchasing the televisions you see in the corner from WalMart. We will gut the insides of the televisions, insert the bomb and repackage them in the original boxes. We will deliver them to our five couriers, who will in turn give one to each of their recruits. On the day after Thanksgiving, nineteen of the televisions will be returned to WalMart. The men will have a four-hour window to get them back to the stores before we access the bomb's computer remotely, and poof! The Americans will see what damage a nuclear bomb can do-not only to the immediate landscape, but to their economy as a whole."

"Nineteen bombs? What happens with the twentieth one that you are building?" Habib asked.

"It is being reserved for the most important target," Mohammed answered." "Our most dedicated soldier has obtained employment with the group that cleans the WalMart headquarters building in Bentonville, Arkansas. They will be in the building late the night before Thanksgiving. He will leave a canister in the janitor's supply cabinet. With the headquarters vaporized, there will be no command post, no way to keep the other stores–world-wide-functioning. Trucks will stop, factories will be idle. America's economic heart will be stopped."

"The President will be helpless to respond," Mohammed continued. "We will take down the infidels without ever touching their federal properties. The people will finally realize that we cannot be stopped; that their government cannot protect them."

"It is a wonderful plan," Habib responded. "You are to be commended for such brilliance. Because you have lived among the enemy for so long, you understand how they operate, what their weaknesses are, how they can be destroyed. You are a great resource for the cause. Allah will reward you greatly."

"But not if we do not succeed," Mohammed cautioned. "We have much work to do and you must teach me how to assemble these bombs so that we can get you safely out of the country before too long. You cannot be absent from your work for months. You are followed too closely by the international watchdogs."

"You are very right, and the there is another reason you need to get these televisions delivered as soon as possible," Habib commented. "You do not need a large concentration of plutonium in one place. It will be harder to detect if it's spread over a large area. It is a risk to store it here as you have been."

"I know, but we had to wait for your conference in Canada to give us an opportunity to slip you into the country," Mohammed defended. "It was cold enough in Canada as it was. We could not have faked a fishing trip any earlier in the season. The season doesn't even open until late May and sometimes the ice hasn't left yet, even then."

"Do you really think anyone in Houston has a clue to the weather in Canada?" Habib laughed. "Americans think that everywhere it's the same as where they are. They all have a limited field of vision and imagination."

"Perhaps so," Mohammed responded. "But for once, that attitude has worked well for us."

"It will work well again on the day the infidels call 'Black Friday'."

Mohammed and Habib spent the next three weeks assembling the first four bombs. By the end of their time together, Habib felt that Mohammed had sufficient understanding to complete the other sixteen devices. Habib was anxious to leave Houston. He had spent most of the time in the dusty warehouse that Mohammed had rented. They had gone out for dinner on rare occasions, careful to avoid places where they might bump into people who knew Tarik and Mohammed. While Habib could physically pass for his cousin, there was no way he could carry on any type of conversation pretending to be Tarik. Besides, Mohammed and Tarik were supposed to be on an extended fishing vacation to Canada. It wouldn't do to be seen in Houston.

CHAPTER 85

"How is your end of the investigation going? Come up with anything interesting?" Dan asked when one of his fellow task force members entered his office a few days later. "From that file you have, it looks like you've been busy."

"Mason Williams has turned into a multidimensional man. He has lots of balls to keep in the air," the man answered. "It seems that he has at least one really big secret to keep, and when there's one, there's usually more."

"So what is Mason hiding?" Dan asked. He would not have thought that Mason had the kind of personality to be any deeper than what you could observe on the surface. At least that is the perception he had from Maggie's comments.

"We checked his wife's passport records to determine which places, if any, coincided with the trips that Mason has taken. Some of them did-the obvious places that the upper class frequents-but even in some of those places, she did not accompany him," his colleague continued. "Then we checked on where Utopia Energy does business, and none of those places fit with Mason's travel, except China."

"That still doesn't mean that he is involved in some seedy operation," Dan injected, trying to be open-minded. "Maybe he just likes to travel to places his wife doesn't want to visit."

"That's certainly one possibility," the man replied. "But there are others. What if he is involved with some sinister group that wants to do harm? Why would he get involved with those kinds of people? What would be his motivation? After all, he's living a pretty good life here in America-what's he got to complain about? He's wealthy, well placed in society, and seems to have one of those high paid executive do-nothing jobs."

"His lifestyle does not fit the profile of a discontented citizen," the man continued. "He represents all the things that we're hated for in the anti-American world. There had to be something else-there always is. So, we put a tail on him and found a world of information on our friend. It seems that Mason has a traveling companion who is red-headed, long-legged and drop-dead gorgeous."

"Her name is Rachel Montgomery and she is the Curator at the Chaffee Museum of Art," Dan's coworker explained. "From her passport records, it seems that she and Mason have been having an affair for several years. They have mutual friends in the art community and frequently work on the same charitable events, but apparently no one has caught on to their relationship."

"Where do they meet, considering Mason is photographed fairly often?" Dan asked. "It would be hard to keep a secret like that for several years without someone seeing them together."

"It took some creative research to follow the paper trail, but it appears that he bought her a condo in the Weiche Building," the man explained. "I have to give him credit for showing more restraint than most men do with a beautiful woman on the side. He covered his tracks deeply. There are lots of shops and restaurants and even offices in the Weiche that can provide plenty of cover for them. They are very discreet and even if they are seen together, it can be explained by their work on various projects. After this long, it appears that they are content with their secret and there are no visible plans of changing the status quo. She may have been warming his bed for several years, but she has managed to carry on a completely independent life. It all seems stable."

"Well, his friends and family may be oblivious to the entire affair, but what if someone else found out?" Dan questioned. "After all, we were able to uncover all of this in just a few weeks. Granted, we have a wealth of tools at our disposal, but so do other groups. Maybe someone is using the mistress angle to blackmail Mason. It could be as simple as wanting the freight contract for Utopia's shipments out of China, or it could be that those shipments are the key to Han and Yi's newly formed partnership."

"It wouldn't be the first time that a beautiful woman got a guy in big trouble," his companion commented. "But Mason having a mistress does not directly connect him with what's brewing in the Far East. If he is involved, there's got to be more to it than Rachel."

"Let's not forget that Mason is not the only team member that has secrets," Dan replied. "We still have to deal with Alex Sheppard. There could still be something to that story."

"We have a team working on that as we speak," his associate offered. "They're over at NASA now trying to see what they can find out. You know that once they make that visit, this investigation gets more visible. Your friends are going to know that Wu is being watched. You need to be prepared for them to confront you."

"Nobody knows that better than I do," Dan sighed as he ran his hand through his wavy hair. "Nobody."

CHAPTER 86

When Dan came into the office the next morning, there was an email from Joseph Lee asking Dan to call him at the Embassy in Beijing. Dan hit the kitchen for coffee and a bagel before settling down to talk with Joseph. From the tone of the email, he had a feeling he was going to be tied up for a while.

"So are you just hanging around the office waiting on my call, or is it true that you have no social life?" Dan joked when his counterpart answered. The two friends always fell into a comfortable banter.

"I'm going to ignore that remark, because we both know that I get around way more than you do in your single-but-settled life," Joseph jabbed back. "You might as well be married, man."

"Time to change the subject," Dan remarked. "Tell me what is so important that I needed to call on a secure line."

"I did some checking into Wu's history here," Joseph began. "It seems the Chinese have never got over his defection. It is still an open wound here. The Chinese are accustomed to other countrie's citizens pledging loyalty to them-especially ones from America. They love to have our secrets passed on to them, but they are very touchy about the other way around."

"Imagine that. I'm sure they are unhappy about his leaving. From what I understand, he is an extremely revered scientist," Dan replied. "The folks at NASA treat him like some type of Einstein. They are quite pleased to have him on our side of the pond, and pay him enormously for his decision to join the US team. Do we know why he left China?"

"The Chinese have no one but themselves to blame for that fiasco, although I'm not sure they could have seen it coming," Joseph explained. "Wu was at the International Space University, near Strasbourg, France, working on the implementation of a summer program to identify and map lunar resources when the Tiananmen Square incident occurred. Many of his friends were caught up in the scene and several of them were killed, including his mentor from his college days at Beijing University. Also killed was the head of the China National Space Administration who was not only sympathetic towards the students' demands, but he was Wu's uncle."

"It was a highly explosive situation and Wu was dealing with a great many personal emotions," Joseph continued. "Somewhere in those days surrounding the turmoil in Beijing, Wu walked into the US Consulate General in Strasbourg and requested political asylum. Considering what was happening in Beijing, and the fact that Wu was considered one of the most brilliant space minds anywhere, we quickly and gladly swept him off to Washington."

"From our reports here, he has been the driving force behind some of America's greatest space developments," Dan added. "It appears that he has assimilated well into our society. He is married with three children and is active in the Houston community. His bank accounts are healthy and there hasn't been anything so far that would raise a red flag."

"I wouldn't be too quick to write him off as a nonissue," Joseph interjected. "Our little intelligence group over here has uncovered an interesting development that may or may not be damning, but it is, at the least, curious. It seems that the translator assigned to Utopia's project team is none other than Wu's sister. She was born several years after Wu and was a young teenager when he defected. She works periodically for the Consul in Chengdu and specifically requested to be assigned to this project. We are working up a dossier on her life since his departure, but I thought this piece of info was important enough to pass along now."

"I'm not sure if it's significant or not," Dan responded. "But is certainly could be seen as suspicious that she would ask to work on a project that has connections to her long-lost brother. Or maybe not. She may not even know that Alex is Wu's brother-in-law. I'll have to toss that one around for a while. Contact me when you get the rest of the information on her. In the meantime, I will pass what we do know along to the rest of the task force."

"Will do. It shouldn't be too much longer-maybe a day or two," Joseph replied. "In the meantime I will be enjoying that social life that you don't think exists."

"Whatever you want to dream, buddy," Dan laughed. "Talk to you soon."

Dan had to smile as he thought of his friend. Joseph was a great guy, out-going, the life of the party. He always had a beautiful lady in his life, and Dan did not doubt for a second that he had one now. But Joseph had sworn off marriage many years ago, after his second wife left him for a cowboy. He may have a social life, Dan thought, but it's not one that will stay with him as he grows old. Of course, Dan knew that he himself wasn't much different. He had no plans to tie the knot again, but he did find great peace in knowing that Sara would always be there. That fact alone made him feel more blessed than Joseph.

The task force was meeting at two o'clock and Dan wanted to brief his boss before the group convened. Jim Keith allowed the task force members to work fairly freely without a set of rigid rules, but he still was aware of all that was happening with each member and the group as a whole. One thing he always insisted on was that he be briefed before each meeting by the team's coordinator. Jim was the one who kept an eye on the big picture while the others got dirty with the details.

The team respected his viewpoints and worked well under his loose leadership. Dan was especially close to Jim, given their history, and felt comfortable going to him with any tidbit of intel or just to discuss those gut feelings that law enforcement people develop over time. Jim was the first to acknowledge those types of instincts. That was where Dan was today: No concrete evidence, but a real feeling that something big was developing in front of them.

"You look like a man either deep in thought or trying desperately to remember why he was walking into my office," Jim commented as he watched the long-time agent slide onto the couch in the corner of the office. "What's up with the confusion?"

"I've got one of those feelings that I just can't shake and yet, at the same time, I can't put all the pieces together to where I can draw any logical solution." Dan sighed. "It's just so aggravating."

"Been there, buddy. Is there anything I can do to help?" Jim asked. He understood that sometimes all that was needed was for the facts to be verbalized. Once that was done, things seemed to fall in place.

"I don't know," Dan answered, frustration apparent in his tone and body language. "We've got a guy who has his hands into some serious business. He is head of China's largest financial institution, he meets at sidewalk cafés and public parks with a known terrorist middleman, and he has a new best friend who happens to be a high-ranking North Korean official who wants to defect-with the five million dollars that our guy is willing to pay him in exchange for who-knows-what. All of this is going on while he sits on a committee to establish a partnership between China and one of Houston's largest business entities. It smells, big time."

"Hmm. That's quite a complex picture you paint," Jim remarked. "I can connect the dots between the North Korean and the terrorist middleman without much effort, but have you decided how Utopia Energy got caught in the middle of this equation?"

"We don't know for sure that they are involved at all. But we do know that Utopia Energy's team leader has become quite chummy with Han, insisting on using Han's company as their freight forwarder, despite objections from other team members. In fact, the contract was signed without the participation of anyone on the team except the head guy. Han's same company is the carrier for food supplies being sent to North Korea as an incentive for Pyongyang to return to international talks over their nuclear weapon program."

"So where does the terrorist fit in?" Jim questioned.

"Han is paying the North Korean five million dollars in exchange for something serious enough that the official feels the need to be out of his homeland permanently. The only logical conclusion is that the guy is going to supply Han with nuclear weapons or materials of some kind. The North Koreans have nothing else of value," Dan continued. "Han is not into the nuclear weapons business, but his terrorist middleman, Cai Yi, could certainly find a buyer for such goods."

"Do we know who Yi's customer is?"

"No, but he works with several radical Muslim groups. The CIA has a tail on him now, trying to determine who he is negotiating with at the present time," Dan answered. "We're also working to find out if Utopia, or anyone in their organization, has ties to known terrorists. If there is a connection, then all the dots line up."

"You realize that this could all be a wild-goose chase," Jim countered. "Obviously there is concern about the Chinese-Korean-terrorist triangle, but it's very possible that Utopia Energy is not even involved in the mix on any level."

"You're absolutely right," Dan replied. "But let's think about the implications. If Han is supplying nuclear weapons or materials to Yi, it makes sense that a delivery has to be made to the terrorists. Yi himself is too smart to ever touch the merchandise, so the logical plan is to have Han handle the shipment all the way through. That also cuts down on involving anyone else in the plot. Is that delivery being made to the United States? I don't know, but it's quite a coincidence that Han has acquired a shipping contract into Houston-apparently an under-the-table arrangement."

"That's certainly something to be considered," Jim commented. "We need to ratchet up the priority of this investigation. The last thing we need is to have nuclear weapons coming through the Port of Houston."

Dan continued for the next few minutes reporting the preliminary findings on the backgrounds of the Utopia Energy project team, as well as the top management of the company. He spent a great deal of time going over Mason's secret life as well as the history of Alex's brother-in-law. By the time he was finished, the task force meeting was getting ready to begin. The two men headed to the conference room equally convinced of a conspiracy and yet completely without hard evidence. It was going to be a long process.

CHAPTER 87

The driveway was full of cars when Alex and Maggie drove up. From the tribe of kids playing in the front yard, it seemed they were the last to arrive. Maggie was more than a little nervous about going to Alex's parents' for the family cookout, but he was convinced that she was overreacting. They were not going to eat her alive, although he was anxious to gauge their reactions. He had not told any of the family that he was bringing a date. He had not wanted to give them time to develop a plan to grill Maggie about her past or their relationship. He knew that his sisters meant well, but he didn't want Maggie to feel as if she had to pass some imaginary inspection.

"I really appreciate your coming along tonight," Alex said as he killed the engine. "I know we only got home a couple of days ago and you're just as exhausted as I am, but this is an important night."

"Are you sure it's okay for me to barge in on your family's time together?" Maggie asked as she nervously shuffled her feet across the floorboard of Alex's SUV. "I really don't want to intrude."

"Everything will be just fine," he tried to comfort her. "Besides, they like surprises."

"Surprises? You didn't tell them you were bringing me?" Maggie reacted. "Oh, Alex, how could you do such a thing?"

"Because I can, and because I know that you will all just adore each other," he laughed. "Trust me."

Before Maggie could make any further argument, he was out of the vehicle, gathering his arms full of the food they had prepared. All Maggie could do was follow him into the house and try desperately to calm her nerves. She would deal with his cute little plan later.

After the initial surprised expressions settled down, Alex made all of the necessary introductions. Maggie was sure that she would never remember all of the names but tried hard to concentrate on each person and to remember things Alex had told her about them. It didn't take long for her to give up that effort and finally she suggested that perhaps she should have brought name tags for everyone. They all laughed and slowly the awkwardness faded away. Everyone was good to keep telling her their names, and before long she was happily ensconced in the kitchen helping with the preparations. Alex decided it was safe for him to head to the patio, where the men had gathered.

When the burgers were declared to be grilled to perfection, the group assembled and Alex began the introductions again, this time with the men. Maggie had calmed down by then and seemed to be enjoying herself. There was a great deal of chatter, more than Maggie was used to since she came from a small family, but the evening was relaxing and fun for everyone. Everyone except Alex's brother-in-law, Collin. He seemed overly quiet and distant from the rest of the family, a fact that was not lost on Alex. It was not like Collin to behave like such; he was usually laughing and joking with everyone. But tonight he seemed worried and did not join in the conversation unless he was specifically addressed.

While the ladies were cleaning up the table, Collin motioned for Alex to follow him back inside the house. They walked in silence to the other end of the spacious home to where Alex's dad had an extensive library. Collin closed the door behind them.

"What's wrong? You've been quiet all evening, and now you're acting so secretively!" Alex asked. "What has happened?"

"Two FBI agents came to the Space Center," Collin began. "They questioned my boss for a long time. He wasn't supposed to tell me the details, but of course he did. They asked about projects I was working on and wanted to know if I had been acting different lately. They wanted to know if I had been doing any traveling, and if so, where. They asked if my boss knew anything about my private life-was there trouble at home, had I mentioned anything about my family in China? They asked a few questions about other people in the department, but mostly about how they got along with me. They wanted to know if there had been any recent turnovers, and they had a warrant for my computer. Why were they there? I have done nothing wrong."

"When did this happen? Did they give any indication as to what they were looking for on your hard drive?" Alex asked bewilderedly.

"They came in a couple of weeks ago, while you were in Chengdu," Collin answered. "They asked all the questions and gave no information out at all, but the Space Center lawyers went over the warrant and said that we had to let them take it. I don't understand. This feels more like China than America. What do I do?"

"Have you told Barbara?" Alex asked, knowing the answer already. His sister was having too much fun tonight to have known that anything was wrong.

"No. What would I tell her? I have done nothing wrong," he kept repeating as he paced around the room. "Do I need a lawyer of my own? I have no idea what is happening, but I haven't slept since this all started."

"The first thing we need to find out is what is going on that the FBI would be knocking at your door," Alex said as his mind was whirling ahead to all possible scenarios. He got nowhere. Collin had obtained his American citizenship years ago and had been a solid member of society. There was no reason to suspect him of doing anything wrong. It was not who Collin was. Alex knew that, but what Alex knew did not carry any weight. They had to find out what was happening.

"Maggie has a friend who works for the FBI," Alex commented. "Let me talk to him and see if there is anything that he can tell us about the situation. I will call him when we leave here tonight. My best advice is to go in to work as usual. I would not change my routine. They are watching for sure, so you need to show them that you have nothing to hide. Most of all, do not say anything to Barbara. She'll freak out, and that won't help. You can tell her everything later-when we know what there is to tell."

"Okay. I don't know how to thank you. I didn't know who else to talk to," Collin replied. "Nothing like this has happened in all the years I've been in America. I'm scared. What if they make me leave the country? What if I never see my children again?"

"Whoa, let's not get too far ahead of the game, buddy. I know you're scared, but you need to try to stay as calm as possible," Alex tried to reassure him. "It's probably just a misunderstanding. If they really had anything concrete, they would have taken you along with your computer. They are not going to deport you-you are an American citizen, remember? I'm sure Maggie's friend can help us. I will call you as soon as I find out something."

Both men left the library feeling burdened. Nothing like this had ever occurred in Alex's family. They were "your typical Americans" who just happened to have a former Chinese defector in their ranks. What in the world could be wrong?

Alex could hear laughter as he came into the kitchen. It was nice to see Maggie relaxed and having a good time. He wished they could stay and enjoy the family a while longer, but after his conversation with Collin he was anxious to leave. The sooner he could talk to Dan, the sooner they might get some answers to this bizarre situation. Alex knew that there must be some kind of mistake, but he also knew that sometimes his government made mistakes that were nearly impossible to correct. He did not have a good feeling about this.

"Would you be too upset if we called it a night?" Alex whispered as he pulled Maggie into a hug. She smelled so fresh, like a spring rain; he just wanted to hold her forever.

"Of course not," Maggie quietly answered, surprised that he wanted to leave. "What's wrong?"

"Something's come up that I need to take care of, and I can't work on it here," he answered vaguely. "I'll explain later, but let's say our goodbyes and get out of here."

The family was disappointed that they were leaving so early in the evening and tried to get them to reconsider. After several attempts of vain persuasion, Maggie and Alex were leaving the party and heading in no particular direction that made sense to Maggie. Alex was quiet, as if he were lost in deep, deep thought. In truth, he was. He was still trying to figure out what could possibly be happening with Collin. He truly loved the man and the joy that he had brought to Barbara. They had three children whom Alex adored. They were an ordinary Texan family. They went to church, worked in the PTA, shot off fireworks on the fourth of July. Why would the FBI be snooping around after all these years? Surely Collin had proved his loyalty to America.

"Are you going to tell me what's wrong, or are you just going to drive in silence?" Maggie finally asked. "Do you even know where you're going?"

The sound of her voice broke Alex's thoughts and he realized that he had been totally ignoring her. He looked around trying to get his bearings when he realized that he was going in the complete opposite direction of Maggie's house. His lack of awareness made him realize that he probably should not be driving at the moment. He pulled into a shopping center and turned off the engine.

"I had a visit with Collin tonight that has me worried," Alex began. "Something has happened, and while I don't understand, it can't be good. I need to talk to Dan."

"Why?" Maggie asked. "What does Dan have to do with Collin?"

"I haven't told you everything about Collin," Alex hesitated. "Many years ago, Collin left China and came to America. But he didn't exactly leave under the normal circumstances: He defected. He had been one of China's most distinguished scientists and they had invested a lot into his education and career. He was the crown jewel of their space program."

"Unbelievable," Maggie remarked, stunned over this piece of news. She had never known anyone who had moved to the US from another country, much less defected. "I imagine the Chinese were not too happy about that. Why would he do such a drastic thing?"

"He told me that he was working in France when the violence at Tiananmen Square broke out," Alex answered. "Apparently some close friends and even an uncle were killed in the mayhem. He had seen enough of the world through his travels to know how controlling his government was with the people. He understood their cries for more freedom, and he couldn't justify the killings of innocent people. So he found an American Consulate and requested asylum. Of course, we were thrilled to have him. His decision to come to the United States was a coup for us, even though we had nothing to do with it."

"I'm sure NASA was equally excited to have him," Maggie commented, trying to absorb all of this information. It was quite a story.

"Oh, that's for sure. They treat him quite well, and from the little I do know, he has been a great addition to their team," Alex continued. "He has been at the heart of some of their most ambitious projects. That's why this is all so unsettling."

"What is unsettling?" Maggie asked. "So far you've told me a fascinating tale but you have not explained what happened tonight that caused you to want to leave so early."

"While we were in China, the FBI came to Collin's office," Alex explained. "They interviewed his boss and had a warrant for Collin's computer. They never asked him anything, just took the computer. Needless to say, he's a wreck. He feels like he's back under a Communist regime."

"Does he have any idea what they are looking for?" Maggie asked. She was just as astonished as Alex. This type of behavior only happened in books or in the movies. Real people don't get visits from the FBI, Maggie thought.

"They were asking about what projects he was working on," Alex answered. "They wanted to know if he had been doing any traveling, and if his family life was happy. It's just too weird."

"So you think Dan knows something about this?" Maggie questioned.

"I don't know, but I have to try to do something. Collin is family. We don't ever think about him being anything but an American, and the subject of his defection is ancient history with the family." Alex sighed as he ran his hand through his coarse salt-and-pepper hair. "Do you think Dan would mind if we dropped by his place?"

"I think we should call first. After all, he might not even be there," Maggie offered. "You head us in that direction while I give him a call."

As Alex pulled out of the parking lot, Maggie called Dan. He and Sara were just leaving a restaurant and were on their way back to his house. Maggie didn't want to go into details over the phone, but just told him that there was a problem that they needed his help with. Dan had a feeling that he already knew what the problem was, but he didn't give any indication that he had a clue as to what they wanted to discuss. He was especially quiet on the way to the house, trying to figure out what angle to take and how much, if anything, to tell if this conversation was about Wu. Sara sensed his concern and, for once, left him alone with his thoughts.

Both couples arrived at the house just about the same time and chatted briefly about nothing in particular as they settled into living room. The tension in the air was palatable, which left Sara feeling as if she was the one left completely out of the loop. She could instinctively tell that both Dan and Maggie were concerned about something serious, and even though she didn't know Alex well, she could tell that he was the most bothered of the three of them. She wanted to offer to fix coffee, but was afraid she would miss something important if she left the room. Still, her mother's manners rose to their rightful place as she asked if anyone wanted something to drink.

"Thank you just the same, Sara, but I really just need to talk to Dan," Alex replied to her offer. "Perhaps later."

"What is on your mind? You seem concerned about something." Dan asked, afraid he already knew what Alex wanted to talk about.

"I need to ask about something that may put you in a bind to answer, but I wouldn't be here if it wasn't important," Alex began. "My brother-in-law was paid a visit by the FBI. It upset him a great deal and he is confused as to what they may have wanted. He asked me what to do, and I am here asking you the same question."

"Did he tell you what they wanted?" Dan asked, trying to feel Alex out without offering too much information just yet. He knew that the time may have come to tell Maggie about what the government was concerned about, but if he could find a way to sidestep the issue, he gladly would for now. He would have preferred to orchestrate this meeting on his own terms, but things didn't always work out to his preferences.

"No, not really. They didn't even talk to him actually," Alex answered. "They talked with his boss and then took his computer with them. They had a warrant." Alex relayed what Collin had told him about the FBI's interest in his work, life and traveling activities. It didn't take long to rehash; there wasn't much to tell.

"Has he been working on anything special?" Dan asked.

"I really don't know. We talk about sports and kids and who's going to fix Dad's gutters," Alex answered, exasperated. "Look, he's just a regular guy, living his life. What would the FBI want with him?"

Maggie had been sitting quietly, listening to this whole interchange, and what caught her attention the most was Dan's lack of concern. He didn't seem uneasy about Alex's family being upset. He hadn't asked any questions about Collin-where he worked, what he did in his off hours, not even his last name. It was as if he already knew the answers.

"Well, it's probably not anything to be too concerned about," Dan remarked, seemingly dismissing the entire incident. "I'll check around, see what I can find out. If anything interesting pops up, I'll give you a call."

Alex just sat there stunned as if he had been reprimanded by the school principal. Dan had effectively ended the conversation as he stood up and headed for the kitchen.

"I think coffee sounds great after all," he called back over his shoulder as he headed into the kitchen. "Anyone want to join me?"

"Did I miss something, or did he just blow the whole thing off?" Sara asked, astounded at Dan's behavior.

Maggie and Alex just sat there, each thinking the same thing as Sara. They did not understand Dan's attitude at all. It was as if having the FBI raid your office was a normal occurrence. About the time Maggie was getting ready to head to the kitchen to confront Dan, he returned to the living room.

"Coffee should be ready shortly," he commented as he slowly sat back down in the chair he had previously occupied, a notepad in his hand. The others just sat there staring at him. Finally, Maggie said what the others had been thinking.

"So that's it? I'll let you know; don't worry your pretty little head over it?" Maggie fumed. "I expected better of you than that, Dan. You're behaving as if this was some sort of school yard incident. What's your problem?"

"My problem is that until I know something, I can't give you any answers," Dan replied patiently and calmly. "It's late on a Friday night, what do you want me to do? Until Monday, I can't do a lot of investigating. You just need to give me some time. I don't have instant answers."

"Don't you think it would help you to know his brother-in-law's name?" Maggie continued, her level of anxiety not lowering even an inch. "You haven't asked his name, or what part of NASA he works for, or anything. How are you going to find out what's going on if you don't even know who you're checking up on?"

"You haven't given me a chance," Dan responded, hold up the notepad he had brought back from the kitchen. "I had to have something to write on. Now, if I can continue, I will get the information I need."

Maggie stewed as Dan asked Alex several questions about Collin and his work. He asked about where they lived and where Barbara worked. He asked if Collin had always lived in the Houston area or if he was from somewhere else. Alex calmly answered his questions, just saying that he had moved here from China several years ago. Alex agreed with Maggie's opinion that Dan wasn't acting too concerned, but he wasn't going to lose his temper just yet. Besides, Maggie was doing a good job in that department. He had already decided that his next conversation with Dan would be without the ladies present.

"Seriously, sometimes an investigation will tread on people who have nothing to do with whatever the Bureau is working on," Dan commented as Maggie and Alex prepared to leave. "I'm sure this is no big deal. Your brother-in-law will probably have his computer back by Monday morning and nothing else will ever come up. There's a lot going on with Homeland Security these days and they waste a lot of time checking out dead ends. Could be as simple as one of his neighbors being too nosey and suspicious and calling the Bureau with some crazy idea that this guy's is a threat somehow. Trust me, we get kooks all the time."

Maggie and Alex left, each unnerved by the evening's events. Meanwhile, Sara was a tad concerned herself. She had never seen Dan act as uncaring as he did tonight.

"So, what was that all about?" she asked when they were alone again.

"Like I said, it's probably nothing. If this guy hasn't done anything wrong, I'm sure this will be cleared up quickly," Dan replied.

"That's not what I meant. Where's your compassion? You were cold. These are our friends," Sara snapped back.

"Our friends were talking to me as a professional," Dan answered. "As a law enforcement officer, I cannot show emotion. It's no different than your personality when you're with me and when you're in the classroom. All of us have a different office demeanor."

Sara calmed down a little, but was still unhappy with Dan's treatment of Alex and Maggie. It bothered her the rest of the weekend, but she did not bring it up again. It wasn't that she was trying to skirt an argument, but more that she was well aware that Dan's mood wasn't much better than her own. He was quiet and reflective. More than once she found that he had walked away from her to answer his phone. He spoke in hushed tones and slipped deeper into his thoughts after every call. It was a long weekend.

The mood was no different between Alex and Maggie. They were both at a loss as to Dan's attitude. Yes, he took down information, but he didn't appear to think that their questions were legitimate. Maggie was particularly aggravated because Dan had been her friend for years and she had never seen him behave the way he had Friday night. In all fairness, Alex offered, Maggie had never had to approach her friend in his official capacity. It wasn't that Alex was trying to defend Dan, but he thought he was looking at this from a different view than Maggie. He was more concerned about what Dan didn't say rather than his tone of voice. Besides, they were both still jet-lagged and he was sure that their exhaustion was contributing in some way.

In Alex's opinion, Dan had asked a lot of questions. It almost felt as if he was interrogating Alex, trying to find out some bit of information that he didn't already know. It was just as much his body language as the questions themselves. Long ago in another life, Alex had been a serious psychology major. He was certain that Dan was holding something back, and he intended to find out exactly what. Monday morning he would show up at Dan's office unannounced. He was de-termined that they were going to have a man-to-man talk.

CHAPTER 88

It was usually in the mornings when he noticed it: the pain of the first few steps, the ache of his hips when he first got out of bed. It was those times that reminded him that he was no longer the twenty-something physically fit man that he had been when he first joined the Bureau. He continually worked to keep in shape and to be able to pass the yearly physical exam without too much distress, but that didn't mean that the telltale signs of aging were not already living in his body. In the past he'd had no trouble juggling all areas of his life. Work, work, girls, and more work just kept his motor fine tuned. Now it took great effort just to get the motor started. The past few weeks were beginning to take their toll. He had been working long hours, often going back to the office after having a late dinner with Sara. While he rarely ever spoke of his work, and never during an active investigation, he had felt overly burdened with the secretiveness of this case. Any way it went, there was going to be tension. His body was tired and his mind was exhausted. He was ready for some piece of information, some offhanded tip, anything that would bring this case together.

This morning was no different. His first steps were taken gingerly and his right hip snarled at the thought of having to move. Dan knew that there was not going to be a cup of coffee strong enough to give his body the energy it needed. It had been a long, tiresome weekend. Besides the cold shoulder he got from Sara, there had been a barrage of phone calls. After his conversation with Alex, he knew they were on borrowed time. He needed to push for answers before he had to talk to Maggie or Alex again.

He figured it would be Alex first. Maggie had been the one who got in his face, who questioned his responses. Maggie had been the one who didn't buy any part of his explanation and yet, while it was Alex's family being targeted, he did not respond. He'd sat silent when Dan had dismissed the entire episode; he didn't join in when Maggie snapped back; he just quietly left. His behavior bothered Dan because it did not fit the norm. Maggie's reaction was what Dan would have expected of Alex. Instead, his response was calm, maybe even calculated. What did that mean? Did Alex know more about the situation than he was willing to admit? Was he trying to see what Dan knew, what hints he might let slip? Or was he simply waiting for a more appropriate time? Maggie was obviously upset; perhaps Alex decided to follow up later, without the drama of his girlfriend. It could go either way, and until Dan knew more about Wu's life, he was not willing to bet on which side of the fence Alex would come down. He hated feeling that way about someone that he really liked. Dan thought Alex was a stand-up guy who obviously made Maggie smile. That alone was enough to earn him points. But Dan could not ignore the bottom line: If Alex was involved in something illegal, then Dan had to stop him. Maggie was going to get caught in the crossfire.

The office was already busy when Dan arrived, machines humming and people buzzing around with cell phones plastered to their ears. It was barely six o'clock and some of these people had been at work for several hours. Some had never left from the day before. Dan had just gone in the kitchen for his daily ritual of coffee and bagels when someone called his name, barely audible above the din.

"There's a call for you from China and one of your buddies is waiting in your office," one of the female agents informed him. "By the way, the coffee's way too weak this morning and the bagels are history."

"Great, just what I needed-no caffeine, no nourishment," he mumbled as he turned to head for his office. "It's going to be a long day."

Dan saw that the man waiting for him was one of the Bureau's field investigators. He had been one of the agents who had been interviewing Wu's neighbors and coworkers and had taken his hard drive. Dan was anxious to hear what he had found out, but the call from China took precedence.

"Hey Walker, hang tight for a moment while I answer this phone," Dan commented as he made his way around his desk. "I'm sure this call is related to your recent activities."

Dan wasn't surprised to hear Joseph Lee's voice at the other end of the line. The legal attaché sounded tired, but then his day was just about over; there was a thirteen hour time difference between Beijing and Houston. It made communication a little difficult at times.

"Do you have something good to share or are you just missing me?" Dan joked as he answered the line.

"You are not my type, sweetheart, so missing you is not why I called," Joseph jabbed back.

"Your loss. So tell me what you've got," Dan replied as he grabbed a notepad and pen.

"Not anything that jumps up and slaps you, but some strange behavior just the same," Joseph answered. "Lilly has led a fairly quiet, but productive life since her brother left. She and her parents were harassed frequently during the first few years after the defection, but authorities seemed to back off as she finished college-without any unauthorized behavior-and later landed a job as an assistant economics professor at Beijing University. She has kept her nose clean and often works as a translator for visiting American and French businessmen. She applied to the consulate in Chengdu for the translator job for the Utopia Energy plant. Haven't been able to find out yet how she knew about the project."

"Have you been able to establish if she and her brother have kept in touch?" Dan asked. "I would think it would be pretty easy these days with the internet."

"Not as easy in this corner of the world," Joseph commented. "The government keeps a close eye on what their citizens are doing on the internet and you can bet that they are watching her, not only because of her brother but also because of her position at the University. If she was using internet cafés, then perhaps."

"Maybe we can find out something from this end about that," Dan replied.

"Check your email. I just sent you some pictures that were taken in Chengdu last week," Joseph continued. "The pictures show Lilly with a Caucasian man, probably American. Let me know if you recognize him."

Dan turned to his computer. When he opened the attachment on the message from Joseph, his stomach knotted up. Not only was the man American, but Dan indeed recognized him. The image staring back at him was definitely Alex Sheppard. He and Lilly looked to be in a very private conversation. He would have loved to know what they were talking about.

"I know him. That's Alex Sheppard," Dan commented. "By the look of the picture, I would say that they know about their family connection. They seem to be quite cozy."

"The guy that took these photos followed them for about half an hour," Joseph explained. "He said they appeared to be familiar with each other, but did not give any indication of intimacy. He didn't believe they were lovers, but definitely friends, more than acquaintances."

"That certainly puts an interesting spin on things," Dan commented, almost to himself as if he were in deep thought. "This gets more complicated with each passing hour."

"Complicated maybe, but we are no closer to finding out what is going on," Joseph replied. "It seems like we are in a holding pattern. The clock is ticking and we still don't know what is happening."

"The only thing we can do is to keep digging. There's got to be an answer and it's probably right in front of us once we find the missing link," Dan said. "I have someone here in my office who might have more information for us. Let me visit with him and I'll get back to you."

"Sure thing, buddy. Meanwhile, I will be checking on the tails we have on Han. Maybe something new has developed," Joseph commented. The two men spoke for a few more minutes before ending the call and Dan turned his attention to his colleague who had been patiently waiting.

"So how is your day starting?" Dan asked the agent who had been waiting during the phone call. "Mine's getting more complicated by the minute."

"Oh, you know, another day making the big bucks," Walker replied. He was a tall man who barely had room to cross his legs in Dan's cramped office. He had been with the Bureau for about ten years and had become one of their better investigators. He had a sixth sense about people-who was lying, who was not.

"The problem with those big bucks is that to get them you spend all your time working and no time enjoying the money," Dan laughed. He knew that Walker-or anyone else for that matter-was not doing this job for the money. They were all too underpaid for the work involved.

"Good point. You know, the long hours are not so bad when you discover something useful," Walker commented. "But unfortunately this weekend did not harvest anything of value. I know that's not what you wanted to hear."

"I'm sorry I pushed you guys so hard, but the secrecy of this investigation is beginning to crumble and I need to fast-track some of this stuff," Dan apologized. "You mean, you didn't find anything?"

"Are you kidding? This Wu guy is squeaky clean. He doesn't even buy a lottery ticket," Walker replied. "In the past two weeks, we've gone through his bank records, his computer, visited his neighbors, even followed him to church. Nothing."

"Did you check his phone records? Were there any calls to China?" Dan asked. "Anything that would indicate contact with his sister or anyone else?"

"Nothing. No calls to China. There were a couple of calls about a year ago to France, but that's it," Walker answered. "And his email seems to be either about his work-to legitimate colleagues-or to local people about soccer games or symphony tickets. He checks his kids' grades electronically, pays bills the same way, but for the most part he doesn't spend time surfing the net, at least not at work. You know, we haven't checked his home computer. There could be an entirely different story there. We're just waiting on the approval to get a warrant. You task force guys need to let us know what to do next."

"We have the go-ahead for the warrant whenever we want to execute it. We're just not sure yet if we want to play that card," Dan replied. "If we go after his home computer prematurely, this whole situation could blow up before we are ready. We're not there yet. Not until we have more information."

"Whatever you guys want. Just let me know," Walker said as he unfolded himself out of the chair. "Not that my opinion matters, but I think you're chasing the wrong rabbit here. This guy's a boy scout."

Dan watched the investigator dip his head as he left the office. He hoped Walker was right. He had always respected Walker's assessments of people and wanted to do so now, but Dan was too close to the situation to take the easy road. He had to be completely convinced by the facts and not just Walker's gut feelings, however accurate they had been in the past.

He turned his attention back to his email, where the picture of Lilly and Alex was open. Maybe Alex didn't know anything about Lilly and Wu. Perhaps she was his lover. It was true that Alex seemed to be totally enamored with Maggie, but he had been going to China for months before Maggie joined the team. He and Lilly could have already had a relationship.

Just as he was trying to decide where that particular scenario would lead, the phone buzzed and startled him from his thoughts. It was the front desk downstairs. He had a visitor who insisted on seeing him.

"Who is it?" Dan questioned.

"He says his name is Alex Sheppard," the receptionist answered.

Dan let out a deep breath as he instructed the young girl to have Alex escorted to his office. He knew it would take a few minutes for security to be rounded up to bring Alex to the fifth floor and he used that time to go over the story he had decided to tell Alex. He hoped it would be convincing enough to buy some time before he had to decide if Alex was a player or merely an innocent citizen who was about to get a rude baptism into the world that Dan operated in every day.

When Alex finally arrived in Dan's office, he entered with the demeanor of a man who was anticipating a fight. Absent was his easygoing personality that Dan normally associated with the man. Dan was not surprised; he knew this was not a social visit.

"You're out and about early today," Dan commented as he took his seat behind the desk. "I'm surprised you have time on Monday morning to stop by here on your way to work."

"I doubt that you are all that surprised," Alex calmly remarked. "You didn't really expect me to leave the conversation as it was on Friday night, did you?"

"I'm not sure what I expected. Maggie was a tad hostile about the whole thing," Dan answered. "I would have thought that you would be the one to be more impatient. After all, it's your family that is involved."

"Maggie was just tired and worried. I don't react the same way she does, and it was obvious that you weren't going to tell us anything that night," Alex replied.

"That could be because I needed to do some digging before I could give you the answers you were wanting," Dan said, trying to let Alex lead the conversation. He wanted to be able to judge just how much information Alex would need to be satisfied.

"Could be. Or it could be because you were stalling," Alex stated. His voice was controlled, but he made no effort to be friendly.

Dan sighed as he leaned back in his chair. This was not going to be as simple as he had hoped, but he did realize that he was not dealing with just anyone. Alex was a professional businessman, well skilled in negotiations, and not someone who was going to be easily dismissed.

"Look, think what you want, but I really don't have first-hand knowledge of every investigation going on in Houston," Dan began. "There are lots of different divisions and they work with other federal agencies. This isn't just a hometown bunch of cops. I did some checking this morning and while I don't know any details-and may not be able to find any out-I did find a little information. There is an ongoing inquiry involving another agency and one of our teams. It seems that Washington received a tip that some sensitive information concerning our missile defense system has possibly been compromised. The people involved have close ties to your brother-in-law's past."

"What are you talking about? You think Collin knows something about our defense system?" Alex asked, stunned that anyone could think that Collin was a spy. "He works for NASA."

"What exactly do you think he does at NASA? Are you telling me that you don't know what he works on everyday?" Dan asked, equally surprised that Alex was not informed of his brother-in-law's importance to the space agency and to the country's defense.

"No, I don't know. Collin has always maintained that agency rules prohibit him from discussing his work. My sister doesn't even know what he does every day, other than being a scientist at NASA," Alex explained. "Now you're telling me that not only does my brother-in-law work on top-secret defense systems but that he is passing that information on to China? This is crazy. I'm telling you, Collin is not doing anything illegal. It's not who he is."

"I'm not telling you anything about Wu, understand?" Dan said quietly as he leaned forward toward Alex. "All I am saying is that an investigation is on-going in a certain area. I don't know any of the specifics and doubt seriously that I ever will be informed. What you have to understand is that you cannot tell Maggie or Wu or anyone what I have told you this morning. There will be hell to pay if you do."

"What am I supposed to tell Collin? He knows I was going to check with you about this situation?" Alex asked. "Am I just supposed to act like nothing's wrong?"

"You can tell him that all I could find out was that an investigation was being conducted on a possible security breach, but that I don't know any more than that. You can tell him that I offered to pass on any information that might come my way, but that as of now, it doesn't seem to be a big deal?"

"Is that true?" Alex asked.

"That it's not a big deal?"

"That you will let me know if you find out anything else," Alex responded.

"I will let you know what I can, but you have to realize that this is not my area. I don't know that I will be able to find out any more than I have already told you," Dan replied.

"Should he retain a lawyer?" Alex questioned. He just wanted to protect Collin. He knew that whatever the government might think, his sister's husband was not a spy. He worried that Collin was being framed.

"Does he need one? That's only a question that Wu can answer," Dan replied. "At this point, he has not been charged with anything. He's not even been questioned. More than likely, they are looking for spyware or such that may have compromised his computer. I think if it were me, I would sit tight and wait."

"That's easy for you to say because it's not you. If it were, you would not be content to just sit by and let people make accusations."

"Who's making any accusations at this point? Remember, you know nothing other than that a possible security breach is being checked out. Alex, I have trusted your character and told you more that I should have, so you have to trust me and promise to say nothing more-not to anyone, including Maggie."

"I won't, at least for now," Alex conceded. "Look, I appreciate your help and I really didn't mean to come off as a jerk, but you have to understand that the FBI is not a part of normal people's lives."

"At least they don't think we are," Dan laughed, trying to end the conversation and leave Alex with less curiosity than he came started with. "Let me walk you out. Security gets a little nervous if someone is just roaming around."

Dan led Alex through the maze of offices and cubicles to the elevator. The two men discussed the upcoming weekend. Their girlfriends had a big cookout planned and both of the men thought there was way too much planning going on for this to be just a "fun time." Dan shook Alex's hand in the lobby and promised to keep his ears open.

As Alex left, he felt as if he had had his pocket picked by a professional. He knew that he was being fed a story on some level, he just wasn't sure what part of it, if any, was true. There was something not right about this situation.

Dan headed back upstairs to his office, feeling that the meeting and the bogus storyline may have bought him some time, but probably not enough. The investigation was going to have to speed up before it came crashing down on Dan's head.

CHAPTER 89

Imad Mubarak hung up his cell phone and stood staring out the window. At this time of night, all he could see was his own reflection, but it didn't matter. He wasn't even looking. The caller never missed a week, calling within a two-hour time frame every Monday night. Imad had begun to adjust his activities around the ritual.

The small voice inside his heart had started growing. It visited his conscious thoughts more and more. How had he come to this point in his life?

Imad had spent his entire childhood wanting to help others. When he was accepted into medical school, he realized quickly that medicine, without a doubt, was his calling. His life in America had been very comfortable over the years. He and his wife were well respected in their community and his children were excelling in their college pursuits.

His work at the Vanderbilt-Ingram Cancer Center had earned him the respect of his fellow oncologists throughout the United States. His research was showing great promise, and he knew that he was nearing a breakthrough. He just needed more time. But time was something he didn't have in great supply. It dawned on him that he now understood how many of his patients must feel, knowing that they don't have enough time for a cure to be found; not enough time to see if a treatment would be effective.

There was a difference, however: His patients had not chosen to have cancer. He had made a conscious decision to follow the path that he was now questioning. Somewhere back in his college days it had seemed important to take a stand against everything his religion condemned. He wanted to be a good servant of Allah. He had pledged his loyalty to a group of extremists who were determined to make war with the "infidels." But he had long given up his radical ways … or so he thought.

He left college, and his comrades, and moved to Nashville to work at Vanderbilt. The position was very prestigious for a young doctor just out of medical school, even if he had graduated at the top of his class. Soon afterward he met Aala and fell in love. They were married and quickly had three beautiful children. Imad's salary afforded him all the pleasures of middle America: the house, the cars, vacation homes. He quietly moved beyond the radical ideals of his youth.

Imad was enjoying a quiet evening at home when the initial phone call had come through. He had thought Aala would answer it, but then realizing that she was out with friends, he picked up the receiver. That had been his first mistake. He instantly recognized the voice and his stomach knotted with dread. He knew this was not a social call. His past had come back to haunt him.

He supposed he could have gone to the authorities at that time, but that option was not in his DNA. He had grown up in a very different world from most Americans and while he shared in their prosperity, he did not believe in their justice system. Going to the police would have just caused trouble for him, and he had enough of that now. He resigned himself to his fate. He had signed up for this in a former life, and now Allah was calling in his marker.

Imad turned from the window and moved toward the fireplace. It wasn't a terribly cold evening by Tennessee standards, but he was chilled to the bone. There was no turning back now. He had gone over and over the situation in his mind for the past fourteen months. There were times, when he was with the group, that he even got a little caught up in the rhetoric of the past. He tried to convince himself that he was being a good soldier. But in his heart, he knew that he was nothing more than a mass murderer.

CHAPTER 90

"Got a minute?" the man asked as he walked into Dan's office. He was one of the field officers assigned to the investigation of Mason, and it was he who had previously reported Mason's affair to Dan.

"Sure. Especially if you have news to share," Dan replied as he sat back in his chair. It had been a long morning of trying to put all the pieces of the puzzle together and he was frustrated that he was no closer than he had been a week earlier.

"I think I've got something you will be interested in," the man offered as he dropped a folder of photos on Dan's desk. "This may be the piece of evidence you were needing to focus on Mason rather than Alex."

"You need to understand the situation better," Dan curtly replied as he reached for the folder. "I want the truth to come out. Do I hope that Alex is not involved? Of course. But if he is, then I still have a job to do."

"Sorry man, just thought you would like this turn of events," the man said as he took a seat. "I never meant to imply that you are anything but professional."

Dan did not respond to the apology, but instead studied the photos in front of him. He was surprised, to say the least, at what he was seeing. This certainly did change the focus of the investigation.

"Where did you get these?" he asked.

"We have had a tail on Mason since we first discovered his little romance. We figured we would watch the way he operated to see if there was any clue to his connection with any terrorist-types," the man explained. "What we saw instead was that we were not the only ones keeping an eye on him. Those men have been glued to him for weeks–along with their trusty camera."

"Do we know who they are?" Dan asked.

"That's the interesting part. They work for Wang," the man replied.

"The Chinese mafia leader?" Dan asked, his curiosity rising with each passing revelation.

"The one and only," the man answered. "They really aren't very good tails, but Mason seems oblivious to their presence, and they seem too preoccupied to realize that we are watching them."

"So what's the connection with Mason and the Chinese gang?" Dan wondered out loud. Somewhere in the back of his mind, he knew some small piece of information that was the key to this mystery. But at the moment, that small piece was evading his conscious thought.

"Hey man, that's why you have the fancy office. I just gather the info, it's your job to figure out if it means anything," the man said.

"Well, you can bet it means something," Dan replied. "Now we only have to figure out what it means and if it's important to the investigation. Let me know if anything else turns up."

"No problem. I will say one thing for the guy, he sure stays busy. Between the girlfriend, the wife, and the job, I don't know where he would find the time to get involved with anything that interested these goons," the man commented as he stood to leave.

"It's probably one of those areas that got him in trouble," Dan replied. "And I'm willing to bet that we can eliminate the wife as the culprit. I'm leaning toward the job–with the girlfriend thrown in for insurance."

Dan spent the next half hour going over the photos. They were taken at all sorts of places: at Mason's home, in the lobby of Utopia Energy, at the Weiche Building. These guys were persistent to say the least, Dan thought. He was certain that the fact that they were tailing Mason was important to the Bureau's case. But how? What was it that still nagged at his brain? He was sure he had read something in one of the dozens of files on his desk that was the answer to his gut instincts.

After another two hours of poring through pages of intelligence, Dan finally found the connection he had been looking for: Wang, the leader of Houston's most prominent Chinese gang, was the brother-in-law of Zhang Han. If Wang was keeping an eye on Mason, it was because Han had asked for the surveillance; that was pretty much a given, Dan decided. Whatever was in the works, Mason was their contact at Utopia.

That should have cleared Alex from any hint of suspicion in Dan's mind, and yet it did not. There was a strong connection between Wu, his sister Lilly, and Alex. Perhaps they were not a part of the bigger problem, but Dan could not ignore the pictures of Alex and Lilly. He wasn't sure if that was because of the investigation or because of Maggie.

One thing he did know for sure: It was time to execute the search warrant for Wu's personal computer.

CHAPTER 91

Dan knew that this was going to be a difficult evening. The girls had planned a big cookout with lots of friends, but despite the growing guest list, Dan knew that he could not avoid Alex. He also knew that Alex was going to be livid.

Agents had seized Collin Wu's home computer on Monday, and so far had not found anything sinister to report. The most damning evidence to a foreign connection was several emails over the past year or two to a colleague in France. It appeared that the NASA scientist was using his friend in France to be a go-between with emails to Lilly. There were no direct emails to the sister, but several messages had been passed through the friend. None of them were vague or suspicious, mostly news about their ailing parents. About a year ago, the emails had stopped. About the time Alex had started traveling to China.

Dan was comfortably sure that Alex was in no way connected to Han and the terrorists, but at the same time he knew he would have to come up with some plausible story to cover up the true intentions of the investigation into Wu's life. Dan was not ready to bring Alex into the fold.

Sara had been at Maggie's house for several hours getting ready for the evening's festivities. When Dan finally arrived, the patio was crowded with a hodgepodge of people. There were several people from each of their workplaces, which made for an interesting mix of conversations. It wasn't long, however, before Alex descended on Dan.

"Why don't you and I take a little walk?" Alex suggested as he approached Dan. "Perhaps Maggie's office would be more appropriate than here."

Dan quietly followed Alex into the house, knowing that this conversation could easily turn into a confrontation. He was glad for the suggestion of a more private place to have their discussion. He had come prepared to face Alex and the sooner he had this over with, the sooner he would feel better.

"I thought you were going to keep me informed," Alex said defiantly. "You do know that they took Collin's home computer. They came into my sister's home armed with a warrant. Do you have any idea how upsetting this all is?"

"I told you that I would let you know what I could find out–which might not be very much," Dan quietly replied. "If you recall, I told you that this was another group's inquiry and that I might or might not be kept in the loop. Besides, what information I did get only came to me today. I knew I would see you tonight."

"So what did you find out? Is Collin in some kind of trouble?" Alex snapped back as he paced the floor. He was trying desperately to remain in control, to keep in mind that this was Maggie's friend, but his actions were falling well below his intentions.

"As best as we can determine at the time, neither Wu's work computer or the one at his house has been compromised," Dan began. "There does not appear to be any electronic security breach."

"So that's it? You invade a man's workplace and his home on mere suspicions and then fail to let him know that you didn't 'find' anything," Alex ranted. "This is what I–and Collin–pay taxes for?"

"I didn't say that we didn't 'find' anything. I said there didn't appear to be any electronic breach," Dan began the story he had rehearsed for the past two hours. "We had been alerted to a possible security breach at NASA by a Chinese informant. Naturally, our first instinct was to check computers. That's a response to living in an electronic world. Sometimes we forget that good old-fashioned surveillance still works pretty good."

"What's that supposed to mean?" Alex asked a little less defensively this time. "You can't tell me that you found any dirt on Collin."

"Oh, we found something, but it wasn't exactly on Collin," Dan calmly replied as he slipped several photos from his jacket pocket and handed them to Alex. He watched patiently as Alex absorbed the pictures taken of him and Lilly. The silence became deafening.

"What are you suggesting?" Alex finally asked. He was unsure as to what the agent was implying, but he knew that at some level he had been busted. He wasn't about to offer any information until he could determine what direction Dan was heading.

"You tell me. You two seem to be quite cozy," Dan answered. He needed to get Alex to open up without having to tell him the truth about the entire investigation.

"Where did you get these? Are you having me followed?" Alex asked accusingly.

"We're not having you followed. In fact, these came to us from a source that wasn't interested in you at all," Dan lied. "You can imagine my surprise when my friend's boyfriend shows up in a photo involved in an international investigation. Now, do you want to tell me what's going on between you and Lilly?"

Alex shot a look at him, surprised that he knew Lilly's name. Alex had no desire to break a confidence he had made with his brother-in-law, but at the same time he saw no advantage to being a suspect in something that he wasn't involved in. After several moments of indecision, he finally knew he had to come clean, with the hope that the government man would not put Collin or Lilly in any danger.

"Okay. I have no idea what you think I might be involved in, but I promise you it is quite innocent," Alex began, his tone very different from the beginning of this conversation. "Lilly is Collin's sister."

"That much I know. What I don't know is why the two of you seem so comfy with each other," Dan replied.

"It's not what you think. I am only a go-between, passing messages and photographs," Alex answered, as he rubbed his hand through his hair.

"What kinds of messages and photographs?" Dan asked, suddenly concerned that there was a problem.

"Family news, pictures of the kids, that kind of stuff," Alex answered. "Collin's parents are old and in poor health. They're never going to get to meet their grandchildren. At least this way, they can have some sort of connection."

"Why were the two of you being so secretive? If this is just about family letters, why all the clandestine meetings?" Dan asked.

"You really don't understand, do you?" Alex asked. "Do you have any idea how upset the Chinese government still is about Collin? If they had any idea that his sister was communicating with him, they would make her life miserable. That's why we're so secretive. Collin doesn't want any harm coming to her or his parents."

"So how did you two get hooked up? How did she know to ask for the assignment to be your translator?" Dan asked, relieved at the story he was hearing, but curious as to how they had made all of the arrangements.

"Collin has a friend in France who has a friend at Beijing University. The Frenchman emailed the information to the friend in Beijing, who in turn told Lilly about Utopia's project. It's been a long and complicated process. We have tried to be so careful, but obviously someone has caught on to us. What will happen now?"

"I can ask my colleague in China to put a tail on Lilly for a while and see if anyone is still watching her," Dan offered, trying to sound cooperative about the entire setup. "When do you return to China?"

"In about two weeks," Alex answered, unsure as to why Dan would want to know.

"I will have him continue to follow her while you are there to see if there is some connection. It's possible that someone is suspicious that she is communicating with her brother," Dan explained. "You need to be extremely careful. You also need to alert her that someone could be watching."

"What about Collin? Can I tell him what is going on?" Alex asked, knowing he would have to give his brother-in-law some sort of explanation.

"I think you should. He needs to be aware of the danger he is putting Lilly in by trying to communicate with her," Dan replied. "As far as the FBI investigation is concerned, you can assure him that nothing is wrong and that he can continue his life as normal. The fact that these photos of you turned up is just a by-product of the investigation. Obviously this was a wild-goose chase, but in today's world, we have to check everything out."

"You know, I understand that position in theory, but when it happens to your own family, it feels wrong," Alex replied. "There should be a better way."

"I can't argue that point, but until there is, sometimes good citizens get caught up in the frenzy," Dan commented. "Your brother-in-law will never get a full explanation from the Bureau, just a form letter apologizing for any inconvenience. Off-the-record, please convey my personal apologies."

"That I can do," Alex replied. "Please understand that my attitude was not personal toward you either. I just needed to defend my family."

"No problem," Dan said. "But there will be major problems if the two of us are not seen helping with this party. We'd better head back outside."

"You're right about that. I'd rather be in trouble with the FBI than with Sara and Maggie!" Alex laughed as the two men returned to the patio.

CHAPTER 92

Dan had to admit to himself that he was relieved that Alex was not involved in any homeland security issue. He was equally relieved that Alex and Lilly were not lovers. Maggie did not need any more drama in her life, although he was sure she was about to get more of it. At least it would not involve Alex. He knew now that he needed to concentrate efforts into learning more about the relationship between Han and Mason. Maggie certainly considered it strange, and Alex had also commented on the unusual arrangement between the two team leaders. His first call was to Joseph Lee.

"Hey buddy, sorry to bother you, but I need some more help," Dan began.

"What else is new? You never call just to socialize," Joseph replied. "What can I help you with?"

"Utopia Energy's team is going to be back in Chengdu in about ten days," Dan explained. "I'd like you to put a tail on Mason Williams, the team leader. I will email a photo to you. I'm especially interested in his evening activities, but would like to have him watched 24/7. Is that doable?"

"You think he is somehow involved with Han and the terrorist?" Joseph asked.

"Don't know, but the odds are leaning in that favor," Dan answered. "He has a couple of tails on him here in Houston-us and a Chinese group headed by Han's brother-in-law."

"Bingo. I told you there were no such things as coincidences," Joseph whistled. "Consider it done. Do you still want us to watch the translator and the American?'

"No, we have traveled that road and feel confident that it is an entirely different issue," Dan said. "Intriguing enough, but not an interest to the current investigation."

"Gotcha. Just let me know when our guy is scheduled to arrive," Joseph replied.

"I'll email you the info as soon as I can. Meantime, do you have any new information about what is happening in North Korea?" Dan asked.

"Nothing new since we talked before," Joseph answered. "The clock is ticking, though, and something ought to surface soon."

"Not too soon, I hope," Dan sighed. "We need a better picture of the scheme before it starts going down. Right now, we just don't have enough info."

"Roger that," Joseph said. "Maybe your guy's upcoming visit will provide what we need to move forward."

"Maybe so," Dan replied. "Maybe so."

CHAPTER 93

After briefing Jim Keith on the latest developments, Dan returned to his office and contacted the Agency's liaison with Interpol. The task force had worked with the international police organization before, and Dan wanted to know what they knew about Cai Yi and his known associates. The agency desperately needed to know who Yi's customer was, and if that customer was in the United States. The liaison office promised to have someone contact Dan as soon as possible. All he could do now was wait and hope that this trail would supply him with a name.

Within hours the call from Interpol's Fusion Task Force came through. Dan was a little surprised that the caller was fellow Texan Brad Robberson. Brad was one of the American contributions to Interpol, but Dan hadn't thought Brad would be the contact point. Brad explained that he was now a member of Project Kalkan--FTF's regional task force for Central Asia, the entity specifically interested in Middle Eastern terrorist groups.

"I understand that you are interested in Cai Yi," Brad commented. "What's going on that landed Yi on your radar screen?"

"He sort of showed up there by accident and we're trying to piece the picture backwards, if that makes any sense," Dan answered. "But why would the Middle Eastern group get this call?"

"Because Cai Yi, while headquartered in China and Southeast Asia, operates extensively with groups from the

Middle East-Afghanistan in particular," Brad replied. "Why don't you bring me up to speed?"

Dan spent the next half hour going over the situation as they knew it, including the suspected threat of nuclear material, but leaving out the part about the North Korean's defection, only naming Yi and Han specifically. He was familiar with the Interpol agent, and while the two groups often worked together, Dan was not sure how much he wanted to share with the international organization. Something as big as a defection, or even as vague as Utopia Energy's role, needed to be played close to the chest at this point in the investigation.

"Well, it sounds like a deal is about to go down, and Yi certainly runs with the lower food chain group. You could be on to something big," Brad commented. "What we can do for you is to pull Yi's cell phone records for the past few months. It will take a while, but maybe that will give you the lead you're looking for. I will tell you this: His favorite customers are Muslim extremists of the worst kind, and if this is where the trail leads you, then you have a huge situation to handle. You will be needing assistance from many sources, so be prepared for this thing to explode."

"I understand, but for now I'd prefer to keep this in-house as much as possible," Dan replied. "Trust me, no one is going to let egos get in the way of bringing down the bad guys. The world's too small for that kind of Hollywood attitude."

"You got that right. The bad guys operate everywhere with each other; we'd be fools not to do the same," the Interpol officer remarked. "It just seems like they do it better than we do sometimes."

"Sometimes they do. That just means we have to work harder ... and smarter," Dan conceded.

"Speaking of work, I'd better get at it," Brad said. "I'll get back to you as soon as I have those phone records. In the meantime, if anything comes up, call me direct."

When the two men finished their conversation, Dan decided it was time for a break. Sometimes you needed to step back from an investigation to be able to see the picture more clearly. For Dan that meant a visit to the gym. It was there that he did his best thinking-away from the phones and interruptions. He needed to plan what step the task force should take next. Was it time to talk to Maggie? Yes, he thought as he headed downstairs, a trip to the gym was just what he needed.

CHAPTER 94

"What is all the secrecy about?" Maggie asked jokingly. "You'd think you were plotting to overthrow the government."

"Just trying to keep someone else from doing that very thing," Dan replied, the serious tone in his voice catching Maggie's immediate attention. "Please, let's walk. There are too many people around here for us to talk."

The two exited the main entrance area and headed toward Duck Lake. It was an early weekday morning and the crowd at the Houston Zoo was mostly still confined to the Guest Relations Building and Kipp Aquarium. They were alone on their walk to the center part of the zoo.

Maggie had been curious when Dan called and asked her to meet him. He acted very mysterious and asked her not to let Sara know that they were meeting. Maggie couldn't imagine what he was up to; it was months before Sara's birthday, so it couldn't be some big surprise he was planning. But he had been so serious, so professional sounding when he called that she immediately left the office to meet him. Now that they were together, his demeanor was doing nothing to calm her nerves.

"So what's going on to spark this top secret meeting?" Maggie asked, trying to keep her tone lighthearted, but failing miserably. "You seem worried."

"I am worried. I need to tell you something that involves National Security and I don't like having to do this," Dan replied. "What I am about to tell you cannot be shared with anyone-not Sara, not Alex, not another breathing soul."

"Are you sure you even want to tell me?" Maggie asked, suddenly queasy. She had rarely seen this side of Dan's personality-his business side-and it frightened her. Her gut told her that this was not going to be a conversation that she wanted to hear.

"No, I don't want to, but I need to," Dan answered. "What I am about to tell you could put your life in danger, serious danger, and that fact upsets me. I wouldn't do this if it weren't necessary. I need your help-your country needs your help-and your promise of total secrecy. You can talk to no one about this except me, and even then, we cannot draw attention to ourselves. We cannot talk in front of Sara and Alex.

"Well, you certainly have my attention, especially with that 'life in danger' part," Maggie responded. "Please tell me what's going on."

"We have reliable information that a Muslim terrorist group is trying to smuggle nuclear material into the country," Dan quietly began as they found a bench and sat down. "We are fairly certain that they are planning on bringing it in through the Port of Houston and may have already been able to get some of it through Customs."

"What's all this got to do with me?" Maggie questioned. "I don't even know anyone who's Muslim, much less a terrorist."

"You would be surprised at what you may know and not even realize it," Dan replied. "In fact, a comment you made a while back is one of the reasons we are having this conversation today. You are the one who sent up a red flag that got this whole investigation started."

"What are you talking about?" Maggie asked, her voice betraying the calmness she was trying so hard to project.

"Remember the night the three of us were at Sara's and I cooked steaks? That night you were complaining about Mason and the backdoor deals he was making with the Chinese.

You mentioned that he had signed a contract with Tiger Eye Enterprises to be the freight forwarder for your compressors."

"So he made a deal without consulting the rest of the team. It was a poor business decision, but how does that fit into your story?" Maggie confusedly asked.

"Tiger Eye is on the Department of Homeland Security's Watch List. You causally mentioned that name, not understanding the implications," Dan continued. "But for me, all kinds of bells were going off. My friend's company was doing business with a group considered a threat to our country. That conversation set off an investigation, which snowballed quickly."

"I'm still not following. What has all this got to do with me being in danger?" Maggie questioned.

"Obviously, I cannot give you all of the details, but we think that Utopia Energy's compressor shipments are being used to smuggle nuclear material into this country," Dan replied. "Our question is: Who is involved? We don't believe that the company is a player, but we cannot rule out an employee, or even more than one employee. People do stupid things for a variety of reasons."

"Are you serious? You think someone in my company is plotting to destroy our country?" Maggie shouted as she stood up, pacing back and forth. "Tell me you are kidding. This can't be real."

"Sit down and lower your voice-now," Dan ordered, his police training coming to the surface. "We don't need to draw the attention of anyone."

Maggie did as she was told and the two of them sat for several minutes in silence. Shaking inside, Maggie's mind was racing as fast as her heart. This kind of situation didn't happen to real people. It only happened in the movies. She trusted Dan, but how could she possibly believe what he was telling her? It was all too surreal.

"Maggie, just knowing about this endangers your life," Dan finally spoke, so quietly that she had to strain to hear what he was saying. "These people will not let anyone get in the way of their plan."

"Then why are you telling me this? What could I possibly know?" Maggie whispered back, afraid of his answer.

"We need your help. We need someone on the inside who can be our eyes and ears," Dan explained. "We have resources in place, but they can only do so much. They are not involved in your meetings; they do not know the personalities of your team; they are not in a position to notice when something out of character occurs. You are. You know these people. You know when something happens that is beyond the scope of the negotiations. You know when someone is acting strange."

"Why me?" Maggie asked. "I'm not some super-spy. I'm a lousy poker player. Surely there is someone else. What about Alex?"

Dan sat quietly, unsure of how to handle this subject. His silence spoke volumes.

"You think Alex could be involved?" Maggie asked, already suspecting the answer.

"Not really, but we can't totally rule out the possibility," Dan conceded. "We've done some investigation, and while it was pretty much a dead end, there are still some areas that could be questionable. For now, we would like to not involve Alex."

"You are all crazy," Maggie shot back. "Alex would never be involved in anything like this. What kind of investigation did you do?"

"As I said before, I can't give you a lot of the details," Dan answered. "You will just have to trust me."

"Trust you? Let me see if I have this right: You tell me something that will put my life in danger, you tell me that the man I love could 'possibly' be involved, but you can't give me any details?" Maggie stormed. "Then you tell me that I have to trust you. What's wrong with this picture?"

"I know I'm asking a lot of you and I would never do it if it weren't so important," Dan responded. "Maggie this is serious. Will you help us?"

"You really can't expect me to answer that right this minute," Maggie retorted. "This is a lot to process. Dan, we've known each other for years, and I have never known you to lie to me, but this is too much. I can't give you an answer."

"That's fair. Give yourself a day or two to think about what I've told you, then give me a call," Dan replied calmly. "But remember, not a word to anyone."

"Dan, no one would believe me if I told them," Maggie commented as she picked up her purse and headed for the exit.

Dan sat there for several minutes, appearing to be absorbing the sounds and smells of the zoo. Instead he was rehashing his rationale for telling Maggie about the situation, for putting her in this position. He hoped he hadn't made a huge mistake.

CHAPTER 95

Maggie left the zoo in a state of total disbelief. Her head was spinning with all sorts of crazy thoughts, but they all came back to her relationship with Dan. She did trust him. She had never known him to act without cause, and despite the bizarre tale he had told her, she couldn't just dismiss his story. She had to think about what he was suspecting, about what he wanted her to do.

Going back to the office was out of the question. She could not deal with the business of her day and think about Dan's theories at the same time. She would have to have some time alone. She called Anne with some excuse about a migraine and headed for Katy. Perhaps if she could get to the quiet of her own home, some of this might make sense. She didn't really believe that, but she didn't know where else to go.

Blinded by the insanity of what she had just heard, she never noticed the dark sedan that followed her out of the zoo's parking lot. Normally she was very careful about watching the traffic around her. She was a woman living alone which triggered some subconscious alarm system that always kept her aware of her surroundings. But today the system was down, totally nonfunctioning. As she wound her way around the Eastex Freeway to the Katy Freeway, the sedan followed, keeping a safe distance but still close enough to keep an eye on the target.

"She called someone before she left the parking lot," the man reported when he answered his cell phone. "She's on I-10 now, headed toward Katy."

"Looks like she might be headed toward her house," Dan commented. "We have a trace on her cell and her home phone, so I should know shortly who she called. Just keep an eye on her and let me know if she decides to go somewhere else, or if someone meets her at home."

"Will do," the man replied. "How long do you want us to tail her?"

"Until she calls me back."

CHAPTER 96

Maggie pulled into the garage and closed the door. For several minutes, she just sat in the car, in the dark, unable to even move. Her mind was racing over the globe, but it wouldn't settle down long enough for her to consider the situation logically. Finally the stuffiness of the car made her move into the house. Once inside, an obsessive need to hide possessed her as she went from room to room, closing blinds and draperies. When the downstairs resembled a tomb, she went upstairs and followed the same pattern: shutting curtains in an attempt to close off the outside world.

In her bedroom, in the safety of the place she had shared with Tom, she collapsed across the bed. Able to muster only enough energy to kick off her shoes, she lay in the darkness with her mind racing. Was Dan right? Was there a sinister plot that somehow Utopia Energy had become caught up in? Who? More importantly, why? Why would any of these men she traveled with want to endanger the lives of others? What could they possible hope to gain by helping terrorists destroy something in America?

She went over each team member in her mind. In no way could she fathom that Paul, David, or John could be involved in anything secretive-they never set foot outside the hotel complex unless they were coming inside or going to the airport. They ate all their meals within the hotel's three restaurants, worked out in the hotel's gym, swam in the hotel's pools. She doubted if any of the three had walked across the street to the park. They were really amazing the more she thought about it: As frightened as she was about traveling to China, she would never have cloistered herself inside hotels as they had done. She might not have been as courageous as Alex, but she would at least have ventured into the park.

Alex. That brought on an entirely different set of thoughts. How could her beloved Alex be a traitor? He would never be involved in anything so insane. What had Dan said about Alex? They couldn't rule out the possibility? But he had also said that their investigation of Alex had been a dead end. Did their investigation have anything to do with Alex's brother-in-law? She had never learned how that whole mess had turned out. Maybe the two were connected.

And then it dawned on her. All the hubbub about Collin was really about Alex. The FBI wasn't looking into Collin per se, but rather to determine if Alex and Collin were somehow connected to this terrorist plot. It was all linked to Alex. Maybe that's why Dan had been so vague when Alex and Maggie had cornered him about the incident: He was covering the fact that Alex was the focus of their investigation.

But it still didn't make sense to her. Why would Alex do such a thing? What would cause a man who had once aspired to be a Navy Seal to turn against his country? Dan just had to be wrong. It was not Alex. But then she remembered Lilly. Alex and Lilly had seemed secretive on more than one occasion. They tried to talk without anyone noticing. When he did get caught, there was always a pat answer: asking for restaurant directions or what time the museum closed. And there was the time in the park when Maggie had observed them. Close, almost intimate, trading envelopes.

The headache that she had faked to Anne was now a full-blown reality. She could not think straight any longer. Shedding her clothes on the floor, she crawled under the covers and willed her mind to stop. Exhausted, sleep quickly claimed her.

CHAPTER 97

Hours later, Maggie stirred. It took her a few moments to figure out her surroundings. When she awoke enough to remember why she had come home, she was nauseated. She continued to lie still for a few minutes, testing whether the headache had truly left or was just waiting to hit her the moment she moved. The room had a much darker feel than it had had earlier. Even though she knew the drapes were closed, it hadn't seemed this dark before. She looked over at the clock and realized it was almost seven o'clock in the evening. She had slept the entire day.

Oh well, she thought. That's what the mind does when it doesn't want to deal with reality...it runs away. Today it ran to dreamland, which she knew was a better alternative than to la la land, where many people retreated when they were overwhelmed. She had to admit that the sleep must have helped, because she didn't feel as overcome with panic as she had been earlier in the day. She was still confused, but calmer. She thought again about Alex, Alex and Lilly, Alex and Collin. There was obviously something there or Dan would not have hesitated like he did, but even Dan admitted that he didn't think Alex was involved in the plot. It wasn't really what Dan had said, but rather the tone of his voice. Maggie was certain there was more to the story, and while she intended to pursue it, she was sure that Alex wasn't involved in a threat to America.

So who did that leave? Mason. She had tons of ill feelings toward the man, but she really couldn't picture him as a traitor. He didn't have the spine for all the cloak-and-dagger that something like that would involve. He wasn't the type to get his hands dirty. But who else could it be? She wondered if Dan had considered Mason. She had been so upset at the zoo that she hadn't thought to ask any questions. She had just reacted to raw emotions. What would cause a man who appeared to have everything to turn on the country that had permitted his success in the first place? Maggie had never been a person who understood the rationale of violence to promote a political agenda. That's what the polling booth was for, to effect change. She sincerely believed that logical people could make a difference without degrading their cause with bloodshed. Maybe that's naïve thinking, she chided herself, but it had been working pretty well for over two hundred years in the United States.

Her stomach growled and she realized that she hadn't eaten since before daylight. She needed to get up, but her body did not want to move. Finally, she forced herself out of bed and into some comfortable clothes. There was no energy or inclination to cook, so she headed for the nearest noise-filled chain restaurant, where she could be lost in the crowd and not bothered. As she backed out of her driveway, the two men in the sedan perked up and prepared to follow their subject.

"She's moving," one of the men said to the person he had just called. "Looks like she's heading out for dinner. She just pulled into the parking lot of Chili's at Mason Road and Katy Freeway."

"Follow her inside and see if she's meeting someone," Dan instructed. "I'm almost there now. I'll wait in the car until I hear back from you. At that point, you can call it a night. I'll take over from there."

"Sounds good to me, I'm starved and ready to be in any position other than sitting," the man replied.

Thirty minutes later, one of the agents walks out of the restaurant and heads toward his car. Parked next to the sedan is Dan, waiting patiently for an update.

"Looks like she's by herself," the agent reported. "She has ordered her meal and is sitting in the back corner on the left side. Walker's staying put until he sees you inside."

"Thanks. I'll go in and visit with her," Dan replied. "You and Walker call it a night."

As Dan walked to the back of the restaurant, he saw his fellow agent leave. Maggie never saw him coming until he sat down across the table from her.

"A lady should never have to eat alone," Dan commented as he ordered a drink from the ever-attentive waiter.

"How did you know I was here? Are you following me?" Maggie asked, surprised by his sudden appearance.

"I wanted to make sure you were okay," Dan answered. "I dumped a lot on you this morning and I was worried."

"Worried about me or worried that I would tell someone about our conversation?" Maggie quipped back.

"Oh, I know the only person you have talked to since our meeting was Anne," Dan revealed. "It's you that I'm worried about."

"You know that I talked to Anne? Do you have my phone bugged?" Maggie incredulously responded.

"Maggie, you're not dealing with the Keystone Cops here," Dan calmly replied. "I am a Federal Agent. This situation is serious. This is the real deal."

They were both silent as the waiter brought Maggie's meal, and Dan's drink order. The interruption in the conversation gave Maggie time to quiet her pulse and to try to regain control of her emotions. She needed to be calm and logical. Deep inside, she believed Dan. The struggle now was between her mind and her heart.

"Okay, let's pretend for a minute that someone is wanting to ship something into the United States," Maggie began, lowering her voice to just above a whisper. "What makes you think that Utopia Energy is involved in any way?"

"There's too much of a coincidence among the players involved," Dan replied, equally quiet. "You have to understand that I can't give you many details. It's safer for you if you don't know any more than necessary."

"Well, it's necessary for me to know more than you've told me so far, if you want my help," Maggie countered. "Look Dan, I understand your position, but remember that you came to me looking for help-help that may put my life in danger. I can't just blindly do whatever you ask. I have to know something about what led you to this point. Surely you can understand."

"Of course I can," Dan conceded, as he sat back in his chair and let out a deep breath. "There is more I am prepared to tell you, but this is not the time or the place. Come by my office tomorrow and we can talk.

"Not acceptable," Maggie replied. "If I'm not going to sleep tonight, I want to at least know the details of why I can't sleep. Finish your drink and then we'll go back to my place and talk. I trust you've had it swept for bugs?"

"You watch entirely too much television," Dan laughed, knowing that a team had already checked her house while they were having dinner. With Wang involved it was a prudent step to take, not only with Maggie, but with Alex and Mason as well.

CHAPTER 98

"I've gone over Yi's phone records for the past year," Brad Robberson began. "Most of the calls are benign, black-market stuff, nothing serious. There was one interesting development. There were several calls between Yi and a guy in Kabul just before Yi started shopping. The contact from Kabul is a known al-Qaeda friendly. It seems that he is an Arab version of Yi, a middleman to all types of bad guys. He has done business before with Yi, mostly drugs and some automatic weapons, but nothing of this magnitude."

"So now the trail leads to Kabul?" Dan sighed, shaking his head. "This is getting scarier by the moment."

"Oh, there's more," Robberson continued. "It seems that our guy in Kabul is a favorite contact for Habib Aghasi, the head of the Atomic Energy Organization of Iran. Aghasi has family living in the US-two cousins in Houston. Mohammed and Tarik Aghasi."

"Bingo. You just made the circle connect," Dan replied, sitting up straighter in his chair. "Do we know if he has had contact with the cousins?"

"We should have that info within a couple of days," Robberson replied. "I can tell you what we know so far: Habib's father has had some very bad associates in the past. He was in the inner circle of the group that took over the American Embassy in Tehran back in the late seventies. Habib has always seemed to take a higher, more intellectual road, but you can't be raised with radicals and not have it wear off on you."

"I wonder if that's true for our two guys here in Houston," Dan said, his mind chasing rabbits. "Were they raised in a radical setting that is just now harvesting what they sowed?"

"It makes sense that they were," Robberson replied. "We need to see how close the cousins' fathers have been during all of these years. We may be looking at the ultimate sleeper cell."

"So it's our esteemed nuclear researcher who is the mastermind of the operation," Dan commented, following the path of communication in his mind. "Or at the very least, he's the point man."

"I would say that is probably more accurate," Brad Robberson replied. "We know that he is just a puppet of the current Iranian regime. This could very possibly be a government sanctioned operation."

"That opens up an entirely new can of worms," Dan responded, his heart suddenly racing. "An international incident is not what we need to be dealing with on top of the bad guys themselves. This could be a nightmare."

"You do realize that this just blew up in your face? You have no choice now but to involve a lot of other people, starting with the State Departmen," Robberson advised. "This cannot be contained within the FBI."

"I know." Dan sighed. "Thanks for your help, buddy. I'm sure we will be talking again."

"Soon, my friend, soon."

CHAPTER 99

"Mohammed and Tarik Aghasi are the American-born children of Aalim and Badra Aghasi, who immigrated to the United States from Venezuela," the task force member began. "The parents both worked in the oil and gas industry and appear to have led quiet lives here before returning to Venezuela five years ago. The sons remained in Houston, both working in the Global Market Complex. Tarik, the younger of the two, works as a financial market analyst for Bailey Worldwide Investments and Mohammed works in the IT Department of Kelly-Jones Communications."

"What do we know about their social activities?" Dan asked. "Are they members of any political or religious groups?"

"Not political that we can determine," the agent continued. "They write checks to a local mosque, but are not active in any of the Muslim groups that we regularly watch. They are both single, have valid driver's licenses, no records-not even traffic violations. They live together, making house payments on time, and pay their taxes early."

"Totally flying under the radar screen," Dan mumbled, almost to himself. "What assets do we have in place with them?"

"None yet. We've just been doing the background work," Jim Keith interjected. "It's too soon to take a chance of being discovered. We need more information before we can blanket their movements."

"I know. We also need to find out more about Yi's customer," Dan said. "I'll contact Joseph Lee to see if there's anything new. Meanwhile, Interpol is working on who might have contacted Yi to begin with. It may take a few days."

"Let's hope we have that much time," Jim commented as he dismissed the meeting and headed back to his office.

CHAPTER 100

"I'm so glad to see that you could join us this time," Han commented as Mason and the rest of the Utopia Energy team entered the meeting room. "Our talks should go much smoother now."

Mason said nothing as he found his place at the table. The other team members stared in disbelief at such a rude comment. As far as they were concerned, the negotiations had gone much better at the last meeting when Mason had stayed home.

"We have a lot of work to do. I suggest we get started," Mason addressed his team as he opened his briefcase and pulled out a stack of papers. His tone was very professional, devoid of the usual friendliness he projected at these meetings. He did not make eye contact with any of the Chinese.

The two groups settled down and worked without breaks right up until noon. They covered a lot of ground, but seemed to make little progress. Even though everyone tried to focus and participate, Mason was setting the pace entirely too fast for quality work to be accomplished. Both sides were visibly frustrated, except for Han. He had positioned himself at the end of the conference table and spent the morning quietly observing the entire process. With an almost amused look on his face, he rarely made suggestions or asked a question, and always kept his eye on Mason. For his part, Mason never acknowledged Han and did not look in his direction, even when Han did interject himself into the talks.

Finally his team members interrupted Mason's nonstop checklist and insisted on having lunch. It had been a long morning and they all felt like they were running a marathon that they had not trained for, especially for the first jet-lagged morning session. Before they could secure their computers and regroup to look for something to eat, Mason had disappeared. No one had paid any attention to him, but everyone was surprised when they realized he had already left the room. Everyone except Han. He had never risen from his seat, instead watching Mason as he scrambled to grab his briefcase and quietly leave the room. Han was amused. He knew that Mason was miserable and afraid. He knew that Mason realized there was no escape; he could stay in Houston, but Han could still destroy him. Yes, Han thought, this was working out quite well.

The other team members made their way to the hotel restaurant, too tired to try to fight the lunch crowds in the local haunts. Even Maggie and Alex opted to join the group. They were all exhausted, not only from the trip over, but by the nonstop pace that Mason was determined to keep up. They weren't sure what his problem was, but they knew that they could not keep up at this level without some serious sleep.

"I feel like I've been run over by a freight train," Paul said as they sat down at their table.

"Yeah, it's called the Mason Express," John White, the maintenance manager, interjected. "We've got to find a way to derail that guy and cut the afternoon session short. I'm so tired that I'm not sure I'm even processing what we're discussing. I have no idea if we've missed anything critical or not."

"That's the truth," Alex agreed. "We will need to revisit everything we've discussed this morning. But I'm going to have to have some rest before I can even do that. What do you think he's taking to keep him so wired up?"

"I have no idea, but remember his strange behavior the last time he was here?" Maggie commented. "He left a day early without so much as a word to anyone."

"Then he didn't come back with us on the next trip," David continued. "He had some excuse about a meeting at Ray Controls. There's something going on with that guy that's making him act weirder than usual."

"Well, whatever his problem is, I've had enough of the marathon running for the day," Alex declared. "We're going to make the afternoon a short session whether he likes it or not. I'm about to fall asleep at the table, so we have got to end this early."

The others agreed to a three o'clock mutiny and then spent the rest of their lunch conversation discussing more pleasant topics. They had all worked together for several years and shared mutual interests and friends, so it was easy for them to fall into a comfortable banter that didn't involve work. After a few minutes of relaxation and nourishment, they felt they could continue with the talks–at least until the time they had all agreed upon to quit. As they filtered back into the meeting room, Alex quietly walked over to where Lilly was standing. He spoke with her briefly before returning to his place at the table. No one noticed, except Maggie.

Mason was the last to return for the afternoon session, and it was immediately obvious that his disposition had not changed during the lunch break. It was as if he were trying to conclude two weeks' worth of work in one day. As in the morning, he focused strictly on business and never once looked in Han's direction. Whenever anyone tried to revisit something that had been discussed in the earlier session, he cut them off as being redundant, and moved on to the next subject.

Even the Chinese group was beginning to feel shell-shocked. What was this crazy American up to? Long before three o'clock, one of the Chinese team members suggested that they call it a day and take up in the morning. Mason vehemently argued for continuation, but everyone else, including Han, cut him off and started packing their computers up to leave. Mason fumed, but finally conceded that they were quitting for the day, despite his objections. Before he could gather his belongings, Han walked up and blocked Mason's way to the door.

"It is good for you to be here, my friend," Han sarcastically commented. "I assume you will join me for dinner as in the past?"

"You've got to be kidding," Mason whispered, afraid that someone would overhear. "I may have been stupid before, but that doesn't mean I'm going to continue to play your sick little game."

"There's no need for you to be hateful. Whatever harm you think has happened, it's your own fault and nothing will change that now," Han firmly replied. "You still have to eat, and I would prefer to keep a close eye on you. You will meet me downstairs at seven o'clock and we will go to dinner. I know you must be exhausted, so we will make it an early evening."

"I don't think that's going to happen," Mason sniped, trying to muster as much bravado as he could.

"You have no choice. Don't keep me waiting or I will have to send my associates to find you," Han threatened as he turned and left the room.

Maggie sat motionless as she tried to absorb what she had just witnessed. While the others were preparing to leave for the day, she was finishing entering her notes when out of the corner of her eye, she saw Han approach Mason. There seemed to be an immediate escalation of tension in Mason's body language and although they were talking quietly, Maggie could hear every word. She didn't dare move for fear that one of them would realize that she had overheard their conversation.

What did Mason mean by "your sick little game"? His words tried to sound strong, but his tone revealed his fear. What had happened to the two men who had once seemed joined at the hip? Why was Han threatening Mason over something as insignificant as dinner? Maybe Dan had been right after all. Maybe there really was something sinister going on. As much as Mason irritated everyone on the team, it seemed to bizarre to think that he was involved in anything so dark as to threaten the United States. Maggie's logic was just not letting her totally buy into Dan's theory.

She shook off thoughts of spies and terrorists and made her way to the doorway where Alex was visiting with the other team members. She and Alex said goodbye to the others and headed upstairs.

"That went better than I expected," Alex commented as he walked Maggie to her room. "It's barely two o'clock and it was nice that the Chinese guys ended the day. I think they were almost as tired as we are."

"I'm not sure that's possible, but I am still thankful that the day is over," Maggie replied. "I could barely hold my head up. I just want to take a nap."

"Amen to that," Alex agreed. "I'll call you around six and we can decide what we're doing for dinner. That will give us enough time to get some rest."

"Sounds good, although I think I could just sleep until morning," Maggie commented. "I need all the rest I can get if we are going to go nonstop again tomorrow."

"Don't worry, because we are not going to. I have no intention of letting Mason pull that kind of stunt again tomorrow," Alex assured her. "I was too tired today to try to argue with him, but you can bet I will feel more like it in the morning. His pace is only going to cause more problems in the long run, because we are not talking out these plans to see what the pros and cons are to each one. I don't intend to have to spend time fixing problems caused from his insane schedule."

"You're right and I'm sure the others would think so as well," Maggie agreed. "But for right now the only problem I want to fix is my exhaustion. We'll talk later."

Alex gave Maggie a quick kiss and headed to his own room to crash. He would have liked to spend the afternoon with his arms wrapped around her, but as wonderful as that sounded, he knew he didn't have the energy to even suggest it. Instead, he found his own bed to be quite inviting and within seconds he was deep in sleep.

Before Maggie would allow herself to collapse, she pulled a notebook out of her briefcase and recorded the conversation she had overheard between Mason and Han. She might think Dan was too caught up in drama, but still something nagged at her conscience and she decided that she would at least try to be observant until she decided what was really going on … if anything.

CHAPTER 101

When Mason reached his own room, he realized just how tired he felt. He had to psych himself up to be able to face Han at the meetings and frankly thought that the pace he had set had been relatively successful. He had managed to avoid interacting with Han, until the end of the day anyway. But still his stomach fought nausea. What else had he expected? Did he really think he could come back to Chengdu and just ignore Han? He knew for sure that he couldn't stay in Houston again. Not only would Baron go ballistic, but those thugs were capable of doing anything. He had yet to figure out how to get out of this mess, and until he did, he didn't need anything to come to the surface, especially not in Houston. He had thought he could keep a lid on things if he returned to China as scheduled and tried to buy some time. Somehow that plan didn't seem to be working so well.

Mason knew that he needed to rest before he had to go out for the evening, but he wasn't sure he could shut his motor down. He had gone to his doctor before leaving Houston and gotten a prescription for anti-anxiety medicine, but he was afraid to take it when he was so tired. If the pills knocked him out and he missed meeting Han, then those goons would come knocking at his door, and he really didn't need that to happen. Still, he needed sleep, so he took one pill, set his alarm and also called for a wake-up call for six o'clock. That would give him enough time to freshen up before dinner with Han. It was going to be a long evening.

CHAPTER 102

As Mason left the elevator and headed across the lobby toward the door, he noticed a beautiful Chinese lady approaching him. Mason always noticed beautiful women, but this one especially caught his attention. She was tall and long-legged with long blue-black hair, wearing three-inch heels and a tight emerald green dress that barely covered her curvy hips. Mason was so distracted that he was surprised when he realized he had bumped right into her. He reached out to steady her as she teetered with her balance.

"I am so sorry, I was not watching where I was going," Mason sincerely apologized.

"It's okay, I'm fine," the girl replied without releasing her hold on his torso. She lingered a half a second longer than necessary. Before she broke contact, she reached up to straighten his tie. "Here let me fix your tie."

Mesmerized by her flawless, pale skin, Mason stood still while the beauty reached up and pretended to straighten a tie that wasn't out of place. When she finished, she rubbed her hand over his chest pocket.

"There you go, good as new," she commented. "Be careful tonight."

"I'll try to watch where I'm going," Mason smiled. "You have a good evening."

He turned to watch her as she entered the elevator, temporarily forgetting that Han's car was waiting for him outside the hotel. She was the loveliest creature he had ever seen in his travels to China. Before he continued his trek across the lobby, he let out a long sigh of regret that he was not spending the evening with her.

Outside the hotel, in a car parked just past Han's limo, two agents smiled as Mason's sigh came in clearly through the transmitter stuck on the back side of his tie.

CHAPTER 103

As Maggie and Alex were getting off the elevator, they saw Mason stopped in the middle of lobby talking with a beautiful Chinese woman. They seemed familiar with each other, as the woman was straightening Mason's tie. Without thinking, Maggie and Alex both slowed their pace as they witnessed the exchange.

"Well, that was very interesting," Maggie commented as they continued across the lobby. "I wonder where he met her."

"I wonder how much he paid to 'meet' her," Alex responded. "I can't imagine that she was attracted to his charismatic personality."

They both laughed as they made their way out of the lobby. When they reached the sidewalk, they saw Mason getting into a waiting limo, but they could not see who else was inside the car.

"My curiosity makes me want to follow that limo," Maggie commented as they turned to walk in the opposite direction. She really needed to see if Han was in the limo also.

"We need to change the focus of your curiosity," Alex laughed. "The last thing I want is to spend an evening watching Mason play whatever game he is playing."

"You think he's with Han?" Maggie asked.

"That seems to be his pattern when we're here," Alex answered. "The two of them have been cozy for a while now, although I don't see the attraction. They seem so opposite."

"Perhaps it's a Chinese honor thing," Maggie suggested, wanting to keep an open mind, despite what Dan had told her. "Maybe Han feels obligated to play host to the American visitor."

"You could be right," Alex responded. "As long as I don't have to be a part of the charade, I don't care what he and Mason do in the evenings."

"Maybe we should care," Maggie replied, her tone suddenly serious. "Mason apparently makes business deals during these evening adventures. Remember our contract with Tiger Eye-the one none of the rest of the team knew anything about until it was a done deal."

"You have a point there," Alex conceded. "But it's not a strong enough argument tonight to get me to follow Mason and spy on him. My stomach has its sight set on Pete's, and somehow I don't think that's where Mason will be dining tonight."

"I certainly hope not," Maggie agreed. "You know, I've had about all of Mason I can handle. I don't understand why he's even on the team, and I'm about at the point to push that issue with Baron. Although, I think Baron already feels the same way."

"If he does, then why are we still having to put up with Mason?" Alex countered. "I've never known Baron to put up with excess baggage for no reason."

"The reason is higher up than Baron, and probably has something to do with Mason's well-connected father-in-law," Maggie suggested. "There's a long history between our CEO and Cynthia's daddy. I'm sure he got Mason the job. Why else would he still be around? It's not because he's brilliant."

"No, he's not. But as far as China is concerned, his presence should be about over," Alex commented. "The project is all but finished. I'm not even sure why we needed the entire team here this time anyway. All we're doing now is fine tuning a few points."

"You're right, but I don't want to have to work with him on future projects," Maggie replied. "You are also correct about the need for us all to be here. I'm not even sure if I could justify my attendance. You and John could have finished this up just fine without the rest of us."

"Ah, but you make a more interesting traveling companion," Alex said, winking at Maggie. "John really isn't my type."

"Good to know," Maggie laughed as they turned down the alley toward Pete's.

CHAPTER 104

"I glad to see that I didn't have to send my colleagues looking for you," Han commented as Mason got into the limousine. "It would have made us late for our dinner reservation."

"It wasn't as if you gave me an option," Mason sniped.

"Mason, you may not like the situation you are in, but you have no one to blame but yourself," Han patiently, but bluntly replied. "You didn't turn down one invitation before."

"I didn't know that I was being set up, that I was dealing with a bunch of thugs," Mason shot back, sounding braver than he felt.

"Let me assure you that we are not a 'bunch of thugs,'" Han commented. "However, you are correct in saying that you were set up. That much is true. You were chosen because you made such an easy target. You let yourself be used. A real man is on his guard at all times, always watching for those who might be trying to take advantage. You allowed your ego and arrogance to guide you instead of your common sense."

"Thank you for the sermon, but I'd just as soon not hear it," Mason retorted. "I don't know why we are going out tonight, pretending as if everything is all right."

"Because everything is all right, my friend, as long as you remember our arrangements," Han answered.

"You have what you want, so why continue the charade?" Mason asked, his voice no longer demanding, but rather more resigned.

"Let's just say it's something about keeping your enemies close," Han replied. "Besides, your friends would be suspicious if we were to suddenly change our normal plans. This way there are fewer questions asked behind your back. We will simply enjoy dinner."

"Why are you doing this? What more do you want?" Mason quietly asked.

"As I told you before, there are some questions you do not want answered," Han replied. "Trust me, it is safer for you to know nothing."

The two men rode in silence the remainder of the way to the restaurant, but the tension was thick. Han remained quite smug, but deep inside he felt a twinge of pity for the proud American. It was a sad situation for an honorable man-or any man-to find himself in. Han could only ponder what he would do in similar circumstances.

The evening dragged on as both men struggled with conversation. Han sincerely wanted to enjoy Mason's company. After all, Han had accomplished his mission, so he could see no reason for them not to be sociable. Mason, on the other hand, was fighting his own demons. He was embarrassed, infuriated, and downright angry. He just wasn't entirely sure if he felt that way toward Han or himself. Han was a personable host and it was difficult not to enjoy his company. That, however was the problem; that was what had gotten Mason into this predicament in the first place.

As promised, Han had made plans for dinner, but no other activity afterward, so despite the seemingly endless meal, Mason found himself back at the hotel at a reasonable time. He was nervous as he made his way to his room, afraid that Han's associates would be waiting, and he had no idea how he would survive another ordeal with them. In spite of his frayed nerves-or perhaps because of them-Mason succumbed to sleep almost immediately. However, the shades of the night offered him no peace; his dreams kept him tossing and turning throughout the wee morning hours.

CHAPTER 105

"Well my friend, you made a good decision in having us follow Mason," Joseph began the phone conversation. "There is definitely a dark connection between him and Han. I'm emailing you a transcript of last night's dinner meeting between the two men."

"Hang on while I check my computer," Dan said as he opened his email. "Here it comes now."

Dan quickly scanned the email and realized that they had indeed picked up an interesting conversation. It was the first conclusive evidence that there was more to Han and Mason's relationship than just building a compressor plant.

"This doesn't give us any details of what has gone down, but it's obvious that Han has something on Mason and he is using it as leverage for what he wants Mason to deliver," Joseph commented when his colleague had had time to look over the email.

"This is great, I mean, it's certainly a start," Dan commented. "We need to find out as many of the details as we can, but I'm pretty sure that at least one thing Han derived from this was getting Tiger Eye the shipping contract."

"So you think Han is using Utopia Energy to smuggle something into Houston?" Joseph asked. "It could be that he's just a ruthless businessman."

"Could be, but then again, it could be a cover to deliver whatever it is that Yi is buying," Dan replied. "I need to try to find out if there is anything else Han has managed to get written into the contract negotiations."

"You want the tail kept on Mason?" Joseph asked.

"For now. I'll get back to you as soon as I learn anything," Dan answered. "It seems we have one more piece of the puzzle."

* * *

"I just wanted to check with you and see how your first day back had gone," Dan tried to sound cheery when Maggie called.

"Brutal. It's always tough the first day, but today was unbelievable." Maggie sighed as she kicked off her shoes and stretched out across the bed while she talked to Dan. "Mason was a man on a mission that just about wore the rest of us out."

"What do you mean?" Dan questioned. "Was he acting differently than he usually does?"

"Daylight and dark different," Maggie responded. "Usually we're not sure that he even pays attention. If you ask him a question, he has this blank look on his face; not involved at all. But today, it was the Mason Show, starring the one and only Project Manager himself-emphasis on the 'only' part. He talked nonstop, ignored questions and concerns from everyone else, and tried his best to cram two weeks of work into one day."

"How did everyone else react?" Dan asked. He was curious if others saw the situation as Maggie did, or if her viewpoint was now clouded by what he had told her.

"Frustrated, aggravated, shell-shocked," Maggie replied. "At lunch we had planned a mutiny for the afternoon session, but the Chinese team beat us to it. Even they were ready to cut the meeting short. Everyone except Han. He didn't seem bothered by the marathon pace at all. In fact, most of the day he just sat there, not participating, but watching Mason's every move."

"I take it that Han's behavior was abnormal as well," Dan replied with more of a statement than a question.

"Yeah. Usually he is very interactive. Sometimes so much so that we aren't sure why the other Chinese members are even there," Maggie responded. "It was almost as if Han and Mason had reversed roles, although Han is never as manic as Mason was today and Mason is rarely as observant as Han was during the meeting."

"Anything else?" Dan questioned.

"I overheard a conversation between Han and Mason today that seemed very cryptic," Maggie continued. "As we were all packing up to leave the meeting, Han approached Mason and invited him to dinner. But it was very insistent and sarcastic, not a polite invitation at all. Mason just freaked out. He said that Han had to be kidding, that he wasn't going to play Han's 'sick little game' anymore and that he wasn't going to dinner with him. Han just smiled and told him that he had no choice and that if he didn't show up, Han would send his 'associates' to fetch Mason. His tone was very threatening and there was no room for misinterpretation."

"That's very interesting," Dan commented almost to himself. "Well, we know that Mason took Han seriously. They dined at the Shizilou Restaurant."

"How did you know that?" Maggie asked, shocked that Dan could know where the two men had gone for dinner. "We saw Mason get into a limo, but didn't know where they went, or even if Han was the person in the limo."

"As I told you, we have people able to watch the outside movements," Dan explained. "We need you to be on the inside."

"Yes, but-"

"Maggie, this is one of those times that you don't need to know the details," Dan interrupted. "It should give you a little peace of mind to know that you are not alone in this. There are good people close by you. Which brings up another subject: Tomorrow at lunch, I need you to go to the park across the street from your hotel. There is a bench in the middle of the park near the playground. A woman will meet you there and give you a package. She will have instructions for you."

"Is that not a tad too cloak-and-dagger? And you think I watch too much television?" Maggie replied, trying to be incredulous rather than scared about the entire situation. It was a futile effort.

"Just do it, okay? Maggie, this is not a game. This is the real-deal bad-guy world. You need to be serious and alert," Dan gently scolded. "It could save your life."

"Okay, okay. Sorry. It's just that this is a little out of my experience realm," Maggie replied.

"I know, but you will do great. Just listen to what you're told and don't go off on some cowboy mission," Dan encouraged. "You can do this."

"Cowboy mission?" Maggie laughed. "You have no idea how far it stretches my comfort zone to even go across the street to the park. You have sure picked yourself a super-sleuth."

"Well, at least one that no one will suspect," Dan replied.

"Let's hope you're right," Maggie replied, the seriousness returning to her voice. "Look, I have to go to sleep or I won't be good for anyone."

"Understood. Take care, Maggie, and call me tomorrow after you have had time to look at the package," Dan replied. "Keep it close to you and don't leave it in the hotel room if you go out."

"Okay. It's a good thing I brought a big purse," Maggie answered, trying to lighten the mood. "Guys always gripe about a woman's big purse until you need her to carry stuff around for you. I will be careful, Dan. Promise. Talk to you tomorrow night."

"Goodnight Mags," Dan replied as he hung up the phone and said a silent prayer for her safety. Sara would kill him if she knew what he was asking Maggie to do.

CHAPTER 106

As Maggie approached the park, she saw a young Chinese woman already seated, seemingly watching a child in the playground. Next to her on the bench was a small manila envelope. Maggie sat down, looking straight ahead, her heart pounding in her throat. Suddenly, she realized what a frightening position she was in.

"It's a beautiful day, don't you think?" the young woman asked in perfect English.

"Yes it is. It seems this is the first clear day since I've been here," Maggie replied, turning her head toward her companion. "It's usually so gray."

"It would be best if you continued to look ahead, or pretended to read some of the papers you have with you," the woman instructed. "We shouldn't appear to know each other."

Pausing briefly as the instructions soaked into her brain, Maggie then opened her briefcase and started sorting through papers as if searching for something of interest.

"Set your briefcase in the bench between us," the woman continued. "When you get ready to leave, put the envelope in the case with your other papers. Do not look at it here. You can open it when you are safely back in your room."

"What's in it?" Maggie asked, her curiosity budding.

"Pictures. We need you to study them and let us know if you recognize any of the people in them," the woman answered. "Dan will call you tonight after you have had a chance to look at them."

"You know Dan?" Maggie asked, shocked at the familiar use of his name.

"We are colleagues. Despite my looks, I am an American," the woman replied, softer, as if she understood Maggie's fear. "There is a piece of paper in the envelope also with a name and phone number. Use it if you find yourself in danger-but only then. Otherwise do not call it."

About that time a small boy, perhaps four or five years old, ran up to the bench and crawled into the woman's lap, chattering nonstop in Chinese. The woman gathered her belongings and the two of them strolled slowly out of the park. Maggie watched them until they disappeared into the street crowd, wondering how a woman with a young child could ever be involved in such a dangerous job.

After a few minutes Maggie checked her watch and as if she had lost track of the time, hurriedly started putting papers back inside the briefcase, careful to include the manila envelope as casually as possible. Her legs shaking, she headed back across to the hotel and straight to the conference room. The pictures would have to wait until the afternoon session was over, but Maggie already knew that those pictures were all that she would be thinking about.

CHAPTER 107

"So, where would you like to have dinner tonight?" Alex asked as he followed Maggie out of the meeting. "I missed you at lunch. Where did you run off to?"

"Oh, I really just needed some fresh air," Maggie tried to casually answer. "I spent a few minutes in the park. It was a beautiful day and I didn't want to spend it inside."

"Well, you are right about it being a pretty day. We don't see many of those when we're in China," Alex replied. "Why don't we find an outdoor café and enjoy the evening as well?"

"Sounds wonderful, but first I need to rest for a while," Maggie responded. "I'm still really tired and I need a nap."

"Want company?" Alex grinned as he put his arm around her.

"As inviting as that sounds, I think I'll pass," Maggie answered. She didn't want to wait any longer to look at the envelope, but she didn't want to make Alex angry either. "I don't think I would be very good company today. How about a raincheck? We can go out for dinner later."

"You have the sweetest way of turning a guy down," Alex laughed as they stopped outside her room. "A raincheck will be just fine. You get some rest and I'll pick you up around seven. How does that sound?"

"Very accommodating. Thank you, Alex," Maggie sincerely answered. "I will be ready."

As soon as the door was closed, Maggie opened the envelope and spread several pictures across the bed. Several of them were of Han, but she did not recognize any of the other men. Curiously there were no pictures of Mason, which surprised Maggie. She had assumed that Dan was trying to show her there was some connection that would prove Mason was involved in this terrible plot. She was still looking over the photographs when the phone rang and startled her.

"I was hoping to find you in your room," Dan said. "Have you had a chance to look at the pictures?"

"Do you ever sleep? It must be five in the morning there," Maggie replied. "Are you at the office?"

"Unfortunately, yes. I wanted to try to catch you before you went out to dinner," Dan answered. "I need to know if you recognize any of the people in the photographs. Have you seen any of them hanging around the hotel?"

"The only one I know is Han," Maggie answered. "Who are the others?"

"The one taken in a park is of Han and a guy named Cai Yi, a very bad player. The one taken in Tiananmen Square is Han and a North Korean official," Dan explained. "The group of men are the top dogs of Tiger Eye Enterprises. Are you sure you never met with any of them in your negotiations?"

"I'm sure. There were no negotiations with them, remember?" Maggie answered. "Mason made the deal without consulting any of us. We never met anyone from Tiger Eye."

"Okay. I need you to study these photographs and try to memorize the faces," Dan continued. "I need you to be on the lookout for any of these guys-especially if you see them with Mason."

"I'll do my best. You know, these guys all look alike to me," Maggie conceded.

"Well, they won't after you stare at the pictures for long enough." Dan laughed. "But remember to keep the photos with you. Do not leave them in your hotel room or in the meeting room."

"I will, but do you think that someone would really look through my room?" Maggie questioned.

"I don't know, but we can't take that chance," Dan soberly answered. "Besides, a maid might recognize someone in the pictures and tell the wrong person that she saw them in your room. I just need you to be really careful."

"I will. I really would like to take a short nap before Alex comes for dinner, so if you don't mind, I'm going to say goodbye." Maggie yawned.

"You do that. I would tell you to give Alex my best, but that wouldn't be such a great idea," Dan commented. "Enjoy your dinner, and stick close to Alex when you're out and about, okay?"

"Don't worry," Maggie quietly answered. "I promise not to go on any adventures."

Maggie gathered up the photographs and put them safely in her purse before lying back across the bed for a quick nap. She knew she needed to study them more, but she was aching for rest and before a minute had passed, she was sound asleep.

CHAPTER 108

Alex and Maggie did not linger over dinner as they normally did when they were in Chengdu. They were both exhausted and not very good company, and so after a few minutes of visiting with Pete, they headed back to the hotel. Maggie sent Alex on to his room while she checked with the front desk for any messages. As she waited for help, she noticed a limo had pulled up to the front door and let Mason out. He did not seem to notice Maggie as he crossed the lobby for the elevators. What caught Maggie's attention was the guy who got out of the car's front seat after Mason had gone inside. He also watched Mason's progress across the lobby, then found a chair, pulled out a newspaper and made himself at home. The limo drove off without him.

The desk clerk handed Maggie just one message: Dan's name and a phone number. As she turned to head upstairs, the man with the newspaper watched her every step.

CHAPTER 109

"You look like you've been up all night. What's wrong?" Maggie asked as Alex hurriedly sat down for breakfast.

"I've been up for several hours. The plant is down and I have been trying to work them through it on the phone, but I can't seem to make them understand," Alex explained as he ran his hands through his hair. "I don't see any way out of not going on-site."

"Today? But we're supposed to fly to Shanghai this morning," Maggie countered, knowing already that she was going to have to go solo on this day trip. "We have a logistics inspection at Tiger Eye's shipping facility."

"I know, Maggie, and I'm sorry, but I don't know what else to do. I have to get the plant running again," Alex replied, his voice softer, less frustrated. "You will be just fine. Lilly is going with you to translate and you will know better than I would if everything is in order. Call me if you have any questions and we'll get together for dinner when you return."

"Great, just what I wanted to do … spend the day with Lilly." Maggie sulked as she set her food aside. "She and I are not exactly buds."

"Lilly's okay, you just haven't taken the time to get to know her," Alex responded. "You know, if I didn't know better, I'd say you were acting like a jealous girlfriend."

"Funny. But now that you mention it, you do seem to spend more time with Lilly than any of the other guys do," Maggie said. "It's like you two know each other better and have things to talk about."

"Well, if you count asking for directions and restaurant suggestions as 'knowing each other,' then maybe so," Alex replied. "She is a wealth of information about the city. Of course, if you're content to stay inside the hotel complex-as the others are-then there's no need to visit with Lilly. Seriously, you surely don't think there's anything between me and Lilly."

"I suppose not, but you can continue to convince me when I return from Shanghai," Maggie winked, trying to lighten the situation she knew she had caused. "We'll see how creative you can be."

"I'll work on it in between getting a multimillion dollar plant back on line." Alex laughed. "No problem. No stress."

CHAPTER 110

"How long does the process take from the time that the trucks deliver the compressors to when the ship actually sails?" Maggie had Lilly ask the warehouse manager.

"That depends on a number of circumstances," Lilly said, relaying his answer. "There can be many complications and delays."

Another dodged question, Maggie thought as she continued walking around the warehouse. The man did not fit her image of a shipping warehouse manager. He was too clean-cut, too well-dressed, and too young to have had very much experience. It was as if he had been hired for the day to appease the American visitors. She wondered if he would act so aloof if Alex had been asking the questions.

"What kind of complications and delays?" Maggie asked, trying to control her aggravation.

"Sometimes there are other orders ahead of yours, sometimes the docks are blocked by other ships loading, sometimes the weather doesn't cooperate," he answered directly, not replying through Lilly.

"Had I known you spoke perfect English, Lilly could have had a day off," Maggie replied smiling sarcastically. "I am aware that such inconveniences would have to be worked around, but in rough terms, how long?"

"Ideally, two to three weeks," the young man answered, all pretense of politeness vanished.

"I would like to see the paperwork on all of the loads that have shipped out so far," Maggie instructed, as she walked around a compressor being crated by several workers. "I will look around here while you gather them for me."

Obviously dismissed, the man walked toward the offices, anger seething with every step. Maggie knew that she had irritated him, but she didn't care. From the moment she had arrived, they had treated her as if she were invading their domain. She needed to remind them that she was the customer, the one paying their salary.

As she continued to mill around, she had an uneasy feeling. Something felt wrong, or perhaps she was just annoyed or maybe even paranoid about everything, thanks to Dan. Lost in her thoughts, Maggie bumped into a crate sitting on the floor. As she regained her bearings, her glance at the crate became a stare. The box contained exhaust manifolds, cast with Utopia's logo. She looked at the compressor being crated, but it was already boxed in enough that she couldn't see the exhaust manifold.

Why were the manifolds in a shipping crate on the floor? Why had they been removed from the machines? None of this made sense. Maggie pulled out her cell phone and made several pictures with the camera. She never saw the worker who witnessed her picture-taking.

She walked toward the offices to ask why the manifolds were lying in a separate shipping container, appearing to be forgotten, when she was met by the warehouse manager.

"Here is the paperwork on all the shipments," he said as he handed her several thick folders. "These are copies, you can take them with you."

"Thank you," Maggie absentmindedly replied. "I have another question. Why is there a crate of exhaust manifolds sitting in your warehouse? Why were they removed from the compressors?"

Hesitating for a split second, the warehouse manager replied, "Those are extra parts that we are to ship to the United States. We haven't crated them for shipment yet."

"Some of them are quite dusty," Maggie commented. "It looks like they have been here for a while."

"Well, we don't ship them very often," the man explained. "Just when we receive enough to fill a crate. It's too expensive to short ship them."

Maggie decided that once again she was being dismissed, not given straight answers. She was sure that she was being lied to. She did not remember any talks about spare manifolds. There was no need for spares; they never needed replacing. The entire visit had felt odd, as if she were invading a space that she wasn't supposed to visit. Something in her gut told her that it was time to leave. She wanted to get back to Chengdu as soon as possible.

When they got into the taxi, Lilly questioned her as to why they were leaving so quickly. Their plane reservations were several hours away.

"I have a lot of paperwork to go through," Maggie replied, pointing to the stack of files the warehouse manager had given her. "I think my time would be better spent doing that than walking around a dirty shipyard. Besides, what else was there to really look at?"

Lilly didn't reply, but instead rode in silence to the airport. She thought Maggie to be a rather odd person, forceful yet fearful, confident yet unsure of herself. Maggie was always polite to Lilly, but was never friendly, not like Alex. But Lilly reminded herself that Maggie did not know about her connection with Alex, did not realize that they were practically family. Better that she not know, Lilly thought. Lilly didn't need any more trouble in her life.

Maggie also rode in silence. What was going on at the freight forwarder's warehouse. She knew in her heart that

Utopia had never ordered shipments of spare manifolds. She was positive. What had she seen? She needed to email the pictures to Dan right away, but didn't want to risk Lilly seeing what she was doing. It would have to wait until she was safely back in her hotel room. Did she dare ask Alex about spare parts? No, not yet, she decided. She needed to talk to Dan first and ask him before involving Alex. She tried to keep in mind what Dan had told her about his investigation of Alex. Dan had never totally cleared Alex of suspicion in whatever was going on. Until Dan felt confident with Alex, Maggie was going to keep her mouth shut. Her life depended on it.

CHAPTER 111

As soon as the American woman and her translator had left, the warehouse manager was approached by a worker who told him about having seen the woman take pictures of the manifolds. The warehouse manager went ballistic. Not only had she seen them and questioned him about them, but then he learned that she had taken pictures with her cell phone. Pictures that could already have been emailed anywhere in the world. This was not a good situation, he knew. He also knew that he had a call to make. He had to let his father know what had happened.

Chen's call surprised Han, and though Han rarely took calls during the team meetings, he knew that this must be urgent. He knew Maggie had flown to Shanghai for the inspection. That was why he had Chen posing as the warehouse manager. Han wanted someone in place who could watch for any trouble, and Chen knew enough about their operations that he could fake being in charge for one day. The fact that he was calling well before the visit should have been over troubled Han immediately. He excused himself from the meeting to take the call.

"She saw what?" Han asked incredulously. "What were they doing lying around where she could find them? Why hadn't they been shipped out?"

"Lack of communication," Chen guessed. "No one really expected her to walk around quite so much. We all thought she would stay in the office area. But there's more to tell you. Not only did she see them, but she took pictures with her cell phone. I have no idea if she emailed them to anyone or not, but either way, this could be a problem."

"Not could be. She IS a problem," Han raged. "We cannot risk everything because of some woman. You did the right thing in calling."

"Do I need to do anything to help," the younger man asked. "Is this something you would rather I handled?"

"No," Han responded. "She is one problem I will be happy to eliminate."

CHAPTER 112

"Did you get my email?" Maggie asked. She had called Dan as soon as she arrived back at the hotel in Chengdu. It was three o'clock in the morning in Houston, but she knew she had to call before Alex came to take her to dinner.

"What email? What time is it?" Dan sleepily asked as he booted up his computer. "What's happened? Are you okay?"

"Yes, I'm fine. I'm so sorry to wake you up, but I have just a few minutes to talk, and then I have to leave again," Maggie apologized. "I emailed you some pictures that I took today at the freight forwarder's warehouse. Things just don't add up."

"Okay, I have them now. What exactly am I looking at?" Dan questioned. "I can see the Utopia logo, but what is it on?"

"Those are the exhaust manifolds for the compressors." Maggie explained. "There was a box with at least half a dozen of them, maybe more. The problem is that those manifolds should never have been removed from the compressors. There's no logical reason for it."

"Did you ask anyone?" Dan inquired, suddenly afraid that someone might have picked up on her suspicions.

"I asked the warehouse manager, who looked like someone from central casting-but that's another story," Maggie rambled. "He said they were extra parts that were to be shipped to Houston when they got enough brought in for a load."

"I take it that his story doesn't work for you," Dan replied. "Any chance he's telling the truth?"

"I suppose there's always a chance, but I don't think so," Maggie answered. "I don't recall ever having a discussion about spare exhaust manifolds. It's just not something you ever replace. I could verify it with Alex, but I didn't think you would want me talking to him about it."

"You're right. Not just yet anyway," Dan agreed. "I know you really need to confide in Alex, but please humor me and don't talk about any of this to him. When you get back home, we will make a decision about Alex. There are some things you need to understand before we bring Alex into the circle, okay?"

"Okay. We'll deal with that later," Maggie replied. "Back to the pictures, what do you think it means?"

"You'll need to give me a little time to mull this over," Dan answered. "It has to be a clue to something, but at this time of the night, I'm not sure. Obviously there's something going on if there's no reason to remove the covers. Were the manifolds missing on any of the shipments that have already arrived in Houston?"

"Not that I heard about," Maggie answered. "I could check, but it would take some digging and would also raise a lot of questions as to why I'm asking. Whatever you need me to do, just let me know."

"Let's think about this for a few hours," Dan suggested. "Are you getting ready to go out for the evening?"

"Yes, Alex should be here any minute," Maggie told him.

"Call me when you get back in from dinner," Dan said. "That will give me some time to think and perhaps have some more questions to ask."

"Okay, I'll call," Maggie agreed. "I have to hang up now- Alex is at the door."

"Be very careful, Maggie," Dan warned. "Be aware of everything going on around you."

"Don't worry. You have me at the paranoid alert level," Maggie assured him. "I'm just praying you don't raise it to petrified."

CHAPTER 113

"How was your dinner?" Dan asked when Maggie called back. "Eat anything I would recognize?"

"We just stayed in the hotel tonight. We both had a very long day and didn't feel like fighting the crowds," Maggie explained. "I had some semblance of roast beef. Actually, it wasn't too bad."

"I've been thinking about what you told me about the exhaust covers," Dan said, jumping right to the point. "I still don't have an answer that I've thought all the way through, but I do have a question about something you said earlier— about the warehouse manager being another story by itself. What did you mean?"

"He just didn't fit the part," Maggie began. "First of all, he was too clean cut. Preppy clothes, clean nails, not your typical dock worker. His English was impeccable. He had to have studied in the States, which doesn't seem likely for a blue collar worker in China."

"Have you seen him before? Was he one of the guys in the pictures I sent you?" Dan asked.

"I didn't even think about the pictures," Maggie replied. "Let me look through them quickly. I know I haven't seen him before but, wait a minute, I think this is him. The photo numbered twelve. I think that is him. Who is he?"

"Number twelve is Zhang Chen, son of your buddy Zhang Han," Dan responded. "How very interesting, but it fits. Chen was educated in the East, Harvard to be exact, and you are correct, his skill set is way above that of a dock foreman. I'm sure that's not his day job, so the question begs to be asked, why was he there? My guess is that Han didn't want you asking too many questions to someone who just might give you an answer."

"Maggie, how many compressors arrive in each shipment?" Dan continued. "And, how often do the shipments arrive?"

"They are supposed to ship ten compressors at a time," Maggie answered. "How often is more difficult to predict. It depends on whether the plant is running up to capacity without any shutdowns. Unfortunately, those are a real problem; they happen quite often. I'll have to check to find out how many compressors have actually arrived and the time frame in which they were shipped."

"I think that would be very helpful," Dan replied. "I have a theory, but without knowing those numbers for certain, it's just that: a theory. See if you can find out when the next shipment is scheduled to arrive. Email me the information as soon as you can. Every minute could be critical."

"I'll get in touch with our corporate receiving office before I go to bed to get you the past history," Maggie said. "But I can tell you that there should be a shipment arriving in Houston just any day. I know one shipped out the first morning of our last visit, so the timing should have it there soon."

"Good job today, Maggie," Dan replied. "I don't know if you found something important or not, but the point is that you were watching, aware of anything that seemed out of the norm."

"These days, everything seems out of the norm." Maggie sighed as she hung up the phone.

CHAPTER 114

"Follow her if she leaves the hotel tonight," Han ordered. "Find a way to spike her drink and get her out of the restaurant-make it look inconspicuous."

"What if she is not alone," one of the men asked. "Do we take her companions as well?"

"No, only the woman," Han answered. "Too many missing bodies would cause trouble. Get her out of the restaurant and make sure she disappears forever."

The two men exited the limo and made their way into the hotel lobby to wait for their prey. Han wanted to follow them to make sure everything went according to plan, but he could not risk being seen by Maggie or any of her cohorts. As he had the driver pull away, his heartbeat was racing. They had not needed any bumps in the plan and the American woman had become a major bump. She asked too many questions and was too curious for her own good. The biggest problem was that she was smart. Han never underestimated his enemies, and he knew that soon enough Maggie would start putting the pieces together. He knew she would never guess about the plutonium, but she would figure out that something was being smuggled into Houston, and Han knew she would go straight to the authorities. He also knew that her disappearance would stir up trouble as well, but it was a risk he was willing to take. He could not afford to let Maggie live.

CHAPTER 115

"I checked the compressor receipts," Maggie said. "There seems to be an odd pattern. Each month ten compressors arrive in the States as scheduled. Eight of them arrive at Utopia's warehouse a week later. The other two are delayed by a couple of days more."

"Every time?" Dan asked.

"So far, it's been every shipment out of Chendgu," Maggie answered. "I can't imagine why two would get separated every month."

"When is the next shipment scheduled to arrive?" Dan asked.

"It should be there within the next week. Why?"

"I think it would be profitable to follow the shipment and find out what happens to those two compressors that seem to get delayed each month," Dan replied. "I have a buddy in Customs. I will get with him to coordinate the arrival time."

"Do you think those two compressors are the ones that the-"

"Careful. Remember that others could be listening," Dan warned. "To answer your question: Yes, I do. It makes sense."

"Sorry. I'm not used to this cryptic stuff," Maggie replied. "Will you let me know what you find out?"

"I will try," Dan replied. "You need to realize that it's safer if I don't tell you everything."

"Okay, but when this is all over you can tell me all of the details," Maggie said. "I understand that you can't at the moment."

"Maybe not even then," Dan explained. "There may be things I can never tell you. But never forget that you are serving your country."

"I'll let you know how I feel about being drafted when this is finished," Maggie shot back. "Keep in mind that I didn't exactly volunteer for service."

"I never forget for a moment who has put you in harm's way," Dan replied soberly. "It weighs on my conscience continually."

CHAPTER 116

"Two more days and we can head for home." Maggie sighed as they got off the elevator and crossed the lobby. "I'm always ready to leave, but this time I can barely stand the wait. I am so ready to be back in the States."

"I understand that feeling," Alex replied. "This has seemed like a particularly long trip. But fortunately this should be the last trip."

"Until something goes wrong at the plant, and you have to fly over to save the day," Maggie bantered. "At least my part of this project will be finished."

"I have no desire to 'save the day,'" Alex responded. "I may rack up huge phone bills, but I don't plan on any more frequent flyer miles to this side of the world."

The two continued to chat as they left the hotel, totally unaware of the men following them. Making their way through the crowded streets, Maggie and Alex finally arrived at Highfly Pizza. It was a loud, busy joint full of expatriates longing for a taste of home. They had to wait for a table, but eventually settled in for a fun evening. Maggie always enjoyed eating here because she was surrounded by English-speaking people. It wasn't that she could really understand any of the conversations, the noise level was way too high, but just the sound of familiar words made her relax.

One of the two men who had been following Alex and Maggie made his way to the bar, while the other waited patiently near the restrooms. At the bar, the man walked up behind the waitress and whispered in her ear as he slid his arms around her waist. Giggling, she pointed to the drinks sitting on a tray in front of her. Releasing his hold, he patted her butt and reached for the tray of drinks. On the way to the table, he sprinkled a powder into the drink meant for the American woman.

"I always like coming here," Maggie said as she took a sip of her drink. "It feels more like home."

"Doesn't it make you homesick?" Alex asked teasingly.

"Nope," Maggie laughed. "There's not enough Texans here for that. But at least it's not all Chinese."

The two continued to visit as they waited for their pizza to arrive. Maggie wanted to tell Alex about what she had seen in Shanghai, but knew that she couldn't break her word to Dan. She couldn't even ask if any of the compressors had arrived without manifold covers without opening up the entire mess, so she just chatted about life in general and tried to avoid talking about the project. The longer they visited, the stranger Maggie began to feel. At first she seemed a little lightheaded, but before too long the room started spinning around her.

"I suddenly don't feel very well," Maggie said as she grabbed the side of the table. "It's so hot in here."

"Are you okay?" Alex asked as he reached out to steady her. "You look really pale."

"No, I think I'm going to be sick," Maggie answered as she struggled to keep from passing out. "Maybe I need to go to the ladies' room."

"Let me help you," Alex said as he stood to help her out of the chair. "I'll walk you there."

"That's not necessary," Maggie replied, not wanting to cause a scene. "I'm sure I will make it just fine. I'll be right back."

The two men watched as Maggie wove her way across the crowded room. They had already made sure that no one else was in the restroom that might offer help to a sick fellow

Westerner. Maggie entered the restroom, sure that she was going to vomit at any moment and hoping that it would make her feel better. Instead, she was assaulted with wave after wave of dry heaves, each one more violent than the one before. She leaned against the wall, fearing that any moment she would hit the floor. After what seemed to be an eternity, she made her way to the door. She needed to get back to the table, to get Alex to help her back to the hotel.

As she opened the restroom door, the two men grabbed each arm and pulled her toward the door. Her mind tried to register what was happening and who these men were who were abducting her. She tried to scream, tried to find Alex, but her head was spinning and before she could make a sound, she fainted.

Alex, who had decided to check on Maggie, was walking towards the restrooms when he saw the two men dragging her toward the door.

"Hey, stop!" Alex screamed above the din of voices. "What are you doing? Stop!"

Running for the entrance, Alex knocked over chairs on his way and caused the entire dining room to stop talking and stare at the man frantically heading across the room yelling at two men who held a seemingly drunk woman between them. The men, aware that they were now the center of attention, let go of their hold on Maggie and ran out the door, disappearing in the crowd. Alex reached Maggie just before her head hit the floor.

After a moment of frozen silence, the restaurant manager rushed to Alex's side trying to help.

"Call an ambulance," Alex screamed. "And call the police."

Before the manager could react, an American man ran up to the group, reaching for Maggie's neck to check her pulse.

"I am a doctor," the man explained. "Please let me help you. There is no need to call the police. They are not very responsive to begin with and when they find out that an American is the victim, they will just walk away. Let's use our energy to take care of your friend."

The man continued to check Maggie's pulse and checked her pupils. As he touched her face, Maggie stirred.

"What happened?" Maggie asked. "Who were those men?"

"Please don't move," the doctor instructed. "Don't worry about the men, just tell me how you are feeling."

"Sicker than a dog," Maggie replied. "I tried to vomit, but nothing happened."

"Do you think you can sit up?" the doctor asked as he and Alex raised her back up against the wall. "How does that feel?"

"Like I'm on a merry-go-around," Maggie answered. "The room is still spinning."

The manager returned with cold rags and a bottle of ginger ale. This was not the first American he had seen who could not tolerate alcohol, but it was his first attempted kidnapping. He was shaking as he handed a rag to the doctor.

"Just sit here for a few minutes with this rag on your head," the doctor instructed. "Let's see if the spinning settles down."

"What did you have to eat?" the doctor asked Alex.

"Our food had not arrived yet, we were just having a drink while we waited," Alex explained. "She was perfectly fine when we arrived, but then in a few minutes she was complaining about not feeling well."

"Did you drink the same thing?" the physician continued with his questioning.

"Yes, we both ordered the same thing. Why?" Alex asked.

"She is not running a fever, so I doubt it's a virus. Which leads me to think that it was some kind of food poisoning," the doctor answered. "But since you had not eaten, then my thought turned to your drinks. The fact that you both had the same drink, yet you are not ill, leads me to think that her drink was spiked. Do you know of any reason someone would do such a thing?"

"No. Absolutely not," Alex reacted. "We know no one here. That's crazy."

"It's not as crazy as you might think, my friend," the doctor replied calmly, trying to reassure Alex. "This is China, and people—especially beautiful women—disappear all the time. It was obvious those two guys were trying to take her somewhere."

No one noticed the waitress who quietly slipped out of the watching crowd. The staff never saw her collect her belongings and slip out the kitchen's back door. She knew that no one would come looking for her if she left, but if she stayed, the American man might try to question her. She did not want to be involved.

After sipping on the ginger ale and being still for what seemed like an hour, Maggie wanted to move. She had been the star attraction for tonight's dinner theatre and she was ready to leave. After Maggie convinced Alex and the doctor that she was able to get up, the men helped her outside, where Alex hailed one of the many green taxis crowding the streets of Chengdu.

"Take her back to the hotel and make her be still," the doctor instructed. "When do you leave to go home?"

"The day after tomorrow," Alex replied.

"Get her to a doctor as soon as you get back," the doctor said. "Have them run a toxicology report and a complete blood workup. I'm sure she will be fine, but it never hurts to check things out. I doubt seriously that they gave her enough of anything to harm her over the long haul, that's not usually how they work, but she needs to be sure."

"Will do. I don't know how to thank you," Alex replied. "I'm grateful that you were there tonight."

"Well, I didn't do anything but observe her behavior," the doctor responded. "But I'm glad my presence made you feel better. Please be careful. This is not a friendly place, and Americans are not the most respected visitors. They love our money, but they don't like us."

"I understand," Alex said. "Thank you again."

As the taxi pulled away, Maggie leaned against Alex and closed her eyes. Before they reached the hotel, she was sleeping. Alex paid the driver and picked Maggie up out of the taxi, carrying her into the hotel and to his room.

This was one night he was not going to let her out of his sight.

CHAPTER 117

Dan's friend at Customs had called him late the night before to tell him that the Tiger Eye ship had docked and was going through the procedures to off-load. The manifest had shown compressors belonging to Utopia Energy, and a little more legwork revealed that the compressors would be leaving the Customs warehouse this morning. Dan had arrived before daylight and was almost ready to give up when he saw the ten tractor-trailer rigs, each loaded with a huge natural gas compressor, leave the Houston Port Authority and head west toward I-610. Following the convoy onto the Westpark Tollway, he watched as eight of the trucks went north on the West Beltway 8, while two of the trucks headed south. Knowing the destination of the eight trucks, he chose to follow the wayward two semis to find out where they were going.

It didn't take long before the two tractor-trailer rigs pulled into a large lot with an eight-bay building. Each of the drivers pulled into a bay and shut their units down. Dan watched as he passed by, but had trouble seeing into the building. He got out of his car, opened the hood, and made a small slit in a radiator hose. Then turning the car around, he drove into the garage lot with steam coming out from under the hood.

"Man, am I glad you guys are here," he said in his best down-home Texas drawl. "My car's steamin' like a locomotive. Think you could take a look at it?"

One of the mechanics strolled outside and opened the hood. When he found the faulty hose, he pulled Dan's car into one of the bays.

While Dan waited for his car to be repaired, he lingered around the shop. Taking his cue from others mingling in the garage area who seemed oblivious to the 'No Customers in Shop' signs, Dan wandered toward the two semis. The mechanics were busy taking off the manifolds and replacing them with different ones that had Utopia's logo stamped onto them.

"What's wrong with those?" Dan casually asked as he pointed to the discarded parts.

"Don't know," one of the men replied. "We just were told that they were defective and we needed to change them out."

Dan walked closer to the rejected manifolds and nonchalantly dropped a set of keys on the floor. On the key ring was a magnet that Dan subtly touched against one of the manifolds. The magnet was not attracted to the metal. As he picked up the keys, he tried to move the parts with his leg. The manifold did not move. Lead, he decided.

"Those things look mighty heavy," Dan remarked. "What do you do with the bad ones?"

"Some guy from the factory comes and picks them up," another one of the mechanics offered. "He comes pretty quick, sometimes before we have them changed out."

Dan continued to make small talk until his car was ready to go. He pulled out of the garage and parked on the edge of the property. Pulling out a map of Houston, he pretended to be looking for a location. There was so much traffic in and out of the garage that no one paid any attention to his dark sedan parked in the corner.

About thirty minutes had passed when a Chevy stake bed truck pulled into the lot and up to the bay doors where the two semis were parked. A dark-headed man, looking to be in his thirties, jumped out of the truck and started visiting with two of the mechanics. After a couple of minutes, the three men loaded the discarded manifolds onto the stake bed. After signing some papers on a clipboard, the men shook hands with the driver and went back inside the garage. The driver pulled out slowly, seemingly unaware of the dark sedan leaving the lot behind him.

Careful to stay far enough away, Dan followed the truck north for almost an hour. He slowed as the truck entered the lot of an apparently vacant steel building in Spring, Texas. Dan pulled into a parking lot a block from where the truck had stopped. From that vantage point, he could see the truck backed up to an overhead door. Dan could see that another man just inside the building was helping guide the driver as he backed the truck inside. Once the truck was inside, they closed the overhead door.

Dan continued to watch the building as he called his office. He needed someone to find out who owned the building. As he finished his call, the two men came out of a side door, got into a parked car and left. Still following far enough back not to gain any attention, he followed the men back into downtown Houston to the Global Market Complex. The driver dropped the passenger off in front of Bailey Worldwide Investments before parking the car in a lot adjacent to Kelly-Jones Communications.

Well, Dan thought, I wonder what the odds are on this being a coincidence.

CHAPTER 118

As Dan waited at the Global Market Complex, he tried to sort out the day's events. Deep in thought, he was startled when a call came through from his office.

"The building is owned by a holding company in Austin," Agent Brock reported to Dan. "They own a lot of real estate in the Houston Metro area."

"Who owns the holding company?" Dan questioned.

"Spencer Exploration, an oil and gas corporation" the man responded. "They're a family company, been around forever, since the early nineteen hundreds. My wife's father retired from there a couple of years ago. They own a chunk of Texas dirt, and about ten years ago formed a real estate division to handle all of their properties. Seems they are pretty good oilfield hands, but didn't know much about real estate management. So they hired an entire real estate team to run the offshoot."

"Does your father-in-law still know anyone who might help us quietly?" Dan inquired. "We need to know who is leasing the building without creating a lot of attention."

"Oh, I'm sure he does. He may be officially retired, but he spends a good part of every day there," Brock laughed. "He calls it 'consulting'. I call it bored with retirement."

"I call it a good situation for us," Dan commented. "Ask him to do a little snooping around."

CHAPTER 119

"My father-in-law just called," Agent Brock said as he walked into Dan's office later that afternoon. "The building you were asking about is rented to a Rick Oliver. No info on him."

"Really? Any chance of getting a look inside?" Dan asked.

"Glad you asked. It just so happens that Spencer Exploration is looking to sell that piece of property." The agent offered. "Seems my father-in-law told them he might know someone interested."

"Sounds like your father-in-law is an excellent consultant," Dan laughed. "Did he happen to set up an appointment?"

"Two o'clock this afternoon," Brock answered. "You are in the internet import business and need a warehouse to store your shipments."

"We need to have eyes on the Aghasi brothers to make sure they are nowhere near that building at two o'clock," Dan warned. "This needs to be a quiet visit."

"Oliver and Hardy have two teams already in place watching each office building and the parking lot," Brock explained. "They have your cell on speed dial should there be any movement."

"What about your father-in-law? Will he be there? Does he know not to mention the Bureau?" Dan asked, trying to think through the situation.

"He will meet us there to introduce us to the owner," the agent said. "Cover story is that I have a buddy who's looking for property. You're the buddy. It's simple, not deep enough for any slip ups and yes, he's cool with the Bureau part. Don't worry, this will work."

"I always worry," Dan laughed. "It's part of my charm."

CHAPTER 120

"The building was built back in the seventies," the real estate broker explained as he unlocked the front door. "There's 16,000 square feet of warehouse space plus another 1500 square feet for offices. I tried to contact my renters, to let them know we were coming, but the phone number they gave me was disconnected."

"How much longer do they have it leased?" Dan asked casually as he pretended to look at the office set up.

"The lease ran out three months ago, so they are just renting on a monthly basis," the broker answered. "They come to the office at the first of every month and pay the rent in cash."

"Cash? That seems an odd way to do business," Dan replied. "What kind of business does they do?"

"I don't really know. Some kind of repair business-computers, televisions," the broker responded. "I think they work for several repo companies. You know, fixing up the stuff so that they can resell it."

The men pretended to be interested in the office layout and made small talk about whom to give each office to if they purchased the building. What was striking about the space was the lack of office equipment.

"Did they furnish the office, or does it all go with the building?" Dan asked.

"This was all in the building from a tenant we had a couple of years ago," the broker answered. "He died, but no one ever came after the desks or anything, not that there's much here."

"It doesn't look like your current renter uses the office at all," Agent Brock chimed in. "There isn't even one computer here."

"Well, maybe you don't need computers for the repair business," the broker replied. "Why don't we head out to the warehouse area? I'm sure it will be quite adequate for your needs."

The men entered the warehouse area and were immediately struck by what was not there. The huge area was empty except for the truck and one workbench with two stools. Sitting on the floor were two unopened Sony television boxes.

Dan walked toward the stake bed truck parked just inside the overhead door. About ten feet behind the truck was a pile of manifolds with Utopia Energy's logo stamped on them. The two manifolds that he had seen loaded earlier from the garage were still on the truck.

"I don't know what all that stuff is," the real estate broker commented as he tried to refocus the group on the building's assets. "Obviously they don't need this large a space. You will notice the eight overhead heaters. They all work and the roof is just two years old. In the back corner, you can see the dock entrance. All of the doors are electric, so you don't have to worry about manually pulling them open and closed."

As the men walked back toward the office, the broker continued to spit out facts that none of them were interested in, but pretended to absorb. Dan lagged behind the others. He had seen something around the corner of the outside office wall and as he detoured to investigate, he had to catch his breath to keep from making any comment. Hanging on the wall were two hazardous materials rescue suits.

CHAPTER 121

Leaving the broker, the three men drove back to Houston. The silence in the car was deafening. The agents had lots to discuss, but did not want to talk in front of their guest.

"I know you guys can't talk about your investigation, but do you realize what you saw back there?" the older man asked.

"What exactly are you talking about?" Dan countered. He wanted to know if the man had seen the hazmat suits.

"Those compressor manifolds. The ones that had Utopia Energy stamped on them," the man replied. "Those have nothing to do with electronics repair-even I know that much-and those brand new televisions wouldn't be needing repair work done either."

"Mr. Stephens, I appreciate everything you have done for us," Dan patiently replied. "I need for you to do one more thing. I need you to forget anything you saw today. I know that is asking a great deal, but there are people's lives depending on your silence. Please do not discuss what you saw today, not even with your favorite son-in-law here."

"Understood. In another life I was with Special Forces, so you don't have to explain the importance of the situation to me," the gentleman respectfully responded. "Today did not happen."

Dan let the man off at Spencer Explorations' corporate office and the two agents finally were able to talk freely.

"I got the tag number off the truck," Brock said. "I'll run it when we get back to the office. Are those the manifolds you saw at the garage?"

"Yeah, that's them. There must have been fifteen or more of them there," Dan replied. "Did you see what was hanging on the side of the office?"

"No, what?" Brock asked.

"Two hazmat suits," Dan replied. "Complete with boots and lead gloves."

"Great to know, now that we've already been in there." Brock sighed. "Think we were exposed?"

"No way to tell what the levels are without measuring equipment, and that will take a warrant," Dan answered. "One thing's for sure: Our bad guys think they need the suits."

CHAPTER 122

"You both had the same drink?" Paul asked, amazed at the story he had just heard. "But you didn't get sick?"

"Same drink, I'm fine," Alex answered. "That's what made the doctor think her drink had been spiked. Apparently, this happens quite frequently, especially to beautiful women."

"It's true," Lilly interjected. "They kidnap women and sell them as sex slaves. Indonesia is full of such women."

The entire group, both American and Chinese, had been listening to a replay of Maggie's adventure at Highfly Pizza. Lilly translated as Alex told the group about the two guys who tried to abduct Maggie.

"Didn't you call the police?" John asked.

"I tried to get someone to call, but the doctor said it wouldn't do any good," Alex explained. "According to him, the police would have done nothing."

"He was probably right," David said. "Crimes to visitors are mostly ignored, the authorities have too many of their own people to deal with to worry about some other country's citizens. They are especially uninterested in Americans. Unless you are some high-ranking diplomat, whose problem might cause an international embarrassment, then you are out of luck."

Mason had been listening to the conversation, but made no comment. He had been too interested in watching Han's reaction to the story. Han, who usually tried to appear at least concerned for the American team, seemed to be angry. He had not said one word, but sat stoically, his jaw clenching and his hands made into tight fists. Mason had seen this look before, and it frightened him just as much now as it had the first time he had experienced Han's wrath. There was more to this incident than Maggie and Alex thought. Mason was sure that Han was involved.

"I know I'm changing the subject, but how was your trip to Shanghai?" David asked. "Was everything in order at Tiger Eye's shipping facility?"

"Well, let's just say that they're not a very friendly group," Maggie said after hesitating half a second too long. "They didn't seem to want to-"

"Enough of this mindless chatter," Han shouted, interrupting Maggie in mid-sentence. "We have work to do."

The Chinese team scurried to their seats while the Americans stood in silence, amazed at Han's outburst. Not only was he rude and out of line, but such a demanding tone seemed totally out of character for him. He had always been firm and somewhat inflexible, but he normally presented himself in a quiet, controlled manner with a slight smile on his face. This eruption was totally unexpected.

No one seemed more shocked than Mason. He knew instinctively that Maggie's trip to Shanghai and her incident in the restaurant were connected. He was not sure how, but he knew, none the less. Somehow this was all connected to the reason Han had used Mason to get the contract for Tiger Eye to be the freight forwarder.

The rest of the group settled around the table and the conversation quickly turned to the project at hand. Everyone seemed to try to focus on business and to avoid eye contact with Han, who had sat back in his chair at the end of the table and continued to stare at Maggie. For anyone watching, the hatred was palatable.

But the only one watching was Mason. As the meeting continued, Mason sat quietly, not participating in the discussions, but rather watching Han and trying to figure out exactly what was going on. There was a connection, he could feel it in his gut. Suddenly the pieces all came together, and he realized that Han must be using Utopia's compressors to smuggle something into the United States, and that Maggie had somehow compromised the situation on her visit to the shipping facility.

Whatever Maggie had seen had almost gotten her killed. Mason was certain that she wasn't being abducted to be sold as a sex slave. Han was behind this; he was going to have Maggie disappear forever. The realization shook him to his core. Han wasn't going to leave any loose ends … and Mason was a loose end also. He knew that Maggie was still in danger, but more important, Mason knew that he could be the next one to disappear. He had to do something quickly to make sure that didn't happen.

As the meeting continued, Mason formed a plan in his mind. Han had already proved that he had a long reach and that he could destroy Mason's happy little world in Houston. As much as that thought sickened Mason, he knew that he had to save his life, even at the expense of his lifestyle. If he could get back to Houston, he could go to the FBI or CIA or somebody and tell them about the smuggling operation. He had no idea what it was that was being smuggled, but it was important enough to Han to make sure Maggie didn't ruin the plan. Mason knew that the authorities couldn't save his marriage, or even his job, but perhaps they could save his life. He had to get to Houston.

When the group broke for lunch, Mason took his computer and headed out of the hotel. He walked down the street for several blocks before hailing a green cab to take him to the airport. On the drive there, he called his American travel agent to arrange an emergency flight to Beijing then on to Houston tomorrow. It would take him two days to get there, since it was already past noon, but at least he would be on his way. He always kept his passport with him, which was all he needed. Anything he had left in the hotel room could be replaced. His life could not.

CHAPTER 123

"We better head back to the conference room," Paul sarcastically commented. "We don't want to upset 'General Han' again."

The group laughed as they gathered their briefcases and left the restaurant. They had spent the better part of their lunch discussing Han's odd behavior. There was no precedence for his outburst, it was totally unexpected. They finally decided that they not only didn't care about Han's problems, but that they are were all ready to leave China. This had been a particularly long trip and an endless project. They were all ready to stay Stateside for a while.

When they returned to the room, the Chinese delegation was already seated, computers running. Han had apparently rattled their chain enough that they were trying not to antagonize him any further. It was obvious that Han's disposition had not improved during lunch. His face was still oozing anger. Even the Americans noticed that he seemed focused on Maggie.

The only one not present was Mason, which did nothing to improve Han's mood. None of the team had seen Mason since the morning session, but that was not unusual. Mason rarely joined the team for lunch, and they were not in the habit of keeping up with him. The thought occurred to several of them that he once again had left early for home. He had done it before, just deciding to leave a day early without a word to anyone. They were not concerned. In fact, not having to travel with Mason seemed like a bonus to them.

"We have not seen Mason since the morning session," Alex explained, tired of Han's attitude and indifferent to Mason's whereabouts. "Let's just finish up here so that we can all go home. Mason's presence is not necessary to complete our work."

"Mason's behavior is unacceptable," Han retorted.

"Perhaps so, but he's not here, so let's move on," Alex replied harshly. "We are all tired and, trust me, you are far more concerned about Mason than we are. He is not a crucial part of today's business. Now, let's continue."

The others in the room seemed to pause for just a split second. The Chinese were surprised that Alex had challenged Han, considering the Chinese leader's foul mood. The Utopia members were a little taken aback by the forcefulness of his tone, but were totally in agreement with his comments. Everyone quickly got back to work, with Han sitting silently at the end of the table. After about an hour, Han abruptly got up and left the room. The others looked at each other and continued their conversation without interruption. No one cared enough to discuss Han's departure.

In the lobby, Han motioned to the two men who accompanied him everywhere. He quietly said something to them and then returned to the conference room. The others looked up briefly when he returned, but did not miss a beat in their discussions.

The two men Han spoke with quickly went to work. They first checked with the concierge to see what he might know about Mason. He thought he remembered seeing the American leave the hotel around lunchtime, but could not be sure. The two men had been in the lobby all morning, but neither one of them had noticed whether Mason had walked through or not, they had been distracted watching the big screen television that was constantly playing in the lobby. They knew that if

Mason had slipped by them, then Han was going to be livid. It was not something they looked forward to experiencing.

They persuaded the concierge to take them to Mason's room and open the door. When they entered the room, they were surprised to find all of his belongings-clothes, toiletries, books. It did not appear that he had planned to go home, since all of his personal items were still where he had left them. If he was leaving the country, wouldn't he have taken his luggage? Perhaps he was just late getting back from lunch, they decided.

The two men decided that before they told Han they had no idea where Mason was, they would do a little more checking. One of the men called a friend at the airport and persuaded her to check the flights that had left Chengdu since noon heading to Beijing. After several minutes the friend reported that Mason had purchased a ticket on China Air just before departure. The flight had left about an hour ago.

One of the men entered the conference room just far enough to get Han's attention and motion for him to step outside. Without even excusing himself, Han left the room and joined the two men in the hallway.

"The American is on a flight to Beijing," one of the men reported. "The flight left about an hour ago. He left in a hurry, leaving his personal belongings in his room and purchasing his ticket just before the airplane left."

Han stood silent, but his anger could be seen just boiling under the surface of his stoic posture. For several moments he said nothing, letting his brain digest the new information and form a plan. The two men remained quiet, knowing that Han preferred not to be interrupted when he was trying to decide what to do next.

"Call the office in Beijing," Han finally spoke. "Have someone meet Mason at the airport. Be sure to make them understand that his body is never to be found."

With that directive, Han returned to the meeting and took his place as if nothing had happened. He did not change his behavior during the rest of the meeting and when the day was over, instead of saying goodbye as the rest of his comrades did, Han picked up his briefcase and left the room. The Utopia team was once again shocked at his actions. It was the last time that they were going to be meeting with the Chinese team, and while none of them expected a farewell dinner, they thought he at least would have acknowledged all of the work that the two teams had accomplished.

Personally, Maggie was glad that Han just left. He had glared at her all day for some unknown reason and she was relieved that he was gone. She had no idea what his problem was, but it was obvious that if looks could kill, she would have been dead hours ago. It had made the whole day uncomfortable and she was so ready to go home. She hoped she never had to set foot in China again.

"Are you up for another dining adventure?" Alex asked. He wasn't anxious to roam too far, but he certainly didn't want to let Maggie dine by herself, especially after last night's event.

"Not really," Maggie replied. "I think I would just rather eat in the hotel's restaurant and get to bed early. I haven't even started packing yet."

"That's a good plan for me," Alex responded, realizing he was relieved to stay in the relative safety of the hotel. "I'll come by your room in a couple of hours and we'll grab a bite to eat."

Maggie was anxious to get to her own room. She had not had a chance to call Dan and tell him about what had happened at Highfly Pizza or about Mason's repeated disappearing act. She had wanted to contact Dan last night, but when they got to the hotel Alex had insisted on taking her to his room. She couldn't call Dan from there and she needed to talk to him, to be calmed by his professional attitude.

"Ah, just the voice I needed to hear." Maggie exhaled when Dan finally answered his cell phone. "You have no idea how glad I am that you answered."

"What's wrong?" Dan immediately asked. He was constantly worried about Maggie, and her tone did nothing to ease his concerns. "Are you okay?"

"I'm fine now, but it has been an interesting couple of days," Maggie replied. "I wanted to call you last night, but I couldn't get away from Alex long enough to talk. There have been some weird things happening here. They may not have anything to do with your investigation, but they're odd just the same."

Maggie proceeded to tell Dan about the incident with the two thugs who had tried to kidnap her. She tried not to leave out any details because she had learned that sometimes the smallest point seemed important to Dan.

"How do you feel today?" Dan asked, knowing in his gut that this wasn't some sex-slave incident.

"Weak, mostly. I have had a dull headache all day, but that could be attributed to our charming host's asinine behavior today," Maggie answered. "I will be so glad to get home."

"Maggie, I know that I have said this before, but you really need to listen to me," Dan warned. "I don't believe for a minute that last night's incident was a random act. My gut tells me that you were a specific target, and if Alex hadn't been watching for you, those guys would have succeeded in snatching you."

"What would be their motive?" Maggie asked, not doubting Dan's intuition for a moment, but wanting to better understand her situation.

"I don't know, but you can bet it has to do with what you saw in Shanghai," Dan replied. "The way that visit played out has bothered me. Han's son being there and the exhaust manifold covers lying around. It just doesn't add up".

"Something else happened today that was odd also," Maggie said.

"Not another attempt on your life, I hope," Dan replied.

"No, nothing that dramatic, and honestly it may be nothing at all, considering the past," Maggie responded. "As I said before, Han was a real jerk today. He was rude and hateful. He stared at me all day. It was evil. His actions were out of character for him. He has never acted so poorly. Even his own countrymen seemed embarrassed. Then there was Mason's little disappearing act."

"What do you mean?" Dan asked, concerned that Mason had been snatched by the same guys who had gone after Maggie. Dan never had believed in coincidences and his training told him this was all connected.

"When we broke for lunch, Mason must have left," Maggie explained. "He did not return for the afternoon meeting. He did this once before: In the middle of the day, he just decided to head for Houston. No message left for us, just disappeared. It looks like he pulled the same stunt again."

"Have you tried calling his room?" Dan asked.

"No, I hadn't even thought of that," Maggie answered. "I just assumed he flew home."

"This is not the time for assumptions," Dan chided. "It could be that the same guys who tried to kidnap you were able to grab Mason. When we hang up, I want you to call his room and check on him. Let me know if he's there."

"Okay. Alex and I are going to stay in the hotel tonight for dinner," Maggie said. "If Mason doesn't answer when I call his room, I'll look for him in the lobby and in the restaurant. I'll call you back before I go to bed, but right now I have to start packing. I don't want any delays in the morning, I just want to get out of this place."

"I know I sound like a broken record, but considering what has happened, I think you understand," Dan said. "Be extra careful."

"I will, promise," Maggie soberly replied. "I'll call you in a few hours."

When Maggie hung up from talking to Dan, she tried to reach Mason in his room. There was no answer, so she decided to call his cell phone, but it just went to voice mail. A sick feeling rose in the pit of her stomach, but she tried to calm herself. She would look around in the hotel tonight. Surely she would see Mason coming or going, as was his regular routine.

In the meantime, she needed to pack. She was finally going home.

CHAPTER 124

"Tonight, late, I want you to go to the American woman's room and take her," Han instructed his two bullies. "Make sure you keep her quiet and get her out of the hotel without being seen."

"Where do you want us to take her?" one of the men asked.

"I don't care where you take her, as long as no one ever finds her."

CHAPTER 125

It is good to see you, Brother Imad," Mohammed said as he embraced the physician. "I trust you have been well."

"Yes, I am well and it is good to see you and Tarik as well," Imad replied, trying to sound sincere. "Let's go inside. I made reservations for us."

"A good thing, I think, considering the crowd," Tarik commented. "This is apparently a very popular restaurant."

"Yes, the Cairo Pyramid is the most popular Middle Eastern restaurant in Nashville, always busy, and very loud," Imad explained. "No one pays any attention to anyone else's conversation and it's too crowded to be remembered."

"Perfect," Tarik shouted as they pushed their way through the crowd waiting to get inside.

Once they were seated, Mohammed scanned the crowd. It was indeed a very diverse group of people, mostly in their twenties and thirties. There were groups of single women having dinner, as well as families with young children. Imad had chosen well, he thought. No one would ever remember them being here.

The three men engaged in harmless small talk until their waiter had brought their food. While there was really no chance of anyone being able to listen to their conversation above the din of the crowd, they did not take any chances. They waited until they were less likely to be interrupted to settle into a serious discussion.

"Are your men still in place, ready to carry out Allah's will?" Mohammed asked.

"Yes, they are," Imad replied. "They are just waiting for instructions."

"Before we leave tonight, we will transfer two televisions from our vehicle to yours," Mohammed began. "You are to deliver them to two of your men as soon as possible. They are to keep them well hidden, even from their families, until they get further instructions. Most important, they need to plug the televisions into electricity and keep them plugged in until they get the call to complete the mission."

"When the time is right, we will contact you with detailed orders," Tarik continued the conversation. "Basically you will advise each man to return the television to a specific Walmart store. They will then find a location within a block or two radius where they can video the event. When the mission is complete, they will send the videos to you. Mark each one as to the location filmed, and send them to us."

"Why video it?" Imad questioned. "Will it not be all over the evening news?"

"Only the aftermath, not the initial explosion," Mohammed interjected. "Besides, we need the uncut versions to show the truth to the world. The infidels are capable of exploiting any situation. We need to be able to have real proof of the event."

"When will this all happen?" Imad continued his questioning, his stomach churning with the thought of so many deaths and injuries.

"In time, my brother," Mohammed answered. "It is not necessary or prudent that you have that information tonight. We will give you plenty of notice."

"We will need to meet with you one more time to bring you two more televisions," Tarik advised. "As well chosen as this place is, we cannot risk coming here again. Be thinking of another location. We will contact you in four to six weeks to set up a meet."

The three finished their meal without further discussion of their intentions. They talked about their college days, and for a little while, Imad was able to enjoy their company and forget about the situation that he had allowed himself to get caught up in.

Not until he was preparing for bed did the nausea return. It was a long sleepless night for the man who had vowed to "do no harm".

CHAPTER 126

Mason had not been able to settle down during the flight from Chengdu to Beijing. During the ride to the airport, he had called his travel agent in Houston who arranged for his flight to Beijing and for his hotel reservation at the Crown Plaza Lido. He didn't want to spend the night, but his flight arrived too late to make any connection to the U.S.

During the flight, he had decided that when they landed in Beijing, he would try to book a flight to some European country. It didn't matter where, as long as he got out of China. He could figure out how to get home from there. Lost in these thoughts as the flight unloaded, Mason did not see the two men waiting just inside the terminal, but they recognized him immediately from the photo that had been emailed from Chengdu. They followed him as he found the men's room and waited patiently for him to finish his business. As he walked back into the concourse area, the men caught up with him, one on each side.

"Good evening, Mr. Williams," one man said staring straight ahead. "I trust your flight was comfortable."

Mason hesitated for just a second, but never stopped walking. "How do you know me?" he asked.

"You are a friend of Han's," the second man answered. "He asked us to meet you and take you to your hotel."

"How did he know I was here?" Mason asked, mostly to himself.

"Han knows everything," the man answered. "We have a car waiting outside."

"I have decided not to stay in Beijing tonight," Mason replied, frantically looking at the monitors as they walked, looking for a flight he could catch. "I am needed at home for a family emergency and I cannot lose a night by staying over."

"There are no flights this evening to the US," the first man explained. "You will have to stay over."

"I am aware of that," Mason responded, trying to sound calm and in control. "I plan to fly to Paris, then to the US. There is a flight leaving in an hour."

"That would not get you home any sooner," the second man stated, as the three of them continued down the concourse, heading for the exit. "You will be more refreshed if you get a good night's sleep."

"Thanks just the same, but I would rather keep moving," Mason replied.

"We are here to escort you to your hotel," the first man firmly responded as he opened his jacket to reveal the gun secured safely within reach. "There will be no more discussion."

Mason walked in silence, trying to decide if he should make a run for it, screaming as he went to try to attract attention. His panic almost chose this course of action until his brain kicked in. He could not speak the language, no one would understand him, and they would shoot him on the spot anyway. This was China-they could make up any story about him and no punishment would come to them. Besides, he would still be dead. He decided to go quietly with them and hope there was some chance to escape along the way.

Outside the terminal, a car was waiting for them. It took Mason several minutes to realize that they were headed in the opposite direction from the Lido. He mentioned this to his escorts, who chose to look straight ahead and remain silent. He tried to get them to respond several times as they traveled, but the men continued their silent treatment of him. They drove for another hour and pulled into what looked like a construction site. The rain had sent the workers home early, so there was no one at the site to witness the car's arrival. The driver followed the construction equipment's path down into a huge hole that was being excavated.

"We get out here," one of the men ordered.

When Mason hesitated, the second man backhanded him with the butt of a revolver, nearly causing Mason to black out. The men yanked him from the back seat and dragged him across the site to an area that was being back-filled. Before he could get to his feet, they had pumped several rounds of hollow-core bullets into his body. He never knew what hit him.

One of the men started up the backhoe, pushed Mason's body into the ravine, and covered the area with dirt. It was all over in less than half an hour. The two men brushed off their suits and returned to the car that had been waiting for them. On the trip back into downtown, they made the phone call to Han.

CHAPTER 127

This was the last shipment of food scheduled to arrive in Pyongyang from China. For the past ten months, Tae's informant in the Foreign Affairs office had alerted Tae when the shipments were scheduled to arrive, and the CIA agent had watched from the shadows as Kim Cheoul-su met each ship and was greeted by Zhang Chen. He assumed tonight would be no different.

Tae was settling in for the wait. The ship was scheduled to dock around ten o'clock but he always showed up at least an hour earlier, just in case the plans had changed. Half an hour into the wait, Kim Cheoul-su's car pulled up near where the freighter always docked. No one left the car. Tae waited.

Soon the freighter arrived and Tae could see Chen waiting on the deck, just as he always did, searching for Kim. About that time, the car doors opened. Kim stepped out, accompanied by his wife who was carrying their son. Tae hurriedly snapped pictures of the family before Kim nervously ushered his family onto the ship. As soon as they were on board, Chen escorted them out of sight. Another man left the ship and drove Kim's car away from the ship, returning fifteen minutes later on foot.

Within moments, the usual Army entourage arrived to offload the food shipment, a task that usually took about two hours to complete. Tae was often bored and drowsy during the unloading of the ship, but tonight his senses seemed more alert. Everything seemed different tonight. In the past, Kim would stay on-board until the military had left and then would casually return to his car and make the thirty-plus-mile trip back to Pyongyang. But, Tae thought, in the past Kim came alone, never with his family. In the past, his car stayed on the dock during the off-loading process. In the past, the hair on Tae's neck did not stand at attention.

On schedule the Army completed the transfer of food and left the port in a long convoy. Tae waited. As soon as the military was away from the area, the men on the ship began to prepare to leave. It was near midnight, long past the normal sailing times. Tae searched the ship constantly with his goggles to try to locate any sign of Kim and his family. There were only sailors visible. Within a few short minutes the ship was pulling out of the berth and headed toward the locks that would allow it to leave Taedong River and enter Korea Bay on its journey back to China. Kim and his family had never left the ship.

CHAPTER 128

"Are you just worn out or am I terrible company?" Alex asked, grinning as they waited on their food to arrive. The restaurant was fairly busy and the service was a little slower than usual.

"I'm sorry. You are wonderful company. I guess I'm just so tired and ready to go home," Maggie replied. "What were we talking about?"

"We were talking about going to your ranch in Montana when we get back," Alex patiently explained. "I know it would be good for you to have a few days to decompress."

"You're probably right. That whole scene last night has left me more shaken than I realized," Maggie admitted. "It would be great to be in the mountains for a while. You will love it there. It's so peaceful and beautiful."

The waitress brought their food and the two of them settled into a long conversation about the ranch and Maggie's memories of the times spent there with her family. She slowly calmed down as the evening continued, but Alex noticed that she watched everyone who walked into the restaurant. He wondered if she was afraid the two men from the night before might return.

"Maggie, last night was an isolated event," Alex finally said. "Those guys are not going to show up here tonight. You don't have to keep watching the doorway for them."

"I suppose you're right," Maggie replied, unaware that she had been so obvious or that he had been watching her so closely. She didn't dare tell him that she wasn't watching for the two men from the previous evening. "I will just be so glad to get out of here."

"I know, I will be happy if I never have to come back, although that's probably just wishful thinking," Alex laughed, trying to lighten her mood. "I have a feeling there will be plenty of problems even after everything is supposed to be finished."

"Don't take this the wrong way, but I'm glad it will be you that has to handle those issues," Maggie admitted. "I'm ready to stay home for a while. Maybe that's what Mason did today. Maybe he had stayed as long as he could and just skipped out early again."

"Probably. It wouldn't be the first time," Alex replied. "But it was rather tacky, you have to admit."

"Yes, but that's typical of his behavior," Maggie agreed. "Still, after what happened to me last night, maybe we ought to check on him. The front desk will know if he checked out. Why don't we stop by there on our way back upstairs?"

"If it will make you feel better, but frankly I think he just split," Alex answered. "Trust me, no one would kidnap him to be a sex slave."

"Humor me." Maggie smiled. "And please don't go down that road. I don't need a visual of Mason and sex in any form."

They finished their dinner and then made their way to the lobby to talk with the attendants on duty. No, they replied, Mr. Williams had not checked out, but none of them remembered seeing him since morning. Maggie asked the concierge to phone the room and when there was still no answer, she convinced him to check the room in case Mason was ill. Alex thought she was overreacting, but went along with her to ease her fears.

When they reached the room, the concierge knocked and when there was no response, he opened the door. All of Mason's personal items were still there. No attempt had been made to start packing, as the luggage was still in the closet. His computer was missing and it didn't look like he had been in the room all day. Maggie knew something was wrong. She needed to call Dan, but had to get away from Alex first.

"He's probably just out for dinner," Alex tried to reassure her, but he was concerned. It was getting late and they had a very early flight. Mason should have at least started packing. The fact that his computer was not in the room bothered Alex as well. Mason would not have taken his computer to dinner.

"Your friend is right, miss," the concierge. "I'm sure he is enjoying a wonderful meal. It looks the same as when the others checked earlier. I am sure he will return soon."

"What others?" Maggie snapped. "Who else has been looking for him?"

"Two men, earlier this afternoon," the concierge answered, realizing that he had said too much.

"Who were the men?" Alex demanded.

"I do not know," the man responded. "They said they were part of your group from the meeting room and that they were trying to find Mr. Williams so that you could get back to work."

"Did you know them? Have you seen them here before?" Maggie asked, her heart racing.

"Yes, I have seen them here many times," the man replied, failing to mention that he had always seen them waiting in the lobby, never going to the meeting room. "Is something wrong? Is Mr. Williams supposed to be with you?"

"No, no he is not supposed to be with us," Alex answered, trying to calm the situation. "We just haven't seen him for a while and wanted to make sure he was okay. I will leave a note here for him to call me when he returns."

The three left the room and the concierge headed back downstairs, happy to be away from their questions. He would watch for the men tomorrow and warn them of what happened tonight. He did not want any trouble from either side, but the Americans were leaving and the two men were definitely Chinese.

"Do you really think everything is okay?" Maggie asked as they headed back toward their rooms.

"No, but the concierge realized that he had said too much," Alex answered. "I didn't want to spook him. We may need him again. Did you notice that Mason's computer was not in the room?"

"Yes, I did. That's not something he would take to dinner with him," Maggie replied. "I don't think he skipped out early, since all of his clothes are still here."

"Something is not right. First, last night's episode, and now this," Alex commented. "I think we might need to contact the American Consulate. Mason may show up tomorrow morning, but considering everything that's happened, I would hate to think that we lost valuable time by waiting until morning."

Maggie knew that she couldn't let Alex call the consulate, not just yet anyway. She was troubled about what to do, but if she went back to her room alone to call Dan, Alex might contact the authorities without her knowledge. She also knew that Dan would not be happy with what she was about to do, but he would just have to get over it.

"Before we do that, I think we need to talk," Maggie said. "And then we need to make a different phone call."

CHAPTER 129

Tae left the dock at Namp'o and made the trip back to Pyong-yang as quickly as possible. As usual, there was little traffic and he was careful not to draw attention. As soon as he was safely in his suite at the hotel, he took his satellite phone from its hiding place. It was a tool he rarely used, but tonight's activities warranted the need.

"Major changes here. It seems that our goose and his gaggle have gone for a swim," Tae cryptically reported.

"We'll have our big eye keep a watch on them," the CIA contact in Dandong replied. "We should visit soon."

"I should be able to leave within the hour," Tae said. "Perhaps you will have more news by the time I get there."

"With any luck, I'll have your vacation plans finalized," the contact said. "Bring your treasures with you."

Tae ended the call with the understanding that his time in Pyongyang was over. If Kim Cheoul-su and his family were defecting, especially with nuclear material, then the govern-ment crackdown would put Tae in too much danger. As loyal as Joo had been as an informant, he could not be depended on to keep his silence. He would be at the center of the inves-tigation because of his closeness to the Minister, and he and his family would be extracted by another team. Tae quickly packed the phone, tablet, and camera into a backpack. He hid the camera's memory card in a slot in the sole of his shoe. He took the stairs and exited a back door without encountering anyone. When he pulled out of the parking lot, it was almost

3 a.m. If nothing went wrong, he would be in Dandong in time for breakfast.

CHAPTER 130

"You've got to be kidding me!" Alex responded when Maggie had finished telling him what Dan suspected. "You think Mason is smuggling an atomic bomb into the States? That's crazy."

"First of all, I said 'nuclear material,' not atomic bomb," Maggie replied, trying to remain calm while Alex absorbed what she had told him. "Secondly, I didn't come up with this theory, the FBI did that all by themselves."

"I think your friend Dan has been watching too many movies," Alex continued as he paced about Maggie's room. "The FBI gets a little nuts sometimes. Remember that they were investigating Collin to see if he had passed on any secrets. They bark up the wrong tree frequently."

Maggie didn't know what to say. She had already decided that the investigation of Collin was really a look into Alex's life, to see if he might be the traitor. She also knew that Dan had found something during that search that made him hold back from involving Alex in this craziness. She had not yet figured out what Dan had discovered, and she wasn't sure tonight was the time to try to find out. Her silence did not go unnoticed.

"What? Why are you not saying anything?" Alex questioned. "What do you know that you aren't telling me?"

"Alex, please calm down. I need you to have a rational thought process right now," Maggie replied quietly. "We could be in trouble here, and now is not the time to chase rabbits that we don't want to catch."

Alex continued wearing a path into the carpet, running his hands through his hair. He had so many thoughts running across his brain, but the one that kept popping to the front was Collin. And Maggie's behavior to his comment. Then it dawned on him: Collin wasn't the target of a federal probe. They had been looking into Alex, and Collin got caught in the crosshairs. The FBI thought he might have been the one involved in a smuggling ring.

"They weren't interested in Collin at all, were they?" Alex asked as he finally sat down. "They were checking me out, to see if I was involved in this mess in China."

"I don't know that for sure, but that's the conclusion that I came to," Maggie replied.

"They have to know that I'm not a part of any of this. I would never betray my country. Besides, they obviously suspect Mason from what you have told me," Alex rambled, mostly to himself. "If they know all of this, why did Dan not come to me instead of you? Why would he put you at such risk?"

"You'll have to ask him that question," Maggie answered, not sure how far to probe. "Look, he apparently had some reason that kept him from using you, but I don't know what it is. Maybe he thought you were too close to the situation in some way."

"Lilly. It has to be about Lilly," Alex finally responded after several moments of deep thought.

"What are you talking about?" Maggie asked hesitantly, not sure she really wanted to hear the answer.

"What Dan discovered in his investigation was that I have a connection with Lilly," Alex explained. "He had pictures of the two of us that could have been interpreted differently from reality. Dan thought that Lilly and I were lovers."

"What kind of pictures would lead him to that conclusion?" Maggie asked, holding her breath.

"Nothing like what you're thinking," Alex continued. "Pictures of us in the park, close to each other, whispering quietly. His conclusion was understandable, but entirely off the mark."

"I could use a little more explanation here, if you don't mind," Maggie responded, trying not to come to any conclusions herself, but failing miserably. She remembered seeing them in the park and in the hotel, and she knew in her heart that she, too, believed that they might be lovers.

"I'm sorry, sweetie," Alex said as he reached for her hand. "I should have been clearer. Lilly is Collin's sister. She and I pass letters and pictures back and forth between her parents and Collin. That's all that's going on, but from the eye of a camera … "

"But why are you being so secretive? What's the big deal?" Maggie asked, instantly relieved and ashamed at what she had thought.

Alex told Maggie more of what had happened to Collin years earlier. He explained how the Chinese government was still angry about Collin's defection and how Lilly and her family were under constant surveillance. He explained the great risk she was taking in passing letters through Alex. They had to be careful, secretive. It was the only way to protect Lilly and her parents.

"I can't even begin to tell you how relieved I am with the truth," Maggie replied. "But you need to be more cautious. If the FBI has pictures of the two of you, the Chinese could as well."

"That was basically what Dan said." Alex responded. "He warned me to be careful."

"So that's why he wouldn't tell me why he didn't want to involve you," Maggie commented. "He was trying to protect Lilly. He didn't want any more people knowing what was going on than necessary. You know, I can appreciate his protection of your situation, but I have to admit, he opened the door of my imagination to scenarios that I didn't want to think about."

"I'm so sorry. Dan and I both put you in a difficult spot," Alex apologized. "I should have been more open with you. If I had, then Dan could have used both of us and not put you in such danger alone."

"Water under the bridge now," Maggie replied, trying to refocus on the immediate situation. "What we have to do at this point is to call Dan and tell him about Mason. He already knows that Mason skipped out of today's meeting. I was supposed to look for Mason during dinner tonight and then call Dan with an update. He's waiting."

CHAPTER 131

Tae was exhausted when he arrived in Dandong. The drive itself was enough to make anyone weary, but the added danger of being captured along the way weighed heavily on Tae's mind. The backpack was stored in a hidden compartment inside the back bench seat, but it was far from foolproof. Tae knew that if he had been caught, he would have been executed. He also knew that even though he was back in China, he was far from safety. He could, however, operate here much easier than in North Korea.

He made his way to the hotel supply business and entered through a side door. His counterpart was waiting for him. It had been a profitable few hours in the intelligence world.

"I am glad to see you safely here, my friend," the supplier said. "I have been worried."

"I too am happy to be out of that mess," Tae sighed as he dropped the backpack on the table. "I have always worried about my exit strategy out of Pyongyang, but it actually was rather easy in the end."

"It wouldn't have been if you had waited any longer," his friend reminded him. "As soon as Kim Jong-un discovers that his Foreign Affairs Minister has flown the coop, it will get ugly quick. Especially if he finds any nuclear material missing."

"So, do we have any news yet? Do we know anything about Kim Cheoul-su?" Tae asked.

"We know that the ship he left on is running wide-open in a path back to Shanghai," the man replied. "Satellite photos have shown a woman and a child on the deck from time to time. We have assets in place at Tiger Eye's warehouse at the port. We will know the moment they dock."

"That's good, but now this asset needs to get some rest. It's been a long time since I last slept," Tae said, rubbing his eyes. "I'm taking over the cot in your storage room."

"What about dinner?" the agent asked. "I thought I could tell you all about your new assignment."

"In the morning, my friend, in the morning."

CHAPTER 132

After talking with the Interpol officer, Dan closed the blinds on his office windows, sat back down, and propped his legs up on the desk. He closed his eyes in an attempt to focus and to calm his breathing. He had to organize all of the thoughts that were racing through his mind and devise some sort of acceptable plan.

Okay, he thought, how does the timeline progress? Habib contacts al-Qaeda, who then calls Yi. Yi then makes contact with Han who in turn, makes a new friend with a North Korean who wants to defect. In the meantime, Utopia Energy's compressors are being shipped stateside with lead exhaust manifolds that are being replaced once they have cleared Customs. Habib's cousins are collecting the lead manifolds, buying lots of televisions, and going on road trips.

They have got to be smuggling nuclear material out of North Korea into the United States using the compressors as a cover, Dan concluded. Han is using Mason to control the shipping contract so that the manifolds can be switched before leaving China. That's what Maggie saw when she visited the freight forwarder's warehouse.

Maggie. Dan suddenly sat straight up, realizing what his first action must be before anything could be done to shut down the operation: He had to get Maggie out of China.

CHAPTER 133

"That must have been a great dinner. It's been hours since we talked," Dan said immediately when his cell rang, doing little to hide his worry. "Please tell me you are okay."

"I'm fine, but Mason may not be," Maggie responded, getting right to the point. "We think something is wrong."

"We? Is there someone else there with you?" Dan asked, his heart racing.

"Alex is here. I've told him everything. Before you get mad about that, just please understand that I had to," Maggie started defending herself. "He was about to call the American Consulate, so I had to tell him what was going on. Why didn't you tell me about Alex's secret, instead of pretending that he might be involved?"

"Because it was just that: A secret. I didn't need to further compromise a delicate situation," Dan explained, relieved that Alex had told Maggie about Lilly. Maybe now Maggie would be safer, with Alex aware of the situation. "Something must have happened to get you to tell Alex what I specifically asked you not to tell him."

"It has, so save your attitude for when we get home," Maggie snapped, the stress beginning to get to her. She just wanted out of China. Now. "I'm sorry, I didn't mean to be rude. It's just all been too much this trip."

"I'm sorry also," Dan apologized. "Tell me about Mason. Why do you think something is wrong?"

"I didn't see him in the lobby or the restaurant tonight," Maggie began. "After dinner, Alex and I checked with the front desk, and Mason had not checked out and none of the employees had seen him since early this morning. We talked the concierge into opening his room. All of his belongings are still there with the exception of his computer. We don't think he would have taken the computer with him to dinner, but we also don't think he would have left for home without his clothes and stuff."

"If Mason had left in a hurry, how would he have booked a flight out?" Dan asked, his mind already miles ahead of Maggie's. "Would he have used the hotel service or called himself?"

"If he had used the hotel, they would have known," Maggie commented. "I doubt he would have made the reservation himself. He would have probably called our corporate travel group in Houston and had them make all the arrangements."

"Okay, here's what I want you to do," Dan instructed. "Do not leave the hotel. In fact, stay together as much as you can. I need you to call the travel agent and see if you can find out if Mason had them book a flight for him today. Get all the info they have. I have to make a couple of calls myself. I will call you back in about an hour."

"Dan, do you think something has happened to Mason, or are we just all paranoid after what happened to me?" Maggie asked, frightened to hear the answer.

"Let's just say that I don't think you're paranoid," Dan answered. As he hung up the phone, he was praying a silent prayer.

CHAPTER 134

"This doesn't sound good at all, my friend," Joseph Lee commented after Dan had informed him of the latest happenings with the Utopia team. "Do you have any information at all on any reservations Mason may have made? Could it be that he just decided to bail out?"

"Well, that wouldn't be out of the range of possibilities with this guy, but I still think he would have taken his luggage," Dan replied. "After what happened to Maggie the night before, it's just not likely that these are separate incidences. I'm afraid our Utopia friends have inadvertently become an issue for Han's business arrangement with Cai Yi."

"That's a very real possibility," Joseph agreed. "What do you need for me to do on this end?"

The two agents spent the next half hour working on the details of a plan to get Maggie and her coworkers safely back to Houston. It would require a great deal of preparation, but they felt it was all justified. Han's stakes were too high to let the whole plan fall apart over a couple of unimportant Americans. The FBI needed to get Utopia's team out of China, quietly, and then work on stopping any terrorist plot in the works.

"I think this will work," Joseph decided after the two finalized their plan. "I will make the call and have agents in place in about ninety minutes. You inform Utopia to be ready to move."

"They will be," Dan assured him. "Thanks for all your help."

"Thank me when they are safely in Houston."

CHAPTER 135

"Mason called the agency in Houston just after we broke the session for lunch," Maggie reported to Dan when he called back. "They booked a flight for him that left Chengdu at two o'clock and arrived in Beijing around 5 p.m. They reserved a room for him at the Crowne Plaza Lido in Beijing." He's scheduled to fly out in the morning at ten o'clock."

"Thanks for the info. I'll check the flights and the hotel," Dan replied. "But first, we have a change of plans for tonight. I need you to have everyone pack up and be ready to leave in an hour."

"Leave? Where to?" Maggie asked, fear creeping into the pit of her stomach. "Who's everyone?"

"Everyone on your team," Dan answered. "Get them to meet in your room. Someone will come to your room in about an hour and move all of you to the Consulate. The accommodations won't be as fancy as where you are, but they will be more secure."

"Secure? You think we are all in danger?" Maggie asked.

"Probably not, but let's look at this logically. You were drugged and almost kidnapped. Mason has disappeared," Dan explained. "We know that there are people surrounding you that have bigger schemes in play than just your compressors. So, yes, it's possible that the whole team has been targeted, but from what you tell me about the level of involvement of the other members, it's a small possibility. Still, it's the premise we're working on tonight to convince the others to go with you to the Consulate."

"How will we know who the people are that are coming to get us?" Alex asked via the speaker phone. "How will we know they are with you and not the bad guys?"

"Maggie will recognize one of the agents who will be coming for you," Dan answered, realizing that the anxiety level was rising for both Maggie and Alex. "You will be safe with them."

"So what exactly are we supposed to tell the others?" Maggie asked. "Surely you don't want them to know what is really going on?"

"No, of course not. Just tell them that I convinced you to report your incident to the American Consulate, and that along with Mason being AWOL, the officials there felt it would be prudent for you to stay in their facilities until you leave for home. We will use the cover story that Americans are being targeted by some of the Chinese gangs."

"Dan, what about when we get to Beijing?" Alex interjected. "Will we be safe there during our layover?"

"Only the others are going to Beijing as planned," Dan explained. "You and Maggie will be heading in a different direction. We'll leave your current reservations in place in case someone is checking the airline's computer. By the time they figure out that you are not on the plane to Beijing, you'll be miles away."

"If they have the power to check the airline records for the flight we're supposed to be on, can't they find out the one we will really be on?" Maggie asked.

"You and Alex will be traveling on different passports, which the Consulate will have ready for you. You are not to tell the others of this change in plans," Dan continued. "We will have some explanation for them in the morning."

"Why can't we tell the others?" Maggie asked, weary from all the covert arrangements.

"Maggie, there are spies everywhere in China. If your team knows about the change and are overheard talking in the car or at the airport, your cover could be compromised," Dan answered. "The locals that work for the Consulate have had background checks, but nothing is set in stone. Any one of them could be persuaded to spy for the promise of money or the threat of harm. That's why nothing important is ever discussed in their presence."

"You're going to have to come up with something better to tell them than Chinese gang activity to justify Maggie and me taking a different flight," Alex suggested. "These guys may not be very adventurous, but they aren't stupid."

"I'm counting on them being a little shell-shocked by the whole idea of the American Consulate coming to get them in the middle of the night," Dan admitted. "Hopefully this will all happen so fast that they won't question too much until we get them back in Houston. By then I will have a better cover story in place."

"Time is slipping by, so you must go to the others and get them ready to leave," Dan continued. "We will talk again when you are safely inside the Consulate."

Alex decided it was safer to visit each of the team members rather than risk using the telephone. He left Maggie to pack and quickly made the rounds before gathering his own belongings. He must have been convincing, because none of the others questioned his instructions.

CHAPTER 136

One of the agents who came for them was the woman Maggie had met in the park, the same woman who had given her the pictures to review. The agents were professional but not friendly, which only underscored the seriousness of their situation. David, John, and Paul were confused, but did not ask any questions. They were taking their cue from Alex and Maggie, both of whom were submerged deep in their own thoughts.

Dan had been correct: The accommodations were not on the Crowne Plaza level, but they were comfortable enough. More important, they were safe. The female agent showed them each to their rooms and then took Maggie and Alex downstairs to a communications area where they could speak with Dan via a secure phone line.

"Did you have any trouble convincing the others of this move?" Dan asked.

"Not really. They seemed to buy into the story," Alex replied. "But I'm not sure how long they will continue to believe it, especially with Maggie and me not leaving with them in the morning."

"It only has to work for another few hours," Dan assured him. "The important thing is that you are safe tonight. Tomorrow morning, the two of you will travel as Carson and Rita Henry. You will fly from Chengdu to Singapore, then on to Tokyo. From there you will travel to San Francisco. You will be met at each stop by a member of the diplomatic security who will pose as a friend who is visiting with you while you are waiting for the next flight. Once you are in

San Francisco, you will be accompanied by FBI agents who will stay with you overnight and take you back to the airport the next morning for your flight to Dallas, where I will meet you and fly with you into Houston."

"Are you sure this is not overkill?" Maggie asked.

"Maggie, we have to look at the big picture," Dan responded. "These guys have gone to a lot of trouble to arrange this entire smuggling ring. There are many more details than I can share with you, but just understand, their investment doesn't remain within the borders of China. Neither does their reach."

Dan's comment sobered all three of them. While only Dan had an insight to the depths of the situation, Maggie and Alex both realized what Dan was not telling them. This was so far outside the range of their life experiences that they were unable to focus. They both realized that at this point they needed to follow the agent's instructions and not even try to figure out some abstract plan that was evolving around them.

"I am totally convinced that this is the right thing to do, especially after what I've learned in the past hour," Dan continued. "Mason was on the flight to Beijing, but he never checked into the Crowne Plaza Lido. There has been no activity on his credit card, so I doubt that he chose to stay somewhere else. We will be monitoring the airport in the morning to see if he catches his flight to the States."

"Could he still be in the airport?" Alex asked, his mind struggling over where Mason could be. "If he was afraid, maybe he chose to stay in a very public setting."

"I suppose that is possible, but I have no way to find out," Dan replied. "I don't have the manpower to cover the entire airport, and the Chinese authorities are not going to help us. Even if they would, the diplomatic channels would not only take forever to forge through, but at this point, we don't know all of the players in the big picture, so we could actually cause more harm than good."

"You aren't very encouraging." Maggie said, exhaustion about to overtake her emotions.

"I know, Mags," Dan responded, feeling helpless. "But I need to be honest with you so that you understand the danger you could all be in. There are bad dudes involved here with a lot at stake. They are not about to let a handful of insignificant Americans spoil their plans. You need to trust me."

"I do trust you," Maggie replied. "I'm tired and scared and I want to be home. I know you're doing everything possible to assure our safety. I just haven't grasped how all of this has happened to begin with. We're just an American firm wanting to build compressors in China. How did something so straightforward get so complicated?"

"Because the people you are working with have an entirely different agenda," Dan tried to explain. "If Utopia had not been there, someone else would have been. There are too many Western-especially American-companies that are doing business with the Chinese. They would have found someone else to exploit."

"Too bad they didn't," Alex replied. "I'd just as soon this was someone else's problem."

"I understand, but that's not the issue at this point," Dan agreed. "Our focus now is on the next thirty-six hours. After that, you will be where I can touch you. We will all feel better then. For now, I need you both to get some sleep. Alex, watch after our buddy there."

"Not a problem," Alex assured him. "You take care of getting us out of here; I'll keep close tabs on her."

When the call ended, Maggie and Alex made their way back upstairs. Exhausted beyond belief, neither one remembered their head hitting the pillow.

CHAPTER 137

Mohammed and Tarik had met Imad outside Nashville four weeks after their first meeting. Once again, they loaded two televisions into his SUV. He was on his way now to deliver one of them to his courier and the second one, stored safely in his garage, was his to deliver when the orders came from Houston.

As Imad pulled out of the Vanderbilt campus, his mind wandered to all sorts of places-a futile effort to ignore the severity of the mission. He planned on driving south on Interstate 65 to Athens, Alabama. There he would meet his contact at the Walmart parking lot. How ironic, he thought, that he was making the delivery at the same store that would soon become a target in the war against the infidels. Allah's war.

As he headed down Charlotte, he tried hard to convince himself that he was fulfilling the will of Allah, that he was being the soldier he had been called to be, but all his brain could focus on was the hundreds of wounded that would be taken to area hospitals. He could hear their cries and screams as the pain racked their mutilated bodies. Surely, this was not Allah's plan.

Imad never saw the carload of teenagers that ran the red light at the intersection of Charlotte and 11th Avenue. Somewhere in the deep recesses, his brain registered the sounds: crunching metal, breaking glass, screams. He felt the slam of the air bag hitting his face and then something hard slamming into his back. And then, his world went black.

CHAPTER 138

"The rescue unit worked for almost two hours trying to get him untangled from the wreckage," the nurse supervisor commented as she watched the trauma team work feverishly over the man. "They said the car was literally wrapped around an electric pole. They had to cut the power to the pole before they could even try to get him out of the car."

"Has he been conscious at all?" another nurse asked.

"No, poor man, not even for a moment," the first nurse answered.

"They're trying to locate his wife. I hope Dr. Mubarak survives until she arrives."

"I never give up on the human spirit, but this time there may just be too much damage to overcome," the supervisor said as she continued to watch the doctors try to stabilize the dying man. "Sometimes, death is the better alternative."

CHAPTER 139

"We just received the info on the five numbers that Mohammed has been calling every Monday night." Agent Brock addressed the task force. "They all live within our fifteen-hundred-mile perimeter and all are to homes of Muslims. And all of them attended UT in Austin at the same time as the Aghasi brothers."

"So we know where they met, do we know if they were a part of any radical groups while in college?" Dan asked.

"So far we haven't been able to tie them to any organized faction, but they were known to hang together, and they were also known to be somewhat aggressive, from sources at the Muslim Student Association. Seems they often questioned those who were preaching against violence."

"Have they kept in contact since college?" Dan inquired.

"Still working on that, but it seems reasonable that they had some sort of communication line or they wouldn't have known how to find each other after so many years," Brock replied. "There's more. It seems that each of these men called three numbers immediately after Mohammed called them. We know who these people are, but we are checking their phone records to see if there are any call patterns with them."

"Contact me as soon as you hear anything," Dan instructed. "We have to get a fix on how big this network is-soon."

CHAPTER 140

"Dr. Mubarak, you have extensive injuries. You have internal bleeding and we need to operate. "We're trying to get in contact with your wife. As soon as she gets here, we'll let you see her."

"I must talk to the FBI … " the injured man responded. "Must talk to them. Urgent."

"You can talk to them later," Dr. Craig answered. "We have to operate now. There is no time to waste."

"Take him to OR-1. We don't have time to get his family's permission," the doctor ordered.

CHAPTER 141

"Dr. Mubarak, it is Layalla," the young nurse said as they raced the gurney down the hallway "We're taking you to surgery. You need to be tough. I will be in the OR with you."

The man opened his eyes, turning his head toward the voice. Recognizing Layalla, he reached for her hand.

"قنابل. يجب عليك أن تخبر مكتب التحقيقات الفدرالي," he whispered in Arabic.★

"قنابل؟ ما الذي تتحدث عنه؟ أين؟" the nurse frantically asked.★★

"نتسويه. Aghasi " Mubarak strained, coughing between the words. "قنابل والعشرون ... Thanksgiv-" ★★★

"Hush, no more talking," Layalla pleaded. "We will talk about this later."

They reached the operating room, the team working rapidly and efficiently. Before he could say anything else, the anesthesiologist administered the medicine that would keep him from feeling the pain of the surgery. Unfortunately, it did not numb the pain in his conscience.

CHAPTER 142

Layalla checked the patient's vital signs. The wreck had caused extensive damage and there would be more surgeries ahead … if he survived the night. She knew that the chances of his seeing another day were slim.

★ *"Bombs. You have to tell the FBI." he whispered in Arabic.*

★★ *"Bombs? What are you talking about? Where is-?" the nurse frantically asked.*

★★★ *"Houston. Aghasi." Mubarak strained, coughing between the words. "Twenty bombs. Thanksgiv-"*

His family had visited briefly, but he was still unconscious and his wife was devastated, crying uncontrollably. Layalla could only imagine how she felt. Dr. Mubarak was just a colleague to Layalla, but he had always treated her kindly. She suspected it was because they were both Muslim. However, he was different from most Muslim men she knew. He was always professional, speaking to her in public and never questioning her Western clothes. Perhaps America had influenced his behavior. Her thoughts were interrupted by stirring sounds coming from the bed.

"Layalla," he whispered.

"Shhh, Dr. Mubarak, you need to rest. You have been through a lot today and your body needs time to recover."

"من فضلكم يتعين عليكم ان تساعد" the man pleaded. "هل الدعوة إلى مكتب التحقيقات الفيدرالية؟ بد لي من التحدث.★المهم"

"There will be time to talk when you are better," the nurse replied. "Please save your energy."

‏‹‹أن بجي لب نوتوميس سانلا نم ريثككلا .تقو كانه سيل›‹‹فقوتي."★★

Suddenly alarms and bells screeched, startling Layalla. The room was filled with nurses and doctors before she could even think to call for help. Doctors were barking orders, nurses pushing drugs through the I.V., but Layalla knew it was too late.

The heart monitor was showing a flat line.

★"*Please, you have to help.*" *the man pleaded.* "*Did you call the FBI? I have to talk to them.*"

★★"*There's no time. A lot of people are going to die.*"

CHAPTER 143

The two men would have preferred to convince the concierge to give them the key to the woman's room, but they knew that Han wanted this handled quietly and there was always the chance that the hotel employee would crack if questioned. There was no activity in the hallway, just as they had hoped it would be, considering it was almost three in the morning.

The taller of the two kept watch as the other man quickly picked the lock. They were silent as they entered the room and waited by the door for a few moments while their eyes adjusted to the darkness. What little light that came through under the doorway and around the window was enough to allow them to easily maneuver around the room. It was also enough to let them know that the bed had not been slept in. There was no one in the room.

They knew that calling Han at this time of the morning, with this kind of news, was not going to be a good experience. But they had no other idea what to do. They surely couldn't wait until morning, for fear that too many hours would have passed to suit Han. Finally, they made the call.

"What do you mean she's not there?" Han exploded. "Are you sure you have the right room?"

"Yes sir. We have followed her several times. This is the right room," the man answered. "She is not here."

"Perhaps she spent the night with the other American, Alex. The tall dark-headed one," Han speculated, trying to form some reason for the current dilemma. "Do you know what room he is in?"

"Yes, we know, but I do not think she will be there," the man replied. "All of her personal items are gone. There is nothing here."

"You do not get paid to think," Han shouted. "Check the man's room and call me back."

The two men made their way down the hallway to the American man's room, knowing that if he were there, it was going to be harder to keep him quiet and especially if the woman was with him. Their breathing settled when they entered the room only to find that it too was empty of all personal possessions. They were glad that they did not have two people to restrain, but they were certain their boss would not feel as relieved.

CHAPTER 144

Layalla shut off the monitors, tears streaming down her face. Why had this happened? Why had Allah allowed this tragedy? Dr. Mubarak was saving lives, finding new treatments. People needed him. Islam needed him. The world needed to see compassionate Muslims, not just the radicals on the nightly news.

She left the hospital, oblivious to her surroundings during the drive home. She always tried to distance herself from the tragedies of her patients, but this was different. This was her colleague, her friend. Her friend, who apparently had a secret. Perhaps he was delirious from the trauma of the accident, she thought. Surely he hadn't known what he was saying. What had Dr. Mubarak done? Why had he chosen to reach out to her? Why did he address her in Arabic? He had never done that before today. Why did he not want the other nurses to hear what he said to her?

Maybe she had misunderstood what he said. No, she argued, she had understood every word. Every word that was going to do nothing but cause a lot of trouble if she told anyone. She knew that if she went to the authorities, not only would Dr. Mubarak's family be judged, so would she. "American born" meant nothing unless you could blend in with the crowd, make no trouble, instill no fear. If she talked, her whole life would change. People would no longer look at her as a trained professional, but would only see a Muslim. *Their* interpretation of Muslim. She and Dr. Mubarak would be labeled as radicals, out to destroy America. She didn't want to face that kind of bigotry.

Layalla had lived a charmed life, compared to most of the women in her extended family. Her parents had moved to Baltimore from Cairo when her father was offered a job at Johns Hopkins. By the time Layalla and her sister were born, her parents were well assimilated into the American culture. Layalla was always encouraged to follow her passions, and they supported her decision to go to college. They often prayed that she would settle down and marry, but they knew she would never accept a traditional arranged marriage. When Layalla moved to Nashville to work in Vanderbilt's Critical Care Center, her parents worried silently, but never stood in the way of her decision. There were times, like tonight, when she wondered if perhaps she had made the wrong choice. Perhaps she should have married. At least she would have had a safe person to discuss the drama of the day with, to share her sorrow and fear. That thought made her smile: If she had been a traditional Muslim wife, she would not have even been at the hospital, much less privy to Dr. Mubarak's odd request.

But what if she had been wrong about Dr. Mubarak? What if he had fooled everyone, including herself? Was it possible that he was part of a radical Islamic group out to inflict harm? But he was a doctor, dedicated to healing. He would never hurt anyone. Layalla was confused and exhausted. Her thoughts were swarming around with no sense of direction or logic. Arriving home, she slumped in her favorite chair, not even bothering to change clothes. Before long, the overwhelming sadness in her heart gave way to a flood of tears. She mourned for Dr. Mubarak, for his family, for all her patients that she had never allowed herself to mourn for before. She felt terribly alone, not for the first time, but tonight the emptiness she normally pushed away washed over her in waves of despair.

Somewhere in the distance, Layalla could hear pounding. It was an insistent sound, accompanied by a muffled voice. Go away, Layalla thought, just be quiet. But the thumping and the voice only became louder. What were they saying? Slowly her reluctant mind realized that someone was calling her name, someone was knocking on her door. Momentarily paralyzed by her sound sleep, she finally made her way to the apartment door, aware now that the voice belonged to her friend, Hala.

"Are you okay?" Hala asked as she stormed into the apartment. "I have been calling for an hour. Did you forget our plans?"

"I am sorry, Hala, but I fell asleep and I never turned the phone on after I left the hospital," Layalla explained. "This has been a horrible day and I just collapsed. I completely forgot that we were meeting for dinner. What time is it?"

"It's almost nine. Aren't you starving? Maybe we could still grab a sandwich."

"Whatever. I am really not hungry," Layalla mumbled, running her hands through her long black hair. "But give me a minute to change, and we'll head out."

"You must have had some kind of a bad day. I've never known you to pass up dinner at Hannah's. Want to talk about it?"

"One of the doctors was in a car wreck today," Layalla explained, not wanting to be say too much. "He didn't make it."

"Oh, Layalla, I am so sorry. Which doctor?"

"Dr. Mubarak," Layalla answered as the tears threatened to spill over her eyelids. "It was so horrible. He was injured too extensively to have ever recovered."

"Look, we don't have to go out. Let me find something in your kitchen to eat and we can stay in and talk. I think you could use someone to vent to tonight."

"No, it's okay. I think I would be better if we went out. Someplace loud," Layalla said.

Talking about what happened was the last thing she wanted to do. Hala was not the one to confide in; she was too opinionated. Everything was either black or white with Hala, and Layalla knew that this situation was most definitely gray.

CHAPTER 145

Layalla was awake long before the alarm went off. She had spent a restless night arguing with herself over what she should do. But when morning finally came, she accepted the answer that she had known she would, despite a deepening fear. She called in sick to her supervisor and then she called Barry, an attorney she had once dated. Luckily they had parted as friends and he did occasional legal work for her.

Within an hour Layalla was sitting in Barry's office telling him Dr. Mubarak's story.

"Are you sure this is what you want to do?" the attorney asked. "You have to know that this could change your life ... in a lot of areas. The authorities may not believe you; your identity will be found out and your community might not react favorably to the attention your actions will focus on them."

"I understand all of that, but I don't see that I have any other choice," Layalla responded. "Barry, this is my country and someone could be threatening it. Do you really just expect me to forget what I know?"

"What do you know? That some guy writhing in pain was talking crazy? You don't even know that there's anything more to this than the ravings of a dying man."

"My experience is that dying men don't rave," Layalla snapped. "This is important, I can just feel this. If you don't want to help me, it's okay, but I am going anyway."

"Not by yourself," Barry replied, reaching for the telephone. "Let me make a call to a buddy of mine, and let him know we are on our way over there. The last thing you need to be doing is talking to the FBI without an attorney with you."

CHAPTER 146

Rusty Coggins ordinarily would have peddled a cold call off on one of the newbies, but this call was different. Barry had been his roommate in law school, and while they had chosen different career paths, they had always remained close friends. If Barry needed to meet with him during business hours, then it must be important, the agent thought.

Within minutes Barry and Layalla were seated in Agent Coggins's office. Barry explained that Layalla had been thrust into a circumstance that might or might not be anything important, but if it was, then national security was at stake. His preface piqued the agent's interest. This was not going to be any ordinary private citizen tip. Agent Coggins encouraged Layalla to tell her story.

"There was a car accident on Monday involving one of the doctors at Vanderbilt," Layalla began. "Dr. Imad Mubarak. He is … was a research oncologist and a well respected doctor. He came into trauma in very critical condition and needed emergency surgery."

"We were on our way to the OR. He was very weak and his condition was deteriorating rapidly," Layalla continued. "He spoke to me in Arabic. He said that he needed to talk to the FBI. Something about bombs. Twenty bombs."

"Did he say where the bombs were located?" the agent asked as he sat up straighter in the chair, his heartbeat throbbing in his ears.

"He said the word 'Houston' and he said 'Thanksgiving'," Layalla replied trying to hold the fear at bay. She knew by the agent's behavior that he considered this something sinister, not just the delirious ravings of an injured man.

"What else did he say?"

"He said 'Aghasi.' That is not an unusual name in the Muslim community," Layalla responded. "He said a lot of people would die and that the FBI must stop them."

"Thanksgiving is in a few days. Why didn't you call us sooner? Isn't that what he asked you to do?"

"Easy Rusty," Barry injected. "She's here now. Just listen to her story."

"I thought he was delirious. I didn't want to believe he was involved in something evil," Layalla explained. "But the next morning in the ICU, after the surgery, he woke up long enough to ask me again to call you. Before I could find out more, he died. I was shocked and grieving and didn't know what to think. I just went home. This morning I knew that I had to tell someone. That's when I called Barry."

"How well did you know Dr. Mubarak?" the agent asked as he started scribbling notes. "Do you know if he was involved with any radical groups?"

"I only knew him as a colleague. We were not close friends. I do know that he was highly respected at the hospital and throughout the medical community nationwide," Layalla responded, her voice getting louder by the moment. "He was often asked to speak at oncology conferences and even testified before Congress about cancer research funding. I cannot believe that he was some crazy radical."

As Layalla rose to leave, she turned and looked directly in the agent's eyes. "Sir, despite what you hear on television, not all Muslims want to kill. Not all Muslims want to destroy this country. Many of us were born here, and we love America. You must stop these crazies before anyone gets hurt. That's what Dr. Mubarak was trying to do."

Agent Coggins watched her leave the room, knowing that what she said was true. He also knew that was not the way it would play out on the evening news.

CHAPTER 147

"Sir, the Nashville office is on line 3, Agent Coggins," the receptionist announced to Jim Keith.

"Nashville? Did he say what he wanted?"

"No Sir, just insisted on talking to the head of the terrorist task force."

Jim hesitated before he answered, wondering why an agent from Tennessee would be calling Houston. "Keith, here."

"Special Agent Keith, this is Agent Coggins. Sir, we have a situation here. I have a statement from a dying man who wanted to warn the FBI about twenty bombs in Houston."

"You certainly have my attention," Jim said straightening in his chair. "Tell me more."

Coggins spent the next few minutes explaining Mubarak's accident and what had transpired at the hospital. He included what background information he had been able to obtain about the doctor.

"I'm sorry that I don't have more to give you, but I believe the man was sincere in trying to warn us. He was very insistent for someone in his condition."

"Dying men are often remorseful," Jim commented. "Likewise, they are usually truthful. In this case, we have other intel to support his claim. Write up your report and email it to me-soon."

"Ready to send, sir. I understand the timetable you're working against," the agent replied. "Thanksgiving is just around the corner."

CHAPTER 148

"They're both gone?" Han screamed into the telephone. "It's after three in the morning, where could they be?"

"Do you want us to talk to the front desk?" one of the men asked, trying to make any offer to calm his boss down.

"No, no, no. At this time of the night, that would only raise suspicions," Han answered as he tried to think through the fog of being awakened again with bad news. "Let me think. I will call you later."

His mind whirling, Han tried to determine what this could mean. If both Alex and the woman were gone, then probably the others were as well. Perhaps they were all anxious to return home and they changed their flight to leave after the last meeting. If that was the case, then they were probably in Beijing. The more direct flights to America left through Beijing, and he knew from previous visits that they always traveled through that city. He was sure that was what happened. One phone call would be all it took for him to find out. He called his son and brought him up-to-date on the situation and advised him to locate the team in Beijing and get the information about their flight out. Han was a very powerful man in China, and in Beijing in particular. He had spent many years and a great deal of money buying eyes and ears in every industry. If the American team was still in China, he would find them.

CHAPTER 149

"Gentlemen, there has been a development," Jim Keith addressed the task force in an emergency meeting he called after talking to the Nashville office. "There's a dead man in Tennessee that just moved the Aghasi case to the top of the list."

The veteran policeman filled the rest of the team in on what had happened with Dr. Imad Mubarak and about the deadline they were now working against.

"That's only days away," Keith continued. "Have we been able to identify the rest of the contacts?"

"Yes, we received that information earlier this week," Dan interjected. "We have been going over their individual phone records. So far we have not seen any further pattern of contact. Of course, there's always the internet, but without warrants to search their homes and offices, the phone records are all we have to go on. We need to devise a plan to bring them all in at once, including the Aghasi brothers. We do not need to give them time to warn each other."

"We are also going to have to bring in some help," Keith said. "It's past time to consult Homeland Security, the CIA, and Interpol. I have called all of them and they are each putting together a team to work with us on the task force. This is still our operation, but I expect everyone to cooperate. Remember, we are all on the same side. The other members will be here this afternoon at four. Until then, let's get a plan formulated and printouts made on what we know so far. I want the other agencies brought up-to-date as quickly as possible."

The task force spent the next two hours working with FBI offices throughout the South to coordinate the mass sting operation. It would take a couple of days to work out the details, which didn't leave them much time to find the bombs and destroy them before the Thanksgiving deadline.

CHAPTER 150

"No answer again?" Tarik asked his older brother.

"No, it goes straight to voicemail," Mohammed answered as he paced across the room. "It's been three days from our appointed call time. This does not feel good. Something is wrong. It is not like Imad to not pick up."

"Were you able to talk to the other four?"

"All of them. Everything seemed in order. I have a bad feeling about this, my brother."

"What do you want to do?" Tarik asked. "We can't call his work if he has been compromised. The authorities would have his phones tapped."

"I think we need to call Habib. We have to go to Plan B."

"Do you have our tickets and passports?" Tarik asked.

"Yes, I took care of that today. We have two round-trip tickets from Houston to Mexico City and then to Caracas," Mohammed answered. "It will be a long flight, but the Mexican authorities will not be looking for us. Even if they cooperate with the American government, they will be looking for the Aghasi brothers. Our new passports and identification papers will not connect us to that name or even to each other. We will be on the same flight, but we will behave as if we do not know each other. Total strangers."

"Too bad we will not be making the return trip," Tarik said. "There are some things I will miss. But it will be good to see our family, to be among our friends."

"We have been in America for a long time and have made a good life, but we always knew that someday we would be leaving," Mohammed reasoned. "We have prepared well; we will be safe in Venezuela."

"I am not afraid to die, but I understand that someone has to lead the war," Tarik said. "Our brothers are the bravest of men."

"Brave and blessed. Soon they will be in Paradise."

CHAPTER 151

"Where's Maggie and Alex?" David asked as the driver loaded their luggage in the back of the Consulate car.

"I do not know about the others," the driver responded. "I was only told to take the three of you to the airport."

The three Americans looked at each other with growing concern. The past twelve hours had been like a roller coaster ride for them. They were quietly preparing for a routine trip home when they were snatched in the middle of the night and deposited at the American Consulate. Now they were being told that their two colleagues were not headed to the airport with them. None of the three felt good about their circumstances.

"We need to know where they are before we leave," John insisted. "We aren't just going to fly out of here without them."

"Please sir, just calm down. The driver only knows what he has been told, nothing more," a man instructed them as he walked toward the car. He was one of the men who had picked them up at the hotel the night before. "The others will go to the airport in a different car. Now, if you will join me, we will be on our way."

Satisfied with the official's answer, the three men got into the car with him and settled in for the drive to the airport. At first the conversation was innocuous, comments about the traffic, the weather, and the desire to be back in Houston. Before long, the talk turned to the events of the previous evening. The embassy man quickly quieted them, nodding his head toward the driver. The three men didn't know what to think of the situation, but they did understand that they were not to talk about what had happened. The rest of the trip was made in silence.

Once they arrived at the airport, the driver quickly handled their luggage while the official escorted them inside. Bypassing security, they were taken to a room off the main corridor. The guard at the door seemed to be expecting them and ushered them in without questioning.

"This is a secure lounge that is used for VIPs, such as visiting heads of state," the Consulate official explained. "I will accompany you to Beijing and see that you are safely on a plane to the States. Both here and in Beijing, you will be loaded before the rest of the passengers."

"This seems a like a lot of trouble over some Chinese gangs," Paul commented. "Are you sure this is still the story you want to stick with?"

The other two Americans watched as the official seemed to struggle with how he wanted to respond. None of them felt comfortable with the situation, and the man's hesitation did nothing to ease their tension.

"You will be better off if you do not ask any questions until you get back to Houston," the man finally commented. "Your life may truly depend on your compliance."

"So who's going to be in Houston to explain all of this strange behavior?" Paul questioned. "How are we going to know the truth? And where are Maggie and Alex?"

"You will be met in Houston by someone from the FBI," the man answered. "Your friends will be traveling separately from you. You will not see them again until you get to Houston. I could not tell you that in the car. You never know who is listening. My advice to you is to act as normally as you can on the flight back and do not discuss any of this until you land in Texas."

The mention of the FBI finally sobered the three sufficiently enough that they asked no more questions. The lounge remained eerily silent as the men waited to be loaded onto the plane. Each was lost in his own thoughts and determined independently that this was his last trip to China. All they wanted now was to land safely on American soil.

CHAPTER 152

The two Chinese men had sat quietly in the loading area, scanning the faces of the people waiting to board the plane to Beijing. There were several Americans, but none who matched the pictures they had been provided of the five Americans from Utopia Energy. As soon as the final boarding call was completed, one of the men calmly walked up to the loading checkpoint. After a few moments of harmless chatter, he showed the woman the pictures. She pointed to three of them and said that they had been priority loaded before any other passengers, along with another Caucasian man, who appeared to be the leader of the group. He was not among the pictures she was shown. No, she had not seen the other man or the woman; she knew nothing about them. The Chinese man rejoined his partner and then called Han.

Meanwhile, in the recently opened Terminal 2 building, Carson and Rita Henry stood in line in Customs waiting to catch their flight to Singapore. They looked like typical tourists: Rita wearing a Panda tee shirt and Carson in one showing the Great Wall and a camera hanging around his neck. They blended in marvelously. It was early in the morning and the short line was moving fairly quickly.

They had left the Consulate in a taxi driven by the woman that Maggie had first met in the park. Their pictures had been taken in their tourist attire and forwarded to Singapore, Tokyo and San Francisco so that the foreign service personnel in those cities could spot them departing the plane. Before they left the Consulate they had been thoroughly briefed on their faux backgrounds and had spoken with Dan one last time.

"Well darling, are you ready for our vacation to be over?" Carson asked as he put his arm around his wife.

"I can't wait to be home," Rita responded. "Although I can tell you that this is one trip that I will never forget."

"Neither will I, my dear. Neither will I."

CHAPTER 153

It took two long days for the task force to outline all the details in Operation Turkey Shoot. There were the usual egos to get past, but in the end, Dan felt good about the plan to stop a terrorist attack and hopefully round up all the international players in the process. There was a lot riding on Interpol's ability to get its member countries to agree to the arrests—especially in China. China was the one weak link that worried Dan. While he was dedicated to stopping any terrorist attack on his country, he was also dedicated to Maggie. If Interpol did not convince the Chinese government to arrest Han and his partners at Tiger Eye, then Maggie's life was still in danger from Han's connections in Houston. The truth was, she might be in danger either way.

Another truth was that the task force would probably be unsuccessful in its capture of Cai Yi. The middleman had been sought by various governments for years, but he always managed to dwell untouched in the bowels of the underworld. The CIA had had a tail on him for the past week and so far, he seemed to be uncharacteristically visible. But, as with any rat, he could disappear into the smallest hole where no one could find him

Dan was just about to call it a day and go to the safe house to check on everyone, when his phone rang. It was his direct line so he knew it was either something about the case or it was Sara. Either way, he had to take time to answer it.

"It's good to know that you are still working," the voice said when Dan took the call. "I'd hate to think that you were relaxing somewhere enjoying a real life."

"What has you calling so early in the day for you?" Dan asked, immediately recognizing his Beijing counterpart. "Please don't tell me it's your dedication to the Bureau."

"My dedication is exhausted. I've been here all night, and you are not going to like what I have to tell you," Joseph Lee soberly replied. He was tired and exasperated and it showed in his tone.

"Whoa, sorry buddy. This sounds ominous. What's up?"

"The ship carrying Kim and his family docked in Shanghai two days ago" Joseph began. "A limo was waiting and took them to a charter airstrip. It appears that Tiger Eye's private jet flew them to Hong Kong."

"Are they still there?"

"No. They chartered a plane that posted a flight plan to Sydney," the FBI LEGAT continued.

"Please tell me that we have eyes on them." Dan sighed, wondering where this chase was leading.

"Well, we did."

"Did? As in we 'don't' have now?" Dan snapped.

"Apparently there are sixty thousand Koreans in New South Wales and they were able to blend in quite well," Joseph explained. "Our guys are working on it, but I wouldn't count on a quick resolution. Craig Deaton is running the trap, but this is a case of reacting rather than anticipating."

"I know, I know. Sorry for the attitude. It just feels like this whole operation is out of control," Dan apologized. "We've got suspects all over the world, all executing their plays, and we don't even know the game plan. It's a little frustrating."

"Well you can bet that Kim has fulfilled his part of the plan because it's obvious that he is on the run," Joseph tried to analyze. "That must mean that Han has received whatever

Kim was peddling and has probably shipped it out. The question is, has it all arrived in Houston and what happens now?"

"Now, my friend, we shut them down."

CHAPTER 154

"This is not good news," Habib responded to Mohammed's story. "Has he ever behaved this way before?"

"Never. Sometimes it takes a second or third call when he gets involved at the hospital, but never this long."

"Do you think he has had a change of heart?" the Iranian questioned, careful not to be too open with his wording.

"I would never have thought so, but the circumstances demand that I at least consider the possibility," Mohammed answered. "Needless to say, I am worried."

"How soon could you be able to travel?"

"We have already made the arrangements," Mohammed answered. "We leave in the morning."

"Very good, cousin. Our plans can still be carried out. The results won't be as widespread as we had hoped for, but the end effect will still be the same. There's no reason that you can't finish the job from a new location." Habib replied. Or that I can't finish it from here if necessary, he thought.

"We will call you when we arrive."

"May Allah be with you."

Habib hesitated only moments before he dialed the number. He had hoped that it would not be necessary to clean up after his cousins, but he had known from the beginning that it would be a possibility. Now it seemed that his forward thinking had been prudent.

"Greetings, my brother, it is good to hear your voice," Habib said when the call finally connected. "It seems we may have a small problem. I need you to check on our esteemed doctor."

"What do I need to find out for you?"

"The lines of communication seem to have closed. I need to know if we have a problem," Habib explained. "We have been unable to contact him and I need you to find out if there is a legitimate reason. Perhaps he is in need of some assistance."

"I was just getting ready to go out. I'll be more than happy to check on the situation. I'll call you as soon as I know more."

Habib felt a small sense of relief after making the call, but still there was a lingering uneasiness that nagged at him. The doctor's disappearance could be extremely alarming for their plan. While he was just one part of the plot, it could all fall apart if he had had a change of heart, if he had contacted the American authorities. His cousins had not considered this possibility because Imad was their friend. But Habib knew that in America, there was no such thing as a faithful-to-death friend, even if you were Muslim.

CHAPTER 155

Alex and Maggie exited the plane looking like the typical tourists who had endured the thirty-hour flight from the Orient. Their wrinkled clothes helped them blend into the throng of walking dead looking for the nearest restroom and coffee shop. As they entered the terminal, a man and woman greeted them as if they were all family. By now, Alex and Maggie had become accustomed to this routine. They had experienced the same situation in both Singapore and Tokyo.

"Any luggage we need to pick up?" the man asked as he shook Alex's hand.

"No, just the carry-ons. We travel light. It makes these long flights easier," Alex responded as he repeated the rehearsed conversation that would identify the agents as friendly contacts.

With contact established the two couples headed out of the building into a waiting car. Both Maggie and Alex could feel their bodies relax just at the thought of being on American soil.

"Man, it feels good to be home." Alex said as they settled into the car. "I thought we would never get here."

"I'm glad you're here also," the male agent responded. "But you are not home free yet. You need to continue with your cover until you are safely in Houston. We have strict orders to keep a close eye on you tonight and get you on the plane to Dallas in the morning."

"Where are we going now?" Maggie asked, weary from the stress of the trip.

"To an FBI safe house," the agent answered. "It's quiet and you will be comfortable there. We have to leave for the airport at eight in the morning. That will give you several hours to catch up on your sleep."

"Those are welcome words, although I would rather keep going until I'm home," Maggie replied. "I really want to be in Houston."

"I can understand that, but you have to realize that we need to stay on script," the man explained. "You cannot arrive in Dallas until Special Agent Kardan is there to meet you. That won't happen until tomorrow. You need to trust us."

"I've been trusting Special Agent Kardan for weeks now and look where it's gotten me," Maggie snapped.

"If you'll excuse the obvious, ma'am, it's kept you alive."

CHAPTER 156

Maggie felt a little better as they boarded the plane for Dallas. She really needed more sleep after the grueling trip from China, but that would have to wait until she arrived home. Home. How wonderful to be back in her own house, safe from the insanity of this entire trip. The thought of sleeping in her own bed kept her spirits and her energy from waning.

"Do you think this is over?" Maggie asked as she and Alex settled into their seats.

"I would like to think so, but I doubt it," Alex answered. "There's just so much I don't understand about all of this."

"I know that a lot has been dumped on you in the past forty-eight hours," Maggie sighed. "I wanted to tell you earlier, but I couldn't. I had promised Dan that I wouldn't say anything."

"I've got a real issue with him over that decision. He put your life in danger."

"Give him a break, okay?" Maggie ran her hand through her hair. "He was still trying to figure out what was going on."

"What is going on? Do you really understand this?" Alex asked, trying to keep his voice low. "Do you think Dan has it figured out yet?"

"I don't know, Alex. I just know that I want our lives to go back to normal."

"I don't know if that is possible. I guess it will depend on how this all ends," Alex conceded.

"Well, I hope the end is near."

CHAPTER 157

"Excuse me, but I was just at Dr. Mubarak's office and it seems that the door is locked. Can you tell me how to find him?"

"Are you a patient of Dr. Mubarak's?" the hospital receptionist asked.

"No, I am not a patient. Dr. Mubarak and I are colleagues. I had a lunch date with him today."

"I am so sorry to have to be the one to tell you this. Dr. Mubarak was killed in a car accident a couple of days ago."

"What? When did this happen? I haven't heard anything."

"It happened on Monday. A car hit him in an intersection just a few blocks from the hospital here," the receptionist offered as she continued to enter data into her computer. "My boyfriend, Travis, drove the wrecker that picked up the car. He works for Morgan Wrecker Service. They hauled the car back over to their shop. You should see it. It's no wonder Dr. Mubarak didn't survive; no one could have lived through that kind of wreck. He was alive when the ambulance got here, but-"

The receptionist looked up only to see that no one was there. The man had disappeared.

CHAPTER 158

Maggie and Alex were sleeping before the plane ever departed from San Francisco. Before arriving in the States, they had always slept in shifts, but now both exhaustion and complacency broke down their vigilance. The plane was preparing to land in Dallas when the flight attendant woke them up.

"Excuse me, but the pilot has received a message for you," the attendant whispered to them. "When the plane lands, please do not leave. When all of the other passengers are unloaded, someone will come for you."

"Do you know who the message was from?" Maggie asked as she tried to wake up from the fog.

"It came from the FBI. Someone named Dan."

Maggie and Alex looked at each other as the attendant left them and prepared for landing. They both felt the familiar uneasiness return. They had thought they were safely home, but apparently they were wrong.

"Do you think something else has happened or is this just overkill?" Maggie asked.

"I'd like to hope it was the latter, but since they did not have us wait when we landed in San Francisco, I would bet that something has happened."

"I was afraid that would be your thought," Maggie said. "I wonder if it has anything to do with Mason?"

"I don't know. We've been traveling for three days now without hearing any news," Alex replied, thoughts swirling through his head. "Something major may have happened. Or maybe it does have something to do with Mason. Or maybe our buddy is paranoid."

"Dan may be a lot of things, but he is not paranoid," Maggie responded. "He's too logical, too analytical for that. No, there's a reason he wants us to wait on the plane, and you can bet it's not going to be good."

CHAPTER 159

"The three others on the American team left on their flight as scheduled, except they were pre-boarded with another Caucasian man, not Alex Sheppard, and there was no sighting of him or the woman," Chen reported to his father after hearing from the surveillance team at the airport. "None of the Americans checked into their hotel last night, but we do not know where they did stay."

"They cannot just disappear into thin air," Han screamed. "We have to find them. We cannot let them get to America!"

"I have a contact in the American Embassy in Beijing," Chen offered. "I will check to see if they are there or if they have been there. Father, we must not overreact. The last of the special delivery compressors will leave this week. We are finished. We need to fly low, under the radar as we always have done."

"What if the woman goes to the American authorities?" Han asked, only slightly less agitated than he had been.

"What is she going to say? That she saw some spare parts? She knows nothing," Chen calmly reasoned. "With the exception of the last installment, all of the money has been received and subsequently hidden from anyone who might decide to look. The last details of negotiations are over; the plant is up and running; you need to let this go."

"You're right, my son," Han slowly answered. "I have let my emotions take over my senses. The only threat we had has been eliminated. The woman is nothing. Thank you for your wise words."

"It is my pleasure, Father, Chen replied. "Please spend the rest of your evening planning how you will spend all of that money."

CHAPTER 160

Alex and Maggie stayed in their seats as the rest of the passengers juggled their belongings and filed out of the aircraft. They sat silently, not knowing what to say. Each was lost in their own thoughts as to what was going to happen next. The flight crew was making their final rounds of the plane when a familiar face sat down in the seat across the aisle from them.

"Man, do you two ever look like the worn-out tourists," Dan laughed. "I couldn't have conjured up a better disguise if I had tried."

"Not funny. None of this is funny," Alex barked. "We're tired and confused, and we are not in the mood for jokes-especially from you."

"I'm sorry. I know this has been difficult," Dan apologized. "I wish things were different, I wish this was all over. It will be soon, but not today. In fact, there's been a change of plans. That's why I had you wait here. We are going to board a Bureau plane that will take us to Houston. We will go out the side door of the ramp. I don't want you in the terminal at all. Right now, I need to get you to a safe place. The next forty-eight hours are critical. If things go as planned, you should be able to go home soon. I'm taking you to a safe house outside of Houston. Sara is there now and has planned a great dinner for you."

"What has happened?" Maggie asked. "Is this about Mason?"

"No. We don't have any more information on him," Dan hesitantly responded. "I'm not sure that we are going to know anything soon about Mason, if ever. My gut tells me that he hasn't survived the game he got caught up in."

Alex and Maggie were silent as Dan led them off the plane and into a waiting car. Neither one of them was even sure they were breathing.

CHAPTER 161

"Well, you look like something the dog dragged up, but I'm so glad to see you," Sara quipped she as took Maggie into her arms and hugged her for what seemed to be minutes. "What kind of mess have you got yourself in, girl?"

"All I did was listen to my best friend tell me what an adventure I was going to have in China." Maggie sighed as she sat down on the couch at the safe house. "No more adventures for me."

"From what little I know about the situation, it is not the adventure I had in mind," Sara replied. "I am so sorry this has all happened, but it will be over soon."

"Is that true, Dan?" Maggie snipped. "Are we going to have our lives back anytime within the foreseeable future?"

"Just a few more days, I promise," Dan replied, trying not to react to Maggie's tone. "I know that you want this to all be over. So do I. We are working around the clock to bring all of this to a positive closure. I need both of you to trust me for a few more days. The important thing is that you're back in the States and you are safe. Sara's the only one outside of the Bureau that knows you are here. I'll be in and out, but you will never be left alone. The two guys out front putting in a sprinkler system are really agents. There's also two agents set up in the house behind us. A gate through the privacy fences connects the two houses, so there are plenty of folks around."

"Dan, do you mind introducing me to the guys?" Alex asked. "I would like to see the layout, and I think the girls may need some time together. Besides, I would like you to fill me in a little better on how this all happened."

The two men left through the patio and headed for the house directly behind the safe house. Maggie decided to clean up while Sara started dinner. Maggie was sure she had never taken a shower that had felt so good. She dressed in fresh clothes and was soon in the kitchen helping Sara and filling her in on the past forty-eight hours getting out of China. They were deep in conversation when Alex returned alone.

"Wow, you look like a new person," Alex remarked as he watched the two friends prepare dinner. "Do I have time to see if a shower will do the same for me?"

"If you hurry," Maggie teased. "I'm starving and don't intend to wait too long while you primp. Where's Dan?"

"He had to go back to his office. He said he would try to be back in a few hours."

"Well, too bad for him because we aren't waiting on him either," Sara chimed in. "He'd better have food stashed in his desk drawer."

Alex's mood sobered as he headed for a shower. After what Dan had told him, he doubted seriously if the Agent was going to have time to worry about food.

CHAPTER 162

The Joint Task Force had turned the conference room at the FBI office into a high-tech operations center. The group divided into teams, each working with a set of field agents who, in turn, were coordinating the actual stings. Jim Keith and Brad Robberson were working together to synchronize all of the domestic and foreign groups to strike at the same time, regardless of the time zone they were in. It was not an easy task, considering this was a worldwide operation. Dan was busy serving as the command post communications point. He was frequently taking calls from China on the location of all of the suspects. The local authorities were working diligently to locate all of the members of Tiger Eye as well as Han's son, Chen, much to Dan's relief. Joseph Lee did not have encouraging news about Kim Cheol-su and his family. It was as if they'd vaporized once they arrived in Sydney. Local officers were poised to round up Wang's Chinese gang just in case Han tried to contact them. Dan had sent Oliver and Hardy's teams to arrest Mohammed and Tarik. He wanted them in custody before any of the other teams moved in. Dan didn't want to take any chance that the two could be tipped off by one of their comrades. He was just about to check in with them when his phone rang.

"We've got a big problem on this end," Agent Hardy reported. "We're at the suspects' house and there's no one here. Both cars are in the garage, the beds are unmade, and there are dirty dishes in the sink. The coffee pot is turned off but is still a little warm."

"It's seven in the morning. Where could they be?" Dan asked, his thoughts swirling. "They don't go to work until nine. If they had gone in early, their cars would be gone."

"Our thoughts exactly, but we still dispatched a couple of agents to the Global Market Complex, just in case they somehow got to work another way than by driving," Hardy replied. "We're still checking, but I don't believe any of the transit buses run through this area."

"Take some men and canvas the neighborhood. See if anyone has seen them in the past few hours," Dan instructed. "They can't have been gone long if the coffee is still warm. Call me back if you get anything."

Dan quickly informed the rest of the group of the problem with the Aghasi brothers. They had previously checked all airlines, bus terminals, and Amtrak for any reservations, but had found nothing. Dan had thought that the authorities had the upper hand, the element of surprise. There had been no surveillance on the two for fear of tipping them off. Now he wanted to kick himself. He should have realized that the brothers might also know about the doctor's death and therefore might have changed the timetable out of fear of the plan collapsing.

"Someone rerun the transportation reservations and see if any last-minute seats were booked," Dan shouted. "Let's get photos of the two in the hands of Houston metro and TSA and put some bodies on the ground looking for them. We need to cover all airports, trains and bus stations."

"Line two for you, Dan, it's Hardy," someone yelled above the chaos.

"Tell me something good," Dan answered.

"Well, it's something, but maybe not good," Hardy replied. "A neighbor was jogging early, about six-thirty, when she saw a Yellow Cab pull up in front of the Aghasi house. She said the two brothers loaded luggage in the taxi and looked like they were in a hurry. Yellow Cab records show that the taxi took its fare to Bush Airport."

"We've got guys on their way there now, but take your team anyway," Dan ordered. "We need all of the eyes we can get out there. I'll get Homeland Security to do a lockdown of the airport and to shut down the wi-fi system and block service to any nearby cell towers. Let's just pray their flight hasn't already taken off."

CHAPTER 163

Locking down the airport turned an already hectic scene into pure chaos. Panic was widespread, with people trying to leave the terminal as well as those arriving for their flights. Police were running everywhere with photos in hand, looking at every passenger. Planes on the runway in line to take off were put on hold as well and were slowly rerouted back to the terminal. A voice over the intercom continued to ask passengers to remain calm, but the announcements only served to heighten the tension.

Tarik and Mohammed had been sitting on opposite ends of the waiting area for United Airlines. Their eyes locked as the intercom announced the airport lockdown. All around them, people started chattering, some storming the boarding desk, trying to find out more information. The two men sat quietly, unsure of what to do next. Tarik lifted his cell phone out of his pocket, but then replaced it as he watched Mohammed slowly shake his head. Mohammed got up from his seat and headed toward the men's restroom. After a few seconds, Tarik followed him.

Once they were in the restroom, they waited until the only other man left before they spoke.

"We need to remain calm," Mohammed explained, trying to convince himself as much as his brother. "They are probably not even looking for us. We do not want to do anything to arouse suspicion."

"What do you want us to do? We never planned for any trouble at the airport," Tarik asked, his voice shaking. "How do we get out of here?"

"We are not going to be able to get out of here," Mohammed replied. "Didn't you hear-they have the entire building on lockdown. Our only hope is that we can get on our flight before they find us. We need to go back and wait. Stay on the other end from me as we have been. We need to turn our phones off. I don't know how much of television to believe, but we do not want them locating us by pinging the cell phone, if that is even possible."

The two men left the restroom separately and returned to the areas where they had each been sitting. Each tried to remain calm but to appear interested in what was happening. After a while of screaming at the airline officials about missing flights, most people had returned to their seats. While they were not happy, the initial panic had seemed to wane. Mohammed calmly pulled out his laptop, trying to see if he could find out what was causing the shutdown. While he waited for his computer to boot up, the people around him started complaining about having no cell phone service. Soon other computer users were griping about losing their wi-fi connection. Mohammed tried connecting to his email, only to find that he, too, had no internet service. It was then that the light bulb came on: The authorities had either shut down the wi-fi or jammed the system. He knew it was only a matter of time.

CHAPTER 164

Agents Oliver and Hardy split their teams up and started at opposite ends of the security area. Houston Metro and Airport Security had the check-in area and baggage claim covered. Police radios were crackling everywhere, since their phones were also affected by the system shutdown. Just as the agents were entering the United Airlines waiting area, Tarik cracked and bolted down the concourse. He was pursued by federal agents and within a few yards was tackled and taken into custody. The waiting area burst into a scene of chaos as passengers panicked and tried to run out of the area, fearing for their lives. Mohammed took this as his cue, grabbing his laptop and trying to get lost in the crowd. He had barely made it into the main thoroughfare when Agent Hardy spotted him.

"Stop, Federal Agents," Hardy screamed as he pushed his way through the mass of bodies. "Mohammed Aghasi! Stop!"

Mohammed surged faster, pushing people out of the way, clutching his laptop as he tried to find an exit. Hardy and half a dozen other agents were behind him, struggling to get through the crowd that seemed to swallow up their suspect. Hardy suddenly realized he had lost sight of Mohammed. He paused for a second when someone in the throng yelled "there he is-he ran into that restaurant!" Looking ahead to where the man was pointing, Hardy saw people running from the establishment as tables fell over and dishes were crashed onto the floor.

As Hardy and his team rushed inside, they saw Mohammed flying through the kitchen door. Following quickly, they were almost overrun by the kitchen staff trying to get out. When they finally entered the area, they saw a very frightened young man in Mohammed's grip with a butcher knife held at his throat.

"Stop or I will kill him!" the suspect screamed. "If you come any closer, I will slit his throat."

Before anyone could think, a falling skillet distracted Mohammed for a split second and Hardy took his shot. The bullet struck the assailant in the left shoulder and he collapsed to the floor, loosening his grip on his hostage. In a scene of total pandemonium, agents overtook the suspect and called for an ambulance. Within minutes, Hardy had found a police radio and dispatched a report to Dan.

Just as the Command Center was calming down and feeling euphoric about their capture of the Aghasi brothers, the calls started coming in from all over China and the US. All of the members of Tiger Eye had been apprehended without incident. Han and his son had been captured, dining together in an upscale Beijing restaurant, his wife left sitting at the table, stunned.

All over the South, SWAT teams converged on twenty locations, including the home of Dr. Imad Mubarak. Bomb squads quickly followed them in, locating the boxed televisions, and dismantling the switches that had been programmed to detonate with a command from a remote computer. Hazmat teams removed the televisions and transported the plutonium-based bombs to safe locations for disposal.

Sighs of relief and congratulations flew around the Command Center after each field group reported in on their successful mission. The last team to call in was from Athens, Georgia. The team leader was not happy. Dan put the phone on speaker.

"We raided the home of the suspect and apprehended him without incident," the agent reported. "There's just one big problem-there is no television here or in any of his vehicles. Needless to say, he has no idea what we are talking about."

"Are you sure that you've checked everywhere, basement, attic?" Dan asked, a sick feeling growing in the pit of his stomach.

"Everywhere, sir. There's nothing here."

"Could the suspect have already delivered it to the target?" Dan questioned, not sure what he wanted the answer to be.

"It could be sir, but he isn't offering anything, except how we are violating his rights," the agent answered.

"He's going to wish he lived somewhere else where there were no rights before we're through with him," Dan barked. "Haul him in."

CHAPTER 165

It was a couple of days before Dan returned to the safe house. The agents assigned to protect Maggie & Alex had been kept informed of the sting operation, but had been told to hold their positions until Dan came and relieved them. By the time he arrived, the tension in the house had dissipated and Maggie and Alex had managed to get caught up on their sleep. They were more than ready to go home.

"Sorry it took me so long to get back, but it's been a little rough on my end," Dan said as they gathered around the kitchen table. "I appreciate your patience through all of this. There should be no reason for you to stay here any longer. I will take you home when you're ready and these other guys will shut down the house."

"Can you tell us what happened?" Alex asked.

"I can tell you most of it," Dan began. "It appears that your buddy Han was involved with a very bad man who acts as a middleman for all sorts of extremist groups. This guy, Cai Yi, paid Han a great deal of money to arrange for plutonium to be smuggled into the United States."

"He used Utopia's shipments to do this?" Alex questioned.

"Yes. It seems that the plutonium was smuggled inside fake, lead exhaust manifolds," Dan explained. "That's what you saw in Shanghai, Maggie. When the compressors arrived in Houston, the original exhaust manifolds were exchanged for the fake ones. Two guys here in Houston took the fake ones, with the plutonium, and made several bombs. They distributed these bombs around the country. Fortunately, they left a pretty good trail for us to follow."

"The really great news in all of this is that we were able to capture most of the players in the scheme," Dan continued. "There is one that is still at large, and one that we never had a chance of arresting."

"Why not?" Alex asked.

"Because he is in Iran," Dan said. "He was probably the mastermind of the mechanics of the whole operation, but he takes his marching orders from someone else. There was no way we were going to be able to go into Iran and get him. However, because of all of this his travel plans have been shut down. He's a very wanted man in many countries of the world now."

"Any news about Mason?" Alex asked. "Do you know where he is?"

"No, I'm afraid not. Like I said before, Mason is probably not going to be found. I'm sure Han knows what happened, but I'm equally sure that he's not going to tell us."

"Is it over for us now? Can we go home?" Maggie asked, finally finding her voice.

"You bet, Kiddo. Go get your stuff and I will take you home," Dan smiled.

As Maggie left to gather her belongings, Alex detained Dan in the kitchen.

"Did you find all of the bombs?"

Dan hesitated before speaking. "Grab your stuff too, Alex. I'll meet you at the car."

CHAPTER 166

The man found himself driving through an old part of town, where he was unfamiliar with the businesses. Watching the street addresses, he knew he must be close. Then he saw it: a plain concrete brick building with a fading sign. Pulling up to the side of Morgan Wrecker Service, he parked the white SUV just out of sight of the front door.

Hearing the bell tinkle when the door opened, the attendant looked away from the television long enough to see a well-dressed man enter the office. It never fails, he thought, someone always has to interrupt me in the middle of the ballgame. Tennessee was playing Florida and at this point, it was anybody's game.

"How can I help you?" he asked, keeping one eye on the game.

"My brother's car was towed here earlier this week. I am here to get his personal belongings out of the vehicle."

"I need his name and the make of his vehicle," the employee asked as he opened the file cabinet to retrieve the information. Maybe he could find this quickly and be able to get back to the television.

"Imad Mubarak. It is a black Mercedes. Late model, but I am not sure of the year."

"I remember that one. I hauled that car in. Man, what a mess," the attendant muttered as he reached for the keys. "Sorry about your brother. My girlfriend works at the hospital. She told me that he di-"

"Thank you, but I'd really rather not talk about it," the man interrupted. "Could you just let me get his things?"

"Yeah sure. Uh, I need to have the bill paid before I can give you the keys. It's two hundred dollars."

The man pulled out his wallet and handed the attendant the cash for the bill.

"Here are the keys. It's sitting at the back of the garage," the attendant explained. "Mind if I stay here and watch the game? You won't have any trouble finding it. Only Mercedes on the lot."

"No problem. Go back to the game," the man answered as he headed for the door. "I can find everything just fine."

The attendant was back in front of the television before the man drove his SUV around to the back of the building. He was able to spot the car immediately and understood why the doctor had died. The Mercedes was hardly recognizable from the driver's door forward. As the man walked around to the passenger side, he pulled a pair of latex gloves out of his pocket and put them on. After tugging on the door to get it to open, he looked inside, searching for anything that he needed to confiscate. A quick glance under the seat rewarded him with a cell phone. It must have been thrown there during the impact, the man thought. He slipped it into his pocket as he headed around to the trunk. Clicking the remote, the trunk lid opened up and the man smiled. Sitting in the trunk, looking perfectly intact, was a television box.

He looked around carefully before gingerly lifting the television out of the trunk and loading it into his own vehicle. As he drove out of the wrecker yard, he hit the speed dial button on his cell phone and waited. After several moments, he heard the call answered.

"Mission accomplished."

EPILOGUE

Children's laughter filled the air as families strolled around the beautiful Jardin Japones, the Japanese Gardens. It was a gorgeous Sunday in Buenos Aires, the temperature a pleasant 79 degrees. Couples meandered arm in arm through the park, deep in private conversations. Families wandered throughout the five acres, spending time both in the park and in the cultural center. There were people from all nations soaking in the summer sun, taking pleasure in their free day before the work week started again.

One couple called to their son, a mere toddler, who had been trying to capture a butterfly. Gathering up the boy, the parents left the park and headed toward one of the outdoor cafés that lined the Avenida del Libertador. Shortly after they found a table, the waiter brought their drinks and took their order, laughing and bantering with the couple. It was obvious that they were regular visitors to the establishment. The customers that afternoon were a melting pot of nationalities, all contributing to the international flavor of the city. Buenos Aires was home to many expatriates, so the Korean couple and their son blended into the human landscape well.

The couple enjoyed a leisurely meal while their son was entertained with a movie on his portable DVD player. The movie captured the boy's attention and allowed the parents to have time to visit and have adult conversation. Had the couple been as attentive to their surroundings as their son was to his movie, they might have noticed the man standing across the street, just inside the gardens, snapping photo after photo of them with his zoom lens.

ACKNOWLEDGEMENTS

This has been a long adventure, filled with potholes and mountaintops. I started drafting this novel while I was waiting for something that never happened. In the waiting, it took on a life of its own, compelling me to finish the story. Fortunately, I was not alone on this journey and the following is a feeble attempt to say thank you to those who traveled with me. The length of time-it was long-may have caused my brain to forget someone. Please forgive if that someone is you. As with any work of fiction, remember this book is just that: fiction. The story is not even based on true events, but rather the ramblings of a mind belonging to someone who (occasionally) has too much time to think.

Mikkel Norse, project manager extraordinaire, without whom this novel would have never been published. Your first-hand knowledge of building facilities in China and other places around the world, was critical. Your persistent encouragement took this project from an idea over coffee to the book you hold today. You forever have my deepest gratitude. Feathers.

Brock Ray, you are the best nephew ever. I appreciate that you volunteered your creative talents to design the book cover, so that you and I could collaborate on this adventure. We both know that I did not inherit any artistic genes, but I am so grateful that you received a double dose. We will always share this memory. Kudos to a job well done.

In today's digital world, everyone needs a computer guru in their life. Mine is Robert Guy. Thank you for sharing your knowledge of cyberspace, for your willingness to guide this project through the technical processes and for your excitement through it all. Your questions and suggestions forced me to dig deeper and even in the wee hours of the morning, that digging led to a better storyline. Ready for the next adventure?

Carolyn Rae, how many hours have we discussed this project? I am grateful not only for your years of love and support, but for reconnecting me with Andy. I am impressed with your networking abilities that defy time and space.

Andrea Nelkin, whew! What a big job you took on in the middle of Covid. My words are insufficient to express my gratitude for your proofreading and copy-editing talents, and for your continued encouragement to see this work completed. You are a hero.

Barbara Verchot and my late brother, Keith Ray: you never gave up. Your excitement and curiosity encouraged me during some of the deepest doubting days. You reminded me that dreams never have expiration dates.

Kim Kelly, thank you for sharing your expertise as an FBI agent. Hopefully, I followed your advice in keeping it real, or at least somewhere near real. I learned so much from you about how television distorts the truth about the men, women, and agencies tasked with keeping us safe. As the title suggests, we often don't realize what tidbit of information sends up red flags to a trained law enforcement professional. Thank you for choosing this career and for your patience with me.

To my oilfield friends (especially the late Joe Voskhul) who, in the absence of the great Jim Carter, answered my questions about natural gas compressors. I hope I understood as well as you described.

John Lankford, the crazy chemistry professor, did his best to explain the properties of plutonium and how a dirty bomb works. Any errors are completely the fault of my non-scientific thought processes.

Andrea Rogers, thank you for the author's photo. I know how little you had to work with, so it was a herculean accomplishment.

And to my beta readers all along the way-thank you for your time and feedback that contributed to a better result: Jody LaFleur, Gina Williams, Gwen Woodhull, Mom, Grant Farrell, Colleen Frost and Jenny Oliver (who still wants to drive the book tour bus).

Most important, my sincere thanks to those of you who chose this novel and trusted me with your hard-earned funds. I hope you will consider it as money well spent.

K. Ray Carter

ABOUT THE AUTHOR

Photo Credit Andrea Rogers

A native of Arkansas, K. Ray Carter has traveled extensively throughout the United States and Europe. With a background in political science and journalism, Carter enjoyed a successful career in the oil and gas industry before turning to writing. Now retired, Carter spends time gardening, volunteering, and exploring historical fiction, especially stories from World War ll.

Visit Carter's blog at thorstravels.wordpress.com for more insights.

Cover Design by Brock Ray

kraycarterauthor.com
Facebook.com/kraycarter.author
Instagram.com/kraycarterauthor

9 798822 957510